THE STRANGER'S SHADOW

THE LABYRINTHS OF ECHO: BOOK FOUR

THE STRANGER'S SHADOW

MAX FREI

*Translated from the Russian by Polly Gannon
and Ast A. Moore*

THE OVERLOOK PRESS
New York, NY

This edition first published in hardcover in the United States in 2013 by
The Overlook Press, Peter Mayer Publishers, Inc.

141 Wooster Street
New York, NY 10012
www.overlookpress.com
For bulk and special sales, please contact sales@overlookny.com,
or write us at the above address.

First published in Russia by Amphora in 2003

Cataloging-in-Publication Data is available from the Library of Congress

Book design and type formatting by Bernard Schleifer
Manufactured in the United States of America
ISBN 978-1-4683-0027-7
FIRST EDITION
1 3 5 7 9 10 8 6 4 2

CONTENTS

Previously in the THE LABYRINTHS OF ECHO . . .

MAX FREI WAS ONCE A LOSER. HE'S A BIG SLEEPER (DURING THE DAY, that is; at night he can't sleep a wink). A hardened smoker, an uncomplicated glutton, and a loafer, one day he gets lucky. He discovers a parallel world where magic is commonplace, and where he fits right in. This is the city of Echo of the Unified Kingdom, a land where a social outcast like Max can be remade as "the unequaled Sir Max."

In this upside-down universe, Sir Max's deadpan humor and new-found talent for magic soon earn him a place in the secret police—night shift only, of course. As Nocturnal Representative of the Most Venerable Head of the Minor Secret Investigative Force of the City of Echo, Max's job is to investigate cases of illegal magic and battle tres-passing monsters from other worlds. With his occupation comes an unusual band of colleagues—the omniscient Sir Juffin Hully, the buoy-ant Sir Melifaro, the death-dealing Sir Shurf Lonli-Lokli, bon vivant and master of disguise Sir Kofa Yox, the angelic Tekki, and the capti-vating sleuth Lady Melamori Blimm.

Plunging back into the threatening and absurd realm portrayed in the first three books of the Labyrinths of Echo series—*The Stranger*, *The Stranger's Woes*, and *The Stranger's Magic*—*The Stranger's Shadow* follows the new adventures and misadventures of Sir Max and his friends in this enchanted and enchanting world.

ONE

THE DARK VASSALS
OF GLENKE TAVAL

"YOU KNOW WHAT, NIGHTMARE," SAID MELIFARO, "YOU OWE ME A great deal of money. I've been keeping a tab. I take your wives— all *three* of them—out to the most exquisite taverns in Echo every day, sometimes several times a day. Now I'd be quite happy with just one, but she brings her sisters along with her on a regular basis. The girls, you see, think that the most horrifying thing that could happen to them is to be left alone with me in a well-lit, crowded room. I don't know where they got their ideas about me. Long story short—pay up."

"Two words, buddy: dream on." I thought I had gotten used to the antics of my diurnal half, but never in my wildest dreams had I expected such brazen impudence.

"Oh, so that's how you treat your old buddy now, your majesty?" said Melifaro. "Well, I'm offended."

"*You're* offended? Did I hear that right?" I said. "Not only are you trying to make me a cuckold—completely unsuccessfully so far, by the way—you also demand that I finance this dubious enterprise out of my own pocket. You'd better thank me for not having a heart attack and dying on you after that statement."

"Thank you. A dead body in the office would be most inappropriate now. It's a lot of fuss and bother, and I'm going out on a date."

"With whom?" I said. "Don't you dare cheat on my wives. It's a matter of honor in my royal family."

"With *whom*?" said Melifaro. "You have three guesses."

"You got that right. *Three* guesses," I said. "By the way, I still don't know which one of them you've set your heart on."

"What difference would it make? You can't tell them apart."

"I can now," I said. "Wait, let me guess. Xeilax has the same revolting taste as you. I saw her a few days ago wearing a bright-crimson looxi—you'd die with envy. But all in all, she's a very serious lady. So I don't think it's her. How am I doing?"

"So far so good," said Melifaro. "Although someone who prefers the shades of fecal matter in his clothing should curl up and crawl into some dark corner instead of criticizing other people's attire. Hold on, where did you see her?"

"What do you mean? At home, of course. Besides three beautiful queens, my dog lives there," I said.

"Oh, okay then," said Melifaro, sighing with relief.

"Why are you so worried, if you're trying to seduce another one anyway?"

"Because they always stick together everywhere they go, that's why. Plus, I still haven't gotten used to the fact that you can tell them apart."

"Whatever. Moving right along. Kenlex seems the most mysterious of the three. A goody-goody with a strong gaze like Juffin's. Nah, I don't think she's got what you're looking for in a girl. So that leaves us with Xelvi. She's the giggly one. I'm willing to bet she's the one you're working on. Right?"

"Wrong," said Melifaro. "You're a lousy clairvoyant."

"Really?"

"Really. Although you were spot-on about Kenlex having a strong gaze." Melifaro jumped off the desk he had been sitting on, dangling his legs. "All right, I'm sick and tired of you, so I'm leaving. I'm going to try and seduce one of your wives. Maybe it'll finally work. You know what? I think you put some nasty spell on them, being the trickster that you are. Ordinary girls would have already been all over me by now."

"You're forgetting that they have a completely different notion of male beauty in the Barren Lands," I said. "You and I just don't cut it. I'm telling you, the girls are suffering from unrequited love for General Boboota Box. All three of them."

"Very funny," said Melifaro. He stood in front of the mirror and straightened the folds of his new looxi. The looxi was bright green, like a lettuce patch in early spring. He was smiling.

Finally the lover boy left his office. I dashed out, too. I had just gotten an excellent idea, and its realization required Sir Kofa Yox.

The Master Eavesdropper had just come out of Juffin's office. Perfect timing.

"I think you mistook me for someone else," he said. "You're look-ing at me as if I'm the girl of your dreams."

"You're spot-on about my dreams," I said. "I desperately need your Ukumbian cloak. Just for a couple of hours."

"Sure," said Kofa. "I never thought you were going to take bread out of my mouth instead of dozing in your office. As far as I know, even Juffin hasn't yet come up with any work for you for today. What's gotten into you, Max? Whatever's going to happen to your reputation as the star loafer of the Secret Investigative Force?"

"I'm not the star loafer," I said. "And I'm not taking bread out of anyone's mouth. I'm just going to have some fun."

"Fun? What kind of fun? Maybe I'll want some of it, too."

"You? I doubt it. Sir Melifaro is going out on a date with my triplets, and it dawned on me that I simply can't skip the show. If they know I'm there, I'll derive approximately a thousand times less pleas-ure from it. So I'll take your cloak and—long live the Dark Magic of the Isles of the Ukumbian Sea! That is, if you don't mind."

"I wholeheartedly support your endeavor," said Kofa, nodding.

"To violate your job description for the sole purpose of having fun is one of the pillars upon which our organization stands. I'm glad you've finally understood it."

"Thanks," I said, carefully taking the piece of old fabric that could turn me into the most invisible person in the World.

"Not at all," said Kofa. "This isn't my personal toy; it's the property of the Ministry of Perfect Public Order. Tell me if you have too much fun."

"That I will."

Then I poked my head in Juffin's office. Maybe the boss is simply incapable of living a day without admiring my countenance, I thought, and I'm off gallivanting about who knows where.

"I am," said Juffin Hully without lifting his head from stacks of self-inscribing tablets piled up on his desk.

"You are what?" I said, taken aback.

"Capable. Of anything. Including living a day without admiring your countenance."

"A hole in the heavens above you! Not only are you aware of the mess that constitutes my head, you can also keep track of my thoughts. I'm so embarrassed. They must be full of bad grammar."

"Not always," said Juffin, yawning. "I mean I don't always read your mind. Today, though, is a day you need to be taken by surprise. As far as I know, it's been a few dozen days. This poses a huge risk. You might relax and think of yourself as an ordinary guy with an ordinary, successful life and career. Go ahead and have fun, Max. It's your right. It looks like I'm going to be stuck here until midnight at least. The year has just begun, and the office is already full of paperwork."

"Anything interesting?" I said.

"I wish. Reports by the Venerable Heads of the Secret Investigative Forces from our blessed provinces. What interest could they possibly have for anyone? And stop shuffling your feet in the doorway. Run away before I change my mind and dump this work onto your fragile shoulders."

"I can take a hint," I said. "I'm good as gone." I ran out of the office. I had to hurry if I didn't want to search Echo high and low for my fantastic four.

I parked the amobiler in a small, cozy courtyard a few blocks away from the Furry House. The magic of the Ukumbian cloak did not extend to the vehicle it was worn in. And when you were about to spy on one of the secret investigators, you had to take extra precautions. I suspected that even in the fog of passion, Melifaro's head was still capable of some sober deduction work.

I walked the rest of the way to my royal residence. I lost a lot of time, but I was also hoping that the sisters enjoyed dressing up for a night on the town and dawdled while they were at it. There was only one problem that awaited me in the Furry House: Droopy, the huge, shaggy sheepdog from the Barren Lands. I was worried that he would sniff me out. Usually the four-legged genius started to squeal as soon as I even thought of visiting him, so I decided to wait outside.

Melifaro's amobiler, parked nearby, testified to the fact that I had gotten there in time. I even had to wait for almost a quarter of an hour. Finally they came out: Sir Melifaro and three unwitting knock-offs of Liza Minnelli. The splendid attire of the sisters made me feel sorry for the rapidly diminishing funds of His Majesty Gurig VIII, who was sponsoring the happy inhabitants of my palace.

When they were getting into the amobiler, I felt like a complete idiot. How was I supposed to spy on them? Long-distance running had never been my forte. Fortunately, the triplets all got into the back seat. The front seat next to Melifaro was empty, so I stole in and bundled my behind into it. In theory, I knew that I was invisible, but it was still shocking to see that the lover boy was completely oblivious to my presence, even though I was sitting an arm's length away from him.

"Where to, your majesties?" said Melifaro. His tone struck a delicate balance between sincere courtesy and killing irony. Lucky for him, the sisters hadn't had much opportunity to study their suitor in action, so they erred in their judgment on the side of courtesy.

"To the *Kumonian Honey*!" they said in unison.

I was surprised at my own ignorance. I had lived in Echo for much longer than the sisters had and still had no clue of the existence of that establishment.

"Haven't you gotten tired of Kumonian sweets?" said Melifaro as the amobiler took off.

"Sometimes you say such odd things," said one of the sisters. I didn't know which one: I hadn't learned to tell their voices apart yet. "One can never get tired of sweet things."

"You don't know how kind fate has been to you, Sir Melifaro," said another sister. "You have been able to partake of sweets every day since childhood. When we lived at home, the best we could get was the berry of the steppes—it gets quite sweet when it's ripe—and that was it. Of course, when our people traveled abroad, they brought us food from distant lands and shared it among all of us. We all got a little bit, but it happened so seldom. If memory serves, they brought us sweets five times, right, Xeilax?"

"Six times," said Xeilax, sighing. "We were very little the first time it happened. I remember my first honey cracker, even though you two don't."

"Poor things," said Melifaro. "Very well, then. The *Kumonian Honey* it will be."

The trip to the New City seemed like a journey around the world to me. When it came to driving the amobiler, this strapping young lad was no different from the rest of the inhabitants of the Unified Kingdom. His top speed was barely twenty-five miles an hour.

To make things worse, the four chattered on about silly things all the way to the tavern. I had to fight the desire to blow my cover and grab the lever myself. The only thing stopping me was the thought that it would scare the living daylights out of the girls. They might start to suspect that I always followed them around, invisible.

At last, the amobiler pulled over to a squat building on the bank of the Xuron and stopped. The signboard, decorated with an intricate design, read *The Kumonian Honey*. I remembered that Shurf Lonli-Lokli lived just a few blocks from here. I had never had time to visit him at his place, even though I had given him a lift home many times. Amazing how I never have time for anything but a harebrained adventure like this one.

I was so comfortable being invisible that I didn't bother to tiptoe or to breathe softly. Even when I accidentally slammed the heavy, carved door of the tavern, no one turned around and looked at me. The tables at the *Kumonian Honey* were only meant for couples, so the group of four had to squeeze around one of them. I sat at a table next to theirs.

The proprietor, a short, dapper old man whose elegant clothes reminded me of the expensive tracksuits of my distant homeland, went up to Melifaro. The old man's fiery red beard reached almost to the ground. His mustache was just a thin, barely noticeable line below his nose.

Judging by the expression on the face of the Kumonian, he was about to die from excess happiness. His courtesy far exceeded the average level of courtesy of other tavern owners in Echo, which, I must say, was nothing to complain about.

It seemed, though, that the mellifluous old man was going to pass me by. The magic cloak made everyone avert their gaze from me, including tavern keepers from Kumon. Without giving it a moment's thought, I followed him to the kitchen. If the food wouldn't come to Max, then Max must go to the food.

Instead of a single male chef, there were five charming women of various ages and constitutions at work in the kitchen.

"It's that venerable gentleman with his identical women again," the tavern keeper told them in a whisper. "Mark my words, those barbarians are beginning to understand that a man must have a harem. Get down to work and make sure that everything is prepared properly this time. That customer regularly refuses our food—the sign of a bigwig."

I smirked, grabbed the tastiest-looking honey cake, took a pitcher of kamra from the burner, and returned to the main hall.

Melifaro, meanwhile, had already moved closer to his chosen one. On his face was an expression of true, undiluted happiness. Then I looked at Kenlex. She looked pensive and slightly guilty. It seemed that the company of her suitor gave her the sort of pleasure she was not yet prepared to experience.

Xeilax, whom I had begun to consider the "eldest" of the three, was looking askance at her sister. Xelvi's glance, on the other hand, was full of undisguised irony. I could easily imagine her making faces and squeaking: "Here comes the bride, fair, fat, and wide. Slipped on a banana peel and went for a ride." Strange that Melifaro hadn't chosen her. In my book, the two were made for each other. Then again, the human heart is a mystery that I, for one, will never solve.

Truth be told, so far the spying hadn't paid off. Instead of having fun, I was moved. I told myself for the hundredth time that I would soon begin the alchemical process of turning barely known acquaintances into good friends. In other words, I would try to get to know my so-called wives a little better. I sometimes find my indifference to the people at the periphery of my life repulsive. And a lack of time is no excuse.

Meanwhile, the keeper of the *Kumonian Honey* came out of the kitchen carrying a huge tray. Melifaro's face clouded over.

"I said I didn't want anything," he moaned. "The order was solely for the ladies."

"This is on the house," said the bearded native of the Kumon Caliphate with servility. "Please deign to accept my humble offering."

"But I'm not hungry!" Melifaro's voice resembled that of a man on death row who had one last chance to plead with a cruel judge.

"Taste it, at least. I beg you!" said the tavern keeper, making a deep bow.

"That's what you said last time, too, and I ended up eating the contents of all six platters, plus some horrible dessert. No, no, and once again no!" Melifaro was adamant.

"Kiebla!" shouted the tavern keeper. "Come here, Kiebla!"

The oldest of the women I had just seen in the kitchen dashed out into the hall and came to a stop a few paces away from the table.

"This gentleman refuses to taste the food you have prepared," said the tavern keeper in a sad voice. "Beg him!"

The old woman sank onto the floor and began mumbling something in a plaintive tone. I was astonished, but Melifaro seemed to have gotten used to the show already. He shook his head and turned away. The sisters stopped eating and gave Melifaro a look of adoration. I had the feeling that the whole surreal scene was being directed and performed for the sole purpose of shocking the young daughters of the Xenxa people, who had just begun to forget the barbarian customs of their remote homeland (about which I knew next to nothing).

The lamentations of the poor woman continued. It became clear to the tavern keeper that they were lost on Melifaro, and he departed back to the kitchen. Soon all five of the cooks were kneeling in front of Melifaro. I could tell that the only thing the poor fellow wanted was to disappear, but he was holding out. Finally, when the bearded proprietor of this hospitable establishment joined his five cooks, Melifaro broke down.

"Fine, I'll taste your sinning food. Just get out of my sight. All of you," he said. "If you don't stop it this instant, we're never coming here again, mark my words. Actually, you know what? After this disgraceful show, we're not coming here anymore, period."

The Kumonians got up off their knees and disappeared into the kitchen, bowing and walking backward.

"Sir Melifaro, were you joking about never coming here again?" said one of the triplets in dismay. "You just said it so they would respect you more, didn't you? How can one live without the *Kumonian Honey*?"

My friend looked like he didn't know whether to laugh or cry. "Well, if you really want to come back here, I guess I have no choice.

But tell me the truth, do you really like honey soup, girls? I mean, I like pastries and other sweet things myself, but stuffing myself with a mixture of meat, honey, and oil . . . It's just unpalatable."

"But it's so sweet, Sir Melifaro!" said Xeilax. "Sweet things can't be unpalatable."

Melifaro let out a quiet moan. I decided to sneak back to the kitchen to eavesdrop. No doubt they were discussing this latest escapade.

"I told you he was a very important gentleman," said the proprietor to the cooks. "He behaves like the First Courtier of Caliph Nubuilibuni zuan Afia. I wonder where that barbarian learned such exquisite manners."

I chuckled, grabbed a tempting honey bun, and returned to the hall. An idyllic scene met my eyes: the triplets were polishing off the sweets, while Melifaro was staring at them, eyes agog. The mixture of tenderness and sadness on his face seemed to me to be the most amazing wonder of this World so generous with wonders. I had no idea that my thick-skinned chatterbox of a friend was capable of such moving, heartfelt looks. If I were Kenlex, I would have melted and surrendered myself long before dusk.

Before long, though, I decided I'd seen enough. If I had stayed a little longer watching that heart-wrenching soap opera, I might have begun shedding tears of pure honey. I decided to leave before it was too late. Besides, the *Armstrong & Ella* was just a fifteen-minute walk away. Tending to my own life seemed much more prudent than sticking my nose into the lives of others. With that in mind, I left the *Kumonian Honey* and set out for the Street of Forgotten Dreams.

It was getting dark. The lilac twilight of the spring evening mixed with the orange light cast by the streetlamps. Silhouettes of passersby cast intricate, angular shadows. I discovered that I couldn't see my own shadow on the colorful tiles of the sidewalk. Apparently, the magic cloak of the old Ukumbian pirate rendered it invisible, too.

I amused myself for a while by examining the shadows of the passersby. Sometimes I saw an elongated dark silhouette trembling in the diffuse light of the streetlamps, and I couldn't tell whom it belonged to. I realized that the shadow's feet should, in theory, touch the feet of its owner, but it appeared that the shadow was gliding down the sidewalk on its own. The person who was supposed to be casting it didn't seem to exist or, at the very least, was nowhere to be seen. I decided I should ask Juffin about it. Maybe shadows in this World, about which I still knew very little, were in the habit of leaving the house without waiting for their masters.

When I reached the front door of the *Armstrong & Ella*, I hesitated. I was tempted to walk in without taking off the magic cloak to observe Tekki for a while. Maybe I would see what she really looked like when she didn't have to be the "mirror" that reflected me or whomever else she was talking to.

I really wanted to do it, but I decided against it. What if Tekki had a cloak like that and decided to spy on me and my own secrets? I thought. I wouldn't like it, to say the least. I was full of secrets I had no intention of sharing with her. The biggest secrets of all were, of course, the dreams I had when I sneaked out to meet her daddy, Magician Loiso Pondoxo. I was also glad that Tekki hadn't been spying on me that warm winter day when Melamori had dragged me to the garden of the former Residence of the Order of the Secret Grass. My memory had played a bad joke on me that day. I had gotten caught in a hurricane of regrets for the unfulfilled, which could have taken me far, far away, if I hadn't been careful. I'm sure it was all very plain to see.

On top of these, there were many insignificant secrets that I wasn't about to let Tekki in on. For example, I wouldn't have wanted her to witness me scolding a lazy courier, or to have seen me during the bloodbath I had made on the beach of one newborn World. True, killing is much more romantic and elevated than picking your nose, but that incident was sure nothing to be proud of.

For all I knew, Tekki might have had the same personal archive with *Top Secret* written on it, too. And that was her right. So I removed the magic rags of the late Ukumbian pirate and stepped inside the hall of the *Armstrong & Ella*, as visible as I could be.

"What a luxury!" said Tekki, smiling. "The evening has just begun and you're already here. What happened?"

Tekki rarely pretended that seeing me filled her heart with unspeakable grief. Today, however, she was particularly happy about my unannounced appearance, and that was fine with me.

"Juffin had a sudden bout of charity and let me out to pasture until almost midnight," I said, mounting a bar stool.

The numerous customers of the tavern looked on in delight. Another episode in the love story between Sir Max the Terrible and the daughter of Magician Loiso Pondoxo, the Great and Mighty, was unfolding in front of their very eyes. It's hard to live in a world without soap operas. Plain old gossip just isn't the same. So it was a great treat for the public to witness a tender moment between Tekki and me.

Tekki, however, was looking at the customers with evident hostility. "I'm not going to kiss you," she said. "Giving the public a free show is not in my line."

"It isn't?" I said. "Oh, well. Too bad, but as you wish." I moved to the edge of the bar stool and began telling Tekki the dramatic details of the adventures of the queens of the Xenxa and Sir Melifaro in the *Kumonian Honey*.

"Kumonians have hilarious customs," said Tekki. "That honey soup is really revolting—I tried it once. The sisters, though, can eat it without wincing and then ask for more. I can only feel for poor Melifaro."

"I feel for him, too," I said. "Stuffing yourself with sweet soup every day—yuck! I'd rather die."

"That is the least of his worries," said Tekki. "It's going to be hard for him to talk Kenlex into being alone with him, not to mention all the rest of it."

"Really? I thought she liked him, too. I'm a lousy psychologist, I know, but this time I'm pretty sure I'm spot-on."

"It's not a matter of liking or not liking someone," said Tekki. "The girls are used to being a trio. Period. The sky will have to fall for Kenlex to realize that something can happen to her alone, and not to the three of them simultaneously. Do I make myself clear?"

"Pretty clear," I said. "Poor Melifaro. If you're right, he's in a real pickle. Say, maybe I should step in and try to help him out? What do you think?"

"Go ahead," said Tekki, laughing. "You're their king—and their husband, besides. Just tell Kenlex that you're offering her as a gift to your friend. That ought to do it."

"Right," I said, shaking my head in perplexity. "Oh, to the Dark Magicians with all of them. I just remembered—you hired some help, right? How about she does the work, and you and I sneak out somewhere? When am I going to get another free evening? There's something depressing about our walks in the morning. It's like going to a funeral, or to buy groceries."

"And where do you propose we sneak out to?"

"I don't know. Somewhere where you'll agree to kiss me?"

"Oh, there are plenty of places in Echo I'm willing to do that," said Tekki.

We spent a wonderful evening together. The romance bug I had caught from Melifaro had a lot to do with it. I even went as far as to send a call to Juffin an hour before midnight saying I was going to be a little late.

Knock yourself out, said Juffin. *I don't need you here. I'm giving you two extra hours in the hopes that I will have finished by then.*

So much paperwork?

That, too. Plus, there's Kofa's present.

A present? What sort of present?

I'll tell you when you get here. You'll have to show up at work, if only out of curiosity.

The boss sure knew how to hook me. For thirty whole minutes I was burning to set off for the House by the Bridge without losing another minute. Finally I succumbed. Tekki had just decided to conduct an experiment to find out what kinds of dreams were lurking in the night, waiting to ambush the dwellers of the Capital of the Unified Kingdom. I thought I'd better not get in her way.

I could count on one hand the number of times I had seen someone occupy the Chair of Despair—the visitors' chair in the Hall of Common Labor, to put it more plainly. Not too many people were eager to visit the House by the Bridge.

This time, however, there were not just one but two alleged victims in the Chair of Despair. After blinking to adjust to the bright light, I saw that the heads of the victims were adorned with huge fur hats, which testified to their Isamonian origin. Since the victims were silent and paid no attention to me, I went to Juffin for more information.

"What happened to our Isamonian friends?" I said. "Did some Evil Grand Magician of some mutinous Order give their hats the evil eye to make them shed?"

"A certain someone was going to stay somewhere for two extra hours," said the boss. "Your curiosity will be the end of you."

"No, it won't. It's one of my few true virtues."

"Fair enough. In answer to your question, I'm not sure myself what happened to them. From what I can gather from Kofa's account, someone they know died under mysterious circumstances. I was just about to talk to them. I didn't count on your coming so soon," said Juffin.

"Not only did you *count* on it, you *knew* I would. Don't bother trying to convince me otherwise."

"All right, I won't. Let's go talk to your friends."

"My friends? Since when are they my friends?" I said.

"Since not so long ago. Not friends, maybe, but acquaintances.

Don't quibble about my words. Those gentlemen attended your coronation," said Juffin.

"Ah, the venerable furriers Mikusiris, Maklasufis, and Ciceric?" I said, laughing. "If anything, they are Melifaro's friends. He was the one who once threw them out of his living room."

"Well, we're only honored by the visit of Mr. Ciceric and Mr. Mikusiris. Wise Mentor Maklasufis passed away virtually in front of Sir Kofa's eyes."

"What do you mean 'virtually'?" I said.

"Kofa's premonitions were up to snuff again and rose to the occasion," said Juffin. "He was about to spend a quiet evening at home when a couple of hours ago his instincts tore his behind from his chair and drove him out on the street—to the *Irrashi Coat of Arms*, to be precise. What wouldn't rise to the occasion was his amobiler, which refused to start. Kofa had to go by foot, and by the time he arrived at the *Irrashi Coat of Arms* it was too late. People were already making a ruckus. Speaking of which, I never could understand why a dead body always attracts so much attention. So many people find it so intriguing to contemplate it. Do you happen to know why, Max?"

"They're glad it didn't happen to them?" I said. "That's a good reason to be glad, I think. Honestly, I don't know. Maybe someone else's death is always a novelty, like a circus act. I personally have never been too fond of such spectacles."

"Magicians forbid! But let's get down to the business at hand," said Juffin. He yawned and got up from his armchair, stretching and cracking his joints. "A hole in the heavens above those Isamonians. This is the last thing I needed right now. Whatever happens, I'm going to sleep until noon tomorrow. You're on your own. I have the right to take advantage of my position as Sir Venerable Head now and then."

We left the office and joined the Isamonians. They roused themselves, looked around uncertainly, and began to snivel.

"Gentlemen, I'd be happy to hear what happened to your countryman," said Juffin. "It is within your power to see that justice is done." He yawned again. The yawn was so contagious that I had a hard time suppressing my own.

"You tell them, Mikusiris," said one of the Isamonians. "I'm a nervous wreck right now."

I remembered that Mr. Mikusiris was the "Grand Specialist in questions of culture for the Unified Kingdom," something of an expert adviser to Mr. Ciceric, who was head of the corporation of furrier tycoons of Isamon. Talking to us was part of his job, for which, judging from the size of his hat, he was compensated handsomely. Now this human think tank was wrinkling his forehead, trying to live up to his patron's expectations.

"We were coming back from a visit to a very important gentleman who is close to the Royal Court," said Mr. Mikusiris.

"You have already divulged the invaluable information about this very important gentleman, as well as his fantastic order for eighteen rolls of fur pelts, to our colleague," said Juffin. "I'd like to know how Mr. Maklasufis died, if you don't mind."

The Isamonians attempted to glare at him in indignation, but a moment later dropped their gaze. I don't know anyone who can withstand Sir Juffin Hully's icy stare. Fortunately, the boss isn't too keen on gloating over the results of his withering gaze.

"We were walking past the *Irrashi Coat of Arms*. Maklasufis was walking beside me, and everything was fine," said Mikusiris. "Then he groaned, pressed his hands to his chest, and fell to the ground. I tried to feel his pulse and realized right away that the caravan had already left. Yes, gentlemen, it was all over. That bastard we met must have poisoned him. I didn't like him from the very beginning. So we brought Maklasufis to the *Irrashi Coat of Arms*, but there was not a single wiseman in that dirty, stinky tavern."

"Of course. Because it's a tavern, not a hospital," I said. I was offended. I had always found the *Irrashi Coat of Arms* a very neat little place. Some dubious gentlemen who wore skintight pants and huge fur hats in public had no right to throw mud at an establishment that served such heavenly Irrashian desserts.

Juffin guessed the reason for my harsh tone. He shook his head at me, restrained a smile, and turned back to the Isamonians. "Was that all?" he said.

"Yes," said Mikusiris. His fellow countryman and employer squinted, looking off into the corner somewhere.

"I seem to remember you mentioning some shadow to Kofa," said Juffin. "Am I right? Mr. Ciceric, I'm talking to you."

"Mikusiris believes I was just seeing things," Ciceric said with a sigh. "I tend to agree with him. Anyone's brains would melt under the circumstances."

"Indulge me, nevertheless," said Juffin. "I'll be the judge of what melts and what doesn't."

"Before my Wise Mentor fell, I had been observing our shadows," said Ciceric. "The streetlamps on that street are arranged in such a manner that each object casts a double shadow. There were three of us and we cast six shadows: three that were dense and dark, and three pale and more transparent ones. I was about to call Mentor Maklasufis's attention to this phenomenon when I noticed there was yet another shadow. Unlike ours, it wasn't a double shadow, nor was it elongated. I was intrigued by this optical effect. See, in my line of work, I'm more an artist than simply a merchant. It is simply my duty to be intrigued by such things." There was so much pathos in this last statement, it seemed as though he was letting us in on the secret that he had had a hand in the creation of the Universe.

"And?" said Juffin.

"I turned around to find the person who was casting the seventh shadow, but there was no one behind us. Not a single person. We were alone on the street."

"I see," said Juffin, frowning. "But why didn't you think that it was one of you casting that shadow?"

"See? I told you," whispered Mikusiris. "Get over it already." He looked happy, as though he had been waiting his whole life for Mr. Ciceric to disgrace himself in public, and now that moment had come.

"The shadow had no hat!" said the furrier. "Or turban. It had no headgear of any sort. That's why I turned around—to see the imbecile who had been idiotic enough to leave home with a bare head."

"Very good," said Juffin, nodding. "Now I really have all the information I need. Thank you, gentlemen. You may go home now."

The Isamonians readily got up from the Chair of Despair and minced along toward the exit.

"May we tell our elders that you will do everything in your power to avenge the death of Maklasufis?" said Ciceric. Once in the doorway, he felt much more confident. "Or else they will come down from the mountains, and then there will be trouble! Big trouble."

"No, no," said Juffin, laughing from surprise. "We don't want them to come down from the mountains. We'll manage somehow."

And the Isamonians left.

"Funny," said Juffin. "Those guys are funny, their hats are funny, and the whole story is funny. Too funny, in my book. Not exactly what a man needs if he wants to sleep until noon the next day. What do you think about this whole thing, Max?"

"Well," I said, "just this evening I was examining the shadows of the passersby while I was on my way home. Mind you, not yesterday or a dozen days ago but this very evening. Moreover, I thought of asking you if shadows in Echo were in the habit of leaving home without their masters. I guess I just have."

"As far as I know, it's not customary," said Juffin, smirking. "Why were you interested in shadows all of a sudden?"

"No reason," I said. "I guess I was also seeing things, like Mr. Ciceric. Granted, no one died right before my very eyes. Maybe it was some kind of premonition. You know it happens to me from time to time."

"You can say that again," said Juffin. "All right, then. As far as I'm concerned, this night is good for only one thing: sleeping. So that's what I'm going to do. We'll save pondering for tomorrow. Don't rush back home in the morning. Wait for me, okay?"

"You're the boss," I said. "Are you still planning to sleep until noon?"

"I love torturing people, but this isn't a good time," said the boss. "Don't fret, I won't be loafing under the blanket. In fact, soon none of us will have much time for loafing anyway."

"That bad?" I said.

"I'm afraid so. But we'll see. Good night, Max. And try to catch some sleep tonight, if you can. The one thing I can't promise you now is a quiet life and several Days of Freedom from Care in a row."

❧

I had to hand it to Sir Juffin Hully. He managed to teach me to respect professional discipline and subordination. Following his orders, I spent the night sleeping on a makeshift arrangement of a desk chair and two armchairs.

"At last you have improved upon your previous design." Kofa's voice woke me up at dawn.

"I have? How?" I said, still sleepy.

"You used to make do with a single armchair and two desk chairs. If someone had to walk over to the window, your treacherous boots would inevitably catch him in the shins."

"I see. I used to be young and reckless. Now I'm old and wise, I guess." I yawned and realized that without a sip of Elixir of Kaxar, my life was not going to get off the ground. Sir Kofa watched the transformation from a sleepy, pathetic creature to a cheerful, contented Sir Max with fatherly indulgence. "What's cooking in the Capital?" I said, enjoying the lively modulations of my own voice.

"Nothing much, save five fresh-dead bodies in the City Police morgue. Five sudden, inexplicable deaths. Identical to what happened to that poor Isamonian," said Kofa.

"Wow!"

"Don't get too excited about it, boy. We can't make heads or tails of this without Juffin, and he's not here yet," said Kofa. "Better tell me how your spying on our lover boy ended yesterday."

"Nothing much to report there, either. I was even moved to tears at the end. The only good thing was that the girls decided to spend the evening in the *Kumonian Honey*. Unlike his beloveds, Melifaro wholeheartedly despises Kumonian cuisine. I can relate. Their honey soups alone can spoil your appetite forever. Yuck."

"Nonsense," said Kofa. "I'm very familiar with Kumonian cuisine. It's excellent."

"Really?" I said. "Well, you know best. The girls would have agreed with you, too. Poor, poor Melifaro."

"He's really up a creek," said Kofa. "To date a girl whose gastronomical preferences are so much at odds with your own . . . that's terrible. I couldn't do it."

During breakfast, I entertained Kofa describing the Kumonian cooks and the antics of the tavern keeper. Granted, I edited the story a little bit, but it was a sacrifice I was willing to make for the sake of storytelling.

"Tell me this, Sir Max," said Juffin, walking into the office. "Why were you never in the movies back in your home World? I'm thinking of displaying you to the general public for money, if only through a keyhole, for starters."

"Never a day goes by that I don't ask myself the same question," I said. "I guess they weren't very smart there in the movie business. Did you not get enough sleep?"

"How very shrewd of you to notice," said Juffin. "I hope you haven't drunk the rest of my Elixir."

"Nope. There's still some left."

"Praise be the Magicians. Give it to me," said Juffin. "Kofa, don't leave. I have something to talk to you about."

"I thought so," said Kofa.

"Now out of my armchair, kid!" said Juffin. After a few gulps of Elixir of Kaxar, Juffin got into a mischievous mood. Too mischievous, if you asked me. He lifted up the armchair I was sitting in—and I wasn't the lightest person by a long shot—and shook me out of it onto the floor like apples from a basket. Sir Kofa was delighted, and I had to contend with a mild shock.

"Hey! That hurt," I said, rubbing my tailbone. "Now I'm disabled. You can deal with your problems on your own. I need a good wiseman."

The boss frowned and waved his hand up and down my back. "Liar," he said. "Not even a bump."

"There could have been," I said. "My goodness, Juffin, that's just plain hooliganism."

"Right you are," said Juffin. "After a night full of gruesome thoughts, I have the right to a little bit of disorderly conduct."

"All right, then," I said. "By the way, how did you manage to lift both me and the chair? Together we weigh quite a bit."

"My dear boy," said Kofa, laughing. "You can't even begin to imagine what this skinny Kettarian can do. I once witnessed him pull a streetlamp out of the ground just to slam one unfortunate fellow with it. Mind you, there was no magic involved whatsoever."

"I believe you," I said. "You have thoroughly intimidated me, gentlemen magicians. I want to go home to my mommy."

The elderly evil magicians snickered. While they were at it, Juffin managed to clear the desk of the remains of our breakfast, send a call to the *Glutton Bunba*, and even order seconds.

"Laughing aside, we're in big trouble," he said. "Up to our ears in trouble, in fact. I wish we could dismiss the testimony of that Isamonian as just his wild imagination, but to my chagrin, I have proof that he was right. The most revolting kind of proof."

"Oh dear, Juffin," said Kofa, shaking his head. "Is this part of your foul early morning mood, or is it—"

"Boy, is it!" said Juffin. "My mood has nothing to do with it. I didn't sleep last night. Instead, I sent my Shadow for a walk around Echo. It got offended and now it's pretending it caught a cold strolling in the cold spring wind."

"That explains why you look like a wreck," said Kofa. "So how was the walk?"

"Horrible," said Juffin. He stretched his limbs, crossed his arms over his chest, and stared into space. My heart sank as I awaited the rest of the story. I hadn't seen Juffin in such a weird mood in a long time. "There are at least a dozen Lonely Shadows hanging around Echo. Maybe more. I didn't run into them, but I sensed them," he said and fell silent again.

"May I ask you to continue?" I said.

"Yes, you may. I keep forgetting that you need a more detailed explanation. A Lonely Shadow is a shadow cast by no one. In my entire life I have only met a Lonely Shadow once. It happened a very long time ago when I was an intern in the office of the sheriff of Kettari. Back then it was the Shadow that was chasing me, not the other way around. I got away, and later Sheriff Mackie finished it off. I helped him do it, so one could say I learned it from him. Generally, they are virtually ineradicable, those Shadows, but thanks to the old hand Mackie, I have one neat trick up my sleeve."

"Are those Lonely Shadows really dangerous?" I said.

"Incredibly dangerous," said the boss. "Once a Lonely Shadow touches the shadow of a living person, the person dies on the spot, and his shadow becomes one of the Lonely Shadows. The worst part is that this can spread like a plague. I already gave orders to the authorities not to turn the streetlamps on at night. No light, no shadows. So the inhabitants are safe at night, at least when they're outside—that is, if they have enough brain matter to take heed of my advice, lock themselves up at home, and not turn on the lights."

"What about the sun and the moon?" said Kofa.

"Yes, the weather is going to pose a lot of trouble, too," said Juffin. "We must see to it right after breakfast. I'm really counting on Sir Shurf: he's the expert in all weather-related issues. Fortunately, this morning the sky is cloudy as it is, so we have some time."

"It does look bad, doesn't it?" I said. "How are we going to get out of this?"

"We will somehow," said Juffin, sinking his teeth into a fresh, crusty bun. "You go ahead and help yourself, Max. Don't pretend you've lost your appetite. I'm not buying that."

"But I have," I said, mechanically popping a product of blessed Madam Zizinda's cuisine into my mouth.

"I can see that," said Juffin. "Cheer up, Sir Max. We're going hunting today. That's a new adventure for you. For me, too."

"I don't understand why you said you had something to talk to me about," said Kofa. "As far as I can tell, this is precisely one of the cases in which I will be of no use to you."

"And that's *precisely* why you will be dealing with the possible consequences," said Juffin. "I'm leaving Melamori with you, and . . . well, that's about it, I think. There's always Sir Lookfi, of course, but I don't believe he's going to neglect his buriwoks and rush to help you, even if the World starts to fall apart and you're left holding up the sky on your own two shoulders. Which is more or less what has already happened."

"I thought as much," said Kofa. "Perhaps you're exaggerating a tad, Juffin."

"I hope so," said Juffin. "Although, it doesn't look like it."

Shurf Lonli-Lokli appeared in the doorway and gave each of us a piercing look. The office suddenly grew much brighter from his snow-white attire.

"Good morning, gentlemen," he said.

"It's good of you to come so quickly, Sir Shurf," said Juffin. "There's a job just for you. If memory serves, the Mad Fishmonger once played a very neat trick on the inhabitants of Echo. I'm referring to the night that lasted three days in a row. The black clouds that let no sunlight through. Ring a bell?"

"Of course," said Lonli-Lokli.

"Can you pull it off one more time?"

"Certainly, but I will have to breach the Code of Krember since I will be working outside in the open and not down in one of your basements."

"That's a no-brainer," said Juffin. "Don't worry about it. Under the circumstances, we can break a few laws. Leave it to me."

"In that case, you can count on me. Please be so kind as to send a call to Jafax. I will be needing a bottle of Ancient Darkness. I am sure they still keep that wine in their cellars. The last time I summoned the storm clouds, I was drinking Ancient Darkness. Back then one could easily get it at any grocer's. My job will be easier if I copy my actions to the letter, without disregarding any detail, however minute."

"You're a sly one," said Juffin, laughing. "For a bottle of Ancient Darkness, I myself would turn day into night and leave it at that till kingdom come. But all right. Grab your chance, Sir Shurf."

The boss fell silent, concentrating, then looked at me and said, "I'm going to have to demote you temporarily, Sir Max. I need a fast driver. Go to the Transparent Gates of Jafax. A messenger from Sir Kima will be waiting for you there with a bottle of something marvelous. The worst part is that, instead of drinking its contents, you're going to have to bring it over here and hand it to Sir Shurf. Will it kill you?"

"It most certainly will," I said. "Then again, my corpse may turn out to be as good a driver as me."

"I'll give you fifteen minutes," said Juffin.

"Pfft. I'll be back in ten," I said. "That is, if Sir Kima's messenger doesn't make me tarry at the gates listening to the comprehensive report on the health of Magician Nuflin."

"One must always hope for the best," said Juffin. "I've given them quite a scare."

I nodded and shot out of the office like a bullet. Two minutes later I stopped the amobiler by the Transparent Gates of the Residence of the Order of the Seven-Leaf Clover. I think I broke my personal record.

A short, fragile young man in a blue-and-white looxi of the Order, Sir Kima Blimm's messenger, appeared out of nowhere a few moments later. He bowed and handed me a woven basket. Judging from its weight, there was more than one bottle in it.

"Sir Kima asked me to tell you that he is so confident of your success that he wishes you to have the means to celebrate it," said the young man.

"Excellent. Please extend my gratitude to Sir Kima, and . . . no, no 'ands.' I will tell him myself. That's what Silent Speech is for," I said.

I jumped into the amobiler and grabbed the lever. I think I drove back to the House by the Bridge even faster, if that was possible.

"Good golly, Max! Eight minutes," said Sir Kofa. "We timed it."

"You can cut half a minute off of that," I said. "I did have to wait for him, but not for long. And now—surprise! We got more than we asked for. Mind you, I didn't cast a spell or enchant anyone."

"You sure know how to turn on the charm," said Juffin, examining the contents of the basket. "*Four* bottles of Ancient Darkness instead of one. I don't recognize good old Kima Blimm. He's always been such a skinflint."

"By the way, I once managed to reconcile Sir Kima with his niece," I said, boasting. "Our Lady Melamori, as you know, is terrifying in her ire. So at least one bottle here is my personal reward."

"I have no objections to that," said Juffin. "You always share your most valuable prizes with us, you silly boy."

"It's because I'm dying for people to love me," I said with a smirk. "I suck up to everyone the best I can."

Meanwhile, Lonli-Lokli took his holey cup out from the folds of his looxi, uncorked one of the bottles, and transfused its contents into his magic vessel. The precious wine did not spill over but froze in a fragrant dark-lilac cylinder above the top of the cup. Lonli-Lokli took a sip from the top of the viscous iceberg. The iceberg began to melt, slowly but surely, until the cup in Lonli-Lokli's hands was full, and then became empty again.

He handed it to me. "Now you drink something out of it, Max. Once, it turned out you were capable of finding strength on this path. You should not pass up the chance now. We will all need a great deal of strength today," he said and sauntered out of the office.

"Is he really going to conjure up magic right out on the street?" I said, watching the door close behind him.

"No need to do it on the street," said Juffin, smiling. "The Epoch of Orders has long gone. I think he'll go up on the roof of Headquarters. I'd do that, if I were him, anyway. By the way, Sir Shurf is known for giving excellent advice. If I were you, I'd stop playing around with his cup and do as he said. Shall I open Kima's present for you?"

"No, no. I remember that just drinking ordinary kamra from this cup has the strongest effect on me, like the night I flew around above the rooftops of Echo, generally doing Magicians know what. I think it makes sense to repeat that experiment," I said.

"Well, suit yourself," said Juffin. "You're no fun, Sir Max. As soon as I find a decent pretext for opening up another bottle of this godsend, you turn me down."

"I'm just superstitious," I said. "I'm worried that if we drink Kima's wine now, instead of waiting and celebrating the success of our mission, there will be nothing to celebrate later on."

"All right. If you're worried, we'd better not take any chances," said Juffin. However surprising this might sound, he took my silly superstition with true seriousness.

I filled Lonli-Lokli's holey cup with excellent kamra from the *Glutton Bunba*—again bemused that the liquid did not drain from it—and drank it down.

The already familiar sensation of lightness, which was difficult to describe, replaced the feeling of wellness. I felt sincerely perplexed about how I had managed to live my whole life in the heavy, unwieldy body I had inhabited just a few moments before. How had I ever dreamed of turning the world upside down or flying in the clouds with a body like that?

"Has there been a palace coup while I was suffering from insomnia?" said Melifaro. He had somehow managed to appear in the office, sit down beside me, and—the most brazen thing of all—snatch a cookie from my plate and shove it into his mouth. "I don't get it," he continued with his mouth full. "Lonli-Lokli is going at it up on the roof. He's throwing bolts of lightning left and right and howling like a banshee. Our poor police brethren are lying around in a dead faint, I'm sure. Has he been drinking, or what?"

"Has he been drinking?" I said, laughing. "He killed a whole bottle of Ancient Darkness in a single gulp. But never mind him. Help yourself to something sweet instead."

My hint missed the mark. Sir Melifaro was interested in completely different matters.

"What on earth are you doing with his holey cup?" he said in the tone of a sufferer. "Are you drinking from it? Oh my, oh my. The World *has* come to an end after all. Now it's going to face its undoing in an ordinary and merry fashion. I was wondering why girls don't love me, and it turns out it's just the first sign of universal madness."

"Girls still don't love you?" I said with compassion in my voice.

Melifaro paused to mull it over. "I don't know," he said. "Sometimes they do, sometimes they don't. It confuses the heck out of me. But what has happened?"

"A hunt for Lonely Shadows has happened," said Juffin, sighing. "Once Sir Shurf is done with the weather, a-hunting we will go. You're staying behind to hold down the fort. I'm going to be busy on the Dark Side."

"Suits me," said Melifaro. "I'm all up for holding down the fort."

I listened to their metaphysical abracadabra talk, ashamed at my ignorance. Juffin noticed my puzzlement and made a dismissive gesture with his hand. "Pay no attention to the jargon, Max. They liked fancy words like that during the Epoch of Orders. After you perambulate the Dark Side with me, you'll become an expert in this phenomenon."

"Do you think I will?" I said.

"Sure you will. You've done it before. Many a time, in fact."

"I've done what before?"

"Oh, nothing. Don't fret over trifles, all right? There are plenty of ways to waste your energy, and all of them are much more pleasant than fretting over the trivial matters you're so fond of. You can take my word for it, if I had the slightest grounds for suspecting you couldn't manage, I would have just kept you here to help Kofa," said Juffin.

"Right you are . . . I guess," I said. "I still don't understand, though. Anything. Period."

"It's tough to be a genius, huh?" said Melifaro.

"No, it's tough to be you," I said. "Now quit gobbling my cookies."

"I'm so glad I don't have children, Kofa," said Juffin. "Imagine coming home from work and having to put up with something like this. I'd go nuts."

Lonli-Lokli returned, sat down into the armchair, and examined a stack of napkins fastidiously. Then he pulled out the cleanest one and carefully wiped off the perspiration from his forehead.

"Are you finished with the clouds now, Shurf?" said Juffin.

"Of course. It was a little tiring, but nothing out of the ordinary— just as I had suspected."

"Nothing out of the ordinary!" said Melifaro, jumping up from his chair. "You should have seen yourself! I can just imagine what kinds of dreams I'm going to be having for the next hundred years. And I don't even want to think about what kinds of dreams the unfortunate passersby will be having."

"That's a dead giveaway that you were born on the day they passed the Code of Krember, boy," said Kofa with an avuncular smile. "It all seems like a novelty to you."

"Come off it, Kofa. Even in the good old days things like that didn't happen every day," said Juffin. "Have you already recovered, Sir Shurf? Can we begin now?"

"I will be even more efficient if I use my cup one more time. I am not suggesting that I need another bottle of Ancient Darkness. Anything will do, except for water or kamra, of course."

"Except kamra, you say?" said Juffin. "But that was what Sir Max just desecrated your holey vessel with."

"I am no match for him," said Shurf, with an expression so full of irony that I felt green with envy.

He turned to me, hiding a smile that played around the corners of his mouth. That is, I was almost positive I wasn't just seeing things.

"In my Order, we believed that kamra was of no use in a situation like this. I prefer to stick to the tried-and-true traditions. I would not mind, however, trying a beverage from another World. Would you be so kind as to fetch something for me, Max?"

"Something that's *not* an umbrella, though, please," said Juffin. "I can't stand the look of them anymore."

"For your information, I stopped fetching umbrellas from the Chink between Worlds long ago," I said, looking around for a nook to stick my hand in.

"What about that blue umbrella with yellow flowers? You produced it not long before the Last Day of the Year," said Lonli-Lokli.

"Pfft. That was like three dozen days ago. An eternity in umbrella years."

"Yes, but in human years it is still three dozen days ago," said Shurf.

"You're killing me with your irony, Shurf," I said.

"Way to go, Sir Shurf," said Melifaro. "If you and I join forces, we'll get him in the end."

"Do you really have to 'get me'?" I said.

"Of course. One has to rid Echo of the evil that has crawled into it from another World. That, in essence, is the ultimate goal of the Secret Investigative Force," said Melifaro in a pedantic tone. "And you are a typical manifestation of evil, if I've ever seen one."

"Oh, in that case, go ahead and 'get me,'" I said. "But don't bother me now, please. I need to focus."

Believe it or not, they did leave me alone. Even Melifaro shut up temporarily. I was able to focus on the task at hand. I stuck the hand in question under the table and began thinking about beverages in general and alcoholic drinks in particular.

Gradually, my mind painted a picture of a stack of shelves with bottles behind the back of a young bartender. His face seemed familiar, although I couldn't remember where I might have seen him. I was busy with something else: my fingers were already wrapped around the narrow neck of a bottle. I still hadn't learned to take full control of my actions during these maneuvers, so I jerked my hand out from under the table. The bottle slipped out of my fingers, made an intricate arc in the air, and landed right in Melifaro's lap. He squealed in surprise, sprang up on the desk, and looked around, trembling. The bottle fell on the carpet but, thank goodness, didn't break. I carefully picked it up and glanced at the label.

"'Johnnie Walker Whisky. Born 1820—still going strong,'" I said in the voice of a professional voice actor in a complete and utter silence that had fallen over the office. "Seriously, though," I added in my normal voice, "it's pretty good stuff. I mean, it could have been worse. Here, Shurf. Take it. But mind you, it's quite strong. It might even be too strong, I don't know."

"A hole in the heavens above you, Max," said Juffin with admiration. "Maba Kalox himself would envy your show."

He sounded as though he was about to ask me for an autograph. Melifaro began to laugh, which made it difficult for him to get down from the desk. Even Kofa gave a few chuckles.

"In fact, you *can* control your movements, and have been able to for a while. Yet you enjoy indulging your childish desire to make as much racket as possible," said Lonli-Lokli, taking the bottle from my hands.

He unscrewed the cap, sniffed the contents, and shook his head in disapproval. Nevertheless, he poured some whisky in his holey cup, played around with it a moment, and then downed it in one gulp.

"It is strong, indeed," he said, "but that is exactly what I need right now. The taste, however, is wanting. If you have been waiting for me, I am ready to go now."

"We're off and running," said Juffin, leaving his armchair. "Good day, Kofa. I'll try my best not to take too long, but I can't guarantee anything, you understand."

"That's all right, we'll manage," said Kofa. "Considering that you only take along the worst specimens with you . . . No, Sir Shurf, I don't mean you. Lookfi, on the other hand, is pure pleasure to deal with, not to mention Lady Melamori. She's far less trouble than your so-called deputies here."

"You think so?" said Juffin. He even paused in the doorway, giving the matter some consideration. Then he gave a short, resolute nod and added, "You're absolutely right, Kofa. It doesn't get any worse than these two."

Melifaro and I left the office, proud as two tom turkeys at a spring farmers' market. Lonli-Lokli walked at the end of the procession. He wore such a vacant, otherworldly expression, you might have thought we had all died a long time ago, and no subsequent event had any bearing on us whatsoever.

In silence, we walked down to the basement and then descended even farther down, where the true underground labyrinths began. One of the narrow passages (although I didn't remember which one) led to Jafax. Where the others led, I had no idea. It was the second time in my life that I was in these dungeons. My first excursion here was neither lengthy nor memorable, and even seemed like an accident.

We meandered in darkness for a long time. I'm not very good at spatial orientation in general, but here I lost my sense of direction right after the second turn. The trip ended more abruptly than I had thought it would.

"You'll stay here," said Juffin to Melifaro. "A good place for a Sentry, don't you think?"

"It is," said Melifaro.

He stopped, took a few unsteady steps to the side, and stood stock-still. Juffin and Shurf moved closer to him. I was still standing where I had stopped, uncertain what to do now.

"Come closer to me, silly," said Melifaro, smirking. "My arms aren't that long."

His arms? What the heck is he talking about? I thought, joining the gang. Melifaro put his arms around the three of us. His arms felt very heavy and warm. The next moment I felt another hand, also heavy and warm, on my shoulder.

"I shall remember you," said Melifaro.

No. It wasn't just Melifaro. I distinctly heard another voice, too. I could swear it was a very synchronous *duet*.

Then Shurf's hand in its coarse protective glove grabbed me by my elbow and carefully pulled me out of the thickening darkness. I turned around again and gasped. A few feet away from me stood *two* Melifaros. They stood back-to-back—two crisp outlines against a background of clouds of whitish mist that had come out of nowhere.

"Looks great, doesn't he?" said Juffin. "Just don't swoon on me now, Max. As if you've never seen a Sentry before."

"A Sentry? Of course I've never seen a Sentry. What's a Sentry? Where would I have seen a Sentry? In my bedroom? There're no Sentries in my bedroom," I said.

"Calm down, I get the point," said Juffin. "So you haven't seen one. Well, take a good look, then. Our Sir Melifaro is one of the best Sentries around. There were only a few of them in the old days; nowadays, they are very rare indeed."

"This is all fine and good," I said. "But I still don't understand what a Sentry is or why we need one."

"Sentries are these special, very useful guys," said Juffin, pulling me behind him into another dark passageway. "We need them to help us come back from the Dark Side. Remember the magic charm you used to have, the kerchief of Grand Magician Xonna?"

"Sure. It was the best thing for waking up out of any nightmare, not to mention its other useful properties. It's too bad it burned up in the den of the Magaxon Foxes. It was one of a kind."

"Well, our Melifaro is something similar to that kerchief—a protective charm for the three of us. While he's keeping vigil we can rest assured that he won't let anyone follow our traces to the Dark Side.

Sometimes it's very important. If something goes wrong, he'll bring us back, and most likely alive, too. That, as you no doubt understand, is a very good thought to hold on to when the going gets tough."

"It sure is," I said. "What about the other guy? Where did he come from?"

"Beats me," said Juffin. "You see, Sentries are peculiar in this way. There's always a double that arrives to help them. Afterward the double disappears. Sentries are strange and mysterious creatures. Then again, many people are strange and mysterious creatures, too. Did you ever stop to think about that?"

"I did. Then I moved on and forgot about it. My head is full of holes, as you know. Smart thoughts don't stay there for long—Hey, where are we?"

I got a little carried away, talking and thinking about Sentries, one of whom was Melifaro, so I forgot to pay attention to what was going on around me. Only then did I notice that we had climbed out of the catacombs and were standing on one of the city streets. Except that I never would have recognized the place. Like a giant quilt, the cityscape around us was woven from all sorts and shades of darkness—which, however, did not prevent one from making out the smallest details. Unlike the ordinary darkness of the streets at night, this darkness glowed and quivered as though it were alive.

"Welcome to the Dark Side, Max," said Lonli-Lokli, turning to me. He looked a hundred years younger and light as a feather. "You cannot begin to imagine how much I love these walks." His smile was so serene that I almost stopped breathing.

"I think I can," I said. "I once saw you looking like that. In a small mountain town near Kettari, where we got rid of Dead Magician Kiba Attsax, remember?"

"Of course I do. Your town is also on the Dark Side. You simply did not know it was called that."

"I told you that you had already been to the Dark Side and back many times. And you did it without a Sentry, mind you," said Juffin, winking at me. "It's bad when you don't know your jargon, isn't it? You think everyone around you is a powerful magician of some sort, and you're not worth a crown? Well, it turns out we just learned a bunch of smart words back in the day, is all."

"But it wasn't so dark in my town," I said.

"Is it dark here?" said Lonli-Lokli, surprised.

"Oh, our Sir Max is a great storyteller," said Juffin, grinning. "He loves telling fairy tales, and believing in them, too. He heard that we were heading to the Dark Side and immediately told himself that it would be dark here. A truly ingenious conclusion, I must admit. Now it's probably easier to kill him than to convince him that it is indeed light in here. On top of that, the place is very, very beautiful."

"Okay, it is beautiful, I'll give you that," I said. "But light? Are you telling me that the sky isn't black? Or that the leaves on this tree—"

"Are bright lilac," said Juffin.

"Oh, no. Everything is a shade of golden yellow," said Shurf, laughing. His laugh was so contagious that I couldn't help but join in.

"Get it?" said Juffin. "The Dark Side is the way we want to see it. In a sense, each of us has his own Dark Side, which, nevertheless, doesn't prevent us from coming here all together, if necessary. Do you like your personal version of this place, by the way?"

"I guess so," I said. "It's beautiful, but somewhat disquieting."

"Of course it's much more quiet and tranquil to be in the reality that you've made yourself than on the Dark Side of Echo," said Juffin. "But we like it here, too, don't we, Sir Shurf?"

"And how," said Lonli-Lokli.

"You are a completely different person here," I said. I couldn't contain a smile, looking at Shurf. His presence was even more soothing to me now than Juffin's.

"I am, aren't I?" Shurf said with uncharacteristic flippancy. "Maybe here I am the real me. The others—Sir Lonli-Lokli and the Mad Fishmonger, among them—are husks; traveling attire, if you will. I believe I am like a person who has set off on a trip with a very large wardrobe."

"Well put," said Juffin. "But a large wardrobe is not necessarily superfluous. For travelers such as yourself, traveling light isn't an option. A large wardrobe is indispensable to you."

"Yes, I know," said Lonli-Lokli.

"And now it's like you're on a nude beach," I said.

"What's that?" said Juffin.

"Well, it's a place where anyone can go sunbathing in the nude, and no one feels embarrassed," I said.

"Must be a fun place," said Juffin. "All right, I think Sir Max has already gotten his bearings on the Dark Side, so we can get down to business. Let's go hunting, boys."

He went rigid, swiveled his head like a beagle, and, it seemed, even sniffed the air a few times. Then he did an about-face and marched on somewhere into the glimmering darkness, which, as I had just learned, was darkness only to me.

"Let us go, Max," Shurf said softly. "You should not be so nervous. Right now we are where we are supposed to be. You and I are both people of the Dark Side. There, where we just came from, we are only visitors. Strangers that many people find unusual and attractive, but will never consider to be one of them."

"You can speak so beautifully when you want to," I said, picking up my pace. "What about Juffin? Is he also a person of the Dark Side?"

"Of course. Otherwise he wouldn't be here. Now Kofa, on the other hand, is a genuine person of the World. He is a keystone in some sense, although it is not immediately obvious. Sir Lookfi Pence is, too."

"Melamori?" I was whispering, as though I was afraid she could overhear us gossiping about her.

"It is much simpler with women in this regard. They are at home everywhere."

"Rather, they are strangers everywhere," said Juffin, turning around to us without slowing down. "That's why most women go out of their way to surround themselves with proof that they can stand firmly on their feet instead of dangling about between the heavens and the earth with a light heart, as they're supposed to. I can anticipate your next question. We haven't picked to pieces my Diurnal Representative. Well, Melifaro is a Sentry. He belongs neither to the World nor to the Dark Side. His place is on the border. Now try not to get sidetracked. I'd be burning with curiosity myself, if I were you, but the circumstances don't favor chitchat now."

"All right, I won't get sidetracked, but please tell me what I shouldn't get sidetracked from. I still don't understand what it is that you want me to do," I said.

"I don't know what I want you to do myself yet," said Juffin. "We'll see how it pans out. Just keep walking close to Shurf and keep your nose to the grindstone. Be prepared for anything. Just in case."

"Be prepared for anything," I said. "Check."

For the next thirty minutes or so, I carried out Juffin's order with all due diligence: I moved my feet along, kept my mouth shut, and admired the surroundings, going out of my way to pretend that I was "prepared for anything." From time to time, the glimmering darkness shone with bright colorful spots. Apparently, I had managed to make slight adjustments to my "fairy tale of the Dark Side," as Juffin had put it.

My contemplative exercises were cut short, quite literally. Something dark and heavy fell on my foot. I howled in pain and grabbed Shurf to keep my balance. He picked me up with one hand like a newborn kitten and put me down on the ground behind his back. Out of the corner of my eye I noticed how he tossed away his protective glove. Here on the Dark Side, Lonli-Lokli's death-dealing left hand shone not white but fiery crimson.

Only now did I realize that that the heavy object that had almost crushed my foot was only a Shadow with a clearly discernible anthropomorphic outline. To be more precise, it was the Shadow's hand that had tried to grab my boot. No sooner did I realize this than the Shadow vanished, turning into a shapeless puddle onto the ground.

"Did we just score a point?" I said. "Jeepers, that Shadow was one heavy son of a gun."

"Indeed, on the Dark Side, any Shadow, not to mention a Lonely Shadow, weighs a lot more than its master," said Juffin, shaking his head. The boss was looking at me with so much reproach that it seemed I was responsible for the record-breaking increase in the weight of those mysterious creatures.

"But Shurf, you killed it!" I said. "You didn't even break a sweat."

"That was a novice," said Lonli-Lokli, sighing. "The Shadow of one of the poor fellows who died last night. It was still soft and did not know anything about anything. Had that Lonely Shadow been a few days older, I doubt I could have done much damage to it."

"What about your Lethal Spheres?" I said.

"Well, mine will certainly not harm them, but you should try yours. Who knows? Maybe they will work."

"It will be silly if it turns out I'm the only expert in eliminating Lonely Shadows in the World," said Juffin, smirking. "After all, I'm the boss. I'm supposed to give orders, not do the actual work. So you, Sir Max, simply must try to kill them somehow. And I won't take no for an answer."

"Okay, okay," I said. "I'll try."

"Please do, at your earliest convenience," said the boss, livening up.

We moved along. A few minutes later, Juffin turned into a court-yard and stopped in the very center of a circular area paved with small, unpolished rocks.

"This place on the Dark Side corresponds to your house on the Street of Old Coins, Max," he said. "It will be much easier for us to fight here, especially for you. Summoning the beasts here is also easy. An excellent spot in all respects."

With these words, Juffin took off his warm winter looxi and tossed it onto the branch of a nearby tree. His gorgeous turban fol-lowed his looxi.

"They'll get in the way," he said.

Now dressed in a thin silvery skaba reaching all the way to the ground, his head shaved, Sir Juffin Hully resembled a fierce priest of some ancient deity. I couldn't take my eyes off him.

Juffin raised his hands in front of him. That motion projected so much power that it seemed as though he had cut through the very fabric of space. I was mentally preparing to hear the sound of it ripping apart when Juffin let out a piercing, guttural shriek. He shrieked for so long that I accepted this sound as the permanent soundtrack of the rest of my life. When the earsplitting shriek ended, I almost choked on the sudden silence.

Juffin spread his arms out wide with powerful effort and erupted in sudden and forceful laughter.

"Why, welcome, my dear fellows!" he said. "You can't imagine how lonely we are here without you. Shurf, cover my back. Max, stand by my side. Even if you can't help, you'll at least learn something useful. See them now? All gathered here together, the bastards."

A gigantic dark mass of something was approaching us slowly and hesitantly.

"This is the way *I* do it," said Juffin. He laughed again with evil glee and stretched his palms toward the darkness that was encroaching on us. The next moment I saw how Juffin, with visible effort, *crumbled* something that resembled a human body. The dark mass dematerialized in his hands rapidly until there was nothing left of it.

"It's not as difficult as it may seem," he said, winking at me and repeating his feat.

"If you think I can possibly learn this, your ungrounded optimism has just gone off the scale," I said.

"I don't need you to learn it. Your method of killing Lonely Shadows is most likely radically different from mine. I simply want you to find out what it is, and be quick with it," said Juffin, killing a third dark silhouette. "There's no special way to do it, so don't try to copy me. Start off with what you can do already."

"M'kay," I said and almost mechanically snapped the fingers of my left hand. I never had any problem whatsoever with launching my Lethal Spheres.

I saw the green fireball fly out of my fingers and approach the huddle of dangerous Lonely Shadows. The dark clump jolted and backed off. My Lethal Sphere, now big and almost transparent, attacked the retreating clump.

"Hey, they're running away from your Lethal Sphere, Max!" said Juffin. "Excellent. Now we can take front-row seats, relax, and watch the show. Look, *look*!"

I looked and saw something incredible. The dark clump was covered in a veil of a glowing green mist and was starting to shrink.

"Looks like your Lethal Sphere is eating the bastards," said Juffin. "Soon, I hope, there will be nothing left of our little friends. See how easy it all turned out to be? Sir Shurf, what's your news?"

"Nothing in the back, so far," said Lonli-Lokli. "But I am not sure that all the Lonely Shadows answered your summons."

"Of course not," said Juffin. "The protagonist of the show, the leader of the gang, isn't here. I can sense that villain, though. It's somewhere near. It can't make up its mind to attack, and it can't run away. My spell is worth something after all."

"Hey! Look what happened to my Lethal Sphere!" I said. "It didn't disappear, it's still there. Are you sure this is normal?"

"No, Max, it isn't," said Juffin, surprised at what he saw.

The dark clump was gone, but the enormous green sphere had become very dense. It emanated a sense of power and danger so clear and apparent, it sent shivers down my spine. It seemed that my Lethal Sphere had a mind of its own, completely independent of my fickle wishes. Any second now it could take it into its head that the three of us made as good a lunch as the Lonely Shadows just had.

A dark-burgundy flash put an end to our anxieties. My Lethal Sphere wobbled like jelly that had plopped onto the floor and disappeared.

"There," said Shurf, smirking and putting his protective glove back on. "For your every action there is a counteraction, Max."

"And I'm so happy there is," I said. "I'm almost positive that my brazen fireball was about to have us for lunch. Those Lonely Shadows of yours weren't nutritious enough for it."

"Well, they are shadows, after all. What kind of nutritional value would they have?" said Juffin with a straight face. He came to the tree on which his clothes were hanging and put on his turban and looxi. "Thank you, Sir Shurf. I am eternally grateful to you. Now I'm going to deal with their leader. I hope that creature is tougher than its minions, and more talkative. I'd love to have a chat with it. When Lonely Shadows begin walking down the streets of Echo all of a sudden, someone has a motive. I wish I knew who it was and what his motives were. Step aside, boys. I'm going to need some room here."

"Come here, Max. Are you stuck?" said Shurf. Then he did the only right thing to do: he grabbed me and pulled me aside. If he hadn't, I would have still been standing there, as though struck by lightning, trying to process the idiotic escapade of my own Lethal Sphere.

"Do not fret," Lonli-Lokli said softly. "That was valuable experience. Everything changes on the Dark Side, including Lethal Spheres. Once we are back in the World, your Lethal Spheres will start obeying your commands again."

"I got really scared," I said in a whisper.

"I can relate. Now look at Juffin. This is quite a rare and fascinating spectacle."

I turned around and saw that the cobblestones in the courtyard were shining a soft golden color. In the middle of that beautiful shimmering stood Sir Juffin Hully, motionless and ablaze like the brightest candle. I noticed that this time, his arms, again spread out on either side of his body, were wrapped in the fabric of his looxi, as though he were about to grab a boiling caldron.

"*Holy cow!*" I said. "Look, Shurf, there's something I don't get. It's just a bunch of shadows—granted, they're a bunch of *Lonely* Shadows —and we've already wreaked havoc so early in the morning. I'll bet you didn't have to stage this show too often even before the Battle for the Code. Are Shadows really so dangerous?"

"Do you think Juffin and I simply wanted to stretch our muscles? Well, even as exercise, it was effective. But these are Lonely Shadows . . . I do not know about other places, but in our World, they are among the most dangerous and deadly of beasts. If we did not take action, in a couple dozen days Echo would become a dead city, its tale recounted in legend. First Echo, then all of Uguland. Not the most enviable fate for the Heart of the World."

"I see," I said with a sigh and stared back at Juffin. "What's going on down there?"

The boss was not wasting any time. A tall, dark shadow was slowly approaching him. Its blurry outline obscured anything human in its shape. Juffin leaned in toward his adversary, demanding and impatient. The Shadow moved faster, as though attracted by a strong magnet. Moments later Juffin was wrapping his looxi around the dark silhouette. The amber light of the courtyard began to fade, and Juffin's body was not blazing anymore. He relaxed, even stooped a little, and came over to us.

"*La commedia è finita!*" he said in the thin voice of an evil gnome. I was stunned. Had Juffin just said something in Italian? "I'm sorry, Max," Juffin said, laughing. "I didn't mean to scare you. On the contrary, I wanted to give you a pleasant surprise. I fished this mumbo jumbo out of your head. What does it mean, by the way?"

"'The show is over.' So you got that right," I said. "But don't scare me like that anymore, okay?"

"All right, all right," said Juffin, pleased with himself. "So shall we go home, boys? Magicians only know how much time has passed in our World while we were partying out here."

"Time flows differently here and there?" I said.

"Occasionally," said Juffin, nodding, "but not necessarily. It's difficult enough to control the flow of time when you travel between Worlds. When you're on the Dark Side, time is absolutely unpredictable. We'd better hurry."

Juffin stood between Shurf and me and put his arms around our shoulders.

"Melifaro!" he yelled like an angry mother calling her son back home for dinner.

"No need to yell," said Melifaro. There was just a single copy of him again, which suited me just fine. Two Melifaros in one room is one Melifaro too many, in my book.

"Where'd you come from?" I said.

"I didn't come from anywhere, *you* did," he said. "What took you so long? Women and wine?"

"Indeed. What else would one do on the Dark Side?" Juffin said in an absentminded voice. Then he looked at me and laughed. "I'll be darned, Max. I'm going to take you to the Dark Side every day from now on. I love seeing that sweet, innocent, idiotic smile on your face."

"Oh, yeah? What did you look like after you returned from your first trip over there, I wonder?" I said.

"The same way I always look," he said and laughed again. "But only because I was incredibly dense. I thought I had dreamed it all up. And that sneaky Mackie was enjoying my idiocy and didn't even try to cure me of my delusion."

"He's not sneaky, he's a great fellow," I said, sighing. "If someone persuaded me that our trip was just a dream, I'd just go back to my quiet life again."

"Dream on," said Juffin. "No quiet life for you, son. Although, in some sense, every trip to the Dark Side is a dream. A dream that only a person who is wide-awake can dream, though. Keep that in mind, if it makes you feel any better."

He walked down the narrow passageway, and we followed him. I sneaked a quick look at Shurf. Even in the semidarkness of the dungeons I could see his face transforming back to the all too familiar imperturbable mask of Sir Lonli-Lokli.

"Putting on your traveling attire, Shurf?" I said in a whisper.

"Yes. Did you like the metaphor?"

"Immensely."

"I am glad to hear that."

He even made a slight bow, as if we had exchanged some stock compliments at a royal ceremony. Yet at the corners of his mouth, I could still discern a daredevil smile that he had smuggled over from the Dark Side.

A half hour later we left the dungeons and marched down the hallways of Headquarters.

"Say what you will, but I'm going home," said Melifaro. "You should thank me for not passing out in the bathroom."

"Thank you," Juffin and I said in unison and laughed at our perfect timing.

"Do you want me to give you a lift?" I said. "You'll be under your blanket in no more than five minutes."

"That would be great," said Melifaro. It was the rare case of Melifaro accepting my help without showing off. He must have been really wiped out.

"I'll be back before you have time to finish a cup of kamra," I told Juffin.

"A cup of kamra would be just the ticket right now," said Juffin, sighing. "All right, go help your friend. See you soon."

It was almost completely dark outside. The sky was covered in pitch-black clouds that hung so low, it seemed you could touch them if you stood on the roof of a moderately tall house. Streetlamps were out, of course, and almost all the windows were shuttered. There were no pedestrians on the streets. While we were gone, the Capital had led a very gloomy existence.

In the amobiler, Melifaro was dozing off and I expressed my compassion to the best of my abilities.

"I'm just glad I don't have your talents," I said, summarizing our little chat. "The job of a Sentry doesn't seem like a walk in the park."

"It is, though," said Melifaro, yawning. "No need to gloat. You just took an awful long time. Thanks, though, you monster, I'm home.

Would you be so kind as to pull over? I don't feel like jumping out of a moving vehicle today."

"Sure thing, buddy," I said, stopping by the door of his house. Melifaro pandiculated and got out of the amobiler.

"Oh, one more thing. Would you please tell Lady Kenlex that I just could not possibly stuff her sisters' stomachs with Kumonian sweets today?" he said.

"With what sweets?" I said, making an innocent face.

"Kumonian sweets. And don't give me that innocent look. I know you were spying on us in the *Kumonian Honey*. I don't blame you. I would have done the same if I were you."

The heavy front door of his house had already closed behind him, and I was still shaking my head in disbelief. *How on earth did he find out?*

On my way back to the House by the Bridge, I sent a call to Tekki. She replied in no time.

No need to explain. Sir Kofa has told me the story of Lonely Shadows five times already. At first, it was amusing. Then it got old.

Five times? How long have I been gone then?

Only four days. Kofa's just having a bad case of unrequited love for my kamra and, well, me by extension.

He's got great taste.

Then we chatted a little more. I had already reached Headquarters, so it was time for us to "hang up." Not for long, I hoped.

Our side of the House by the Bridge was empty. Even couriers were nowhere to be seen. In the office, Kurush and Juffin were the only living souls, and the buriwok was fast asleep.

"Is Shurf already on the roof?" I said.

"Not yet. I think he's in the restroom," said Juffin.

"He frequents it, too?" I said.

"Apparently. You could have come back sooner, though," said Juffin in a grumpy tone. "You said you'd be back before I finished a cup of kamra, and I have already started my third."

"I was practicing Silent Speech. One has to do it sometimes," I said. "On the upside, I'm not going to bother asking you how long we've been gone. I know it's been four days."

"I don't see that as an upside. You're going to ask me something else," said Juffin, sighing. "For example, where Kofa and Melamori are."

"I'm sure they're asleep at home. Changing into their pajamas, rather," I said. "I guess they didn't have much time to sleep while we were gone."

"You guessed right, although life in the Capital was pretty uneventful in our absence. Even criminals are scared of Lonely Shadows, which is wise of them. The inhabitants have simply been staying home. How about we don't tell them that everything is over? We'll get a few days of the best vacation ever."

"That's an excellent idea," I said.

"Sir Juffin," said Lonli-Lokli, entering the office, "do you think I should take care of the sky over the city?" To my surprise, he wasn't wearing his turban and generally looked disheveled.

"The sky can wait," said Juffin. "I'm going to finish my kamra and interrogate our captive. Who knows, maybe we'll need to expect more guests as early as tonight."

"Do you believe that is possible?" said Lonli-Lokli.

Juffin just shrugged.

"Shurf, you're all wet!" I said, finally realizing what was wrong with him.

"Of course. I recommend that you follow my example. A trip to the Dark Side calls for a good shower. To be perfectly frank, a full bath is in order, but there are no bathing pools in Headquarters."

"Well, if you say so, I'm going to go wash," I said.

"Keep in mind, though, that this falls into the category of completely useless advice," said Juffin, laughing. "It's pure superstition. It was all the rage in Shurf's Order of the Holey Cup two hundred and something years ago."

"Well, it certainly can't do any harm," I said.

When I returned to the office, Juffin was helping himself to another cup of kamra.

"Ha! Another one dripping wet," he said. "This is what the Minor Secret Investigative Force has descended to. How are we supposed to instill fear in the Universe, looking like wet rats? And for your information, ordinary water won't do. Back in the old days you could go to the Murky Market and pay an arm and a leg for a pitcher of water from the Ukli Sea, the only water to chill the hot heads of fearless travelers to the Dark Side."

"Is that true, Shurf?" I said, smiling.

"Of course not. Sir Juffin has just invented this little tidbit for reasons known only to himself."

"I have done no such thing," said Juffin in a voice that betrayed a hint of genuine indignation. "My superstition is about five centuries older than yours. As a consequence, it was dropped a little sooner than yours. But never mind superstitions. Dry off while I interrogate our captive."

Then Juffin closed his eyes and apparently fell asleep. I stared at my boss, blinking in disbelief. To the best of my recollection, his actions had never so belied his words. Juffin opened one eye, visibly annoyed.

"Will you please stop drilling a hole in me with that gloomy gaze of yours?" he grumbled. "I'm not yet so powerful a magician that I can interrogate a Lonely Shadow in person. I'm trying to have my Shadow talk to it. It's easier for them to find a common language. Now be so kind as not to disturb my slumber. Okay?"

"Okay," I said, submitting.

My head was spinning from all of this, my recent shower notwithstanding. Maybe I should have used the legendary water from the Ukli Sea, if only I could have gotten hold of some.

For a few moments, Shurf and I just sat there quiet as mice, trying not to wake up Juffin. I didn't even dare chew.

A thunderous clamor shattered the ringing silence. It was coming from behind the door to the small enchanted room where we locked up the more dangerous prisoners from time to time. Alarmed, I jumped up and gazed around. Lonli-Lokli, however, didn't move a muscle, and Juffin continued dozing. From this I derived that every-thing was going according to plan.

"It is all right, Max," said Lonli-Lokli. "Juffin has simply begun his interrogation."

"In that room?" I said.

"Of course. That room is sufficiently isolated from the rest of the World. It is even possible to contain a Lonely Shadow there for a short time. While you were taking Melifaro home, Sir Juffin locked the beast up in there lest it distract him from enjoying his kamra. I must confess that you missed a very instructive spectacle."

"I'm sure I did," I said, still worried, listening to the ruckus com-ing from behind the wall. "Is this going to take a long time?"

"We will see," said Lonli-Lokli. "You have failed to take into account the fact that, just like you, it is the first time I am witnessing an interrogation of a Lonely Shadow. Never before have I dealt with them. There is no need to whisper, by the way. Sir Juffin will not wake up before he is finished, even if you and I start breaking dishes."

"I don't think I'm in a dish-breaking mood right now," I said.

"It is entirely up to you," said Lonli-Lokli. "I was simply inform-ing you that it was perfectly acceptable in this situation."

Then an earthquake started up out of nowhere. The floor began to shake; the windowpanes trembled. If Shurf hadn't been there, I would def-initely have considered an evacuation plan. But Shurf yawned and grabbed the pitcher of kamra that was dancing on the brazier with a careless ges-ture. I got a grip on myself and pretended that an earthquake was as ordi-nary an event as any other. I don't think I was very convincing, but at least I managed to keep myself from screaming and jumping out of the window.

The next moment, the earthquake and the racket stopped, as though someone had flipped a switch and cut off all those special effects that were already getting on my nerves.

"Phew! That was quick," I said, addressing the ceiling.

"No, no, Max. It is just the beginning," said Shurf. "*Now* they are going to talk."

"Well, at least the natural disaster part of it is over," I said. "You can't imagine how happy I am about that."

"Indeed, you seemed very restless. It is amusing how your reaction can be absolutely unpredictable sometimes."

"And how, pray tell, was I supposed to react to it?" I said. "All my life I've thought that Shadows were completely harmless, incorporeal things—optical effects. And then I witness *that*."

"But of course. Yet you have been living with the heart of one such 'optical effect' beating in your chest for almost a year," said Lonli-Lokli. "You are indeed a master at ignoring facts if they do not satisfy you."

I opened my mouth to tell him he could cut some slack to a person who had had no idea about the existence of the first degree of Black Magic just three years ago, but realized I had better shut up. I didn't need anyone to cut me any slack.

My friend was obviously aware of my internal monologue. In any case, he looked at me with visible approval and was considerate enough to pour some more hot kamra into my cup to reward my mental exercises.

"Glenke Taval," Juffin said suddenly. "I see now. Who would have thought?"

I turned to him, startled. The boss had woken up and was now looking at his hands, studying them.

"You'll have a long day tomorrow, but there's still time," he said. "Right now, I'm exhausted. You can disperse the clouds now, Shurf. I don't think we'll be needing them. Max, since you're moonlighting as a personal chauffeur, I'd like to ask you to drive me home. Kimpa will be vexed, of course, but I have no strength left in me to wait for him to pick me up. With you behind the levers, on the other hand, the trip goes quickly and imperceptibly, like dying peacefully in your own bed, which is unlikely to befall either of us, praise be the Magicians."

"That was one heck of a long-winded metaphor," I said, almost choking on my kamra from Juffin's compliment and prophecy all rolled into one.

"A metaphor like any other. Sir Shurf, if you need another bottle of Ancient Darkness, you'll find it in the bottom drawer of my desk."

"That will not be necessary. Dispersing clouds is simple."

"Good. More booze for us, then. Let's go, Max. I'm wiped out. The darn beast has sucked all the life out of me, I swear."

Juffin was hardly exaggerating. All the way home he was dozing off in the back seat of my amobiler. It was so unlike him that I began to worry.

"Go back to Headquarters, Max," he said when I pulled over by his mansion. "Tell Shurf he can go home if he wants to, and I'm sure he does. Melamori will come to replace you in a couple of hours. Kofa made sure that the lady didn't tire herself too much over the past four days, so she can do some work now for a change. Then you can do whatever you please, including sleep, until tomorrow noon. At noon, come to the House by the Bridge, and be prepared for anything. Got it?"

"'For anything,' as in . . . ?"

"As in 'for anything.'"

For a few moments, the boss contemplated the fretful expression on my face, enjoying what he saw, and then condescended to elaborate on his remark.

"Maybe I want you to be prepared for a long journey. I'm not sure. Frankly, I haven't decided anything yet. We'll talk tomorrow, all right?"

"All right," I said.

What else was there for me to say?

I took my time driving back to the House by the Bridge. I stopped now and then to look at the sky. Marvelous things were going on up there. Thick, dark clouds that Sir Shurf Lonli-Lokli had covered the heavens with were now floating slowly to the horizon in the west, unveiling the clear blue sky up above. As they retreated, they changed their shapes, and some of them were so fanciful that it seemed they knew I was watching them and were doing their best to amaze me.

The chief culprit in producing these unusual natural phenomena had already been occupying the armchair in the office for some time.

He was casting glances full of disdain at the mess that constituted the top of Juffin's desk.

"That's nothing," I said, entering the office. "You haven't seen a real mess yet."

"Can you imagine, not only have I seen a mess but I also have made one in my time," said Shurf. "Now, however, I am in the phase of my life when a mess does not improve the mood."

"That I can imagine," I said. "By the way, Juffin says you can leave these horrible messy premises and go home. That is, if you feel so inclined."

"Perhaps I do," said Shurf. "Are you staying?"

"I am. I have a date with Melamori. The idea is that she's going to replace me in a couple of hours, so I've nothing to complain about, either."

"I see. In that case, I do not think I am going to stick around."

Lonli-Lokli yawned, covering his mouth with an elegant motion of his huge hand in its protective glove. I thought to myself that it was the first time I had seen him yawn—a marvel in and of itself.

He left, and I was alone in the office with Kurush. The buriwok wasn't in a talkative mood. He was busy pecking at the remains of a pastry.

"Would you by any chance happen to know what time it is?" I asked Kurush without much hope.

"About two hours before sunset," he said. "Strange. You're the first person who has ever asked me that question."

"Well, I'm a unique person in many respects. For example, I completely lack a sense of time."

"I thought as much," said the buriwok. "Would you wipe off my beak please?"

I wiped off Kurush's beak and looked out the window. The sky was clear again; pedestrians had ventured outside. The Capital of the Unified Kingdom was recovering after a short nightmare. I didn't doubt that as darkness fell upon the city, the streetlamps would come on as they were supposed to. Still, something was not right.

I was certain. I *knew* that it wasn't just my imagination running wild. Something almost imperceptible had changed in the World, the World that I had long ago stopped perceiving as a permanent shelter. Well, I thought, all the more reason for me to touch its mosaic pavements even more gently—almost like a kiss, almost like goodbye.

"Are you worried about something, angry with someone, or just sleeping in the chair?" Melamori's voice came from behind my back.

"Oh, I didn't hear you come in," I said. "Your third guess comes closest."

"I thought so," she said, nodding. "Those evil sorcerers have beaten the last drops of energy out of you, poor thing. They must be sleeping at home in bed, while you're sitting here, dozing off heroically in the armchair."

"I could have gone home if I wanted to, but I decided to wait and chat with you a tad."

"Really?" said Melamori, cheering up.

"Really. I'm sure you haven't yet had the opportunity to hear the story of Melifaro's epic battle over the honeyed treats of the Kumon Caliphate, have you?"

"No. Tell me, tell me!"

I took pleasure in telling the saga again. Melamori was in raptures over it—a response that was truly worth the effort.

"So what have you been up to for four days?" I said when she stopped laughing.

"What can one be up to when Sir Kofa is left to run the show?" she said. "We ate. *A lot.* And that was about the only thing we did. People were scared to poke their noses outside, let alone commit a crime. Policemen were on vacation, too, as far as I know. Oh, there were two dead bodies, though: a man and his wife. They desperately wanted to celebrate their hundredth wedding anniversary in their garden with a candlelit dinner. The Lonely Shadows got them in no time—the reckless couple were the only two people who dared to use light. They must have lost their minds."

"Maybe. Or maybe they made a conscious decision. Maybe they wanted to die a romantic death together on the very same day instead of facing another century of boring married life. Why not?"

"Oh, Max," said Melamori, "they were real people, not characters in some romance novel. People normally tend to love life, don't they?"

"Sure, normally. But there are crazy people, as well. Those guys are capable of anything."

"I guess you're right." She paused, then said, "You know, a ship from Arvarox arrives in a couple dozen days."

"To take you away?"

"To finish off that poor filthy Mudlax. Then we'll see."

"That's a healthy outlook," I said, nodding. "In such cases one should always improvise."

"I'm scared, Max," Melamori said very quietly.

"Me too," I said. "Sometimes I feel like making a storm and sinking that sinning ship from Arvarox so that everything stays the way it is now. If you leave with Aloxto, it will be devastating. If you stay, it will be even worse. I don't want you to lose the battle with your own fear. There are battles one should never, ever, *ever* lose, even though defeat would be so easy, so sweet . . ."

"The last thing I want to do is admit to myself that you are absolutely right," said Melamori. "And yet I like what you're saying. How come?"

"Because I'm trying to help you. Not to run off with your Prince Charming, of course, but to—" I cut myself short and then remembered Juffin's words. He said them in passing, but they were stuck in my head forever. "I want to help you dangle about between the heavens and the earth with a light heart."

"I . . . I think I understand what you're trying to say," Melamori said, and she turned away to the window. "You know, Max, I think you should go home now. I don't have enough courage to talk about it, and chatting about something else would be . . . I mean, we could

60

do that, but it would sound so fake, don't you think?"

"I do," I said. "To be perfectly straight with you, I can't say I have enough courage to talk about it, either. Maybe courage just doesn't exist. Maybe all the so-called heroes are just ordinary people with atrophied imaginations. You and I, though, have plenty of it, eh?"

"I'll have to disagree with you," said Melamori, smiling. "I personally know a few recklessly courageous fellows who have as much imagination as a person can possibly have. Take Sir Rogro, for example."

"Oh, Rogro doesn't count," I said. "He's an astrologist. He can calculate his own horoscope, convince himself that he's out of harm's way, and then plunge into any adventure."

"Hey, you're right!" said Melamori, brightening up. "I never thought of that. But you really should go home now, before I change my mind. Or I'll want you to stay here and talk to me all night."

"Tempting, very tempting, Melamori, but my body has been engineered in a very lousy manner. It almost always wants to sleep," I said and even yawned to prove my point. "Plus, tomorrow is going to be one heck of a day, if one is to believe Juffin's promises."

"Really?" said Melamori, turning glum again. "I thought it was over. Well, in that case, get out of here, Sir Max. I can't stand looking at your beautiful eyes for another second."

"Are they really beautiful?" I said, hesitating in the doorway.

"It depends. Don't forget they keep changing."

A new episode of the soap opera that was threatening to take over my life was waiting for me at home.

Tekki, looking pensive, was sitting at the bar. Across from her sat one of my beautiful wives. It was not easy to tell the triplets apart, but I would have bet anything that it was none other than Lady Kenlex. What's more, she was *alone*. Her sisters were nowhere to be seen.

"Well, well, well," I said, smiling. "I thought you only went out as a trio. Glad to see you, Kenlex."

"You recognized me!" she said.

"Um, not really, no," I admitted, sitting down next to her. "But I guessed that you were the one looking for a piece of good advice. I've got to warn you, though, I'm not the right guy to turn to in such cases."

"Yet it's *your* advice she desperately needs," said Tekki softly. "Not mine, nor anyone else's, but yours. How do you like that?"

"It's nice to know there are still naive people in the world." I stopped short and gave Kenlex an apologetic look. "I'm sorry, Kenlex. I just have this stupid way of saying things. You'll get used to it. Tekki, I must be the most predictable person in the world, and—"

"And you want kamra, of course," she said, nodding, and put a ceramic pitcher in front of me. I switched to Silent Speech.

Actually, what I really want is to be in your bedroom. Preferably not alone.

That sounds tempting, but this girl has been sitting here for more than two hours. It looks like she's at loose ends.

I can imagine. It's late, she came here alone, and she probably walked, too. She doesn't drive.

Believe it or not, she does drive, and she does it well. Do you think everybody's an imbecile or just a select few?

No, I guess I'm the only imbecile here.

I turned to Kenlex and spoke out loud. "So what seems to be the problem?"

"As if it's so hard to guess," said Tekki.

"Guessing in these matters will get us nowhere. What if all my guesses are wrong and bear no relation to reality? Happens to me all the time."

"What *would* you guess?" said Kenlex.

"My guess, huh? I think you're going to ask me what to do about that annoying, pesky, but very cute Sir Melifaro. Did I guess right?" I said.

"Actually, I was going to ask you what to do about myself. I really like your friend, but Xeilax and Xelvi really don't like it that I really like him . . . I'm sorry, I don't know how to explain it."

"You're doing just fine," I said. "Just fine. But look, I don't have a twin brother so I'm not sure what kind of relationships you have with your sisters. In any case, your business is your business, and no one else's. A person's heart belongs to the person in whose chest it is beating, and that person alone."

"They say I could lose my fate if I take an interest in men," Kenlex whispered, embarrassed. "And I think their words are true and that I should listen to them, but I can't. Not anymore. I don't know how it all happened. In the beginning, everything was so easy and sweet. Your friend came to visit us every day, took us out for a walk or to a tavern, and nothing was required from me. I mean, I didn't have to make any decisions. It was all going so well, for me, at least."

"I see," I said. "And then? Did something change?"

"It did. He was gone for four days. Well, you know that—Sir Kofa said you had been gone together. And I was sad. I never thought I could become sad just because someone stopped visiting me. Today he sent me a call and said he wanted to see me alone, without my sisters. I know what it means when a man wants to meet a woman alone. I got so excited and happy, and I couldn't say no. Now I don't know what to do. Should I send him a call and tell him I changed my mind? But I don't want to say that, and I'm afraid of meeting him alone. Oh, why is this so complicated!"

"It's not that complicated, Kenlex," I said, laughing. "At least, there's nothing to be afraid of. Sir Melifaro is a true gentleman, though that may be hard to believe. Are you worried that once you're alone he'll immediately fall victim to his burning lust? I don't think that's possible. Echo is a big city. Try as you might, you two would be hard-pressed to find a spot where there would be no one else but you. Trust me, Tekki and I have tried it on many occasions and failed miserably. I'd go so far as to say that one can meet strangers in one's bedroom sometimes."

Tekki gave a few vigorous nods. Poor thing, she had run into many a Secret Investigator coming to see me in the doorway of her bedroom.

"But we'll still be alone," said Kenlex. "Strangers don't count. What would they want to do with us?"

"Mark my words, you'll be proven wrong about that," I said. "Go on your date, Kenlex, and don't be afraid of anything."

"I'm not afraid," she said, laughing. "I just don't know what to do and how to behave when I'm alone with Sir Melifaro. I mean, I don't know what to do so as not to hurt his feelings, and at the same time—"

"I get it," I said and yawned, unable to suppress it.

I was overcome by drowsiness so abrupt that it seemed as though the kamra I had just finished was laced with a generous portion of sedative. I shook my head, but it didn't help. Rather, it had an even more lulling effect on me. Meanwhile, my fair ladies were staring at me as though I were a prophet. Tekki, of course, was just curious what I was going to do in this tricky situation. On the one hand, I was supposed to uphold the interests of my friend. On the other, I had no right to give Kenlex a piece of outright bad advice. But I was too tired. To heck with both of them, I thought. Let them figure it out themselves.

"Here's a great tip for you. Works every time. Give him some baloney, and keep doing that until you figure out what it is you really want. You can pull this trick off indefinitely with most men. Even with me. So everything will be all right, trust me. Now I'll have to say good night. I'm sorry, girls, but I'm dead beat. And you don't want a dead body on your hands at this late hour, now, do you?"

I crawled down from the bar stool and went upstairs to the bedroom.

All my talk about needing someone to keep me company in the bedroom turned out to be a hoax. Tekki finally managed to wake me up in the morning, and that in itself was a miracle. I was sure she had had to resort to magic, but I didn't have the dagger with the magic-measuring gauge nearby, so I had to limit myself to ungrounded assumptions.

"What kind of advice did you mean to give Kenlex last night?" Tekki asked me when I began showing signs of life.

"Whah?" I said. "What are you talking about? I was so exhausted I could have said anything."

"You told her to give him baloney, for some reason," she said.

"Oh, that. Yeah, a solid piece of advice, by the way," I said. "What else should a girl do if she doesn't know what she wants?"

"Hold on a second, Max. Let's take it from the top again. What does a piece of smoked sausage have to do with any of it?"

I began to see my mistake. "A hole in the heavens above my silly head! I should have realized that no one would know that expression here."

"So it's just an expression?" said Tekki. "And what does it mean?"

"It means to talk foolish and deceptive nonsense, is all."

Tekki began laughing. "Oh, Max! You know, I think the girl took it literally. She considers you to be a very wise adviser, so you can imagine the consequences."

"Heh. I sure can. But you know, it's all for the better. They'll never forget their date for the rest of their lives."

Tekki wanted to continue our discussion, but I had to wrap it up. I had only two hours at my disposal, and I was not going to waste them discussing someone else's love affairs. Praise be the Magicians, I had an affair of my own, and I preferred to fulfill it rather than discuss it, here and now, while the earth was still down here and the heavens still up there. There was no guarantee that Fate would keep smiling down on my happy existence and not try to destroy the idyll.

Idylls aside, at noon I was at Headquarters, as Sir Venerable Head of Everything had ordered.

To my disappointment, I was the first one to arrive. Juffin was running late. In fact, Headquarters were totally empty save for one young courier, who was sleeping peacefully on a small couch by the entrance to the Hall of Common Labor.

I went into the office. Piled up on the desk were numerous pieces of evidence of its prolonged exposure to Melamori: a glass with the remains of some thick orange liquid at the bottom; a crumpled copy of yesterday's *Royal Voice*, which she had used to make an origami ship; and, of course, crumbs of cookies she had been feeding to her spider Leleo. Having contemplated this charming mess for a few moments, I woke up the courier and told him to clean it up. Then I sent a call to Juffin, whose absence still puzzled me to no end.

Look, this isn't fair. I'm already here and you're not.

Indeed, but I'm on my way. My coming is imminent.

What about the rest of the gang?

The rest of the gang is in position. Melamori is enjoying her much deserved rest, Lookfi is in the Main Archive, as usual, and the rest are abusing my good nature and shirking, using a variety of pretexts. Instead of torturing me with questions, you'd better send a call to the Glutton *and order us something. I haven't had breakfast yet.*

If I only had it my way, I'd be carrying out commands like that day in and day out. Juffin showed up at the office at the same time as the courier from the *Glutton Bunba*. The boss looked at the trays, gave an approving smile, sat down in his armchair, and began his breakfast.

"What special pretexts are there for shirking work?" I said. "It sounds like useful information to have." I can be such a bore sometimes.

"No special pretexts. Just about any will do," said Juffin. "Not for you, though. So you can go ahead and die of envy. Well, all right, all right, I'll tell you. Sir Melifaro was candid enough to tell me he finally had the chance to seduce one of your wives. I would have been a swine not to let him go. Kofa is just enjoying the rare opportunity to have breakfast at home. Both of them, however, will be here in an hour and a half or so. Great things await us today. Well, you three, rather. As for Sir Shurf, he managed to catch a cold yesterday. It breaks my heart, frankly. Deep inside, I am sure that a cold is the worst thing that can befall a man."

"And you are so right. Although I'm sure Shurf knows of a couple of breathing exercises for the occasion. Where did he catch a cold? On the Dark Side?"

"On the roof, of course, where else? He climbed up there to disperse the clouds with his hair still wet. I am shocked, to put it mildly. I have already gotten used to the thought that Sir Shurf is the only perfect creature in this mad World. Then I learn that he, too, is still capable of making silly mistakes like that."

"No wonder, though," I said. "He was really taking it easy yesterday. Now give me the rundown on the great things that await us. I'll bet anything that you called me up here so early just to gossip about it."

"Close, very close," said Juffin. "But the manner in which I am going to 'gossip' about it is not exactly the manner you're familiar with. Are you finished eating?"

"Well, I was going to have a second helping."

"Your second helping will have to wait, if you don't mind."

"I don't, but what kind—"

"Just close your eyes and keep silent for a few moments, that's all I'm asking. I am going to gossip, but not exactly with you. And don't you dare start to panic. You're in the House by the Bridge with me, not in the reception room of that monstrous wiseman from your World who specializes in teeth. Just relax."

I smiled and pulled myself together. Then I closed my eyes and relaxed as Juffin had told me to. Nothing happened, or at least I didn't feel anything. Moreover, I even dozed off for a moment without noticing it.

"That should be it," said Juffin in a cheerful tone, bringing me back to reality. "Wake up. You wanted a second helping, right?"

"Of course you're right. Are you ever wrong? I don't think Nature was generous enough to give you that talent," I said, filling my plate. "What kind of unspeakable curse did you just put on me, though? Or is it a secret?"

"It is. It's one of those secrets that keep themselves, without any extra help, because telling them would require words that don't exist in any human tongue known to me. Let's just say I had a small chat with your Shadow."

"The one you once took a spare heart from for me?"

"The same. Or do you think you've got more than one?"

"What did you do to it this time?" I said in a suspicious tone.

"Nothing I'd be embarrassed to talk about in mixed company," Juffin said and laughed. "What's with the worried look? I just taught your Shadow a few tricks. Perhaps you will both be better off with them. Or not. You never know for certain."

"I don't understand," I said.

"You don't need to understand it. Just know that if worse comes to worst, your Shadow stands a good chance to save your ass, along with the thing it's attached to."

"Why would my ass need saving?" I was still worried.

"Because you're about to get yourself in a very dangerous situation—you, Kofa, and Melifaro. But you more than them. Just bear with me a tad longer. They're going to be here any minute now, and then I'll tell you everything. It's much more practical than individual orientation sessions for each one of you."

"It must be true if you say so," I said, feeling gloomier than ever.

"Aw, don't give me that tragic look now. I told you many times it's not your forte. Just accept it."

"What is it that you're supposed to accept, you monster?" said Melifaro. He stood in the doorway, radiating joy like the midday sun. His new crimson looxi was so garish that I almost went deaf as well as blind, metaphorically speaking.

"From the looks of it, I'm going to have to accept everything," I said.

"Right you are." Melifaro ran to the armchair and jumped into it. The armchair gave out a plaintive squeak. Juffin raised his eyebrows and stared at Melifaro as though he were an inexplicable natural phenomenon.

"What's with the joy on the face of my Diurnal Rep?" he said.

"Girls love me again," said Melifaro. "So the World isn't coming to an end after all. Not now, at least. Prepare to take on the role of a deceived husband, Nightmare. You're going to need it in the near future, I swear by all the vomit-inducing honey of Kumon, may it drown in its own sugar toppings."

"How does one prepare for that occasion, exactly?" I said. "Are there some exercises I need to know? Anyway, tell me what happened. It's a family matter, so to speak. Besides, I know you're going to burst if you don't. I can see it with the naked eye."

Melifaro glanced at Juffin. The boss stuck his fingers in his ears, sat like that for a few seconds, and then crossed his arms on his chest and laughed.

"Max is right. Sir Melifaro, you are both in grave danger. If nothing is done about it, you will burst from overwhelming emotions, and he from good old curiosity. On top of that, I don't believe things have gone so far that you can't talk about it."

"If they haven't, they will," said Melifaro. He couldn't keep a straight face for more than a second. He, too, laughed and said, "You wouldn't believe what that girl was doing! Sinning Magicians, man, those savage customs of the steppes are really something else."

"What did she do?" I said, although I began to guess.

"First, everything was pretty decent. Lady Kenlex finally agreed to meet me without her suite, except she demanded that it take place in the morning. I've noticed that many girls deem us men to be some enchanted evil spirits that are rendered completely harmless in broad daylight. A dangerous delusion, I would say. Anyway, she said she wanted to meet in the morning, but then she also said she wanted to go to a tavern that served baloney. Well, I didn't think much of it at first. I was just glad she wasn't dragging me to that blasted *Kumonian Honey*."

I couldn't hold it in any longer and burst out laughing.

"I knew it," said Melifaro. "I just knew you had something to do with it."

"Don't stop," I said. "Mind you, I was upholding your best interests."

"I wish I could believe that. In any case, it wasn't all that bad. I took Kenlex to the *Happy Skeleton*. They serve good, simple food there, including baloney, right up until dusk. First, we just sat there and chatted about this and that. Kenlex kept looking around, probably making sure there were people around us, but also that no one was making love right there on the dinner table so I wouldn't try it, either. The *Happy Skeleton* is a respectable establishment, praise be the Magicians, so the girl's worries soon disappeared.

"Then they brought us our food, and that's when the unbelievable part began. Kenlex interrupted me in the middle of a sentence, grabbed a piece of baloney from her plate, and handed it to me. I was too dumbfounded to do anything with it, so she just placed it on my head and grabbed another one from her plate. Now I understand what people mean when they claim to be shocked about something.

"Little by little, I began to submit to her whims. I decided that it could very well be one of the poorly studied customs of her homeland. Maybe, I thought, that was what a girl did to someone who had a special place in her heart. I was grateful she wasn't trying to cover me in menkal dung, for crying out loud. I relaxed and just enjoyed her attentions. I think the customers of the *Happy Skeleton* were as happy as the skeleton itself. Even the chef came out of the kitchen to look at what we were doing. Kenlex paid no attention to the customers or the chef. I didn't dare hurt her simple, innocent feelings by interfering in the process.

"It went on for some time. I was all covered in slices of baloney, which had begun falling off and landing on my looxi, but she was just getting started. When she ran out of baloney, she stroked my head, gathered up the pieces from my head and looxi, and put them back on her plate. I thought the ceremony was over, but I couldn't have been more wrong. After she put the baloney back on her plate, she began covering me with it again! I didn't mind, though."

"You liked it that much?" I said.

"Yes, especially the finale. Kenlex got so carried away with it that she kissed me in the end. Apparently, covering a person of the opposite sex with baloney inevitably boosts the passion. Then the girl asked me, very politely, if I would mind her behaving in that manner from then on. I said that my head was at her service at any time of day or night. I had to run back home to change and take a bath, but for Kenlex I'm prepared to make a much greater sacrifice." Melifaro took a breath and gave me a meaningful look. "So it is your doing, isn't it? I can read the confession on your forehead, so don't try to deny it."

"I wasn't going to," I said. "But it wasn't 'my doing,' at least not directly. An ordinary misunderstanding of a linguistic nature."

"What do you mean?" said Juffin.

"Where I come from, we have an expression: 'to give someone baloney,'" I said. "It just means to talk nonsense, disregarding the interests of the other party. I said it when I was talking to Kenlex. How on earth was I supposed to know that she would misconstrue the meaning and take it literally?"

Juffin's and Melifaro's guffaws answered my question.

"I guess I don't need to apologize for showing up late," said Kofa, coming in. "I see you're having a great time."

"I was planning to start getting mad at you in a minute or two," said Juffin, "so you barely made it."

"I just shouldn't be allowed to have breakfast at home," said the Master Eavesdropper. "It was such a rare pleasure that I simply couldn't stop."

"I can relate," said the boss. "Well, since everyone is here, I'm going to have to change the subject and talk about Glenke Taval, former Grand Magician of the Order of the Sleeping Butterfly, who was—and, alas, still is—one of the best sorcerers who has ever burdened the World with his existence."

"Do we have to talk about that wearisome gentleman?" said Kofa. "I think it's pretty clear what we must do. Tear off his head and throw it in a swamp. Better late than never, as I see it."

"You are correct," Juffin said drily. "I was going to propose you do something to that effect. Things have already gone too far, however. An entire army of Lonely Shadows guards Glenke now. But the Shadows are not your problem. Max can easily deal with them."

I gulped and swallowed both the saliva in my mouth and the objections in my head. If Sir Juffin thinks I can easily deal with a whole army of Lonely Shadows, he probably knows what he's talking about, I thought.

The boss gave me a look of genuine compassion.

"I can see you're somewhat surprised, but one of your Lethal Spheres might be more than enough to take care of them," said Juffin. "The critical part is to launch it in the right direction, and you're usually good at that. Our main problem is that Glenke Taval exists in the World and on the Dark Side simultaneously. An unsurpassed and rare skill. I have always been fond of his talents."

"Too fond, I might add," said Kofa. "If you hadn't bargained for his life with Nuflin, we wouldn't have this problem now."

"That is true, Kofa. But back then I was obsessed with the idea that the life of every person chosen by Xumgat was a precious gift that no one had the right to take away unless it was absolutely necessary. I still hold to this idea, partially."

"Well, you are the boss," said Kofa. "By the way, under what conditions was he granted his life and freedom?"

"The usual," said Juffin. "Glenke was never to set foot in Uguland, meet with other members of his Order, have students, and so on and so forth. Besides, when I talked to him personally, he swore he'd limit the area of his explorations to True Magic. I have to hand it to him, though, he has honestly kept his word. According to the Lonely Shadow that I captured, he still sits quietly in his mansion somewhere around the Great Lake Munto and leaves it only to take a walk on the Dark Side. There is also no Apparent Magic that I can detect in what he does. Nominally, he's clean—with one small exception, however. That madman brought us to the brink of an abyss when he began taming Lonely Shadows. I could almost cry from despair: if only some sweet person like Lieutenant Apurra Blookey or Sir Rogro were naturally endowed with his talents. But no!"

"You seem to be too upset about it," said Kofa. "Is he really worth it?"

"It's easier for you," said Juffin. "You couldn't stand him from the outset, although I never quite knew why. Glenke and I used to be good friends, very good friends. I can't say that the fact that we need to kill him makes me happy."

"You should have gotten used to it by now," said Kofa. "You've always specialized in killing your former friends. Go for it, I say. It's a good job, and it puts bread on the table."

Their exchange seemed to be growing rather tense when all of a sudden Juffin made a hopeless gesture, laughed, and said, "Thanks, Kofa. You can always improve my mood. Such a shame, though. An imposing, elderly gentleman, yet so immoral."

"You should discuss this with Magician Nuflin, who is a much more elderly and imposing gentleman. He will tell you that morality is an invention of sated, powerful, and very shrewd people so that all the rest would spend their free time trying to sort out who among them was right and who was wrong. And so that no one would bother the sated ones, and they could just keep eating."

"Spoken like a true former police general," said Juffin, smiling. "And you, boys, are going to Landaland in the company of this old cynic, looking for my old friend Glenke Taval. I don't envy you."

"Hold on a second," I said. "You haven't even begun to explain anything."

"Ah, it is clear that you haven't been with the Investigative Force long enough," said Melifaro. "This is a classic business meeting here: Sir Juffin and Sir Kofa bicker until midnight, while the others make bets on when they're going to fight. At the end, Sir Juffin says that we should improvise and take action according to situation, and then he goes home. Am I right, sir?"

"You're close," said Juffin. "But just for the benefit of Sir Max's pretty eyes and frayed nerves, I will deviate from tradition. Kofa and I can cut down on our bickering and stop right now."

"Thank you," I said. "So we go to Landaland and combine our efforts to bite off the head of your friend Sir Glenke Taval, right?"

"Brilliant thinking," said Juffin. "Now here's something you should know about killing Glenke. You will have to kill him in the World and on the Dark Side *at the same time*. Otherwise he'll slip out of our clutches and we'll never see him until the end of time. That's why I'm sending all three of you. You, Kofa, will kill him in this World—I'm sure you will derive a great deal of pleasure out of it. Max will work on the Dark Side. And you, young man, you—"

"I'll be hanging around on the border, like I always do," said Melifaro.

"Precisely."

"When do we leave?" said Kofa.

"The sooner, the better. You can leave right now."

"Oh, no. That won't do. I don't know about you, boys, but I need to pack," said Kofa.

"Everybody needs to pack," said Melifaro, almost falling off the armchair, overwhelmed with emotion. "And I need to say goodbye to a certain beautiful lady."

"When you first started working here, I gave you a piece of advice," said Juffin. He was smiling, but his eyes were as cold as water under a crust of ice. "I told you that our job was full of perils, and that each time you come to the House by the Bridge, you should always say goodbye to those you hold dear as though you're leaving forever. Remember?"

"Yes, I do," said Melifaro. He was serious. "That was exactly what I was going to do, originally, but I don't yet know how to say goodbye to someone forever with baloney sticking out from under my turban."

"You don't particularly like that advice, do you?" said Juffin, turning to me. "And yet it pertains to you, too. Keep it in mind in the future." He paused and then addressed us all. "All right, guys, you can leave tomorrow morning or at noon. Whenever you wake up, in other words. With Max behind the levers, it doesn't really matter. You'll get to Glenke much faster than I dare hope."

"At noon, then. Please?" I said.

"Fine," said Juffin with equanimity. "As I said, it's up to you."

"It's been a while since I had the chance to get away from Echo for a long time," said Kofa. "It's hard to believe that I'm getting such an opportunity. I'm even beginning to warm up to Glenke. If it weren't for him, I wouldn't have a vacation at all."

"I have been telling you to go somewhere and get a good rest for years," said Juffin. "You wouldn't hear of it."

"You know I hate wasting time on such trifles. But a business trip to Landaland, now, is just what I need."

"Good, then. At least someone is happy about the mission." Juffin yawned one of his contagious yawns and extended his hand toward a half-empty pitcher of kamra. Then he waved off his impulse and got up from his armchair in one resolute swing. "I'll see you tomorrow, gentlemen. I intend to abuse my position as your boss and go home. And I wouldn't envy the reckless hero who dared stand between me and my bed now."

The boss winked at me, then suddenly grabbed himself by the collar and threw himself out the window in one fell swoop. He disappeared before he hit the ground. I saw only a small cloud of pale mist left hanging in the air outside. I stared at it, blinking, as it took the shape of a large question mark and then evaporated.

Sir Kofa shook his head. "He's come up with a new one. All right, boys, I think I'm going to do some work before we leave tomorrow. Don't worry, Max, I'll replace you right after midnight. It's in my own interest. The last thing I want is to travel to the ends of the earth in the company of a sleepy driver who's pumped himself to the brim with Elixir of Kaxar."

"When did I pump myself to the brim with it?" I said. "I'm an extremely moderate, if a tad wearisome, guy. I don't have bad habits. Only harmless quirks."

"Extremely young is what you are, and all your so-called habits are not worth a crown," said Kofa, laughing. "A habit is only worthy of mention when it's at least a couple hundred years old. Good night, boys."

Melifaro and I were alone in the office now. Thank goodness he wasn't in any hurry to leave.

"Some trip we're going on, huh?" he said after a courier brought another tray with food from the *Glutton*. Melifaro's voice was gloomy and lifeless.

"You mean that mysterious, disgraceful task we're supposed to perform on the Dark Side?" I said in a no less gloomy and lifeless tone.

"To Magicians with the Dark Side. We'll manage that somehow. What's bothering me is that we'll be in the company of our Master Eavesdropper-Gobbler. I wish you and I were going alone instead. That would be fun."

"What's wrong with Kofa?" I said, surprised. "He's a pleasure to work with. I have plenty of evidence of that."

"Of course. That was in Echo, right?"

"Sure. What difference does it make?"

"You'll see," said Melifaro. "I'll just say this: There is the Sir Kofa Yox you know here—a well-fed wiseman, a gourmand, a ladies' man, and an all-around sweet person. But as that venerable gentleman gets farther away from the Heart of the World, he turns into an unbearable person. Even his appearance changes. I once had the misfortune of accompanying him on a trip to the ends of Uryuland and back. I still can't fathom how I managed not to lose all my marbles."

"Oh, I wouldn't say that. You've lost them, all right," I said.

"Yeah, yeah, make fun of me all you want. You'll be singing a different tune tomorrow evening. You'll beg me to let you run away to the Dark Side before it's time, but I won't let you, buddy. Mark my words."

"Speaking of which," I said. "I'd be eternally grateful to you if you explained to me in plain words the fundamental principles of our further interactions."

"Oh, that's easy," said Melifaro, laughing. "I'll be going out with your wife, you'll be trying to smash my face, and I'll be resorting to self-defense to the best of my abilities. Neat, huh?"

"I wasn't talking about my wife. I was asking how I'm supposed to behave in the presence of a Sentry. In other words, how am I supposed to use you?"

"'Use me'?" said Melifaro. "Well, you *are* a monster! How dare you speak to a Sentry in that manner?" He made a feeble show of indignation, but his mouth broke into a broad smile despite his efforts to resist it. "'Use me,' eh?" he repeated and laughed again.

"Of course," I said. "If you came with a manual, I would just glance over it and call it a day. But since you came 'as is' . . .'"

"All right, all right, stop making fun of me, already. There's really nothing you need to know. When the time comes, I'll take you to the Dark Side and then bring you back. You can call me any time in between, too, and I'll come and rescue you like an overprotective mother. That's all. I hope this doesn't overtax your diminished mental capacities."

"It does, but I'll persevere. Let's consider this briefing over."

We never touched upon the subject again. Of course, I wanted to ask Melifaro about his mysterious double, but somehow I couldn't muster up enough courage to do that.

He left a couple of hours later. When Juffin has the presence of mind to put me in his armchair, skipping out on work becomes too easy. My colleagues had gotten used to the fact that they didn't have to ask my permission. All they had to say was "good night," then boldly go wherever their whims took them.

Before I could allow myself to enjoy my solitude, I ordered that the remains of my tête-à-tête with Melifaro be cleared from the table. Then I ordered myself another pitcher of kamra, put my feet on the desk, lit up a cigarette, and gave Kurush an expectant stare.

"Tell me about this Sir Glenke Taval," I said. "Only drop the official tone. Make it sound like a fairy tale."

"The story of Grand Magician Glenke Taval cannot be made to sound like a fairy tale," said Kurush. "Even if his life were full of spectacular and amazing events, they would forever remain the personal secrets of Magician Glenke Taval."

"Fine, then. Tell it however you can."

"Glenke Taval was born in Landaland to a family that was on close terms with the Order of the Sleeping Butterfly, allegedly between the years 2740 and 2760 of the Epoch of Orders. It is known that he became an apprentice to the Order in 2832, when he was still very young. There is virtually no information about that early period in his life. In a unanimous vote cast at a meeting of Senior Magicians on the third day of the year 3008, Glenke Taval was made Grand Magician of the Order of the Sleeping Butterfly, immediately after the sudden disappearance of former Grand Magician of the Order Avves Tirak. I have information that there were many rumors regarding his disappearance, but I am not familiar with them. It is commonly held that it was the policy introduced by Magician Glenke Taval that made the Order of the Sleeping Butterfly one of the most powerful Orders in the Unified Kingdom. It is worthy of note that he had virtually no interaction with the World outside, almost never left the Order's Residence, and had almost no enemies, which is unusual, considering the customs and morals of the Epoch of Orders."

"I'm sorry for interrupting you, Kurush, but I was just wondering, what were *you* doing during the Epoch of Orders?" I said.

"I was not doing anything," Kurush said with dignity. "I left my egg on the sixteenth year of the Code Epoch. Are you still interested in Magician Glenke Taval? I'm afraid I don't have the information you're looking for. Nothing that resembles a fairy tale, only the names of his assistants, the date of the official declaration of the Order of the Sleeping Butterfly on its nonsubmission to the Royal Decree calling for its disbandment, the date of Sir Glenke Taval's arrest, the date and conditions of his exile, and so on. If my notion of you is anywhere close to reality, your area of interest lies elsewhere. Why don't you talk to Juffin? As far as I can tell from today's conversation, he has a great deal more of the kind of information about Glenke Taval that you are interested in. People are normally inclined to express their views on the lives of their friends."

"Oh, you *are* the wisest creature in the World, Kurush!" I said. "I think I'm going to go ahead and risk spoiling Juffin's R and R."

Without hesitation, I fulfilled my threat and sent him a call.

You're not asleep yet, are you? I began cautiously.

Believe it or not, no. I should have gone straight to the Street of Old Coins. I would have been watching a movie now, happy and content. Instead, I'm lying in bed, trying to find familiar words in one fascinating book. So far I've found a dozen or so. Let me guess, you're going to squeeze more information about my old friend Glenke out of me? Frankly, I'm not sure I want to divulge the story of his life to you.

How come? You've already told me so many secrets. What difference will another one make?

Secrets have nothing to do with it. Glenke, the way I remember him, was an amazing fellow. I think you might even get along with him. But since you're going to kill him—

I'm not supposed to develop empathy toward him? Is that what you're trying to say?

Precisely. Put it out of your head. Ordinary people can change, sometimes drastically. Let alone powerful Magicians.

Okay, I'll try to put it out of my head. But could you at least tell me something that might help me defeat him?

The most important thing to keep in mind is that Glenke Taval is a powerful adversary. At the same time, he's almost helpless. It's very easy to kill him. At least it's not going to be a problem for you. He never really learned to kill others or to defend himself. His strength lies elsewhere. He's almost at home on the Dark Side.

And how am I supposed to catch him, in that case?

Unlike Glenke, you are *at home on the Dark Side. You'll be surprised to see how easy it is for you to be there. There's something else you should never forget, even for a second: while on the Dark Side, your words have a special power. So don't you dare start shooting off your mouth there. Your garrulousness is the only true danger for you on the Dark Side. Who knows what you might blurt out? Remember what happened between you and the Tipfinger?*

I'll never forget it! Thanks for warning me, Juffin. I always talk nonsense when I'm nervous. Now I have good reason to keep my chatterbox shut.

Well, good, then. Good night, Max. And don't be upset about Glenke. I've had all kinds of acquaintances throughout my life: some good, some not so good.

Good night, Juffin.

I poured myself some kamra, stroked Kurush's feathers, and suddenly realized that now I could carry on living. A heavy load that had been sitting on my chest was lifted. It had disappeared while I was chatting with Juffin, although he hadn't said anything soothing or particularly reassuring to me. If anything, the contrary was true. Hmm, I thought, I can't say the situation is altogether unfamiliar.

Sir Kofa came right after midnight as he had promised.

"Go home, Max," he said. "I can get the two hours of sleep that will transform me from a useless wreck into a human being again right here in this armchair."

"I still envy you," I said. "You need so little sleep. You're good to go twenty-two hours a day."

"Wait a minute, boy," said Kofa, surprised, "why twenty-*two*? I do need two hours of sleep after all."

"That's what I'm saying. Out of the twenty-four hours of the day, you sleep for two. Hence, the twenty-two hours of activity. No?"

"You've got your basic arithmetic right," said Kofa, "except that there are twenty-*two* hours in a day. Didn't you know that?"

"A hole in the heavens above me!" I was stunned by the sudden revelation. "I never thought of that. So that's why I never have enough time for anything!"

"Did you never bother to take a close look at a clock? Well, don't fret. It's not the end of the world."

In the morning it turned out that Juffin's advice about saying goodbye as if you were going away forever was by no means impossible. Some part of me rejected the very idea, but its voice was weak enough that I could ignore it.

In fact, it was easy to do. I just had to admit to myself that there was no guarantee, no piece of paper with a royal seal affixed to it, saying I would always come back from any adventure safe and sound. Not now, not ever. So there.

As soon as I realized this, true serenity replaced my fake nervous cheerfulness. It was a change for the better. Tekki sensed the shift in my mood right away and reflected it like a mirror—that was her nature. It even seemed to me that she felt an immense relief, just as I had. I gave her a peck on the nose, and she, not expecting that, laughed, took a step back, and winked at me, as though we had just conspired to play a harmless prank on a mutual acquaintance.

I was the last to arrive at the House by the Bridge. Sir Kofa and Melifaro were already busy stowing their travel bags under the seats of their amobiler. It even seemed they had dressed up for the occasion. I, on the contrary, had put on an old looxi of a dark swamp-like color, thinking, as naive as I was, that this was what traveling attire should look like.

"You're getting ahead of yourselves," I said to my companions. "Now you'll have to take your luggage out."

"How so?" said Melifaro. He was worried that he would fall victim to another one of my pranks.

"Because we're taking my amobiler," I said. "It's better. I don't know how, but I think I got the best and most durable set of wheels under the sun by accident. You wouldn't believe me if I told you what it's been through, and yet it still looks and runs as good as new. But the greatest part is that it's more spacious. It may not seem like a big deal to you now, but when you get tired of sitting during a long drive and you fancy lying flat on your backs, you'll thank me."

"The boy is wise beyond his years. I always suspected it, but now I know for certain," Kofa said. "We should also bring a few spare crystals with us. It must have never occurred to you that anything could happen to the crystal. A slow hike to Great Lake Munto is not exactly in line with my plans for the coming century."

"Ah, thanks for reminding me. Where do I buy them?"

"At the same store you bought your amobiler. But don't worry about it. I already asked them to set aside half a dozen for us from the Headquarters' supply."

"Excellent," I said. "So shall we go hang on Juffin's neck before we leave?"

"What about the parting scene with General Boboota?" said Melifaro. "Are you going to deprive me of the show?"

"I am. To the Dark Magicians with General Boboota. If he starts to cry, it'll break my heart, and I might decide to stay."

And we went to our side of the House by the Bridge because a cup of kamra in good company was just what a man needed before a long journey.

To my surprise, when I entered the Hall of Common Labor, I saw that Juffin, Melamori, and Lookfi Pence, who had come down from the Main Archive, had been joined by Lady Kekki Tuotli. Instead of the uniform of the City Police Department, she wore an ostentatious, very informal looxi—Melifaro would have envied her if he were a girl. Kekki caught my stare and stuck out her chin coquettishly.

"I'm not just visiting," she said. "I work here now."

"Really?" I was surprised. "Hey, that's great news! I've always said that the police uniform clashes with the color of your lovely eyes. In what capacity?"

"In the capacity of Kofa. I'll wear his magic cloak so it doesn't get too dusty. These gentlemen think that the Secret Investigative Force should not be left without a Master Eavesdropper for long. They also think I'll manage to replace him."

"Of course you will. It's not the hardest job in the world," said Kofa.

"We'll get to test your assumption in practice soon," she said.

"This immoral gentleman has an unbearable habit of pushing his protégées into the cushy jobs," said Juffin, laughing. Then he winked at Kekki. "Don't get offended. That jab was aimed solely at our mutual friend here."

"I'm not offended. Say what you will, I still like it here better than back at my old side of the Ministry."

"But of course," I said. "We're the cream of the crop. Speaking of the best, where's Shurf? I don't believe he's still sniffling and snuffling. He's a bore and a pedant, sure, but that'd be too much even for him."

"He stopped sniffling and snuffling yesterday," said Juffin. "I decided that Sir Shurf could have another day of rest."

"Right. That hero desperately needs to go to the library after yesterday," said Melifaro. "Everyone has his own way of combating a hangover."

We chatted a little more, had some kamra, and then I knew it was time for us to go. I didn't want to go through saying goodbye forever to my colleagues, too, but I knew I had to do it, and I had to do it now.

I glanced over the spacious Hall of Common Labor, rested my gaze on the contemplative face of Melamori—she hadn't really said a word the whole time—and forced myself to think that it could be the last time I see her. There was no way of knowing for sure.

It worked again. The same way it had worked earlier in the morning with Tekki. Instead of grieving or becoming frightened, I once again felt a sense of freedom. It seemed a slight gust of wind could have swept me away. Granted, there was no wind inside Headquarters. Not even a draft.

Juffin gave me a nod of approval. "I couldn't hope that you'd take my advice to heart," he said. "Well, I'm glad you did. Kofa, I have a small favor to ask of you. Since it all pans out that way, could you also . . ."

He came up to Kofa and whispered something into his ear. Kofa smiled and gave a few vigorous nods.

It goes without saying that I was burning with curiosity. I gave Juffin a pleading look, but he shook his head.

"No way, mister. Can't a man have a secret?"

"Absolutely," I said reluctantly. "Let's go, guys. By the way, does anybody know where we're going exactly?"

And then all of my colleagues burst out laughing. Even Sir Lookfi

Pence was laughing, knocking over empty and not-so-empty cups. They probably thought I was joking.

Five minutes later we were already driving across the Royal Bridge. Our route took us to the Left Bank and then farther down to the gate that went by the name of the Breach of Toixi Menka. Back in the day, Toixi Menka, Prince of the Old Dynasty, singlehandedly demolished the city wall, built by his father, King Joxira Menka, in that location. That was how the northernmost gate of the city got its name. The prince's actions rendered a service to the inhabitants of the northern suburbs, but if one were to believe the ancient chroniclers, they also became his undoing.

Either the prince wasn't acquainted with the ancient legend, which foretold that the demise of his family would come from the North, or, unlike his father, the prince didn't believe in superstitions, but soon he and all of his numerous relatives had disappeared under mysterious circumstances. No one, however, bothered to ask where the misfortune had come from—the North or the South. In any case, the Old Dynasty had expired such a long time ago that any attempt to uncover the mystery of that tragic event was merely an exercise for the mind.

Once we were beyond the city limits, I tore along so fast in the amobiler that I couldn't afford to get distracted by engaging in conversation with my colleagues. They were having a lively discussion in the back seat, but I wasn't listening. Finally Melifaro moved up to the passenger seat next to me.

"Kofa's asleep," he said glumly. "Boy, are you driving fast! We're far enough from Echo for . . . Okay, Max, say goodbye to your old friend, Sir Kofa." He sighed and then smiled again. "Look, I simply must tell you that your stupid baloney joke is beginning to grow on me. Combined with that piece of advice from Juffin to say farewell as though one is leaving forever, a piece of smoked sausage produces phenomenal results."

"Oh, yeah?" I said, listening with half an ear.

"Oh, yeah."

"Have I been officially cheated on already or not?"

"You've been a cuckold all your life," said Melifaro, laughing.

The expression on his face suggested that the process of giving and accepting baloney had not been the innocent pastime one might have assumed. I felt as though I had suddenly become the father of a grown-up daughter. I desperately wanted to give the young seducer a lecture on the instability of the minds of young girls, who should be treated decently under all circumstances. I'd probably throw in the basics of contraception into the bargain.

Fortunately, I quickly assessed how ridiculous the situation was, dropped my role of worried parent, and laughed with relief.

"Tell me, young lover, how well do you know this area? Is there some neat little road tavern around here? I don't know about you, but I'm starving."

"You should have thought about that earlier. We're already way past Cheli. The closest town now is Chinfaro. Although, at this speed, we'll arrive at the outskirts in about an hour or so. Can you hold on for an hour?"

"For an hour I can, I think," I said.

"In any case, we should stay there for the night. That will be our last chance to get a good rest. We can wash our feet before going to bed, use a heated bathroom, and drink kamra that is still distinguishable from slop. Farther north of Chinfaro lie territories that are almost uninhabited. Then we'll have to make a turn onto a really bad road, through the infamous woods of Uguland, followed by the even more infamous mires of Landaland. That Glenke Taval knew where to settle to make it tough for anyone who would dare go looking for him. The lands around the Great Lake Munto are not for the faint of heart."

"You sure are full of ominous prophecies today," I said.

"These are no ominous prophecies; they are cold hard facts. And don't look at me as though I was the one who created that useless piece of land just to annoy you."

"How should I know?" I said. "That's just the sort of thing you might do."

"No, no. That's not my area of expertise," said Melifaro in an absolutely serious tone.

About an hour later I saw that we were approaching a fairly sizable town. I even had to slow down: the road was already getting full of competitors. Most of the competition was farmer's carts, but there were a few amobilers of the most whimsical shapes, as well.

"What's with all the noise?" I heard Kofa's annoyed voice coming from the back. "Oh, we're near Chinfaro already. Well, it could have been worse."

I turned around to reply to him. Good thing I had slowed down. I might easily have lost control of the amobiler when I discovered a lanky fellow with a long, horselike face and a beautiful nose sitting in the back seat. I got a grip on myself, however, pulled over to the side of the road, stopped, and then went into shock.

"As if you never noticed before that my face is not an immutable feature of my body. What kind of a brain do you have?" grumbled the unrecognizable Sir Kofa.

"The face, yes, but the rest of your body has been pretty immutable so far," I said.

"It doesn't matter what has or hasn't been so far. The intensity of the emotional changes you are currently undergoing testifies to your low mental capacity. For this reason, you shouldn't waste your time on vain intellectual efforts but rather keep driving and find some decent place for the night."

Sir Kofa's new appearance had indeed rendered him very unpleasant to deal with. It seemed like Melifaro hadn't been exaggerating a bit when he warned me of the possible horrors of the journey. I was so blown out of the water that I obediently grabbed the levers and set the amobiler in motion. Only then did I become outraged. I couldn't find the right words, though, so my indignation remained mute for the time being.

"I told you," Melifaro whispered in my ear.

"Yes, you did. And I didn't believe you. I still don't. Please pinch me so I'll wake up." I said.

"You didn't believe what?" said the long-faced fellow whom I still refused to call Sir Kofa.

"You should spend a little more time on vain intellectual efforts," I said, boiling over. "Maybe then you'll understand."

Kofa didn't reply, and Melifaro looked at me with open admiration. It seemed he had already abandoned the thought of trying to resist the disaster that had befallen us.

Suddenly I heard a strange monotonous sound coming from behind me, so I turned around again. The unrecognizable Sir Kofa was stretched out comfortably on the back seat. In his lap he held a miniature barrel organ. He was turning the carved handle of its crank and looking pensively into the sky.

"That's what I was most afraid of," Melifaro moaned. "Last time he almost drove me insane with his music. Kofa wouldn't let the damn box out of his hands even in his sleep. Mind you, there's no way we can explain to him that it's annoying. He just doesn't give a flying fig."

"You two are incredibly unmusical," said our companion. "This wonderful tune calms one down and stimulates the thinking processes. You should be grateful to me for the joy I give you at no cost whatsoever."

"Thank you kindly," I said, laughing, and turned to Melifaro. "Sir Kofa is absolutely right. See, he's so generous. He could have asked us to pay for the concert, and yet he's charitable enough to let us sit through it for free."

Melifaro smiled a nervous smile. He had definitely been ill at ease since Kofa had woken up. Perhaps he just couldn't cope with the thought that someone else had hijacked the role of most unbearable member of our team.

"Take a left here, Max."

Kofa's new commanding tone could bring down anyone except me. Back in the day I changed jobs many times, and compared to some of my former bosses, Kofa still seemed like a sweet guy. Having pondered the situation, I decided to ignore his new appearance, along with his new disposition, and instead behave as though he was still good old Master Eavesdropper-Gobbler, sweet-natured and indulgent.

"Yes, sir!" I said. "I don't doubt for a second that you know the exact address of the best lousy inn in this backwater of a town."

"Occasionally you seem to be capable of coming to an accurate conclusion," said Kofa. "Pull over by that yellow two-story house there. The *Old House* isn't what one might call a decent inn, but that hardly matters. None of the local inns is a place where one could hope to spend a satisfactory night. At least the meals are good in the *Old House*."

"Did I ever tell you that you could find a cozy place with good cuisine even in Hades?" I said, smiling.

"You have, on many occasions. It is still nonsense. I don't think Hades, judging from your description, can possibly have any taverns or inns in it. Provided that it even exists at all, that Hades of yours," Kofa grumbled.

He took his travel bag out from under the seat and got out of the amobiler. Amazed, I looked at his figure, which had grown a whole head taller. For some reason, I found that fact the hardest to come to terms with.

By the time we caught up with him in the spacious lobby of the *Old House*, Kofa had already cornered the innkeeper and extorted the keys to his best rooms. I was almost certain that Kofa would keep all three keys to himself, but he shared the loot evenly among us.

I threw my bag in the far corner of my room—quite cramped, compared to traditional apartments of the Capital, but cozy—and went down to the dining hall. Melifaro was already there, hesitating about which of the numerous empty tables to occupy.

"I've always liked sitting in the farthest corner, preferably by a window," I said. "So if it's all the same to you, we can—"

"It makes absolutely no difference to me," said Melifaro. He sighed and sauntered in the direction I was pointing. "So how do you like our magnificent Sir Kofa Yox now? Isn't he just horrible?"

"Horrible? No. Actually, I think he's okay. Compared to some of the people I used to deal with, he's a sweetie."

"Is that so?" said Melifaro. "Well, I've always suspected you grew up among werewolves. For your information, that's the real Kofa. I mean, he was born with that long face and unbearable disposition. For the first hundred and twenty years, he poisoned everybody's lives. Then his own father got fed up with it and put a spell on him. He improved his disposition and his appetite a little. As Kofa moves away from the Heart of the World, the spell's powers trail off and we get to see the real son of the legendary Magician Xumka Yox in all his primordial glory."

"Kofa's dad was legendary?"

"Oh, yes! He was one of the seven Great Founders of the Order of the Seven-Leaf Clover. Grand Magician Nuflin was his student, like many other older members of the Order. For a millennium Magician Xumka did some unfathomable things, and then he suddenly retired, had a family, and delved deep into culinary experiments. It looked as though he had grown tired of his own powers and decided to become a regular inhabitant of Echo. Of course he couldn't do that, but he tried very hard. What he did succeed in was getting old and dying. Oh, here comes our precious Sir Kofa. Let's change the subject."

Melifaro and I had a great dinner. The food at the *Old House* was almost as good as at the *Glutton Bunba*. As for Kofa, he said he had to adhere to some special "diet." I didn't understand what it boiled down to from his explanations, but Kofa went to the kitchen several times to personally oversee how each of the dishes he ordered was being prepared. Then he polished off the contents of the numerous bowls and plates at his table. While he was doing this, his face betrayed not a hint of enjoyment. After he finished, he went upstairs, claiming he had to ponder some "further action." As if it needed pondering.

"Want to go for a walk?" I asked Melifaro.

"Right. I'm going to drop everything and run around admiring the paint peeling off the turkey farm fences on the outskirts of the glorious town of Chinfaro," he said with contempt. But then he smiled and added, "This is my only chance to get some decent sleep. I haven't had much of it back home recently, what with all the baloney all over me."

"Don't you think that the 'intensity of the emotional changes you are currently undergoing testifies to your low mental capacity'?" I said, mimicking Kofa's arrogant tone.

Melifaro burst out laughing. "I underestimated you. You are much worse than Kofa. Good night, Monster. Don't get lost in the town."

He ran off upstairs to his room, and I went outside.

At first, any unfamiliar city seems beautiful to me, and Chinfaro was no exception. I like to treat an unfamiliar city like some men treat a girl on a date—I gently touch the cobblestones with my feet and take shallow breaths, accepting each whiff of air, permeated with unusual smells, with gratitude, like a kiss. I do many other things so that the city doesn't think I'm a thoughtless brute like all the others, and I tell it, completely in awe, "You are the most beautiful of all the places I've ever been to. There are no places better than you!"

I say it with utmost sincerity—at least, I believe it myself—and the city believes me and reciprocates in kind. Soon after, it asks me point-blank if there is anything it can do for me. Maybe that's why I've never really felt uncomfortable anywhere, except, perhaps, for the city where I was born. But back then I didn't know how to charm anyone. Or any*thing*.

It was already morning when I returned to the inn. I was elated and emotionally drained, as though I had just returned from a date with a beautiful stranger. In fact I had tortured my feet, circling around Chinfaro's old downtown lit by the bluish light of the gas-filled spheres hanging from all the trees.

Without further ado, I slipped under a thin blanket and fell asleep instantly. It was a wise thing to do because that cruel Melifaro burst in and woke me up before noon.

"What's the hurry?" I said. "Are we late for school?"

"Just wanted to ruin your day from the get-go," he said, staring at me with imploring eyes. "Get up, Max, I beg you! Let's go already. I can't stand loafing around in this blasted empty inn. Also, it's no fun without you."

"Really?" I said, fumbling in my bag for the bottle of Elixir of Kaxar. It still was the only way I knew to put myself to rights in record time. "You could have suffered a couple more hours. You were doing just fine without me for the first hundred fifteen years of your life."

"I was, but you're like a bad habit I can't get rid of. I fear that if things keep going the way they are, I'm going to have to move to your place," said Melifaro. "Also, how come you're so sleepy? What have you been doing all night, you monster? Murdering good people again? Orphans, widows, and other innocents that villains like you usually murder?"

"You mean like their best friends?" I said, yawning, and went to the bathroom. Melifaro followed me there and sat down right on the floor so as not to interrupt the conversation. I was about to demand my right to privacy during such an intimate procedure as brushing my teeth, but then I changed my mind and said, "What's Kofa been up to?"

"He's eating. And thinking. And cranking his dratted barrel organ. The dining hall is totally empty now. No one could muster the gumption to stay there and listen to its sounds. I'm about to snap, too. *Ma-a-a-ax!* Let's get out of here! *Puh-lease.*"

We went downstairs, where I had the chance to verify Melifaro's words. The monotonous sound of Kofa's barrel organ didn't exactly facilitate a warm and friendly atmosphere. A few years ago I definitely would have gone insane if that had been the soundtrack of my life. But now I had Shurf Lonli-Lokli's breathing exercises at my disposal. They came in handy as they never had before.

As a result, I didn't go insane. Instead, I had a quick cup of kamra and headed for the exit.

"Finally." Kofa's grumpy voice came from behind my back. "I thought we'd never leave. Still, it was a mistake on your part not to have anything to eat. It's going to be quite some time before our next opportunity to stop and have a snack."

"I couldn't care less," I said. "Say what you will, but I just can't stomach anything in the mornings. I can always fetch something from the Chink between Worlds. By the way, if you feel like eating while we're on the road, just tell me and I'll get you something yummy."

"I am not eating any garbage from another World," said Kofa. "My stomach is the national treasure of the Unified Kingdom. One could easily end up in Xolomi for maltreating it."

I wrote off his tirade as a joke, although I had my doubts about whether it really was.

By noon we were already driving down the country road. It was too narrow and rough for my taste. It was flanked by dense woods that looked wild and uninhabited. This wasn't exactly how I'd imagined a journey from one province of the Unified Kingdom to another.

"The main road—the one that the farmers take to go to the fair in Numban and back—lies farther off to the side," said Melifaro. "These, though, are the backwoods, in the most literal sense of the word. You should get used to the thought that it's only going to get worse from here on out. *Much* worse, in fact."

"Yes, and all thanks to none other than Sir Juffin Hully," said Kofa, "who sent us to wander about the swamps looking for his former friend, who is even nuttier than that raging Kettarian himself. A worthy task, I'll hand him that. Me? I prefer different forms of entertainment."

He never stopped cranking the handle of his horrible miniature barrel organ. Now it was producing some new tune that was no less tormenting than the first one. I focused solely on steering the amobiler and soon was able to tune out the concert.

Two hours into the journey, the road became so bad that I had to slow down. Sir Kofa was still torturing us with the barrel organ. I noticed that Melifaro had stopped complaining about it. On the contrary, he had assumed a placid, even dreamy air.

"Has the music grown on you?" I said. Melifaro didn't reply, and I thought he was sleeping with his eyes open.

"He can't hear you," said Sir Kofa. "Nor can he hear anything. He had to resort to earplugs since his backwardness and lack of taste prevent him from enjoying exquisite music."

I had to laugh. Melifaro gave me a puzzled look.

"Did I miss something?" he yelled.

I shook my head. Melifaro nodded and went back to staring at one spot. I'd never thought the fellow could sit motionless for hours, not to mention remain silent. At the same time, he looked as contented as if he had been dreaming of this opportunity his whole life.

Suddenly, the music stopped. Perhaps some local deity had been merciful enough to grant me a break. I praised the mysterious deity and focused on my driving again. Soon my nostrils started quivering as they picked up the appetizing aroma of good food. The temptation was too strong for me. I broke the rules of safe driving in all the Worlds known to me and turned around to look.

What I saw was worth the risk I had taken. On Kofa's lap stood an intricate structure that looked like a dollhouse with the roof removed. I peered closer and saw that I hadn't been mistaken by much. It was a miniature replica of a kitchen, complete with stoves, ovens, tiny cooks, and dishes. Even the fire looked very realistic, and pungent steam was emanating from the tiny pots and pans.

"I suggest you either stare at me or focus on the road," said Kofa, "but not both at the same time. I don't relish the thought of an accident during my luncheon."

I opted for pulling over to the side and stopping the amobiler because averting my eyes from Kofa's toy was simply beyond my power. Now I noticed that the tiny figures of cooks were moving. Not just moving but *cooking*. One of the figures came a little closer to Kofa and handed him a plate with a tiny sausage. The sausage, however, only seemed tiny from my perspective. Compared to the cooks that had made it, it was enormous.

"Can I please, oh *please*, have a bite?" I said.

Kofa looked at me askance, frowned, and then broke off half the sausage for me.

"Here. And don't even think of asking me for more. You can rummage around in your Chink between Worlds, or whatever you call it, and fetch yourself whatever garbage you can find there," said Kofa. "There's hardly enough for me. They take their time cooking as it is, and the portions are tiny, as you can see."

"Thank you," I said, munching on the treat. "Mmm, it's so good!"

"Of course it is. This toy is the acme of my late father's genius, so to speak. He had to go completely mad at the end of his life to finally invent this useful gadget. The old man didn't want to leave it for me, but he had to. He had no other heirs."

Melifaro livened up, took out the earplugs, and looked at me, his eyes full of envy.

"You managed to cajole it out of him?" he said. "Lucky you. I've never had a piece for as long as I've known him."

"Kofa, will you please give him a piece?" I said. "It's not fair. I'll get you my grandmother's apple pie for it. It's the best thing ever in all the Worlds. Well, except maybe for Chakatta Pie."

"I don't want your grandmother's pie. I told you I'm not going to eat any garbage from another World."

The tiny cook handed Kofa another sausage. The lucky owner of the magic portable kitchen hesitated a while, then snipped off a microscopic morsel and passed it to Melifaro.

"Today is your lucky day," said Kofa. "But no one is getting anything from me again."

"Pfft," said Melifaro. "As if I'll ever ask you again." But after he swallowed his portion, he melted and added, "Thank you, sir. It's very good and very tiny. What was it that you said about your grandmother's pie, Max? I'd gobble down just about anything now, be it a pie or werewolf's ears, as long as it's tasty."

"Since we've stopped anyway, I guess I should fetch us something," I said. "I can't bear that smell on an empty stomach. I knew our journey would require extraordinary courage, but I never thought it would come to this."

"Well," said Melifaro. "There's courage and there's courage."

I hid my hand under my seat and tried to focus on memories of my grandmother's pie. My skills still weren't perfect, and instead of Grandma's pie, I ended up with some other generic variety. It wasn't too bad, but it couldn't hold a candle to my grandmother's baking.

"Sorry," I said. "It's a different pie. And not the best kind." I felt nervous, as though I were responsible for upholding the reputation of apple pie before Melifaro.

"It's very good, though," he said. "Or maybe I'm just too hungry to be discriminating."

I realized that we could move our jaws while driving, too, and sped off. The journey became more and more difficult: the road deteriorated with each new mile, and the aroma coming from Kofa's "field canteen" was killing me.

An hour later, Kofa's commanding voice rang out in back of me: "We're about to turn left. You need to slow down. This road is only good for birds."

"For birds?" I said.

"Yes, birds. You know, the creatures that flap their wings to stay up in the air? That's why they don't need roads," Kofa shot back in a rude tone. "Here's the turn. Don't miss it!"

"Miss it?" I said. "How can I miss it, crawling along at this pace? Or do you still think I'm driving too fast?"

This new road was barely maneuverable. It was just a path running through the murky, dense woods.

"Holy mackerel!" I said.

"Yes, and it's going to get even worse than this," said Kofa.

After a couple of hours of battling bumps and potholes at a snail's pace, the amobiler's wheels started getting stuck. I persevered a little longer and then finally gave up and stopped.

"Good thinking," said Melifaro. "Your pie was great, but I'm still hungry. Fetch us something else."

"That I can do, but that's not the reason I'm stopping. We can hardly drive any farther."

"If it is only 'hardly,' than that's no reason for stopping. We should keep driving while it is still possible, no matter how hard, and only stop when it becomes *im*possible," said Kofa.

"If we keep driving while it's still technically possible, I'll end up wrecking our only amobiler," I said. "We'd better come up with a plan B."

"You'd better focus on getting us food," said Melifaro. "Then you can come up with any plan you wish."

I stuck my hand under the seat again. This time it took me a lot longer before I sensed the familiar numbness in my fingers. My efforts resulted in a skillet full of ordinary fried potatoes. Melifaro, however, liked it. He even referred to it as a delicacy. Kofa looked at us with disgust but didn't say anything.

While they were munching on their respective provisions, my mind cast around frantically for a solution to our transportation problem.

"Tell me," I said, "among those movies that you all watch so fervently on the Street of Old Coins, were there any about war?"

"Is this dinner conversation, or are you actually trying to make a point?" said Kofa. "Frankly, I still don't know which of the numerous disasters that beset your horrible homeland you call war. Is it when one man chases another around with some sort of shooting device in his hand?"

"No, that's probably a detective movie. Well, okay, forget war.

Maybe you saw a transportation vehicle with tracks instead of wheels? They are these long, sort of crawling . . . things . . . at the sides. Heck, I have no idea how to explain it," I said.

"I think I know what you're talking about," said Melifaro, his mouth full. "Why, though?"

"Because my next question is: Would you, O mighty magicians, work some magic and transform my amobiler into one of those things? Because we're not going to get far on wheels."

"We could try, I suppose. Can't you do it, though?"

"I don't even know where to begin."

"Actually, I don't know either," said Melifaro, "but I can still try."

"You know what would really be great?" I said. "It would be great if you could transform this buggy into some sort of flying machine."

The two stared at me as though I had asked them to strip off all their clothes and play hopscotch.

"You probably didn't know this," said Kofa, "but it takes a great deal of the power of the Heart of the World just to launch yourself into the sky. Such things are only possible in Echo, and then not for everybody. I myself have only done it four times, and have no inclination to repeat those experiments. And you want us to make an *amobiler* fly?"

"Okay, fine. You can't make it fly. I get it," I said, sighing. "What about the tracks? Melifaro, could you try it?"

"Not me—*we* could try it. Or did you think I was going to sweat it here alone while you and Kofa are off in the woods picking flowers?" said Melifaro.

"I could stand by and try to sweat, too, to keep you company," I said.

"Do as you please," said Kofa. "I am not going to do any physical labor. You are both strapping young lads, full of energy. You can have all the fun you want. But spare me."

He got out of the amobiler, gave the dense woods around us a scornful look, and began filling his pipe. Melifaro was also looking around.

"See, Max, I can't create something out of thin air," he explained. "So you and I are going to have to remove the wheels from the amobiler and make some kind of prototype of the tracks. Doesn't matter how bad it looks as long as it looks like *anything* at all. Turning a bad thing into a good thing, that I can do. Making something out of nothing, that's not my line."

I was beginning to regret the whole idea, but after taking a few paces down the path, I realized I had stopped the amobiler just in time. It was so swampy that even my boots got bogged down immediately. We needed an off-road vehicle, and we needed it badly. Otherwise we'd have to headhunt for Magician Glenke Taval on foot.

"All right," I said. "Let's make a prototype. But we don't need to remove the wheels. We'll put a few thick branches on them and wrap some rags around the whole thing. It'll make one heck of a travesty of what we need. I just hope you can do some wicked magic on what we come up with."

"And where do you propose we get 'some rags'?" said Melifaro.

"I suspect you brought a few changes of clothes with you," I said. "I'm sure Sir Glenke Taval wouldn't mind if you came to his funeral dressed in your traveling attire."

"Don't even think about it!" said Melifaro. "My clothes are a memorial to the money I spent on them. For your information, I order my clothes from the best tailors in Echo."

"Oh, really? It's not evident to me. Don't fret over it. You'll write a note to Sir Dondi Melixis, and the Treasury will reimburse your for your irreplaceable loss."

"It's *your* wardrobe that deserves to be sacrificed, if anyone's does," said Melifaro, offended.

"That may be true, but I only brought one spare looxi with me, and it simply won't be enough."

"What about you, Kofa?" Poor Melifaro made one last desperate attempt to save his wardrobe. "Have you brought any clothes that you'd be embarrassed to wear in public?"

"Stop running off at the mouth," said Kofa, launching a puff of smoke directly into Melifaro's face. "Do you think I will let you ruin my garb for some silly experiments in magic? I sometimes think that people under the age of two hundred should be isolated from society. Every last one of them. Young fools are more dangerous than madmen."

"I sometimes think society should be isolated from smokers," Melifaro snarled back.

"I'll bet both of you are going to bury me alive. I'm way younger than two hundred, and I'm going to smoke now," I said, taking out a cigarette from my pocket.

My companions seemed to like the idea of burying me alive. They even stopped bickering. Then we got down to work. One would be hard-pressed to think of a more moronic activity. I really hoped Melifaro hadn't come up with his prototype idea just to get back at me. But when I saw him take out a revolting yellow looxi from his suitcase as his contribution to the project, I knew he wasn't playing a prank on me. Melifaro was a first-class prankster, but not at the expense of his garments.

Kofa didn't lift a finger to help us. He stood a few yards away, smoking and staring at the sky that was beginning to turn gray. In about half an hour, he put away his pipe and ambled toward the road.

"I hate standing in one place," he said. "I'm going for a walk. Finish up here and catch up with me."

"Are you sure it's a good idea?" I said. "Taking walks alone in the woods doesn't sound too wise to me."

"I'm a big boy now," said Kofa and laughed. His tone suddenly became very tender and warm. "You're so funny, Max. Don't worry, though. No wolves will attack me."

I watched as his figure, unusually tall and slender, disappeared behind the trees. Sir Kofa had been a "big boy" for a very long time, true, but if I had had my say, I wouldn't have let him go alone.

"Kofa knows this place well," said Melifaro. "I don't think there's a single swamp in Landaland that he hasn't explored. Kofa used to specialize in busting local bandits. He hunted them at least twice a year, so you don't need to worry about him. Aw, look at you. You look so much like my mommy now that I'm tempted to ask you for cookies."

"Go ahead and try," I said, snarling. "You'll be sorry you did."

"Do you need help?" A friendly voice called out from behind my back.

"I sure do," I said. "It would be kind of you to hold this branch right here while I'm trying to tie it up—Oh!" Only then did I realize that a stranger had snuck up on us. Common sense suggested that I should have been startled enough to assume a defensive stance.

Meanwhile, the short, bearded man in ridiculous fur overalls took hold of the branch I was pointing at. I grabbed the chance and tied it to the wheel. By the time I had finished, I decided against being scared or startled. First, the stranger seemed like a good-natured fellow; second, Melifaro and I were also "big boys." No comparison to Kofa, of course, but still. Melifaro gave our "apprentice" a puzzled look but didn't say anything.

"Thank you kindly, sir," I said. "If it's not too much trouble, would you also hold this branch?"

"Sure," said the man. "I'm good at holding branches. What are you doing here, by the way?"

"Fixing up the amobiler," I said. However honest the reply may have been, it didn't sound very convincing in view of our idiotic activity. Nevertheless, the stranger nodded and grabbed the branch. All in all, he turned out to be a great help: silent, thoughtful, and friendly.

In about an hour we finished the task, and sat down on the damp grass.

"Do you live around here?" I asked the man.

"Yes. It's a nice place."

"That's a matter of opinion," said Melifaro, laughing.

"You helped us a great deal," I said. "Can we do something for you in return? We don't want to take advantage of your time and effort."

"Do you have money?" Our helper sounded naive and excited at the same time.

"As a matter of fact, we do." I couldn't contain a smile. This bearded fellow seemed surprised that we had money, as though Melifaro and I looked like ordinary beggars.

"Could you give me one, then?" said the man.

Now Melifaro and I both had to laugh.

"I'm sorry, the way you said it was funny," I said, handing him a crown.

"Thank you," said the man. "Oooh, this is a big one! I could stay in the *Middle of the Woods* for a whole week with it."

"Stay where?" I said.

"In the *Middle of the Woods*. It's a big house down the road. They have good food there. And they also give you bitter colored water, but I don't like that. You can sleep in a bed there, too."

"Where do you sleep?" I said.

"Why, in a hole, of course," said our new friend. "You?"

"Here and there," said Melifaro, getting up and walking to the amobiler. "Mostly there. Now try not to distract me, and look away please. It's a crucial moment."

The man and I did an about-face.

"So you live in a hole?" I said in a whisper. I was quite surprised. We hadn't ventured *that* far from the Capital of the Unified Kingdom, yet we had already met someone who lived in a hole in the ground. He could have at least built a shack from the trees, I thought.

"Yes, in a hole. It's nice in there," said the man. "But there was one time that I found money—not as big as the one you gave me, though. And I went to the *Middle of the Woods* and then slept in a bed for two days straight. That was great!"

"Why not get your own bed?" I said. "I can give you some more money, and you can buy whatever you need, including a bed."

"You have other money? Oh, would you give them to me? I know what I'll do with them. I'll bury them until winter. And in the winter I'll go to the *Middle of the Woods*. I'd love to have my own bed, but it wouldn't fit in the hole."

"Oh, that's too bad," I said, giving him three more crowns. Excited, he rubbed the coins against his cheek and clenched them in his fist.

"Okay, you can turn around now," said Melifaro. "I think I did a pretty good job, if I do say so myself."

I turned around and froze in disbelief. Not only was Melifaro a powerful magician, he also turned out to be an excellent industrial designer. I couldn't have imagined that an amobiler could look so sleek with tracks instead of wheels. In fact, it looked even better with tracks.

"Now we only need to make sure that this monstrous fruit of our insanity can move," said Melifaro. "Hop in, Max, and let's go. It's almost dark already."

I was somewhat nervous, but to my relief the amobiler jerked into action and started moving. I turned around to wave goodbye to the friendly local, but he was already gone.

"Where did he go?" I said.

"See those two red lights in the bushes? That's your new friend following you with a grateful stare."

I shrugged and looked at Melifaro with disdain. He could have come up with a better one.

"Oh, Max, you don't understand," he said, laughing. "He's a shapeshifter."

"Who's a shapeshifter?" Melifaro was right, I didn't understand.

"That guy there. We got lucky he was a peaceful one who was willing to help and entertain us for a bit. How much money did you give him?"

"Four crowns. Think I shouldn't have done that?"

"Probably not. What would a shapeshifter do with money? He'll lose it. Those creatures have a short memory. Once they transform themselves into something else, they forget everything about their previous form."

"What did this one transform into?" I said.

"No idea. You never know with shapeshifters. Why the puzzled look? Didn't you know there were shapeshifters in the World?"

"I didn't know. Should I feel ashamed now?"

"You should. It's common knowledge."

"Enlighten me, then. I'll take lessons in common knowledge."

"Lessons cost money," Melifaro bantered, "and my lessons cost a lot."

"I'm on a Royal Stipend for Outstanding Achievements," I said. "You can mention you gave me private lessons in your report to Sir Dondi Melixis about the tragic fate of your yellow glad rags. His Majesty Gurig VIII shall see to it that thou shalt not be stinted."

"Will you drop this shapeshifter business already?" said Melifaro. "Yes, there are these animals in our woods that can turn into humans when they get bored. Big deal."

"Hold that thought. They're animals?"

"Of course. What else would they be?"

"I thought shapeshifters were *people* who occasionally turned into animals."

"Of all the nonsense! Only powerful magicians can turn into animals. There used to be a great many of them in the old days, but now . . . although I don't know. Maybe there are still quite a few left. From what I've heard, it's not a very difficult trick."

"Really?" I said. "Hmm. Maybe I should learn it?"

"But why?"

"I don't know. Just so I can, I guess. Say, don't you think we should have caught up with Kofa already? Despite all it has suffered, the amobiler is still quite agile."

"I guess you're right. Hey, your new shapeshifting buddy said something about a house where they give you food, remember? There must be a tavern somewhere around here. Or even an inn, since they let him sleep in a bed there once."

"Good point," I said. "Then I'm not worried. If there is a tavern nearby, I'll bet you anything that Kofa is already sitting at a table there. Those places are like magnets for Kofa."

Lo and behold, two minutes later we did indeed come upon a small, three-story house with a pointy roof. On the sign that hung over the door, one could barely discern the faded letters that read *The Middle of the Woods*. The house stood a little ways off the side of the road and was surrounded by a few other smaller buildings. The owners, however, had made a neat pathway to it and hung bright lanterns over the door, so it was impossible to miss it.

"Oh, this is excellent!" I said. "And you said yesterday that Chinfaro was our last chance to get a good night's sleep."

"People are predisposed to make mistakes," said Melifaro. "I am a typical human being, unlike some monsters that shall go nameless. Besides, I'm pretty sure that the guests of this hospitable place have to go behind a tree to answer nature's call."

"Let's find out." I came up to the porch and opened the heavy door of the house.

Inside it was warm and cozy: clumsy wooden furniture, numerous pots with plants, and the same lanterns that were hanging outside.

Kofa was already there, of course. He was sitting on a bulky stool, sipping something out of an enormous clay mug—seemingly without much appreciation for the contents. Granted, his new face was lousy at expressing any positive emotions anyway.

"What took you so long?" he said. "I was beginning to get worried. The woods are crawling with shapeshifters."

"That was precisely what took us so long—shapeshifters," said Melifaro. "Max gave them money for a keepsake, then they sniffed each other, and so on. He finally found his soul mate."

"Yeah, very funny," I said. "If it hadn't been for the shapeshifter's help, we would still be fixing that miracle of contemporary engineering now."

"A shapeshifter helped you fix the amobiler?" said Kofa. "Good. Physical labor has a positive effect on primitive creatures. Can that cart move across swamps now?"

"And how!" I said.

"Very good. I'll be needing it," said Kofa. He got up off the stool.

"Where are you going now?" I said.

"You are sorely mistaken if you think I am going to report my intentions to you," he said. "I just need to go someplace. It should take about two days, I believe. That's all you need to know. Then I'll return and we'll go cut Glenke's head off. You'll wait for me here. It's not a palace, but you'll survive. Good night, boys."

As soon as Sir Kofa left, I sent a call to Juffin. I don't like stoolies any more than the next person, but desperate situations called for desperate measures.

Kofa just said he had to leave for two days. He told us to wait for him in this tavern in the middle of nowhere and then just up and left. Is this normal, or should we run after him?

It's absolutely abnormal, but let him be. Once Kofa gets something into his head, there's very little chance you can do anything about it.

I don't doubt that for a second, but what do we do now?

Nothing. Just wait, as he said. Enjoy a spontaneous vacation, clean air, and water from forest streams. From my experience, Kofa makes a blunder once every hundred years or so. It's been only sixty since he made his last one, so you're good.

What was the blunder he made sixty years ago?

That secret is not meant for your ears. You are not even of age according to our laws. You're a minor.

Sure, when I need to go to the Dark Side, I'm an adult, but when I want an update on the gossip, suddenly I'm a minor.

Brilliant deduction. It's a pleasure to do business with you, Sir Max, but I'm afraid I'm going to have to say goodbye now. I'm ambushing someone. We have a little situation here, another blast from the past, as it were. This fellow believed that it would be oh so much fun if he bit my head off. I took issue with him on that point, we argued, and now I'm hunting him down.

Whoa, just whoa! He's no danger to you, though, right? Right?

Right, right. Unless you keep distracting me with your chatter. Good night, and buy something sweet for Melifaro.

I had to laugh, remembering the hell Melifaro had been through in the *Kumonian Honey*. I turned to him and said, "Juffin thinks Kofa is so great that he can do whatever he wants. So you and I are going to call these woods home until he comes back. Not to worry, though, we won't get bored. A shapeshifting friend of mine lives somewhere nearby, and I'm sure he has a few furry female friends. We can visit them for a cup of kamra. I wonder if shapeshifters can make kamra?"

"I doubt it," Melifaro grumbled. "I don't even think people make it in these backwoods. Oh well, I'd hoped to get a good night's sleep, and now it looks like my prayers have been answered. I remember reading somewhere that there's nothing worse than when your most cherished dream comes true. I used to think it was nonsense, but now I see how wrong I might have been."

"Do you really think it's that bad?" I said, sitting down on a wobbly stool.

"Nah," said Melifaro and laughed. "I just wanted to practice grumbling. Even you can do it—why can't I try?"

"Speaking of grumbling, thanks for reminding me. Where are the proprietors of this establishment, I wonder?" I said.

"Over there," said Melifaro, pointing to a room next door lit up by the light from a short, fat candle. I followed his finger and saw two pairs of curious eyes staring at me.

"Would you be so kind as to come a little closer, gentlemen?" I said. "First, we want food and drinks. Second, we need a room. Do you have a room?"

"Oh, we have *two* rooms," said a jolly, portly red-haired man dressed in a clean but very old looxi. I broke my head trying to deduce what color it had been at the beginning of its career, but to no avail. "What do you want to eat?" he said. "I can cook *five* dishes."

"Five dishes you say? Oh, my," said Melifaro. "Well, bring all five of them, then. Maybe one of them will be edible."

"Bemboni! Warm up all the food! We've got hungry clients," the red-haired man commanded. Then he stared at us again with the most charming naivete in his eyes and said, "Will you give me money?"

"Of course we will," I said, smiling. "Do you think we're going to eat up all the food you have and leave without paying?"

"Well, I couldn't just send hungry people back into the woods again. Besides, you couldn't eat up all the food we have. We've got a lot of food stocked."

"And we have a big appetite and loads of time to kill, so we're going to try anyway." I said.

I took a crown out of my pocket and gave it to the plump man. He stared at it with the same excitement in his eyes as my shapeshifter friend earlier.

"It's a big one," he said. "Thank you! Do you want me to show you your rooms while Bemboni's warming up your food?"

"Sure, go ahead," Melifaro said and winked at me. "The best one is mine!"

"What if they're the same?" I said.

"Then I don't know. No, one must be at least a little better than the other one. There are no two identical rooms in the World. It's a law of nature. And speaking of nature"—he turned to the red-haired innkeeper—"does your establishment have facilities?"

"Of course," the innkeeper said proudly. "We have an outhouse. My grandfather built it. It's close by. I'll show you the way."

"He has to 'show us the way,' Max. Did you hear that?" said Melifaro in a cheerless voice. "I'll never forgive Kofa for this."

We set off on our little field trip. The outhouse was a small building in the backyard. Inside, it was warm and even comfortable, although there were no bathing pools to speak of. Instead, it had an enormous, clean, albeit old, washtub. If we had a hippo, we could easily have tried washing it in the tub.

Melifaro was inspecting the "facilities" with the expression of a person being drowned in a swamp. I just shrugged. I had lived in far worse conditions once upon a time and had endured them for far longer than two days, yet I had survived.

Then Melifaro and I went back to see our rooms. First, we went up to the second floor, where we found a spacious room with two windows. This was a naive version of a deluxe-style room. In addition to a large old bed on short legs, it had an enormous mirror in a luxurious frame that occupied almost the whole wall. The floor was covered in an old, but still neat, green carpet. Another distinctive feature was the colossal armoire.

"Okay, I'm sleeping here," said Melifaro in a tone that brooked no argument.

"But of course, my dear," I said. "That armoire is just the right size for your clothes. To think of how many happy hours you will spend in front of that mirror! Who am I to deprive you of such simple, innocent joy?"

"As if your joy is so much more complex. Or sinful," he said.

Next we went to the third floor. It must be written in my fate that I always have to end up in the crummiest places. My room was so tiny that I wouldn't have been surprised to learn that it had once been used as a pigeon loft. The roof was sloping on both sides, and kitchen pots with plants stood on the windowsills. There was no furniture, only a rolled-up bed—completely in line with my taste. In a way, I was glad that Melifaro took the "presidential suite" on the second floor.

"Max, if you want to, we can ask them to put up a second bed in my room," Melifaro said, his voice quavering. "You won't survive here."

"Believe it or not, I like it," I said, laughing. "So don't fret, I won't be using your armoire. Besides, I get a warm, tickling sensation when I think of how I'm going to stomp around in my boots on your ceiling right after you fall asleep. I like pacing the floor."

"And I sleep like a log," said Melifaro. "So stomp all you want."

"We'll see what kind of tune you'll be singing tomorrow morning," I said. "Let's go eat now. Our food is probably getting cold again. The next thing we know, they'll whisk it away to warm it up again, and it will go on and on until dawn."

"It's so surprising to hear words of wisdom coming from your mouth sometimes," said Melifaro. And we went downstairs.

The hospitable red-haired innkeeper was waiting for us in the company of a pleasant-looking woman with completely gray hair and a young, ruddy complexion. That must have been Bemboni, who had warmed up our food. Five clay pots and two large wooden plates stood on one of the tables. The woman was inspecting the crown I had given to the innkeeper with unconcealed curiosity. It seemed she didn't get the chance to see money very often.

Our entrance distracted the woman from the coin. Now she was staring at us with the impudence of an ill-mannered child. When we began eating, the woman's beautiful eyes opened even wider. The red-haired man gazed at us with similar intensity. At first, their staring annoyed me, but soon I was able to filter it out. If they wanted to study my manner of chewing food, let them stare all they wanted, I thought.

The food—stewed meat and vegetables with an unusual spicing of wild herbs—was decent, although I couldn't quite fathom why the plump man thought he knew how to cook five different dishes. To my taste, all the pots contained approximately the same dish.

"Do you have any beverages?" said Melifaro.

"I have a kossu herb liqueur," said the man. "Bemboni, could you go fetch it from the cellar?"

The gray-haired lady got up from her stool and disappeared behind the door.

"What's that?" said Melifaro.

"It's delicious, and then it becomes really pleasant," said the innkeeper.

"Can you make kamra?" I said.

"Oh, yes, and I'm good at it, too. That tall man you were talking to, he had three mugs of it," the innkeeper boasted. "Except that he refused to pay for it. But he didn't criticize it, either."

"I see. Well, if he didn't criticize it, could you make some for me?" I said.

"I already have. I'll warm it up," the innkeeper said, and went into the kitchen.

"Are you too scared to taste his liqueur?" said Melifaro.

"You'd be scared, too, if you were me. If it turned out it had the same effect on me as your Soup of Repose, then I wouldn't envy anyone here. Including myself."

"Ah, that's right. You've got those quirks."

"Quirks, yes. I've got lots of them. Do you know how my affair with Tekki began?"

"I'm sure it was nothing like normal people begin their affairs," said Melifaro, laughing.

"Right you are, mister. Tekki gave me some local potion and killed me."

"Oh, that explains the smell. I've been puzzling over it, and now it turns out you're just an ordinary decomposing corpse." Melifaro prepared to laugh and then stopped himself short. "Wait, are you serious?"

"*Dead* serious. Although then Juffin arrived and brought me back to life. It's going to take him much longer to get here, so I think I'll pass. Death is a nasty business. I didn't like it one bit."

"Some life you've got, buddy," said Melifaro. "Now I'll tie you up and gag you myself if you decide to taste that liqueur."

"Deal," I said, helping myself to more stew. "You, on the other hand, can knock yourself out on it. In fact, gulp it all down."

"Do you remember what happened to you after you died?" said Melifaro.

"Praise be the Magicians, I remember almost nothing," I said, my mouth full. "But I do remember the process of dying itself. A most unpleasant experience. Here's a piece of advice for you, buddy: try to become immortal. On second thought, forget it. I'm sure everyone has his own death. Maybe yours will be a cute young lady with a corpulent bust. That's more like your style."

The rosy-faced woman returned and put a small pitcher and a tall, thin ceramic glass on our table. She blushed but managed to say, "It's a hundred-year-old kossu herb liqueur. We try not to waste it. We only give it to people who give us money."

"It's great to be rich! Thank you, miss," said Melifaro and made a gallant bow.

He took a cautious whiff of the contents of the pitcher, poured a little into his glass, and took a sip.

"It's really good," he said. "Poor Sir Nightmare. It's so sad to be a monster from another World. No fleeting pleasures for you, I guess."

"Don't worry about me," I said, smiling. "I'll make up for it. As for pleasure, I have more than I can handle. I've always been a lousy hedonist."

"The words you use sometimes . . ." said Melifaro. He shook his head as though I had been cursing left and right for three hours straight in the company of several dozen frightened women and children of the upper classes.

The innkeeper came back with a large mug of kamra for me. The kamra wasn't any good. Kofa was right when he refused to pay for it. He probably didn't criticize the innkeeper for it only because he knew it was too late for the poor fellow to learn how to make a good mug of it. Still, it was better than nothing. I leaned back, resting my back against the warm wooden wall, and lit up. It felt great.

Melifaro finished his pitcher in no time. Judging from his expression, the effects of the mysterious potion were not much different from those of regular Jubatic Juice.

"Now it's best not to go outside until the morning," the innkeeper told him suddenly. "After such a big helping of the kossu herb liqueur, I always become afraid of darkness, just like a child."

"Huh?" said Melifaro. "What do you mean?"

"I mean I just get very scared, is all."

"How quaint," I said. "Do you want me to walk with you to the outhouse, sonny?"

"No," Melifaro grumbled. "I want to go to bed."

"That's a sound idea," I said. "Even I want to go to bed. Some day it has been, eh?"

※

We said goodbye to the innkeeper and Bemboni and went upstairs.

At the door to his room, Melifaro suddenly froze, hesitating.

"Max," he said, pulling a fold of my looxi. "That red-haired fellow wasn't lying. I don't feel like going in the room."

"Ha!" I said. "But it's not dark in there. There's a candle burning."

"Right, but it's still dark in the corners." Melifaro was becoming difficult. "Max, could you sit with me for a while?"

"I'd love to, but I feel like smoking and I know you can't stand the smell," I said.

"We'll open the window," said Melifaro. He was adamant.

"Are you pulling my leg?"

"I'm not, I swear. I'm really scared. A hole in the heavens above that fat joker and his poison! I've never been scared of darkness before in my whole life. Even in my early childhood."

We went into Melifaro's room.

"I don't think anyone's afraid of darkness in his early childhood," I said, settling down by the window. "The fear comes later, when a nanny tells you spooky stories about the bogeyman that gobbles up misbehaving boys and girls who don't want to go to bed."

"Goodness me!" said Melifaro. The fear in his eyes was very real. "Is this what actually happens in your homeland? A bogeyman that eats children seems even scarier than a mad werewolf. Hey, he won't come for us, will he?"

"Of course he won't," I said, laughing. "The bogeyman doesn't exist, I'm telling you. He's a made-up character, along with many others from spooky ghost stories."

"What other spooky ghost stories?" said Melifaro.

He clearly felt torn between his craving for new information and the desire to stick his fingers in his ears lest he hear another word of it.

I was beginning to have a great time. Fate was giving me a unique chance to scare Sir Melifaro with a silly ghost story. I thought it would be unwise of me to pass up such a rare opportunity. Still, I felt sorry for Melifaro's poor drugged head and decided to tell him the least harmful one.

"Have you heard the one about the Black Hand?" I said in a typical spooky-tale voice.

"The Black Hand? Just a hand? Without a body? Yikes!"

To my utter delight, Melifaro jumped out of the bed and sat next to me.

"Listen then," I began, suppressing my laughter. "It is the story of a little girl who is at home all alone at night because her parents have gone to a party. And then the radio turns on all by itself. You know what a radio is, don't you?"

"Yes, I've seen it in films," Melifaro said in a wooden tone. "It's not supposed to turn on by itself, right? You need to press the button."

He moved even closer and clung to my stool as though I were the dearest and closest thing to him in the Universe.

"Right," I continued. "So the radio turns on by itself and a voice comes on saying, 'Little girl, little girl, the Black Hand is walking down your street. Little girl, little girl, the Black Hand is entering your house. Little girl, little girl, the Black Hand is coming up the stairs.'"

I spoke in howling intonations, drawing the vowels, just like my cousin, from whom I had first heard the story of the Black Hand. I had barely turned five and remember being paralyzed with fear.

Melifaro was grinding his teeth and clenching my wrist.

"'Little girl, little girl, the Black Hand is knocking on your door,'" I said in a demonic whisper.

Melifaro gave out a single, constrained moan.

And then we heard quiet knocking on the door. Now it was my turn to moan and jump.

"Max, there it is!" Melifaro said in a hoarse voice.

"What?"

"The Black Hand! It's coming to get us." He was absolutely serious. The knocking came again.

"Don't be ridiculous," I said. "I told you the silliest ghost story I've ever heard. That must be the innkeeper. He brought you another pillow or something." I looked at the door and said in an angry tone, "Come in!"

"No, don't!" said Melifaro.

But it was too late. The door opened with a long drawn-out chilling creak, just as it was supposed to in scary stories. In the doorway stood a gigantic black hand. Just a hand, without body or head. The sight was horrifying.

Before I had time to realize what I was doing, I snapped the fingers of my left hand and launched a Lethal Sphere. A little ball of bright-green light flew toward our visitor. Instead of destroying it, however, the Sphere went right through the monstrous extremity and hit the door behind it. Then the Sphere grew momentarily, became transparent, and disappeared.

At first I thought that Melifaro and I were sharing the same hallucination. The hand was approaching us, slowly but surely. Deep inside, I was sure it wasn't a hallucination. It was an actual, factual monster, dangerous and invincible. I wish I knew why I was thinking that.

And then it dawned on me.

"I can't kill it," I said. "I can't kill it because it's the incarnation of *your* fear, not mine. But you can kill it. Easy. Just don't be afraid of it. You're not afraid of it. You're not afraid of anything. Ever. You're the most heroic fellow in the Unified Kingdom. And it's not you, it's the darned liqueur in your stomach that's fearing it. But you've got a lot more than a stomach. Such as your bright, brilliant head. Actually, this Black Hand is funny. It's hilarious. Look, look at it. Imagine this thing dropping by General Boboota's office!"

"Boboota's office?" said Melifaro and gave out a nervous laugh.

The next second he burst out laughing, let go of my poor hand, and jumped up. He folded his hands as though he were holding a Baboom slingshot.

"Boom!" he yelled and made a graceful gesture with his right hand.

His impression of firing a Baboom was so perfect that I could almost see the trajectory of the tiny explosive projectile. The "hallucination" disappeared at once, as though it had never existed.

"Brilliant!" I said. "Now *that's* true magic."

"Thanks, Monster." Melifaro fell in his bed. "All thanks to you. Once you thought of General Boboota, the vision disappeared. You were right, one shouldn't experiment with unfamiliar drinks. I think I'm completely healed now. You don't have to babysit me anymore. In fact, you shouldn't, because I'm really falling asleep."

"Yeah, but now I need you to babysit me," I said, "after all that just happened. Unlike you, I'm not the most heroic fellow in the Unified Kingdom. I don't need a Landaland herb liqueur to get scared."

"It's your own fault, though. You shouldn't have tried to scare me to death," said Melifaro. "I've heard about Magician's Horror many times before, but I never thought it would happen to me."

"What's Magician's Horror?" I said.

"What you just witnessed. When a powerful magician becomes truly afraid of something nonexistent, that 'something' materializes and becomes as existent as it gets. It can be pretty dangerous, too. Only its conjurer can destroy it, and he can't do it while he's afraid of it. If you hadn't reminded me of General Boboota, we'd have been in big trouble now. By the way, I imagined that the Hand came into Boboota's bathroom at home rather than his office."

"Right," I said, "and just sat down on a porcelain throne right next to his. That's even better."

And we both laughed.

"Look, now I'm really scared," I said after I finished laughing.

Melifaro looked at me askance. "Do you want me to walk you to your room? I'm sure you're joking again."

"I'm not joking, but you don't have to walk me. I'm not afraid of darkness or the Black Hand. I'm afraid of myself. You can't help me there. Good night, hero. Tomorrow night I'll tell you a story about a hearse."

Melifaro laughed with relief. His laughter seemed to light up the stairs better than any lantern. At least I didn't see anything spooky in the darkness there.

I went up into my room and almost hit the low lintel of the door frame with my head. I sat down on the big soft lump that was my bed and stared through the window at the sharp outline of a slice of the slightly greenish moon.

I felt very uneasy. It was as though that Magician's Horror was a trap designed specifically for me. Juffin was right when he said I was especially good at believing the fairy tales and ghost stories I tell myself. If one of my silly fears materializes one day, just like that, I thought, what then? Thinking of General Boboota is not going to save me. Unlike Melifaro, I'm no hero.

"Go to sleep, man," I told myself out loud. "You know you want to."

Well, once you give yourself a piece of advice, you'd better follow it. I unrolled the bundle of furry blankets, lay on the thickest one, and covered myself with the others.

What I wanted most was to send Juffin a call and discuss the Black Hand with him. I wanted to hear Juffin say that the idea that I'd ever have the power to bring my fears to life was just vanity, pure and simple. But I didn't dare disturb Juffin. What if he was still ambushing whoever it was and I distracted him at the most inappropriate moment? Also, I had my doubts that the boss would comfort me. He'd be more likely to say he couldn't figure out why something like that hadn't happened to me sooner.

I closed my eyes and then remembered that I knew someone with whom I could discuss Magician's Horror or anything else under the sun. Sir Loiso Pondoxo was happy to meet me whenever I wished.

It had been a while since I dared to dream of visiting Loiso. I had been telling myself that I needed a break from miracles, but in fact . . . In fact, I was scared. Not so scared as to grab the first friendly hand I saw but scared enough to keep telling myself: Not today.

Not today, tomorrow maybe, that's what lazy people say. Where did I hear that silly rhyme? In any case, it's not just lazy people who say it. It's also frightened little boys when they don't want to climb up to a scary, dark attic that they absolutely must climb up to.

"One Loiso Pondoxo please. Shaken, not stirred," I said.

Loiso had told me that just saying out loud that I wanted to see him would be enough. Good, then. The meeting had been scheduled. There was no way to cancel it. There was nowhere to retreat. No point in doubting or fretting. My only option was to live, no matter what happened.

Nothing extraordinary happened. I simply fell asleep. I dreamed of the gently sloping hill covered in pale, stiff blades of sunburned grass, the place where Sir Loiso Pondoxo, former Grand Magician of the Order of the Watery Crow, and I always had our rendezvous.

This time I immediately remembered that I needed to walk to the top, and I meandered up following a barely visible path. I must have made the path myself during my previous visits—the place wasn't exactly a popular resort. There was no one but me and Loiso here, no one who could be called another human being.

I reached the top, sweating and panting, giving the lie to the popular notion that people go to sleep in order to rest.

To my surprise, there was no one on top of the hill. The yellow translucent rock on which Loiso had been sitting before was empty. I looked around. Bummer, I thought. It took me so long to muster enough courage to come and see Loiso, and it looks like nobody's home.

"I'm right here." Loiso's mocking voice came from behind. "Did you think that on top of all the rest of my misfortunes I was also glued to that rock?"

I turned around and saw him. Loiso had just come up the opposite side of the hill, but his breathing was as shallow and steady as that of a sleeping person. The peculiarities of the local climate didn't seem to bother him one bit. His face, still looking shockingly like mine, remained pale, his forehead dry. Even the hot wind that bent down the dry grass so that it almost touched the ground hadn't disheveled his hair. Loiso's snow-white garments looked neat, as if he had at his service all the laundromats in the Universe.

"No, I didn't think you were glued to it," I said. "After all, you did get up from it the other day to give me a kick in the butt."

"Nonsense. Even as a kid I never did such indecent things. I did indeed give you light push on the side so you would return home quickly. By that time, you had already been baked. I could have sprinkled you with lemon juice and served you on a platter. You're one rancorous fellow, aren't you? Is that why you haven't come to see me all this time?"

"Oh, no, not at all," I said. "I only just remembered about you kicking me . . . pushing me. I thought you never made mistakes."

"If I never made mistakes, I wouldn't be here to begin with," said Loiso, smiling and sitting down on his favorite rock. "Why didn't you come sooner, then? Because of the heat?"

"That too," I said, sighing. "You know, I told myself that I needed a break from miracles, whereas in fact, I was just scared. Stupid, huh?"

"Not at all. Fear is an ordinary human emotion. Perhaps the most ordinary and most human of all. I can relate."

"I came back when I realized I couldn't afford the luxury of being afraid. Just tonight a friend of mine overindulged himself a little on a kossu herb liqueur, and I witnessed Magician's Horror with my very eyes," I said.

"I know what you're talking about," said Loiso, nodding. "Once that liqueur almost killed me. I still can't believe how many times I managed to escape all the traps that were set for me by my own silly fears."

"So you're familiar with silly fears that come out of the blue?"

"Am I ever! I even know for certain *where* they come from. I have all but forgotten that nasty feeling now, but in the beginning I was really scared. *Very* scared. All the time, with no lunch breaks. I was walking on the edge. All the wonders of the Universe were on the one side, on the other . . . The other side was filled with me and everything I strove to love. Back then I thought it would help fill in the frightening void in my heart. On the border of the two was a strip of fear. That was where I was hanging about. For too long, as I've realized by now. I was painstakingly looking for a way out, a path, a road, a passageway that would lead me away from that border. I had to learn to hate, because hatred turned out to be stronger than fear. That's the answer to the riddle of the origins of the Great Evil Loiso Pondoxo. Scared boys make for excellent evil magicians. Do you know what I'm talking about, Max?"

I shrugged.

"Oh, that's right. Your life is easier, whatever you might think about it yourself. As for Magician's Horror, I don't think it poses any danger to you. You lack the ability to focus on anything, including your fears. Normally, that's your biggest flaw, but in this situation, it'll do you good. Then again, almost anything will do you good. You're always lucky. Come to think of it, *I'm* the one who should be surprised that you know the feeling of fear, not the other way around."

"How come?" I said.

"Well, for starters, because there are a whole bunch of people looking after you. An army of indefatigable wise old men and women, charmed by your good fortune, will shield you with their own chests when the winds begin to blow harder from the Dark Side. In my book, they are overprotective. Me? I have always had to stand alone against the unknown, like a child lost in a graveyard about which he has heard innumerable scary old stories. I've been alone for as long as I care to remember. Now I realize that solitude suits me better than the best company, but I haven't always been this wise, trust me."

"I do," I said. "You've made me ashamed of myself. Here I am, blubbering about my fears, which, as it turns out, are very ordinary, third-rate fears. Why am I whining?"

"That's all right," said Loiso. "Whine away. It's even cute. And you shouldn't have feared coming here. You're not afraid of the Kettarian, are you?"

"On the contrary," I said, smiling, "Sir Juffin Hully is the most potent medicine for fear. At least for my fear."

"See? But of the two of us, he is the more dangerous one. For example, I don't send you to the Dark Side. I don't send you anywhere. I just tell you fairy tales that you love to hear, that's all."

"True," I said, sighing. "The thing is, I never used to wake up with scratches on my face. Dreams with you in them are a tad too realistic for my taste—that's what's scaring me now."

"The dreams in which you met Juffin belong to the same category," said Loiso. "It just so happened that you never got scratches on your face in them. And don't even get me started on your journeys through Xumgat. You're not going to tell me those were just peculiar dreams now, are you? I'm sorry, Max, but right now you look like an old lady trying to persuade her fifth husband that it was he who took her virginity."

I laughed and immediately realized that laughing was not among the luxuries I could afford under the circumstances. Nauseating colorful rings began swirling around in my eyes. The blasted heat was getting to me.

"Uh-oh," said Loiso. "Time to go home, Max. What will happen to my reputation if I have to resort to quackery?"

"I still haven't asked you why your Order had such a stupid name," I murmured, grabbing my head, which suddenly felt like it was made of lead, with my hands.

"At least someone realizes that it was stupid," said Loiso, laughing. "It's a long story, Max. I'll tell you some other time. You'll have another pretext to come see me. It is unbearably hot here, but that's just about the only thing you should be afraid of in this place. This may very well be the safest place in the Universe for you."

"How's that?" I said, making the first unsteady step down the sunburned side of the hill.

"Because it is in my interests to keep you away from trouble. I still don't doubt that you'll set me free, sooner or later."

"You might want to get yourself an AC unit, if you like my living body more than a piece of well-done steak," I mumbled, making another step.

I felt queasy but tried to maintain a vertical position by walking slowly and carefully. My previous visits here had all ended up the same: I fell and rolled down the slope, grabbing the sharp blades of grass, and then I woke up in my bed, dirty and covered with scratches on my skin. This time I desperately wanted to break with tradition.

I was going downhill for what seemed like an eternity. Each step I took cost me an incredible amount of effort. When my vision went totally black, I realized that it was indeed dark around me and I was still descending not the slope of a hill but a flight of squeaky wooden stairs. I had already reached the second floor where the Slayer of the Black Hand, Sir Melifaro, was catching forty winks. I had to go back upstairs.

That's a sick joke on your part, Sir Loiso, I thought. What is it going to be next time? Will I find myself walking on the window ledge outside?

I got back to my room; took off my clothes, which were drenched in my sweat; and blacked out.

My sleep was sound and very long. When I finally woke up, it was way past noon. I felt peaceful and quiet, as though I had spent my whole life in this house in the woods and my waking up today had been no different from thousands of similar awakenings before. I dressed, moaned a little, remembering the distance I had to cover between my room and the outhouse, and set off.

I ended up washing with cold water. I was almost sure there was a way, some trick—some fortieth or even hundred fortieth degree of Black Magic—that could turn cold water in the tub into hot water, but I was not capable of performing such miracles. At least not for now.

I found Melifaro in the dining hall. He was sitting at the bar, listening to the red-haired innkeeper. I don't know what that amiable fat man was telling him, but Melifaro looked as though he were listening to a fascinating story from his favorite book.

"You *are* the biggest sleeper in all of the Worlds," he said, turning to me.

"You can say that again," I said. "But recently I've been thinking of branching out and becoming the biggest glutton in all of the Worlds."

"Would you like me to make you all five of my dishes?" said the innkeeper. "Or would you like any one of them?"

"Just make me some kamra, please," I said. "Do you have cookies or some pies?"

"Bemboni always bakes something, but guests usually don't express any interest in that. I'll get some for you," said the fat man.

He disappeared behind the door and soon returned with a pitcher of kamra and a large dish with a pile of ugly gray crackers. I winced and took a tiny bite out of one of them.

It turned out my wincing was uncalled for. The gray cracker could take a shot at, and even win, a baking contest—even now, when cooks and bakers in Echo were allowed to use a little magic, which they often abused.

Melifaro watched me with eyes full of compassion. I think I looked like a poor homeless orphan from a fairy tale.

"Want to try it?" I said, my mouth full. "Hurry up, though, or there won't be any left."

My mumbling was the best advertisement. Melifaro grabbed a cracker and shoved it in his mouth. His face bloomed with pleasure.

"May I go, gentlemen?" said the innkeeper. "We have lunch at this hour, and it's our custom to sit together at the table."

"Go ahead, Kekula," said Melifaro, nodding. "A family lunch is sacred."

As soon as the innkeeper left, Melifaro jumped up on his stool and stared at me in triumph. "Guess what! You won't believe this!" he said.

"I will," I said. "I've been very gullible recently. It's much easier and simpler that way. So what's the news?"

"These people think that their woods are the entire World!" said Melifaro.

"Could you run that past me one more time? They think what?"

"I'm telling you. There's the woods and there's their house in the middle of it. That's it."

"Are you saying they've never heard of Echo?"

"Echo? Boy, they've never even heard of the Unified Kingdom, or anything else for that matter. Moreover, they think that their house is the only building in the Universe, and that that the rest of the people—including you and me—just live in the woods. Want to know how I found out? That fat guy asked me how we managed to sleep in the woods and remain so clean. He said he had tried to spend a night in the woods a few times, but every time he returned home as dirty as a swamp tussock. Can you believe that?"

"What did you tell him?" I said.

"I was a little taken aback, so I told him we made nests in the trees. Kekula was happy—one less mystery to rack his brains over."

I laughed as I imagined an enormous nest with Melifaro's bright-yellow boots hanging over the edge of it.

Then I said, "Okay, so they think there's nothing beyond the woods. Where do they get the food and all the rest, then?"

"They make almost everything themselves. They have a huge setup here. Also, a man comes here a few times a year and brings them a cart full of food, probably from around Chinfaro. He takes all the money they have collected over time and then leaves. The innkeeper thinks that the cart with food just comes from the woods and then the cart just goes back," said Melifaro.

"Okay, but what about other travelers like us? They must tell them something about the rest of the world, don't they?"

"They probably do. But many people hear only what they want to hear and filter out the rest. Remember our friend from Isamon, Rulen Bagdasys? He remained deaf except for those rare occasions when he desperately needed some information. Most people are like him, though Bagdasys was an extreme case, of course. Plus, shapeshifters who suddenly become rich probably visit this inn more often than city loafers like us."

"This is all just too bizarre," I said. "How did it happen? Where did those two come from anyway?"

"There are more than just those two. Our friend Kekula and that cute Bemboni—she's his sister, not his wife, by the way—are the oldest. They have three brothers and two sisters. They live in the next house and keep the inn together: carve out the dishes, work in the garden, forage in the woods for berries, and so on. They were all born in this house. Their late parents told them that there was nothing in the World save for this house and the woods around it. I don't know why they told them that. Maybe they believed it themselves, or maybe they had reasons for holding a grudge against the World and the reasons were strong enough to make them just reject its existence. Nobody knows, and the folks have been dead for a long time, so you can't ask them. Unless you want to dig them up and throw a family reunion for Kekula, Bemboni, and the rest."

"Thanks, but no thanks," I said. "Boy, what a story, indeed."

"A story like any other," said Melifaro. His voice was full of sadness. "Most people live entrapped in such delusions all their lives, only their delusions are not as funny. Our friendly innkeepers believe that the World is the woods; some uneducated farmer thinks that the Unified Kingdom and a dozen smaller countries nearby are the World. More sophisticated people believe that the World is a lot of water with small islands floating in it, upon which little serious-looking people run hither and thither. By the way, not twenty years ago I was convinced that this was true. Now you and I think that the World is the World, plus the Dark Side, plus other Worlds, plus the mysterious Corridor between them. But there's no guarantee that we're any smarter than these funny forest people. We just happen to have a little more information, but it's not all there is to know, not by a long shot. We're not much different from them."

"Can't argue with that," I said, surprised.

"Of course you can't."

Melifaro grabbed the last cracker from the plate, waved it like a victor over a defeated enemy, and popped it into his mouth. The sad philosopher had disappeared, and now the all too familiar natural disaster, better known as Melifaro Junior, was fidgeting on the stool. I liked him much better this way. All the more so, since I still had to spend at least a day in his company, and I was completely incapable of keeping a straight face for more than a few minutes running.

Sir Kofa returned only at the end of the next day. He looked important, mysterious, and very pleased with himself, almost like in the good old days.

"You look like you have seduced all the women on all the farms in this part of Landaland," said Melifaro. "Figures, though. You've become such a pretty boy ever since we left Echo. Maybe you should keep this look back home, too? It's too bad Kekki can't see you now."

"Kekki is a smart girl," said Kofa. "She couldn't care less about my looks. If she needs to see someone beautiful in her bedroom from time to time, she can just put up a mirror. Let's go, boys. We've already lost a lot of time."

"Oh, *we've* lost time, have we?" said Melifaro. "Also, where do you think we're going to go now? It's almost nighttime."

"What's wrong with nighttime?" said Kofa, surprised. "What difference does it make?"

"I usually sleep at night," Melifaro grumbled.

"That's a stupid habit. But it's all the same, you can sleep in the amobiler," said Kofa.

"Yes, let's go," I said, agreeing with Kofa. "The sooner we leave, the better. Are we close yet?"

"Fairly close," said Kofa. "If there were an ordinary human behind the levers, we'd be entering Glenke Taval's estate tomorrow night. You drive much faster, even on this awful road. I'll give credit where credit is due: you found a good substitute for the wheels."

"And you did the field test," I said, smiling.

"Indeed. That's exactly what I've been doing all this time," said Kofa.

We said goodbye to the odd inhabitants of the *Middle of the Woods*. The red-haired innkeeper was very sympathetic. He was convinced that we were going back to our uncomfortable nests in the treetops. He probably thought that we had run out of money to pay for his hospitality. I almost felt that he was torn between the altruistic desire to let us stay for another couple of nights free of charge and the cold pragmatism that required him to take compensation for room and board.

The pragmatism won out. Kekula promised, somewhat sentimentally, that next time he would let us sleep in beds "for only one small money," he liked us so much. I was so moved that I left a few more crowns in the *Middle of the Woods* on the sly: one on the porch, one on the doorway of the outhouse, and one more by the gate. I liked to think that finding the coins from time to time would make these people happy.

Sir Kofa was watching with great interest.

"Conjuring magic?" he said.

"Nah, just fiddling around," I said.

"Okay, then." He lost interest in my strange actions and demanded, "Max, are we ever going to leave?"

"We are," I said, getting behind the levers of the amobiler.

This time Melifaro got in the back seat, announcing that he needed to get more sleep.

"Be my guest," said Kofa. He sat next to me in the front and put his "field canteen" on his knees. Thank goodness he didn't take out his barrel organ. Apparently, today Kofa didn't need any calming down or stimulation of his thinking processes.

After my amobiler had been transformed into a travesty of an off-road vehicle, driving through the woods became quite pleasant. Granted, I couldn't afford the luxury of speeding up for real, but we weren't exactly crawling. Melifaro was snoozing on the back seat. The son of the great traveler paid no attention to such trifles as the lack of a bed, pillow, or blanket.

"You can catch a few winks yourself, too," said Kofa. "I am quite capable of sitting behind the levers for a few hours."

"Thank you," I said. "But it's not going to work. First, I'm not sleepy yet. And even if I were . . . I'm very conservative, Kofa. I need a real bed. Although I'm not sure I'd be able to sleep even in a real bed now."

"Why not? Are you nervous?" said Kofa. "That's unnecessary. Nothing extraordinary is required of you. You'll stroll through the Dark Side, launch a few Lethal Spheres, and then call it a day. Nothing to get all worked up about. Fretting on the eve of any event that you consider to be extraordinary is one of your numerous bad habits."

"Maybe you're right," I said, nodding. "Maybe this is nothing extraordinary. Maybe. Fine, I believe you. But it's still a dangerous undertaking, to battle Lonely Shadows and their suzerain. Don't you think?"

"It is. But so what?" said Kofa. "Numerous perils threaten each one of us on a daily basis. Take your crazy driving through the woods, for example. Do you see me fainting from fear or even fretting over it?"

"Okay, I get your drift. Now please share your dinner with me. I don't believe you've turned into a simpleminded tightwad. It's not your style," I said.

"I am not greedy; I am mean," said Kofa, handing me a tiny morsel of some wonderfully smelling mixture. "And don't pressure me, Max. You can't begin to imagine how tiring it is for me to be the good-natured portly fellow you've known for all this time."

"But you've always been the same person inside, right?" I said. "Melifaro told me that a long time ago your father put a spell on you that turned you into an affable, respectable gentleman. But you didn't actually change, did you? Before my trip to Kettari, you turned me into a cute girl and Lady Sotofa made me drink Heavenly Half, but neither of you could teach me good manners. Have you heard of that potion?"

"Of course. What made you think of it?"

"She said back then that after a person drinks Heavenly Half he remains himself but everyone around sees him the way he wants them to see him. Did something similar happen to you?"

"Similar, but not quite the same," said Kofa and smiled suddenly. "Everyone sees me the way Xumka wanted them to see me. It wasn't my choice. Generally, however, you're right. Even such an accomplished magician as my father couldn't have changed a person completely. Of course I'm always the same, but . . ."

Kofa fell silent, as though he was weighing whether I deserved to be trusted. Finally he decided in my favor and continued.

"In reality, I don't resemble either of them: the fat one or the tall one. Yet I constantly have to be in the shoes of one of them. It's great that there is a way for me to switch between personalities so easily once I grow tired of one of them: to leave the Capital or to come back. Even though it was hardly his intention, Xumka did me a great favor."

"You weren't exactly on good terms with him, I take it?" I said, remembering my own father without much enthusiasm. I think he would also have put a spell or two on me if he could have. Then again, raising your children is, in and of itself, akin to putting evil spells on them. Day after day your parents try to turn you into someone you desperately don't want to be. More often than not, unfortunately, your parents succeed.

"To say we weren't exactly on good terms is putting it mildly," said Kofa, smirking. "But to Magicians with Xumka. I'd rather not talk about him, especially at night in the middle of the woods. Do you want another piece?"

"You bet!" I said, smiling and taking another piece of perfectly cooked meat from his hands. "If it's too taxing on you to be kind and affable, I can stand you this way until we return to Echo."

"I'll let you in on my biggest secret. It makes absolutely no difference to me whether I'm kind or mean," Kofa said. "I don't give a flying fig, as you would have put it."

I was so shocked to hear that that I almost choked on my piece of meat.

By morning I began to feel drowsy, but as it turned out, I had lost my only chance to kick Melifaro out of the back seat.

"We're almost there," said Kofa. "Let's find a place to hide the amobiler. And me."

"You?" I said.

"Yes. I'll have to stay in the woods while you're loafing around on the Dark Side," he said. "It would make no sense for me to go to Glenke's house now while the Lonely Shadows are still guarding him."

"How will you know when it's time to go?"

"Simple. Melifaro will tell me."

"Tell you what?" Melifaro's sleepy voice came from the back. He had just woken up and was turning his head every which way, trying to shake off the remains of the sleep.

"What you're supposed to tell me," said Kofa. "Max, do you think that grove over there is just what we want?"

"It's your call. You're going to be the one staying there," I said, turning into a group of trees covered in vines. Behind the trees began a dense thicket of fragrant evergreen bushes. I thought my amobiler would be very comfortable there. I hoped that Kofa would, too. To be honest, I felt pretty wretched—small, tired, and empty inside. It still hadn't quite hit home that I, and not someone else, was the one who would soon enter the Dark Side. Moreover, I'd be all alone because that lucky guy Kofa could stay here enjoying the new dawn, and Melifaro would be guarding an unfathomable border between two worlds—this one and the Dark Side. I still lacked the imagination necessary for understanding what exactly I was supposed to do there.

I knew what was supposed to happen in theory, but that was purely academic knowledge. It was just enough to spoil the mood but insufficient to make me start taking action. I could use Lonli-Lokli's holey cup right now, I thought. To drink some lousy drink from it and feel lightweight and omniscient. But Shurf and his cup had stayed in Echo. It looked like I'd have to rely on my own modest abilities. That thought only worsened my mood, which was already far from cheerful.

"What's wrong with you, Max?" said Melifaro. He looked dumbfounded. "What have you become, you monster? I can't help wanting to cry, just looking at you."

"If you can't help crying when you see me, then I have turned into an onion," I said in a glum voice. "Right?"

"Right," said Kofa and laughed. "Leave him alone, Sir Melifaro. Let him indulge his misery if he has nothing better to do."

"Look, guys, I'm really sorry about this," I said, smiling a guilty smile. "I know I'm being a jerk, but I'm really scared. No, it's actually worse. I only *think* I should be scared, but I can't be, no matter how I try."

"Do you really want to be scared?" said Melifaro.

"Well, no . . ." I said.

"Then there's nothing to worry about. You don't want to be scared, and you're not. What's with the gloomy face, then?"

I grinned and began studying the trajectory of the load that had been lifted from my mind. I didn't know why it had been lifted, but it was very considerate of it to desert me, nevertheless.

"Max, we'd all be better off if you'd stop fretting about it and just go there already," said Kofa. "Nothing is going to change if you keep dawdling here in the bushes for another dozen days. You'll only lose the remains of your precious omnipotence."

"You're right," I said. "Melifaro, buddy, could you please walk with me to the bus stop? I don't even know which direction it is."

"I've never heard anyone call the border between the World and the Dark Side the bus stop, whatever that is. I guess I haven't watched enough movies to get your joke. Anyway, give me your hand and close your eyes. It's getting light and you'll be distracted. You're so bad at focusing on anything."

"That I am," I said, closing my eyes. "Kofa, if I don't come back from the Dark Side, take my dog, okay? I think Droopy likes you."

"You should write a last will. You'll be embarrassed when you return," said Kofa.

"I won't be," I said, laughing.

Melifaro pulled me somewhere in the direction I was facing. I took a few unsteady steps and realized that walking with my eyes closed was truly pleasant. If you trusted your guide, that is.

"Just don't open them," Melifaro said. "Or I'm going to have to start all over again. And it can be quite taxing with a trailer like you stuck to me."

"Who's the trailer here?" I said.

I felt easy and tranquil, as though I had just emptied a good dozen of Lonli-Lokli's magical holey cups. A joyous power had flooded into me as soon as I took the first step toward the unknown.

We walked for so long that I got used to wandering in voluntary darkness. I even got used to the fact I had gotten used to it, and that in itself takes a long time.

"There," said Melifaro, letting go of my hand. "You can look around now."

I opened my eyes. It was still dark, so Melifaro's advice to look around sounded like he was mocking me. I raised my hand to my face and noticed that it was glowing with a dim green light. Then I looked at the other hand, but it remained an ordinary human extremity—no illumination whatsoever.

"Never mind that," said Melifaro. "Just one of the tricks this funny place loves to play on us. I'm staying here, Max. You can choose any direction you wish from here. Wherever you go, you'll end up on the Dark Side and nowhere else. If you want to talk to me, just call out my name and speak to me out loud. You don't have to shout, I'll hear you anyway. And don't worry. If anything happens, I'll pull you out and save your butt in no time."

"That's good to know," I said. "I wouldn't want anything to happen to my butt. Anyway, if that's all, I'll be off. Or is there another savage ritual involved?"

"Well, one more savage ritual."

"Just admit that you love hugs, given a good opportunity."

"Sure, especially from some unshaven fellow who reeks of some otherworldly tobacco I can smell a mile away," said Melifaro, laughing.

Still laughing, he lowered his heavy, warm hands onto my shoulders. His double was already standing behind me. I could feel his hot breath on the back of my head.

"I shall remember you," two identical monotonous voices said.

"I sure hope so," I said. "I used to know many people who also thought I was unforgettable. So long, guys. And don't you dare tell each other any spooky stories."

I made a few uncertain steps into the darkness and looked around. Two identical, clear outlines were shimmering in the dark. I thought I saw them both grinning. But of course I could have just been recalling the jolly Sir Melifaro, whom I knew was no longer here.

I kept walking because staying there was pointless, if not impossible. The border between the World and its Dark Side is not a place where one can linger indefinitely. My feet were carrying me forward for a while, and then they decided to turn left.

It was still dark, but it was the familiar, comprehensible, permeable darkness of an inhabited place.

"Enough," I said out loud. "Sure, I'm a dork, and I love to tell myself idiotic fairy tales. My tale of darkness on the Dark Side may be the acme of idiocy, but I'm positively tired of wandering in the dark. Let's bring on the lights already."

That was it. Easy as pie. Suddenly, the world around me flashed out in such beautiful lights and colors that my head began to spin.

I looked around. The place I found myself in was an unusual version of a forest. It was still, glittering, and somehow *muttering*. There was wind, but it didn't move the colorful branches of the trees or the folds of my looxi, which had turned emerald green, a color so bright and saturated that Melifaro would die of envy if he saw it. The wind here was easier to see than to feel. Its silvery streams moved toward me, slowly, and then rushed to the side, never touching my face.

"Oh, it's so wonderful here!" I said.

It was an absurd habit, to talk out loud when I was alone. Yet now I knew that the wind and the trees were pleased with my praise.

I pressed on. I didn't know exactly where I needed to go. I didn't have an epiphany, nothing suddenly dawned on me, no mystical knowledge sprang into my head, no voice from the heavens fell onto my ears, if only to give me a weather forecast. I was as clueless as ever. A special, easygoing mood took possession of me, however. It was so overwhelming that I didn't even *want* to stop and think where I was headed.

I feared no more. A sculptor doesn't fear clay; a mason doesn't rush away when he sees a bucket of mortar; a painter doesn't scream in horror at the sight of a smudged palette. Part of me knew full well that there was nothing here on the Dark Side that I couldn't handle. Praise be the Magicians, it was that wise and placid part of me that was in command, and the other components that comprised my personality took the back seat of my consciousness and waited.

With each step I took, there seemed to be less and less of me. Well, effectively, I was still there—legs, arms, head, and other scenic spots of my body—but I was less and less sure that I really knew the person who was wandering among these glimmering trees, sinking deeper and deeper into the boggy lilac light of his own footprints.

Forward, forward, on you go / Till you find your friend or foe / Don a hat, eat a rat / Scratch your head or drop dead. A children's rhyme kept ringing in my head and I couldn't get rid of it. Good thing I didn't recite it out loud. I didn't mind a hat, but rodents always gave me indigestion, not to mention the dubious outcome foreseen in the last line. *Forward, forward, on you go* . . . And then I remembered that I had come here on business. Better late than never.

For a few moments I pondered over where I should begin. *I guess I should first destroy all the Lonely Shadows and then file a request for an audience with their creator and master,* I thought. *Shadows, eh? Very well, then. Excellent.*

I remembered the mind-boggling acrobatics Juffin had performed to force Lonely Shadows to come closer, but I knew I'd be a fool to even try to copy them.

I felt like a hopelessly useless and backward creature when I yelled, "I command all Lonely Shadows to gather around me in the firing range of my Lethal Spheres!"

Then I shut up and felt despondent. What if they didn't obey my command? A Lethal Sphere was a good weapon, but what was I supposed to do if it decided to have me for dessert? It looked like I was better off without using Lethal Spheres. Juffin had told me that my words had the power of magic spells on the Dark Side. *Let's see if it was true,* I thought. *I'll command them to hang themselves. Or go jump in the lake. Or maybe disappear, vanish forever? Tough call.*

I leaned against a tree and waited. It could very well be that the Lonely Shadows didn't give a damn about my orders. What then?

But they did come. Almost a dozen enormous, dark anthropomorphic silhouettes. Thank goodness the creatures didn't venture to approach me—they didn't even dare to attack. They hovered at a safe distance, listless and tame, like patients in a doctor's waiting room. I was no better. I stared at them, trying to figure out what to do next. Should I command them to die? The main thing was to be clear and concise. Bad speaking skills or garbled words might have very dire consequences.

But my poor excuse of a head refused to work. Reality was slipping away from me, dissipating in a thick fog, as I tried—and failed—to collect the remains of my haphazard thoughts in these murky white woods, to gather them, line them up single file, draw up a roll call, and mobilize them. I began to pick up the scent of certain domestic rodents in the air.

"They are still dangerous in the World, but not here. And certainly not to you."

A soft, deep male voice came from somewhere behind me. I felt that its owner was breathing on my neck, although there shouldn't have been anything but a tree trunk behind my back.

"Who's that?" I said.

"I am the one standing behind. Go ahead and destroy them. What are you waiting for?"

The voice, whomever it belonged to, was talking business. I should have finished off the Lonely Shadows before finding new acquaintances. I still couldn't come up with an eloquent command. Instead, I just shouted at them:

"I want you to be gone for real."

The dark silhouettes disappeared, as though the local special effects team had gone on strike.

"You got lucky, but next time you'll need to express your desires more clearly," said the voice. "Sloppiness is inadmissible in such things."

"Who *are* you?" I said and almost lost my balance. The thick tree trunk I was leaning against was gone.

I turned around in a flash, ready for anything—to fight, to die, to kill, or to be surprised. The latter was the option I was hoping for.

Behind me stood the same tree. Now it stood no more than three feet away, but I saw no other changes.

"You're looking at me *wrong*," said the same calm voice. "I only seem like a tree. I look like a tree, but I'm not a tree. Trees don't talk out loud, even on the Dark Side."

I stared at the tree. What does he mean I'm looking at him "wrong"? And how am I supposed to do it "right"?

I blinked a few times, just in case. Needless to say, it didn't help. I could only rely on the power of my own words.

"Stop looking like a tree," I said. "I want to see your true form."

The tree disappeared. Well, not exactly disappeared. I suddenly realized—no, I *recalled*—that the tree had never existed. Only thick reddish grass that must be pure pleasure to roll in. I fought the temptation to lie down, close my eyes, and forget everything—life, death, the hunt for Glenke Taval, the return trip home, and even myself. Myself first and foremost.

"You said you wanted to see me," the voice reminded me. Why, thank you kindly, I thought.

"I did. The tree's gone, but I still can't see you. Or are you the grass?" I said.

"No, I'm not the grass. I'm just standing behind you again. Would you mind if I didn't show myself to you for a little longer? I don't want you to look at me yet."

"Fine," I said. "Everybody has his quirks. Still, I'd love to know who it is I'm speaking to. Who are you?"

I dropped down on the grass wearily. The sleepy torpor had passed, praise be the Magicians, but my legs buzzed as though I had been working out on a treadmill.

"I will introduce myself a little later, if you don't mind. You are not afraid of me, are you?"

I ran down a quick check of my feelings and said, "I don't think so."

"That's good."

"It sure is," I said. "I do stupid things when I'm scared, and the Dark Side is not the place for doing stupid things, from what I gather, am I right?" I said.

"Correct."

"What is it that you want with me?" I said. "Or did you just miss having company?"

"No, I didn't. And I do indeed want something from you. But before that, I want you to remember one story. It's really nothing. Just an epigraph for the favor I'm going to ask you."

"What do you want me to remember?"

"A thick book in a dark-blue, almost black cover. Two books, rather. Identical in everything but the numbers on the spines. They stood next to each other on the bookshelf in your parents' room, too high for you to reach them. But you did reach them when you were nine, or even younger, by standing on a chair. Do you remember them?"

"A two-volume edition of H. G. Wells!" I was surprised and I laughed. "Of course I remember them. I wasn't nine, though. I was seven and a half. Why did you ask? You're not H. G. Wells's ghost, I hope."

"Oh, no, I'm not."

"Okay, that's good. Do those books hold some kind of terrible secret?" I said.

"It's not terrible. It's a wonderful secret," said the stranger. "There was one particular story in those books. It's the reason you're here. It changed your life, absolutely and drastically. The story about the green door in the white wall. Do you remember it?"

"I do," I said. "I remember it very well."

"I also remember it. Do you want me to tell you what happens in the story? It was a story of a lonely daydreamer, a little boy—probably the same age as you were when you first read it—who was wandering through the city and found himself on an unfamiliar street.

There he saw a white wall and in it a green door. He went in and ended up in a beautiful garden. What followed were a few pages of meaningless, sweet nonsense. The idea was that the boy found Paradise, and when authors try to describe it, they usually fail because no one has ever been there. I'm still not satisfied with that piece, but we digress. You got the impression that the boy loved that wonderful garden, nevertheless. That was good enough. Then the protagonist, as is often the case in fairy tales, broke some rule or other and ended up back in his hometown on an unfamiliar, dirty street. He stood there and cried, so miserable was he. An unspeakably sad episode."

"Yes, but worse things happened afterward," I said, picking up the thread of the story. "That lucky boy bumped into his magic green door several more times in the most unexpected places—boy, was he lucky! And every time he just walked past. Once because he was running late for school, then because he had an exam at college, then something else got in the way. I really wanted to give him a good kick, I swear!"

"But he did open that door one more time," my invisible interlocutor said. "He was found dead in a shaft near a train station, and the friend to whom he had told his story of the Door in the Wall the day before could not figure out whether the poor fellow had indeed found his green door or whether he'd only dreamed it up. But you, you decided it was a good ending anyway."

"That's right," I said, smiling. "That's exactly what I thought. Word for word. But how do you know all this? And why did you remember that particular story?"

"Because H. G. Wells never wrote it," said the voice. "Now, however, the text exists, and not only in your two-volume edition in the dark-blue cover. As far as I know, over time it has appeared in other editions. You see, I wrote it."

"What!" I was flabbergasted.

"Yes, I wrote it. Upon the request of our good friend Juffin Hully. He thought I was the only one who could do it. He was no doubt right. They once called me the Master Steerer of Chance. That was before I became the Grand Magician of the Order of the Sleeping Butterfly."

"So you're Glenke Taval!" I said. I should have guessed sooner, but it somehow hadn't occurred to me.

"Indeed. I'm certainly not H. G. Wells," he said, laughing. "I hope you're not going to kill me before we finish our little chat."

"You've got my number," I said. "To kill you and not get the answers to a million questions? No way."

"Well, that's good. I have just one request: don't hurry with your bloody mission. You'll get your chance. It's very easy to kill me—didn't Juffin tell you that?"

"He did."

"And it is true, unfortunately. Now you can turn around, if you wish to. I don't mind. I was afraid you'd recognize me. Did Juffin tell you what I look like on the Dark Side?"

"You'll be surprised to learn that he didn't even bother telling me what you looked like in the World," I said. "He refused to tell me anything about you. Well, almost anything. He only told me that you were good friends once."

"Ah, so he's not *that* mad at me after all, since he gave us a chance to talk in peace," Glenke said, sounding relieved.

He finally approached me and sat nearby. I looked at him, and frankly, I felt sorry that he hadn't stayed behind my back. Glenke had no face. None. Just a blob of emptiness surrounded by disheveled dark hair, soft as that of a baby.

"Normally I look like a regular person, but here . . ." he said in a guilty tone, covering the emptiness that was his face with his long, thin hands. "Unpleasant, isn't it?"

"Not so much unpleasant as it is . . . well, unnerving," I said. "Don't worry, I'll get over it. Will you please explain the meaning behind that H. G. Wells story that is actually your story? Why did you do it?"

"Because Juffin needed you, but he couldn't transport you from one World into another without your consent. Well, not just that. Simple consent wouldn't have cut it. You had to *wish* for it to happen. Wish for it with all your heart. Some are easy to tempt with a promise of special powers; others can be enticed with a promise of love. Juffin was sure that you were the kind who would only buy into a myth. That's why we fed you the myth about a man who opened the Door between Worlds, the oldest myth in the Universe told in a language you understood. And his plan worked. You read that story and became obsessed. You must have forgotten already, but back then you swore to yourself that—"

"That I would look for that dratted door," I said. "And that I would open it without a second thought when I found it, no matter what other pressing business I had. Good golly, I completely forgot about that!"

"You did, didn't you? But that doesn't change anything. Your words have special powers, not just on the Dark Side—at least sometimes. From that moment on, you began destroying your life without realizing why you were doing it. From then on you never went with the flow. You jumped out of it and took a turn onto the road that eventually led you to Green Street. Mind you, *Green* Street. Talk about coincidences."

"Well, maybe," I said, shrugging. "Just *maybe* it all happened the way you are describing. But why me? Am I special? Did I win some mystical jackpot?"

"Something like that," said Glenke. "You won it by virtue of birth. You were born an Origin, and in our World, Origins are very rare. The last Origin I know of was King Mynin."

"An Origin?" I said, frowning. The term reeked of dangerous romantic nonsense I could smell a mile away. "What kind of a sick thing is that, an Origin?"

"You should know," said Glenke, smirking. "But this is why your words have a special power, cities from your dreams materialize, and all your wishes come true sooner or later, somehow or other. A dangerous quality, if you think about it, especially since in the beginning every Origin thinks he's an ordinary human being and begins collecting other human problems with gusto. In our World, Origins are born very, very seldom, and it's a blessing. Your home World, on the other hand, is teeming with them. But what's the use? Usually Origins are unbearable. The ones who don't know what they are doing are spoiled by their powers. Juffin's idea was that you would have a desire so fundamental, so strong and unfulfilled, that you wouldn't have the time or strength to waste on other trivial concerns. I came up with the story of the Door in the Wall especially for you, and Juffin snuck the edited book into your parents' house. I don't know how he did it, but he did."

"Okay, so I'm an Origin. Fine. Could be worse, I guess," I said. "But to Magicians with my life story, I'll figure it out myself somehow. Why did you send the Lonely Shadows to Echo? Were you bored or something?"

"No, not really," said Glenke. "Juffin had his own plans for you, and I had mine. When the Kettarian asked me to make up a good fairy tale for you, he promised that someday you would take care of my problems. Alas, I have no time left. No time at all. You see, I'm dying. Here on the Dark Side, I'm still doing fine. Perhaps my powers have even grown stronger, since I was capable of raising an entire army of Lonely Shadows and making them work for me. But there in the World, you'd have to talk to a dying old man. A *witless* dying old man, even, which is the worse part. The disintegrating mind of the semidead Glenke Taval is incapable of sending Juffin a call to demand that he hurry up and keep his promise. Or, rather, hurry up and send *you* to keep his promise—which, as far as I can tell, you didn't even know about. That sly old fox, let me tell you, can be notoriously leisurely when it comes to dealing with someone else's business. The Lonely Shadows were like an angry letter addressed to both of you. It happened in just the way I expected: Juffin learned that the Lonely Shadows had appeared in Echo by my command and sent you to take care of me. At the end, I managed to turn the tide of chance once again—this time for myself."

"No wonder they called you the Master Steerer of Chance. It'd be strange if you didn't manage," I said. "And why do you need me, Glenke? What are your plans regarding me? You didn't go through all that trouble just to discuss your literary talent with me. The story is excellent, by the way, don't get me wrong. It really got me. I should thank you for it. But that's not enough, I take it?"

"Naturally, that's not enough. Use your head, Mr. Secret Investigator. You still don't understand what I want from you?"

"Nope. I might be an Origin, but I'm one heck of a brainless one."

"You don't need much brainpower to understand it," said Glenke. "What is the one thing a dying man might want? The Origin can grant a new life and freedom to anyone, even a dead man. In my case, it's especially relevant. All my life I've been groping for some freedom that I myself never understood completely. Was it freedom from human fate that I wanted? I desperately tried to break through beyond the limits of the World, but I could never get beyond the Dark Side. Now I am dying and my powers are not enough to withstand death. I want to try one more time, and all I need are a few words from you so that instead of the unknown of death, another kind of unknown will accept me. You did this once before—for Red Jiffa from the Magaxon Forest. Without his requesting it from you, by the way."

"Oh, I get it now. Sure, I'll do that for you. After all, that's why I came here."

"Ah, but not exactly," said Glenke, laughing. "You came to kill me, didn't you?"

"You don't know me well enough," I said. "From the get-go I was almost sure I wasn't going to kill you. Maybe send you to some far-off place, what with all the Worlds in the Universe, inhabited and not. Juffin, I'm sure, also knew it. I'm also sure he was satisfied with that outcome; otherwise he would have sent Lonli-Lokli instead of me. But hey, you were risking a great deal when you started all this! And then those Lonely Shadows of yours—they killed several poor souls that had nothing to do with you, or Juffin, or me, or H. G. Wells. That wasn't right."

"Agreed on all counts," said Glenke. "But what choice did I have? I'm as good as dead anyway. If you were in my shoes, by the way, you would have eradicated the entire populace of Echo without a moment's thought. And don't pretend you're shocked to hear that."

"I guess you're right," I said reluctantly. "Okay, one last question then. Why did Juffin start it all? I mean, what does *he* want with me?"

"I think you should address this question to him," said Glenke. "It was his idea, I only helped him a little. But knowing Juffin, I don't think he requires anything in particular from you. Juffin doesn't need anything from anyone. What I'm saying is that he'll never ask you a personal favor like I did. Maybe he's just happy to help you harness your own powers, and of course he's burning with curiosity to see what you will do next. A fascinating experiment, quite to his taste."

"Yes, it sounds just like him," I said, smiling. "Well, are you ready, Glenke? I'm going to—"

"I've been ready for many, many years. But please come up with some good wording. So much depends on it."

"Okay," I said, nodding.

Suddenly, I was overcome by a strange sense of paralysis. Nothing remotely like this had ever happened to me before. I became indifferent toward everything: the fate of Glenke Taval, my own mysterious fate, the books of H. G. Wells's stories, the Door in the Wall, and many other things. Yet I was prepared to pay up, to give Glenke Taval what was his due.

"Go to a place where you can be alive, Sir Glenke Taval," I said. "I want you to break free of your fate, disappear from this beautiful World, and end up someplace where everything will be different."

Glenke vanished before I finished talking. I felt drained and bone-tired. I sat down on the soft red grass and closed my eyes. No good. I could still see the glowing sky and the gorgeous landscape of the Dark

Side. Either my eyelids had become transparent, or here on the Dark Side we don't use our eyes to see.

"Melifaro!" I called. "Take me home."

"Aw, the little baby wants to go home. Want me to buy some candy on the way, too?" said Melifaro, helping me get off the ground. Around me it was dark again. The mysterious double of my friend had already disappeared, praise be the Magicians. It was all for the best— I had had it with incomprehensible creatures for today.

"I wouldn't turn down some candy right now," I said, smiling and trying to stand up on my wobbly legs. "Let's get out of here. I'm exhausted."

"Believe it or not, me too," he said, yawning. "So close your eyes and try to walk on your own two feet, okay?"

"I'll try," I said.

Soon Melifaro gave me a gentle push with his elbow.

"You can open your pretty eyes now. And let go of my arm. You're clenching it like you're trying to rip it out to sell at a fair in Numban," he said.

"I didn't know I could sell stuff like that there," I said, opening my eyes. "I'll keep it in mind, in case I come across a spare limb somewhere."

In the World it was nighttime. The night was warm, humid, and windless. Nearby stood my amobiler, now equipped with menacing tank tracks. From it came the annoying sounds of the barrel organ.

"What have you been doing there all this time, Max?" grumbled the owner of that ingenious musical instrument. "What have you done to our felon?"

"Did you visit him at home?" I said. "Well, what happened there?"

"'What happened there' you ask?" said Kofa. "I spent almost a dozen days sitting here in your jalopy, entertaining the local shapeshifters.

There were a bunch of fellows that hung around here and turned into squirrels at night. They came to listen to the music. At first it was quite entertaining, but then I thought I'd go crazy from their chitter-chatter. And I had to put up with all that, only so I could eventually go to Glenke Taval's castle and find a half-dead crazy old man who had the temerity to disappear right in front of my very eyes."

"That's right," I said, happy. "That's very close to how I imagined it. Don't get mad, Kofa, but Glenke Taval doesn't exist anymore. He's neither dead nor alive."

"Oh, really?" said Kofa, with a cunning squint.

"Well, at least he doesn't exist in this World, which is what was required of us. I'm sorry you had to take that unnecessary walk there. If I had known beforehand it would be so easy, you could have just stayed at home. Or, say, in the *Middle of the Woods*. Beats sitting in the bushes, surrounded by man-squirrels hopping around you all night."

"If you had known *anything* beforehand, it wouldn't have been you. It would have been someone old and wise," said Kofa, smiling. "I don't blame you, boy. What I would really like to do now is to kick our Sir Venerable Head's butt. Although I don't think I'm going to succeed. Back in the day I tried to perform that noble task on many an occasion and, alas, always failed. Why on earth did he have to get *me* involved in this undertaking in the first place?"

"Didn't you want a vacation?" said Melifaro. "You did, and so did I. So Juffin gave us a vacation."

"Right. Didn't you like it?" I said. "I thought the trip went great. I have nothing to complain about."

"Especially the music," said Melifaro and laughed. "And the happy days you and I spent in the *Middle of the Woods* about half a mile away from the outhouse. Granted, your story of the Black Hand was kind of cool. All right, let's head back home. Home is the best place in the world. Plus, your wives are waiting for me there."

"Kumonian honey is what's waiting for you there," I said.

"Don't remind me," said Melifaro, stretching out on the back seat. "On second thought, leave me here. Maybe those musically inclined man-squirrels will accept me into their herd and later make me their leader. I'm pretty good at making disgusting sounds myself when I . . ."

He didn't finish because he had already fallen asleep. I wished I could have followed his example.

Of course, I could have off-loaded the driving responsibility onto Kofa's iron shoulders, but we had already spent way too much time on this "field trip." According to Kofa, he had been sitting here for almost a dozen days. Our only chance to get back home at one go lay in my crazy driving. I took a sizable gulp of Elixir of Kaxar and grabbed the lever.

"What's going on in Echo?" I asked Kofa. "Last time I spoke with Juffin he was taking care of some pesky problems. Another old friend, from what I could gather. Did you send Juffin a call?"

"I sent him several calls a day, and not just him. I hope you don't think my intellectual needs could be satisfied by personal contact with man-squirrels. We come from different backgrounds. That's why the initial bond that we formed did not withstand the test of time."

He lit up his pipe, taking his time, and then continued.

"Everything is fine in Echo, and that sly Kettarian fox is particularly fine. They are having loads of fun, too. The ship from Arvarox arrived two days ago. Sir Aloxto Allirox finally gave filthy Mudlax a warm welcome, congratulated him on the occasion of his early parole, and formally executed him right by the ferry crossing, much to the delight of the inhabitants of Echo. That's it in a nutshell. Feel free to amplify the details with your imagination."

"I can't," I said, smiling. "I have a lousy imagination. How has Lady Melamori been reacting to all this?"

"You should ask her. I believe that currently she's not reacting to it at all. She's dragging her Arvaroxian pretty boy along with her to the various fashionable taverns for novice rich people. You know, the kind where they serve those disgusting sweet liqueurs."

"Oh, so you hate them, too?" I said.

"That is the only response to them," said Kofa. "I'm happy that you understand me."

We talked about this and that as our off-road vehicle gobbled down the distance separating us from the beautiful Capital of the Unified Kingdom.

The morning caught up with us as we were passing the *Middle of the Woods*.

"Want to drop by?" I said. "I was told that I could always count on room and board in that place for just 'one small money.'"

"Frankly, I'd rather not," said Kofa. "Their cooking is disgusting. If you keep going at this speed, we'll make it to Chinfaro by dusk. That's where we can eat to our heart's content."

"Agreed," I said and sped up a little more. The sounds of pine-cones crunching under the tracks became even more frequent.

We arrived at Chinfaro not by dusk but soon after lunchtime. The locals eyed my track-equipped amobiler with suspicion. I didn't blame them. If I were them, my jaw would have dropped, too.

Melifaro woke up only after I had come to a screeching halt by the *Old House*.

"How long did I sleep? A day? Two days?" he said, still groggy. "This has never happened to me before."

"You didn't sleep for more than a dozen hours. It's just that Sir Max has gone completely crazy, praise be the Magicians," said Kofa. "Never before have I met a person who could go crazy at such an opportune moment."

"We're in Chinfaro already? Holy smokes, Max!" said Melifaro. "You saved more than just my life, Monster! But if I don't take a hot bath right now, I'm going to die in your arms."

"Liar," I said. "What you meant to say was that you'd die if you didn't change into something bright crimson right this minute."

"Of course, I'm going to change, too," said Melifaro. "And so should you, by the way. You look like a poor farmer from the outskirts of Landaland in these shabby duds. I wouldn't be surprised if the innkeeper asks us to pay in advance after he takes one look at you. Want me to lend you something decent?"

"By 'decent' you mean something garish?" I said. "Let's give it a try."

The bathing pool with warm water seemed to me like the best place on earth. Thirty minutes later I noticed I was beginning to doze off. I got out, dried myself, and began to dress. The bright-yellow looxi that Melifaro had donated to me was as comfortable as its color was revolting. I have always been a sucker for things that other people have worn before me. I don't know why.

I dressed and went down to the dining hall.

Melifaro wasn't there yet, but Kofa was already munching on the contents of the many tiny bowls surrounding him. He looked like he was in a hurry to pay his final dues to his special "diet." He wouldn't have time for it when he was back in Echo, that much was certain.

Kofa scrutinized me long and hard, from top to bottom, and was visibly dissatisfied with what he saw.

"Maybe you should get a good night's sleep after all," he said. "Right now you look more like a Lonely Shadow than a human being. Are you sure nobody put a spell on you?"

I shrugged and ambled along a crisp, elongated shadow cast by one of the customers. He didn't even notice my maneuver.

"Well, the fellow is still alive. That means I'm not a Lonely Shadow. I'm an ordinary human being," I said and winked at Kofa.

"You still look terrible," he said.

"As if he's ever looked *not* terrible," said Melifaro. He was in a good mood. "For Nightmare is his name."

Melifaro looked like someone who would grace the cover of a lifestyle magazine. Even his new attire seemed (who would have thought?) modest: he was wearing a new looxi of an acceptable periwinkle-blue color.

My looks notwithstanding, I had the appetite of a tiger. After I had gobbled down an enormous amount of food, I finally reconciled myself to the idea that I would have to resign from the position of driver for the next leg of our journey. I think I fell asleep at the table, my head resting on a mug of kamra, and hardly even woke up when I was moved back to the amobiler.

It was already dark when I woke up. Kofa's barrel organ was silent. The amobiler was crawling past one-story rural cottages and houses surrounded by thick trees at a whopping speed of barely thirty miles an hour.

"How come we've stopped?" I said sarcastically.

"And how come there's so much venom in a man who has just woken up? You should siphon it off into some special vial from time to time," said Melifaro. "Also, I can easily take offense and start a fight. Before you dropped down on our heads, I was considered to be a fast driver."

"Were you really?" I said. "My goodness, you must have even outrun pedestrians on a few occasions. I know that's considered an achievement among the official drivers of the Ministry of Perfect Public Order."

"Your waking up is very timely," said Kofa. "I was just about to take your place."

"Go ahead," I said. "I'm going to get behind the levers and hope that we make it out of Chinfaro today. Better late than never."

"We're already about to pass Cheli suburbs, by the way," said Melifaro, offended.

"Is this still night, or is it morning? How long did I sleep?"

"It's around midnight," said Kofa, yawning. "Go on, free up the seat."

"Midnight is the best time for ghost stories," I said, getting in the driver's seat.

Melifaro, who had been fuming for a few moments, couldn't continue his act. He smiled from ear to ear.

"All righty, then. Tell me another one," he said.

"In a very dark World stood a very dark forest," I began in a sepulchral voice. "Through the very dark forest ran a very dark road."

"Ooh, this sounds so familiar," said Melifaro. "Go on."

"Down the very dark road drove a very dark car . . . I'm sorry, a very dark amobiler, of course. The very dark amobiler drove up to a very dark city, meandered through the very dark streets, and stopped by a very dark wall. Two men dressed all in black got out of the amobiler, and one of them said to the other . . ." I made a dramatic pause and then blurted out, "'Hey, Boss! This looks like a good place to take a leak.'"

Melifaro laughed. Even Sir Kofa grinned in approval, but then he said in a grumpy tone, "Will you please let me sleep?"

We mustered up all our remaining willpower and shut up for a whopping five minutes.

Kofa slept for no more than a couple of hours, but when he woke up we were already approaching Echo—I had been doing my best to make up for lost time.

"Whoa, we're almost home," he said.

His familiar good-natured, kindly manner, which I had already begun to forget, had returned to him. I even turned around to make sure that it was indeed my good friend Sir Kofa in the back seat. Sure enough, it was him: the long-nosed, arrogant fellow was gone.

"Woohoo, Kofa! Finally. Boy, have I missed you!" said Melifaro.

"I did get on your nerves, didn't I?" said Kofa and smiled.

"Will you be shocked if I tell you that I enjoyed your company the same way I always do?" I said.

"Are you saying I'm always that obnoxious?"

"You're wonderful, Kofa," said Melifaro. He was moved. "You're probably the best person in the World, but you owe me at least a dozen dinners. Your music alone is worth it. Admit that you can't stand it yourself."

"Oh, no. Whenever I get the chance to get home, I always take out that toy," said Kofa. "It calms me down and stimulates my mental faculties. I have no idea why everyone gets so riled up about it."

An hour later we drove through the Breach of Toixi Menka.

"Ah, home, sweet home," said Melifaro, yawning. "I'm going to hibernate until fall as soon as I get to my blanket."

"I'm afraid your hibernation will have to wait," said Kofa, shaking his head. "At least for another half hour. Max, go right to Juffin's house. I just sent him a call. It was a fatal mistake: He said he was waiting for us. Eagerly."

"Oh, no. What does he want with *me*?" Melifaro sighed a deep sigh. "What can a Sentry tell him that is even remotely interesting? That I stood on the Threshold and gazed through the mist with two pairs of eyes? He knows that already from his own experience."

"Juffin is also a Sentry?" I said. "He can do that?"

"He can do anything," said Melifaro. "Who do you think tutored me on all that Sentry nonsense? My mom and dad?"

"You don't need any tutoring in that department. You have an inborn talent for nonsense," I said as I turned to the gates of Juffin's garden.

Juffin was standing on the porch, burning with curiosity and anticipation.

"Just what have you done to the amobiler!" he said. "It's hideous!"

"Perhaps," said Kofa. "But it can now easily cross any swamps in which we would have definitely gotten bogged down, thanks to your friend Glenke. That was quite some place he chose as his final abode. I'm sure it took him a long time to find it."

"Glenke didn't choose where to settle. It's his ancestors' abode. They settled there back in the days when Landaland was considered to be the driest province of the Unified Kingdom. No swamps to speak of," said Juffin. "Sir Max, if you are planning to drive around the city in this monstrosity, you don't even need to wear the Mantle of Death. Just looking at it will make everybody run the other way. And I will be the first victim. Let's go inside. Enough of your demonstrative pandiculation already, Melifaro. I am very much aware that you are tired, but I regret to say I don't give a damn. I missed you, and I wish to talk to all of you. For your information, you have been gone for fourteen days. Of course, it could have been much worse." Juffin talked nonstop while we were seating ourselves in his soft, comfortable chairs.

"Is Chuff asleep?" I said.

Juffin's dog was my first friend in this World. I had never once left this place without having my nose thoroughly licked.

"He is. He'll probably wake up soon," said Juffin. "What you and I need now is lots and lots of good kamra, and maybe something a bit stronger. I don't think we should wake old Kimpa up for that."

He raised his arms above his head. It was a magnificent, powerful gesture. Such would be the gesture with which one would create a new Universe, or at the very least exorcise a few demons. But when Juffin lowered his arms, there was merely a tray full of various bottles and glasses in his hands.

"Impressive, isn't it?" he said. "I sometimes feel ashamed of myself. Such a respectable old man with such a passion for cheap special effects. Still, at least I didn't have to raise my backside off the chair. That fact alone is worth a great deal. Oh, before I forget, Kofa, did you bring me what I asked for?"

"Of course," said Kofa. From the pocket of his looxi he produced a tiny box. "You owe me three more crowns, though. The price has gone up, unfortunately."

"Thank you." Juffin smiled from ear to ear and fumbled in his pocket for the money. Of course I was intrigued. The boss looked at me askance, smirked, and shook his head. "Don't even think about it. I'm not telling. I have the right to a personal secret, don't I?"

"Of course you do," I said and let out such a deep sigh that it should had been obvious to anyone that I was about to die right then and there, in the prime of my life and at the peak of my career.

Juffin was unflinching. He carefully put the box away in his pocket and looked at us. "Well, tell me everything," he said. "Not you, Max. We'll save your story for dessert."

Over the course of an hour, I helped myself to the multitude of snacks Juffin had conjured up. Kofa and Melifaro took the lead in relating the story of our adventure. In their rendition our trip sounded like a mixture of a lighthearted traveler's tale and a dramatic reading of a story of lonely souls lost in the darkness of the Universe.

At some point, Juffin took mercy on the somnolent Melifaro and even asked Kofa give the poor fellow a lift home.

Then Juffin and I were alone.

"My turn to tell the story?" I said.

"No need to," said Juffin, smiling. "You did the right thing setting Glenke free."

"But how come you didn't tell me I was supposed to set him free and not kill him from the start? What if I had defied him? What would have happened then?" I said.

"Oh, come on. Do you think I should make the decision about what to do with your life for you every single time? Or provide you with a fresh instruction manual every day, for that matter? Tough. Glenke Taval has his own fate, and you have yours, and I have nothing to do with either of them. The best I could do was to make sure you two met and then see what happened. You both did a great job, so I can file away your encounter under Things That Improve My Digestion. That is not to say that you didn't have the right to kill Glenke if he had made a mistake. Why not, after all?"

"I still can't wrap my mind around all this," I said. "What about the story that he told me? Is it true?"

"Well, how shall I put it? Of course Glenke told you the truth," said Juffin. "Rather, what he *thought* was the truth. The problem is, the truth always lies beyond words, in that vague, incomprehensible area somewhere between what has been said and what has been concealed. I'm afraid the answer to your question transcends the ordinary yes or no. Let's just say that you have heard another myth—the myth of the Origins. As a bonus, you also learned about the foreword to the story that had impressed you so much in childhood. Mind you, it was a *foreword*, not an *afterword*, for a true myth never ends."

"Actually, there's only one question the answer to which has any practical significance to me now. Tell me, Juffin, is my life going to change somehow after all this?"

"That's a good question," said Juffin, visibly excited. "It's good, yet funny, too. Your precious life, Max, is definitely going to change 'after all this,' as you put it. But it's changing all the time anyway. Haven't you noticed?"

"I sure have," I said. "So does this mean that you and I are even older friends than I used to think? And if it hadn't been for your connivance, I might have become a regular, complacent bore living a happy life? I always wanted to try that, and you ruined my chances."

"There is no such thing as a happy human life," said Juffin, turning suddenly serious. "There are only people, some people, who are dumb enough to consider themselves to be happy. Or to die happy. And don't you tell me that you are jealous of them—I won't believe you. In any case, that wasn't going to happen to you. Even if you had devoted all your allotted time to fulfilling all the numerous trivial desires, you would never have been able to hide from the desperate longing for magic. Yet you would have never figured out what it was you were so desperately longing for. How's that for an option?"

"Not too great," I said. "But it didn't happen, Magicians be praised, so there's no point in talking about it, right?"

"It's getting light," said Juffin and yawned. "Did you lift that load from your two anxious hearts, Max? Or not yet?"

"I don't know," I said. "Maybe there was no load to begin with. I just didn't like the term 'Origin.' It implies something grand, something launching lethal fireballs from its eyes, like Sir Shurf's gloves. It's so unlike me. But it's just a word. It doesn't change anything. I don't care what someone is called. But I did learn a thing or two about myself, and that's not bad. Still, there's something pretty darn attractive about ignorance, isn't there?"

"There is indeed," said Juffin, his face looking very serious again. "Although, one could say the same thing about knowledge. The important thing is to retain a good balance between the two."

"You know what I think? I think that heartrending story about the Origins is just like the one about my ascension to the throne," I said. "It boggles your mind, shakes you to the core, disrupts your sleep, but it doesn't really mean much."

"My goodness, Max," said Juffin. "When did you become so wise? Did you catch something on the Dark Side? Speaking of your throne, some representatives of your poor people came to Echo last night. Right now they are probably sleeping in your palace. They declared war on their neighbors—just what the wiseman ordered. His Majesty Gurig is delighted. He has been pondering a pretext for inciting a large-scale attack by Xenxa warriors on the neighboring tribes, and your subjects just happened to indulge His Majesty's secret desires. Isn't that a miracle?"

"Maybe the King is also one of the Origins?" I said and smiled a malicious smile. "My, my, my, Juffin, how could you have missed that?"

"No, I don't think so," said Juffin, smiling. "But you're going to have to talk to the ambassadors. Please find some time for them tomorrow after you get up. They desperately need you to lend them your royal ear. The fellows from the Chancellory of Concerns of Worldly Affairs have already prepared a detailed set of instructions for them. You just need to hand it to the messenger with due grandeur."

"They have already prepared it? What about our sovereignty? Your words hurt my national pride!"

Suddenly I felt tired of my jokes. I was tired of everything. It was time for me to hit the sack.

With great difficulty, I got up from the armchair that had enveloped me in its comfy softness. I didn't leave, though. I shuffled my feet, trying to come up with something to say, something epic and earth-shattering instead of the usual "good night." The boss was watching me with the cold-blooded curiosity of an entomologist.

"Thank you," I said. "Your bait—the green door in the white wall—was wonderful."

"I couldn't agree more," said Juffin. "Believe me, I derived a great deal of pleasure out of the whole thing myself. You know, before I met you, I had no idea there were people who could be snared by such a trivial thing as a book. You were so serious about ink on paper. That story turned my notion about the power of the written word upside down. Good night, Max. Oh, and don't get it into your head that royal duties somehow relieve you of your primary responsibilities. I expect to see you at Headquarters tomorrow before dusk."

"Sir, a person who has known you for longer than half an hour would never dare think any such thing," I said, suppressing a yawn.

No more than thirty minutes later, I was already struggling with Tekki for the right to cover myself with a few square inches of the blanket. While I was gone, she'd learned to wrap herself in it completely, without so much as a scrap hanging free. When she finally sensed someone else in her bed, I had to prove that someone was me. Fortunately, I was very persuasive.

That night I didn't get enough sleep, nor did I have time to take a breather the next day. At noon a courier from the Ministry of Perfect Public Order woke me up. Juffin had sent the instructions for my subjects.

I should have paid more attention in my history classes, I thought, sitting in the bathing pool with warm, fragrant water, desperately trying to pull myself together. But who knew it would ever come in handy? I could have drawn up a plan based on some epic battle from ancient history. Maybe the experiences of Alexander the Great would have come in handy.

My very first attempt at being a politico was interrupted by Tekki, who came into the bathroom. All the better, I thought. Who knows what dangerous nonsense I would have come up with if I was left to my own devices a little longer?

"Max, have you turned into a fish already?" she said. "Not that I would mind if you did, don't get me wrong. I love fish, but maybe that can wait? Melamori is here to see you. She says she must talk to you right away."

"Well, meeting her in the bathroom is out of the question," I said, laughing.

"Do you think that would shock her?" said Tekki, grinning.

"Not her—me. Tell her to wait just a bit longer. I'll come up in a second."

"Do you know what it's going to be about?" said Tekki.

"I can guess. I know the ship from Arvarox is here already."

Tekki smiled a sad smile and left. I got out of the bathing pool and began to dress.

Melamori was waiting for me in the den. Tekki brought in a tray with some delicious light morning snacks and, as tactful as she was, disappeared after telling us the old legend of some mysterious clients that were allegedly waiting for her.

"It's great you're back so soon," said Melamori. "They say some Magicians who left for the Dark Side thought they spent only an hour there, but in fact returned many, many years later. Don't worry, I'm not going to start whining. I'm still frightened, and I still think I'm making the biggest mistake of my life, but I'm going to do it anyway. That's final. I just wanted to ask you, will you come say goodbye to me?"

"When are you leaving?"

"Tonight. Everybody thinks Aloxto's leaving in three days' time. He says it himself, and everybody believes the word of an Arvaroxian without giving it a moment's thought. But I explained to Aloxto that words were just words, and that a person could tell an untruth once in his life. My overprotective daddy and uncle Kima are busy figuring out how to keep an eye on him when he leaves, and where to hide me that day so I don't go with him. I'm up to my ears in family intrigues, not to mention other kinds."

"Does Juffin know?" I said.

"I think he knows everything there is to know—even things that are none of his business," said Melamori. "In any case, if it weren't for him, I probably wouldn't have had the guts to leave."

"The boss talked you into leaving?" I said, surprised.

"Talked me into it? What nonsense, Max! How on earth would he do that?"

"What did he say then?"

"Oh, nothing much. I asked him why he had never taught me anything special. I mean all those wonderful things that happen to the rest of the gang: the Dark Side, the Corridor between Worlds, and Magicians know what else. I've been working at the Secret Investigative Force for what seems like an eternity, and I still can't do any of that. You know what he said? He said that the journey to the Dark Side begins with another journey. That one morning a person wakes up, leaves his home, and walks out into the unknown. Then he laughed and gave me some menial task. And when I was done, he praised me for an unnaturally long time. Do you see what I mean? Of course, I could pretend I was a dummy and go on with my life as though nothing had happened, but—"

"But you would have made a lousy dummy," I said. "Even if you started bashing your head against the wall."

"Exactly," said Melamori. "That's why tonight I'm boarding that sinning *Surf Thorn*, and may the rest of the World go up in smoke!"

"You're doing the right thing," I said softly. "Of course I'll come to say goodbye. Do you know how to say goodbye forever? It's the coolest thing going."

"Of course I don't. It's not something they teach ladies from respectable families. But I'm going to try anyway. Because I might very well never come back. I'll be sending you calls from time to time, Max. I know you hate Silent Speech, though—"

"All the more reason for me to practice it," I said. "Look at me, such an all-important mister big guy, yet I stumble over my words like a baby. Sometimes I'm even ashamed to send a call to a courier."

"Well, I guess that's about it then," said Melamori, sighing. "I'll send you a call around midnight. It will make things much easier for me if you come say goodbye to me. I'll be embarrassed to shiver in trepidation and shed tears in front of you. I don't want you to remember me with red eyes and a swollen nose."

"We'll see who's going to have a swollen nose and red eyes," I said. "I'm about to start sniffling and snuffling myself."

"Don't," said Melamori. "You're meeting your subjects. If they see you crying, they'll think we pick on their sovereign, and they'll declare war on us. Good day, Max. See you tonight."

Melamori rushed out and left me sitting alone in the living room. My mind was empty, my two hearts skipped now and then with vague premonitions, and my eyes actually did begin to water—something I hadn't expected of myself. I shook my head a few times and then went downstairs. I walked into the empty dining hall of the *Armstrong & Ella*, sat down on a bar stool, and gave Tekki a guilty look.

"Will you be able to tolerate me for a dozen days in the foulest mood possible?" I said.

"A foul mood? You? For a dozen days? Ain't gonna happen," she said, grinning. "You won't hold out for thirty minutes."

"Drat it, you're right," I said. "But thirty minutes I can still manage."

"Then go to your palace and pour your foul mood onto the heads of your subjects. They'll take anything from you. Unlike me."

"I guess I'll do just that. Except that my mood isn't so foul as to throw a cup of kamra in your face if you decide to treat me to it before I go."

"Really? Oh, I'm lucky then," said Tekki and laughed. "Here, your majesty."

"Sometimes you really remind me of Melifaro," I said, taking a sip of the best kamra in the World. "Why is that, I wonder?"

"Because sometimes Melifaro is the very person you desperately need to chat with. He's nowhere to be found, so I'm sitting in for him today," said Tekki, turning serious suddenly.

I looked at her, bewildered, but decided not to touch that dangerous topic.

Eventually Tekki sent me off to the palace. Sometimes her sense of civic responsibility can outdo anyone else's.

The meeting with the delegation of nomads turned out to be fun. There was even a lively recklessness about it.

Droopy was so happy to see me that he literally bowled me over as soon as I stepped onto the threshold of the Furry House. I deserved such treatment for abandoning him for so long. As a result, my subjects were given the rare opportunity to watch their heroic king fight a huge shaggy monster. Droopy refused to behave according to protocol. Then again, the same could be said about me.

Eventually, I mustered up enough strength to push aside three hundred fifty pounds of barking fur and muscles. Then I remembered my own theory, according to which I was supposed to talk to my subjects while sitting in the doorway. Since that was where I was sitting already, it was time to start the show.

"Do not waste words. I know why you have come. Your king knows of the heroic battle his subjects are engaged in," I said with a pathos that contrasted with my behavior just moments ago. "Right, so who is the leader of the gang today?"

The head of the delegation, a tall, muscular fellow in bright-crimson shorts, wearing a headband of the same color, came up to me. I handed him an envelope with the recommendations that the specialists at the Chancellory of Concerns of Worldly Affairs had been working on all night. Needless to say, I had never bothered opening it and reading what they had come up with. Now I felt like a bad student at a midterm exam. Granted, unlike a bad student, I could tell the professors to go jump in the lake and take their questionnaires with them. Being a king had its advantages after all.

"What is this, sire?" the head of the delegation said in a timid tone, fumbling with the envelope.

"It tells you what you're supposed to do in written form," I said. "It's better than giving commands out loud. At least I'll be sure there won't be any confusion or misunderstanding. Take this to your general. I hope Barxa Bachoy is still riding at the head of our mighty warriors."

"Of course, sire," said the fellow, bowing. "That is why he could not come and see you. I will be happy to give him these papers with your wise letters written on them."

"Goody," I said, then stopped myself. "Hold on. Can you read?"

"We cannot," said the hero in crimson shorts.

"Bummer," I said. "I should have thought of that."

Actually, it was the royal advisers who should have thought of that, but now it was too late to blame anyone.

"But some of your subjects can read, O Fanghaxra," said Crimson Shorts.

I heaved a sigh of relief. Phew! One less problem to worry about.

"Some? Who exactly?" I said. I wanted to be sure, just in case.

"Fairiba can read, and so can five of his pupils. Barxa Bachoy can read; Xenli, Barxa Bachoy's daughter, can read; Oitoxti can—"

"All right, all right," I said. "I get the picture. In that case, I don't have to worry about it. Go home, guys. I think you'd better hurry. I hope everything's going to be all right. And tell Barxa that I'm rooting for him."

"Thank you, sire!" said the gang in an out-of-sync but rapturous chorus.

Pfft, I thought, as if I'd root for any other team.

That was where I had to bid my subjects farewell. I also wanted to have a few words with my harem, but the girls weren't home. Little by little they were becoming busy ladies of the world. I wouldn't have known where to find them.

All my roads still led to the House by the Bridge, and that was where I set out to.

I never made it to Juffin's office. In the hallway, I was swept up by a bright-orange tornado. Upon closer examination, the tornado turned out to be Sir Melifaro. He whirled me around and around and around and sucked me into his office.

"Don't fret. Juffin's occupied, and the others have gone Magicians know where," he said. "Except Melamori, of course. She's taking her handsome Aloxto out to air one last time, of course. Sneaky Kofa's pretending to teach Kekki the tricks of his trade. I have to hand it to him: he's the first man to finagle a way to take his girlfriend out to the best taverns in Echo at the Royal Treasury's expense *and* get paid for it."

"Okay, that covers Kofa," I said, "but what about Shurf?"

"Beats me. He left looking like he was about to save humanity from impending doom. I didn't dare ask. Naturally, later it'll turn out he just snuck out to the library. Anyway, they all left me, and I'm stuck here covering their backsides instead of enjoying a dozen Days of Freedom from Care, which I'm sure I deserve after my trip through the swamps in the company of two unbearable fellows."

"There were no swamps there, stop making things up. By the way, now you're going to be covering my backside, too," I said, carefully putting my feet on his desk. "You see, I have a war going on and don't have time for trifles. So you're going to work two shifts now, and I'm going to grieve over the fate of my long-suffering people. Isn't that awesome?"

"Two words, buddy: dream on," said Melifaro.

For a few seconds I stared at his gleeful face. Then it dawned on me, and I laughed. Of course, he was repaying me for one of my comebacks with my own words!

"You're one rancorous son of a gun," I said.

"You bet, mister," said Melifaro. Half an hour later he was gone, saying something about everybody but him having loads of fun, and I went to see Juffin.

Juffin was uncommunicative. He sat at his desk, upon which self-inscribing tablets and—oh, mercy!—*papers* were piled up all around him.

"You should busy yourself with something boring, too," he said. "Routine is the best sedative. Just what a man needs right now."

"Want me to help you with paperwork?" I said.

"No, this magic is well beyond your humble skills," said Juffin with a sigh. "Don't even think of touching it. Better yet, grab yourself a newspaper. It has the same effect."

I went to the Hall of Common Labor, sank into an armchair there, and, following Juffin's advice, buried myself in a fresh copy of the *Royal Voice*. In less than an hour, I was already beginning to doze off. Juffin had been absolutely right: the newspaper bored the heck out of me.

Juffin's voice woke me up. "Magicians be praised, Max. Another dark patch in my life is over," he said, running past me. "Good night."

I opened my mouth to discuss Melamori's escape with him but closed it almost right away. Nothing had happened yet, so there was nothing to talk about.

Juffin hesitated in the doorway and gave me a long look. Then he smiled a smile that was sad and mocking at the same time but didn't say a word. The door closed behind him, and I was alone.

Melamori sent me a call around midnight. She and Aloxto were waiting for me at the Makuri Pier.

I seem to remember you had a water amobiler, she said. Her voice lacked confidence. *Am I right?*

You are. Do you want to take a ride in it?

Indeed. To the Admiral's Pier. You know, it's being guarded. I don't want them to see Aloxto and me there together. My daddy can't seem to mind his own business.

I woke up Kurush. "Looks like you're going to have to hold down the fort alone, buddy."

"You have been gone for fourteen days," said the buriwok. "You could have stayed at work for a change, at least for one night."

"I'd love to," I said, sighing, "but the circumstances are beyond my control. Want me to bring you a pastry?"

"Indubitably," said the wise bird.

A few minutes later I parked my amobiler at the Makuri Pier. I couldn't have missed it if I'd wanted to: I had spotted Sir Aloxto Allirox's snow-white hair blocks away.

"I am happy to meet you, Sir Max," Aloxto said in a polite whisper. His "whisper," however, was the kind that made leaves shake on the trees.

Whatever had happened to his patented Arvaroxian imperturbability? He looked not just happy but also lost, almost stunned. He probably still couldn't believe that he was about to snatch Lady Melamori away, luring her with his beautiful eyes or his beautiful songs about his no less beautiful Arvarox.

"I'm also happy to see you, Aloxto," I said. "It's too bad the pleasure will be so short-lived."

"And will never happen again," Aloxto added.

"Ah, but you never know," I said.

"I do," he said softly. "I will never see this city again. Nor will I ever see you. I am one who knows his fate."

"Oh, in that case . . ." I fell silent. What was there to say?

"Evening, Max. Where are you hiding your formidable sea vessel?" Melamori said. She was peeking out from somewhere under her gigantic boyfriend's elbow like a rabbit out of a magician's hat.

"I'm not hiding it," I said, smiling. "It's just moored. Let me go set the poor thing free. Wait here."

I ran to fetch my water amobiler, which, along with a few dozen cousins, was tied up, rocking to and fro in the lulling waters. A sleepy old man came out of his hut to help me, his face expressing annoyance. He looked at me with an almost superstitious horror. I don't think it was my Mantle of Death—anyone who decided to take a ride down the river at midnight wouldn't instill much trust.

I gave the guard a crown, which improved his humor a bit.

"When are you planning to return?" he said.

"Not sure. Why?"

"I'm here all the time, but I'm usually fast asleep in the morning. Just wake me up if you need anything."

"Oh, no worries," I said. "I'll tie it myself, it's not difficult. Thank you, sir, and have a good night."

The old man nodded and hurried back into his little hut. I motioned to Melamori and Aloxto, and they joined me promptly.

"Where are we going?" I said. "Oh, yes, the Admiral's Pier. Does anyone know where it is?"

Melamori let out a nervous laugh, and Aloxto took my question more seriously. His was the correct attitude—I had never navigated the Xuron at night. The dark mirror of the water and the orbs of blue and orange lights on the opposite bank were beautiful, but their beauty didn't help me find my bearings one bit.

"Do you see that spot of darkness to the right of Xolomi Island?" said Aloxto. "Just keep it in sight."

"All right, chief," I said, maneuvering with great care and difficulty among the moored vessels. "Listen, Aloxto, there's something I wanted to ask you. What happened to the gift that Melifaro gave you? I mean the signet ring."

"The one with a magical man inside? Oh, the gift is doing well. I did as Sir Melifaro suggested: when a great sorrow overcame me, I threw the signet under my feet. A man came out of it. He was very angry, yet his anger was not real. I mean to say that he was not angry the way the warriors of Arvarox get angry."

"I'll bet he wasn't," I said, remembering Rulen Bagdasys, the Isamonian who had once made poor Melifaro hopping mad. To the best of my recollection, no one else had managed to do that to Melifaro since. Not even me.

"And what did you do to him?" I said.

"I was honored. Toila Liomurik the Silver Bigwig, Conqueror of Arvarox, himself agreed to accept that gift from me," said Aloxto. "Now the Conqueror of Arvarox owns that magical man. He brings much joy to the Conqueror."

"Good golly!" I said, laughing. "Finally that fellow brings joy to someone."

I am still grateful to Rulen Bagdasys. If it hadn't been for him, we would have had to talk about some terrifying things, such as life and death, or fate and eternity. Or worse—we'd have had to remain silent, and boy, do I hate awkward silence.

Before I knew it, we were at the Admiral's Pier, where *The Surf Thorn* lay rocking on the waves, ready to cast off.

"Fare thee well, Max," said Aloxto. Now *that* was a man who knew how to say goodbye forever.

He made a mind-boggling jump, turning every notion of the limits of human ability upside down, and flew onto the deck of his ship almost like a bird.

"You should leave now," he said, bending down over the railing. "It is bad luck when someone stays behind and watches a ship cast off."

"Yes, I remember," I said. Then I looked at Melamori.

"So I'm leaving after all," she said. "I still can't believe it, though."

"You are leaving, for sure," I said. "And I can't believe it myself."

"I feel like you've come to my funeral," she said. "I even want to ask you indignantly why you're not sobbing. Although I'd probably be even more indignant if you were."

"Okay, then we'll skip the sobbing part. Now go join Aloxto before you decide to spank me for bad behavior."

Another bird flew up on the deck of the ship from Arvarox.

I grabbed the levers and tore off so fast, it looked like every single scary monster of every single horror film was after me at once. It helped me not to look back, which I desperately wanted to do. I thought that something terrible would happen if I looked back.

But I didn't look. Not once. Instead, I broke a couple of nails tying up my toy by the Makuri Pier, bestowed a few exquisite curses upon the World, and went back to the House by the Bridge. It felt like there was a huge gaping hole filled with cold river wind in my chest, but it was better than the pain of grief. At least it didn't hurt.

I fed Kurush, settled in the armchair, and even managed to catch a few z's. I dreamed of the dark waters of the Xuron and two birds soaring in the sky—a large white seagull and a tiny black swift. I enjoyed watching them. Too bad in the dream I didn't have bread crumbs, or seeds, or anything else the birds would have been interested in.

"Enough working, Sir Max. You need to rest sometimes, too."

Juffin's mocking voice woke me up at dawn. I opened my eyes and stared groggily at the boss, trying to figure out who he was. While I was at it, I also tried to figure out who I was.

"You'd better start looking for a good hideout," Juffin said merrily. "Sir Korva Blimm is going to chase you down the streets of Echo wielding one of the precious swords from his collection—there's no two ways about it. And no Mantle of Death is going to protect you. He'll show you what happens when you assist girls from respectable families escape with unsavory foreign gentlemen."

"Very funny," I said, sighing. "I'll think of something. If worse comes to worst, I'll spit at him."

"Of course it's funny," said Juffin. "And don't you dare start getting all sad and soppy on me. When a good person finally accepts her destiny, it is no reason for grief. Rather the contrary. Okay, fine. Do you want me to give you my word that she's going to be all right?"

"Your word, huh?" I said, cheering up. "Better yet, give me an official paper to that effect. I have an unshakeable trust in the printed word."

"Ah, much better now," said Juffin, smiling. "Go home, Max. There's someone waiting for you there. Also, when you have the time, think about how we're going to manage here without our Master of Pursuit."

"I have a feeling that, when push comes to shove, I'm going to have to hop around standing on people's traces. The crime rate will plummet overnight because they're all going to die—both the guilty and the innocent."

"I was thinking very much along those lines," said Juffin. "Now I think we're going to be fine if you make an effort and at least try to control your gift. I don't want to hire a replacement for Melamori because—"

"Because she's going to come back?" I said, my heart doing a flip-flop.

"We'll see. On the other hand, what is she going to do there? I'd be surprised if studying the ancient culture of Arvarox would be the only pastime for the rest of Melamori's long—and trust me, it *is* long—life."

"Do you see me levitating?" I said. "It's because you've just taken that heavy load off my mind."

"Good riddance."

"Now if you would only tell me what was in that box that Kofa brought for you . . ." I said, my voice trailing off.

"No can do. I'm going to carry that secret to my grave," said Juffin.

"Okay, then. I'll keep thinking that you keep a jack-in-the-box."

"A what?" said Juffin.

"I'm sorry, sir, but that is a secret that I'm carrying to *my* grave," I said.

When I opened the bedroom door thirty minutes later, I froze in horror: Tekki wasn't here.

It wasn't in her nature to get up so early, so I was really scared. I even forgot to send her a call. Instead, I dashed into the living room. She wasn't there, either. Frantic, I rushed downstairs, although I couldn't imagine her standing behind the bar at this early dawn hour.

Yet she was there after all. What's more, she was not alone. I found her in the company of some strange creatures. Calling them human would have stretched the truth beyond recognition. At first I thought the Lonely Shadows had returned to Echo. Then, after I took a good look at them, I saw that the creatures were something else altogether.

"Hi, Max," said Tekki. "Meet my brothers. I told you about them, remember? They decided to drop by, and we stayed up late."

"Oh, your brothers' ghosts," I said and laughed, relieved. "Phew! Morning, fellows."

"Something wrong, Max?" If anyone, Tekki knew me like the back of her hand. She could easily tell my nervous laughter from genuine mirth.

"Nah, I'm just . . . You know, I got really scared when I didn't find you in the bedroom."

"Did you think I had slipped away to Arvarox with some yellow-eyed beauty boy?" she said.

"Good morning, Max." The rustling whisper of one of the apparitions interrupted our exchange. "I hope you're not too shocked by our visit. People generally don't take kindly to our company."

"Oh, not at all," I said. "I'm happy you dropped by to visit your sister."

The situation was rather hilarious: Who else would be happy to catch his girlfriend in the company of sixteen ghosts? I laughed.

"I've never seen a living human being so joyful," said one of the ghosts approvingly.

TWO

DOROTH, MASTER OF THE MANOOKS

"**I** HOPE IT DOES NOT SHOCK YOU THAT I DID NOT INVITE YOU INSIDE," said Lonli-Lokli. "This evening does not dispose one to shutting oneself up in a living room."

I smiled from ear to ear. We had just made ourselves comfortable on a few of the thick branches of a spreading Vaxari tree growing in the nether reaches of his garden.

"What really shocks me is not that you told me to go climb a tree—that's pretty routine. I could never have imagined, though, that you'd manage to crawl up here yourself."

"Did you really think I didn't know how to climb a tree?" he said, surprised. "Strange. It does not take much brainpower."

"I'm sure you can climb anything. It just never occurred to me that you'd do it voluntarily," I said. "Such a lighthearted pastime doesn't really jibe with your image."

"What image might that be?" Shurf said. "And whence the peculiar words?"

I laughed. "The peculiar words are knocking about in the depths of my powerful intellect. And all I meant was that climbing trees isn't really your style."

"In good weather I spend as much time in this tree as I do in my study. Especially if I want to read in peace. I do not invite just anyone here. You're the first. Proximity to trees gives you a tranquility unlike any other. And that is just what you are lacking. Trees can teach us a great deal: peace of mind, for instance."

"Neat," I said. "Too bad I don't have my own garden, what with all my homes. And if I tried to find peace of mind by climbing a tree outside the House by the Bridge, people might get the wrong idea about me."

"They might, indeed," Shurf said. "But even if you had a garden, what good would it do you? You never have any time for anything. You seem to just devour it whole."

This was true. Since the Great Hunt for the Lonely Shadows, nothing extraordinary had happened in my life. Sir Korva Blimm hadn't even given me grief for assisting his only daughter in her escape to Arvarox. Yet my days slipped through my fingers like sand through a sieve. Several days before, Tekki had mentioned in passing that summer would soon be over, and I was floored. Summer? Over? But it had hardly gotten underway!

"Do you remember my friend Anday Pu?" I said.

"Certainly. It would be strange if I had forgotten such a great poet so soon. Incidentally, I lost track of him long ago. Perhaps you know how he is faring these days?"

"He's in Tasher. He publishes a picture-newspaper and earns heaps of money. In short, he's enjoying life to the hilt in the wondrous land of his youthful dreams. And he sends me calls on a regular basis to complain about how tired he is of the 'Tasherian plebs,' who, he is convinced, 'just don't catch.' He had to go all the way to the edge of the World just to pick up his old saw in a completely new place. But the reason I recalled him just now was that the poor guy was always broke as a joke, even after I landed him a job at the *Royal Voice*, and was in the habit of bemoaning the nasty habits of those 'little round things' that kept running away from him. I have the same problem with time. It keeps running away from me, and I'm powerless to do anything about it."

I started feeling like a hopeless slob, and my spirits plummeted accordingly. I don't know how it happened.

"In any case, there is no reason to be so out of sorts," Shurf said. "There are two roads ahead of you. Either you change your life, or you allow it to continue as it is. I seem to have been mistaken in thinking my tree could bring you any peace and tranquility. It is more likely that *you* will teach *it* to fret over trifles."

"I hope not. It might decide to uproot itself and start running around town, trying to get its thoughts in order. And then we'd be chasing after it."

"I do not think it will come to that," Lonli-Lokli said. "I have a question for you, Max. All those books from your World that you so kindly acquire for me from time to time—I must admit, the selection is quite baffling. Tell me, they all represent the same genre, do they not?"

"Yes. I would even say . . ."

I broke off, unable to pin down a fleeting thought. I had to think about it. Over the past half a year I had pulled out several dozen books from the Chink between Worlds. All of them fit more or less my definition of science fiction. Still, I hadn't found a single familiar title among them; even the authors were unknown to me. Pretty strange, if you consider that back in the day I had been up to my ears in the genre, to put it mildly.

"What are you thinking about?" Shurf said.

"About those sinning books. There's something wrong there. You know, recently I've managed to be pretty adroit at fetching things I really wanted. If I needed cigarettes, I got cigarettes—even my preferred brand. Consistently, without any bloopers. Not a single silly umbrella."

"Yes, you are learning that art surprisingly quickly."

"Perhaps," I said, sighing. "But as soon as I reach for a book . . .

I've tried to fetch some specific titles for you. Some were things I think are funny. Others I was sure would completely turn around your notions of my homeland. But it doesn't work. I keep getting books written by unfamiliar authors. It's almost like I'm taking them off the same bookshelf in some inconceivable library."

"I see. Well, the reason I brought it up is that I wanted to ask you whether there is some principle that guides you when you choose these books for me and, if so, which one. But now I understand that you have no control over it. You know, I very much like your idea about an 'inconceivable library.' There is a legend about the library of King Mynin. Have you heard it?"

"No. What kind of library is it? Was it assembled by this very same legendary king?"

"No, he did not found it. He *found* it somewhere on the Dark Side. The legend goes that it contains books that were never written."

"Huh?"

"Well, consider this. Have you ever thought to yourself, I could write a good book, if only . . . ? You can insert any excuse there: 'if I had time,' 'if I knew how to write books,' 'if so-and-so had not already written something similar,' 'if I really wanted to,' and so on."

"If only you knew how often I've entertained that idea," I said, smiling. "But hey, I guess this means that you've thought about it, too, on more than one occasion. Imagine that!"

"Let us just assume that I can imagine in *theory* what it would be like," Shurf said. "In any case, the library that King Mynin found was a collection of books whose authors had never written a line. The legend goes that King Mynin realized this when he found his own book there—or, rather, the book he had wanted to write when he was a prince studying at the Royal Elevated School. He never wrote it, of course. Then he found books there written by his own childhood friends who had never become writers. He even discovered several familiar plots. He recognized them because they had been a topic of discussion among his friends many a time."

I was flabbergasted. "But if that's the case, the library must be almost infinite!"

"That is what the legend says. It describes the library as infinite and claims that it constantly changes location," said Shurf.

"Are you saying I managed to find a way to stick my hand in there?" I said in disbelief. "That's just too weird."

"But why? It is right up your alleyway. It 'jibes with your image.' There. Is that how you say it?"

"Right on," I said, laughing in delight.

"I certainly did not bring up King Mynin's library so you would lose your last shred of sanity over it. I simply thought it might be interesting to corroborate the rumors, if the opportunity presents itself."

"Well, if it presents itself . . ." I said uncertainly.

Maybe it was true that Lonli-Lokli hadn't brought it up so I would lose my last shred of sanity. Nevertheless, that's exactly what happened. I kept thinking about the legend of King Mynin's library all the way to the House by the Bridge. Surprisingly, I managed to avoid crashing into one of the numerous streetlamps. Must have been just my luck.

What oppressed me the most was the thought that one of the shelves might contain the pathetic fruits of the myriad stupidities that had once knocked around my good-for-nothing noggin. And to think that they all had my real name on them, and not some innocuous pseudonym. My only hope was that King Mynin—who had disappeared a couple thousand years before, never to be seen again, and with this extravagant flourish had put an end to his long and tempestuous reign—was the only visitor to this mysterious bookmobile.

"Have you read today's *Royal Voice*?" Sir Juffin Hully fired the question at me as I crossed the threshold.

"Certainly not. Don't you know how I read the papers? I have my own method. First, the paper has to lie around for a while on my desk—I'd say no fewer than half a dozen days. It's always good if it has been trampled on a bit. This increases the information density. It's also a good thing if they've tried to throw it away a few times, and I heroically rescued it from the hands of a trembling janitor. Only after every point in this ritual has been observed do I get down to reading it. By then the news has lost its relevance. It has become history, one might say. Thus, instead of trivial rubbish intended for mass consumption, I read a virtual chronicle of bygone days. What do you think of my method?"

"I approve," Juffin said. "I like everything you do without exception. Observing you is like watching cartoons. Nevertheless, you should acquaint yourself with the contents of today's issue without delay. Congratulations, Lord Fanghaxra. Your heroic people won the war against the whatchamacallits . . . you know . . . Oh, a hole in the heavens above me!"—Juffin jabbed at the paper—"the Manooks! Those fellows really went overboard with their gift for you, didn't they, Max?"

"For me? As far as I remember, His Majesty King Gurig VIII was the only one who stood to gain anything from this war. Let him be the one to rejoice," I said with a yawn. Then I grew indignant. "Wait a minute. Why do I have to get that kind of news from a newspaper? I'm their sovereign. Where is the official delegation of my loyal subjects? They're supposed to appear before my stern but benevolent gaze to boast of their achievements and congratulate me with the victory. No?"

"I think he's caught on," Juffin said, laughing. "Don't worry, Scourge of the Steppes. A delegation of your subjects is already on the way. The publisher of the *Royal Voice* has a good friend in the suite of the Dark Sack. And both of them, in contrast to your brave nomads, have a command of Silent Speech. This means that Sir Rogro receives information from the Barren Lands even before His Majesty Gurig does. Then again, that's his job, isn't it?"

"It is," I said uncertainly, "and he's good at it. So these brave lads are coming here any day now? And I'll have to sit through a formal reception on the occasion of victory and all that jazz? Bummer."

"Yes, I'm afraid you won't be able to get away with a casual half-hour chat this time around," Juffin said. "You'll get over it, though. It won't be today, nor even tomorrow, so you can forget about it for the time being."

He rolled up the newspaper, then placed it carefully on the floor and stomped on it a few times. Then he handed me the desecrated publication, straightened out the folds of his silver looxi in a stately manner, and headed for the door.

"Judging by the dreamy expression on your face, you are making your way to the Street of Old Coins," I said.

"What superhuman perspicacity," the boss said. "'Judging by the expression on your face,' he says. I go there every evening, and you know it. Good night, Max."

"Good it will be," I said in a conciliatory tone and sat down in the now unoccupied armchair. I unrolled the flattened newspaper. Juffin had really gone overboard with the stomping.

The night was suspiciously uneventful. All signs pointed to something nasty that was about to happen—something like, say, a dress rehearsal for the End of the World.

We had basically been twiddling our thumbs since spring. I couldn't remember when the Secret Investigative Force had been spared unpleasantness for such a long stretch. All my colleagues had managed to finagle dozen-day vacations for themselves, hightail it somewhere, and return here. Now they were already getting cabin fever again. All of them but Juffin and me. The boss continued acquainting himself with the cinematographic arts of my homeland, and I held down the fort in our office at the House by the Bridge. In fact, this suited me to a T. There's something soothing about reporting daily for work. At that time, for better or for worse, it replaced the hard ground that I could hardly remember ever having under my feet.

❋

The morning brought no alarming news, however. The same could be said of the following day and night. The lull continued for a few more days, until the arrival of my subjects.

Lady Xeilax's call reached me at sunrise. I had just managed to doze off in my armchair, but her Silent Speech jolted me awake. Until then, not one of the sisters had sent me a call, although Tekki had been boasting for a long time about how easy it had been to teach the girls this skill. They were already quite uninhibited around me these days. Life in the Capital of the Unified Kingdom and regular contact with the dubious characters from the Secret Investigative Force would probably put anyone at ease.

Excuse me for disturbing you at this hour, but a delegation of your subjects headed by my uncle—Barxa Bachoy—has just arrived at the Furry House, she said.

Fine, I said. *I'm glad they've come. Please help them settle in. I'll be there in the evening.*

Again, I'm terribly sorry to disturb you, but these people have come to tell you about their victory, Xeilax objected. *It has long been our custom for the commander who won the war to greet his king with the Victory Dance. And Barxa Bachoy has already begun his dance. You know, Sir Max, the dance has many complex moves, and uncle Barxa, unfortunately, is getting on in years. I doubt he'll last till evening.*

But can't he just retire to a room to rest and begin toe-tapping again toward evening?

The Victory Dance cannot be interrupted once it has begun. Uncle Barxa could fall under an eternal curse!

Got it. I'm on my way. Thanks for the heads-up, Xeilax. And you were so good to send me a call. I'm really very grateful.

I took a hefty swig of Elixir of Kaxar—without that wondrous concoction I would have perished long ago—and sent a call to Kofa. He was the only person I could disturb at that hour without terrible pangs of conscience.

Could you take over here? I said.

Has something finally happened? He was excited.

Yes, but not to us. Just to me. The time has come for me to fulfill my duties as sovereign.

Poor kid, Sir Kofa said with honest sympathy.

At that moment I felt just as sorry for myself.

I parked the amobiler a block away from the Furry House. It was impossible to get any nearer—a herd of menkals was ambling about, blocking the road. Their antlers were bedecked with a record number of trinkets. I assumed they must have been trophies of war.

Several dozen nomads awaited me in my house. Since the time I had taught them to tie their headscarves like pirate bandannas instead of babushkas, the Xenxa warriors had acquired some sense of style. Now all I had to do was teach them to stop dragging around their enormous sacks everywhere they went. Well, and their knee-length bellbottoms didn't quite fit the image of fierce nomad warriors who reigned supreme on the field of battle. The hems of their trousers could be let out to, say, calf length so they could get used to the change gradually.

My plans for government reform were not exactly what you would call ambitious.

At one time I had announced to my subjects that I would always confer with them sitting on the threshold of the reception hall. I said the sovereign occupied the space between his people and the heavens to separate and protect one from the other—I was on a roll when I came up with that one.

Now I had to follow protocol. I sat down cross-legged on the threshold. A bearded giant, the ferocious commander Barxa Bachoy, made a beeline for me with a mincing ballet step not at all in keeping with his demeanor. From time to time he executed a dexterous little leap that ended in a somersault. I was astonished at the ease with which such a hulk of a fellow could defy gravity. In fact, it was beyond belief.

When he was very near, he carried out such an intricate sequence of flips that I began wondering whether my eyes had deceived me. After this, however, Barxa Bachoy ceased challenging the laws of nature with his acrobatics and stood rooted to the spot in a reverential pose.

"We have been victorious, O Fanghaxra!" he said, raising his hairy, muscular arms to the sky. "We smeared the Manooks and captured Esra, their leader. Along with him we captured his brothers, sons, daughters, servants, and menkals."

"His menkals, too?" I said.

It was the first time I had encountered such an attitude toward enemy steeds.

"Yes, the menkals, too," my "general" insisted. "We banned the Manooks from pitching their tents by the holy springs of your lands, we banned them from raising their prayers to your heavens, we ordered them and their children to remove their hats, we received one thousand sacks of tribute from the Manooks, and we told these poor people to remain at home, awaiting your commands in fear."

"In fear—right-o," I said, trying to stay serious.

"You have brought us luck and victory, sire," said Barxa Bachoy.

"And you have brought *me* luck and victory. Good job." My speech-making skills were wanting, but I gave it my best shot.

"What should we do now, sire? Command us."

My general spoke with such fervor that I grew ashamed of my own frivolous indifference to the matter. Should I die, for Pete's sake, and be born again a new man?

"Now you must rest," I said. I couldn't think of anything else. "You have traveled a long road and are weary, so you must sleep a good sleep. I haven't had much sleep myself, as a matter of fact. I suggest we continue our discussion in the evening. In my palace you will find plenty of chambers and servants, and you will all be very comfortable. If you should need something, don't hesitate to ask. You are my honored guests."

Then I had a brilliant idea. Arriving at one of the local taverns with these handsome lads in tow—what a spectacle that would be!

"I hereby invite you to dine with me," I said.

"What an honor, sire," Barxa Bachoy said, breathless with awe. "Never before has a king of the Xenxa shared a meal with his subjects. Heretofore, even the royal family was only permitted to observe this marvelous event while seated on the threshold."

"That may be, but you deserve this honor," I said. "I'll fetch you at sundown and we'll set out together. For now, take your rest."

When I had finished my royal duties, I hightailed it home, to the little bedroom above the *Armstrong & Ella*. I hoped that any further call of royal duty could wait until noon, at least.

Strange as it may seem, wait it did. I didn't get a single call demanding that I dash off somewhere on the double. When I woke up, I felt wonderful, as though I had managed to come by a brand-new body.

"I've already read the morning papers. Looks like a whirlwind of social activity has commenced for you," said Tekki.

She had guessed that I was awake and was standing in the doorway of the bedroom. In the bright light of the noonday sun, her silhouette looked almost transparent. Still groggy from sleep, I almost doubted her reality and felt a jolt of alarm. If there was anything I feared, it was that I would one day discover she was only a clump of preternatural, silvery mist like her ghostly siblings.

But Tekki was real. In the flesh. I had been seeing things.

"I'm still hoping that my social life won't be too frenzied," I said, smiling, and embraced my beautiful mirage. "But tonight I plan to treat my subjects to dinner. I just haven't decided which little tavern is fated to endure our intrusion. Maybe you can suggest a place? Do you have any sworn enemies among your fellow tavern keepers, honey?"

"I wouldn't wish that upon my worst enemies. The main thing is not to bring them here."

"Magicians forbid. Did you think I'd drag my vassals to a two-bit dive where you can't even get a morsel of food? These fellows are ignorant barbarians, of course, but they're still decent family men and not some worthless boozers."

I could have continued my tirade for another hour or two, but I was forced to shut up. In a most pleasant way, I might add.

Still, half an hour later I was already sitting in Juffin's office. I was scheduled to pay a visit to His Majesty Gurig VIII to receive further instructions for the nomads, and the boss had agreed to accompany me. So sweet of him. Let's just say that even though I had managed to travel unaccompanied through the Corridor between Worlds and wander around the Dark Side, that still didn't mean I was ready to venture into Rulx Castle all alone. It would be easier to die, as our idiosyncratic Arvaroxian friends were wont to say.

"All right, let's get going," Juffin said, stuffing a pile of self-inscribing tablets into his desk drawer. "If I don't escape this scribbling duty soon, I'm going to mutiny and join some conspiracy or other."

"And that will be the beginning of the end of the Unified Kingdom," I said.

"Exactly."

When we went outside, Juffin headed toward my amobiler but then seemed to change his mind.

"The castle is a stone's throw away, and it would be a shame not to stroll along the Royal Bridge on a day like this. The weather is perfect."

"But why is the king expecting us in Rulx Castle?" I said. "The king is usually in his summer residence at this time of year."

"Our king is simply capricious, like anyone with a bit of life in him. And this summer the king is really living it up. He announced that the interiors of Anmokari Castle were in dire need of a makeover. Moreover, he has had sudden urges on a daily basis to admire the panorama of the Left Bank as seen from the window of King Mynin's study on the top floor of Rulx Castle. In short, Gurig has flatly refused to move to his summer residence, and I support him in this decision. If you consistently follow convention, you risk losing your wits."

"Yes, you do," I said, like one who knows.

Once inside the castle, we were surrounded by ancient walls steeped in the alarming scent of forgotten mysteries. Stern bearded sentries threw garments woven from a sort of metallic netting over our shoulders. These symbolized our helplessness before the might of this hallowed place. Then we were seated on palanquins—the means of transport that royal etiquette decreed for the express "comfort" of every visitor to the castle, but which defied common sense, as far as I was concerned. After this, we were borne away to the Minor Royal Reception Hall.

His Majesty Gurig VIII was off on his break, officially mandated by royal protocol. We had to wait for him almost ten minutes. The king was in such a splendid mood that I couldn't help but envy him. It seemed that he considered the modest victory of my touching subjects over their neighboring tribe to be a historic occasion of major importance.

"Everything is simply marvelous. We've been very lucky with these nomads of yours, Sir Max," said the king, indicating that we should sit down in some comfy armchairs by the window. "I must admit I didn't expect them to conquer the Manooks so easily. Apart from them, the Xenxa had never had any serious rivals. The Chancellory of Concerns of Worldly Affairs claims that your subjects and the Manooks are the only sizable tribes inhabiting the Barren Lands. Other peoples number only four or five dozen men, women, and children. It is hardly likely that they will unite against a common enemy, and if they do it will be too late. By that time the Barren Lands will already have become our territory. Here, take this," he said, holding out to me a pile of papers. "These are instructions for your general. He's done us proud, this Sir Barxa Bachoy. I have half a mind to keep such a commander for myself."

"He's already working for you as it is," I said.

"You are very right, Max. Now let them know that they must subjugate all the Barren Lands. They should be able to do so in a trice. That bunch of papers I gave you contains a detailed map of the Barren Lands. Indicated on it are arable land, water supplies, and populated (in a manner of speaking) areas. I found an erudite courtier familiar with the cartography of the Xenxa to make it, so your subjects won't have any problems. Sir Mulex swears up and down that this is so, in any case. Give your people one year to complete the task. My advisers assure me that even half a year would suffice, but why burden the people unnecessarily? One year will suit me just fine."

"Matters of state should not be rushed. Otherwise they don't carry enough weight," I piped up.

"You are absolutely right, Sir Max," said Gurig. "I always said you would make an excellent monarch. Well, shall we consider the matter decided? I hope you'll agree to drink something in my company, gentlemen?"

"Have no fear," Juffin said. "This, dare I say, *colleague* of yours can drink a sea of kamra at one sitting. Especially when he is a guest at someone's table."

"A very admirable quality," the king said earnestly.

"Pardon me, Your Majesty," I said. "One more matter, to conclude our discussion. My subjects are asking me what they should do with the conquered Manooks. It's all the same to me, but . . ."

"Me too. They may eat them, if that would be your pleasure."

"I don't think that would really be our pleasure," I said, distraught.

"If your people do not wish to eat their captives, let them bring their king here to the Capital," Gurig said. "He must swear eternal fealty to you, according to the customs of the steppe tribes. Then let the people live as they see fit. The main thing is that they don't interfere in our efforts to subjugate the Barren Lands. Now I propose that we change the topic. Sir Hully, you promised last spring to tell me the story of the Lonely Shadows, and I still haven't heard it. Perhaps now is the time?"

For the next hour I enjoyed life to the hilt. I guzzled the royal kamra and listened raptly to the story of my own adventures. The king gazed at Juffin like a child listening to a fairy tale at its grandmother's knee.

It was all so pleasant that I would have liked to stay in Rulx Castle until deep in the night. Alas, when two monarchs and one Venerable Head of the Secret Investigative Force find themselves in one place at the same time, their tête-à-tête is not destined to last long. The official consensus is that we are all terribly busy, though I for one would not consider that claim to be axiomatic.

Juffin, in any case, was evidence to the contrary. He looked askance at the entrance to the House by the Bridge, shrugged, and strode off in the direction of the *Glutton Bunba*. I followed obediently at the heels of the boss.

"What do you know about King Mynin's Library?" I said, sitting down at my favorite table between the bar and a little window looking out onto the courtyard. This cozy nook seemed tailor-made to fulfill each of my many desires without exception.

"Almost nothing at all, like the rest of humanity. Apart from King Mynin himself," the boss said. "What made you think of it all of a sudden?"

"Shurf told me the legend not long ago, but his account was very abridged. While we were being whisked around Rulx Castle on those absurd palanquins, I kept looking around and wondering which dark corner concealed the library's secret door."

"The door to Mynin's Library? What a thing to search for!" Juffin looked at me with genuine interest. "Why does that whet your curiosity?"

"I don't really know. It just intrigues me. I'd like to poke around in it for a while, just for fun."

"You'd better be careful what you wish for," said Juffin. "Otherwise you might get lost and end up in that sinning place for good. How would we even begin to look for you? That mythical library is just a tiny piece of another inscrutable Universe. They say that Mynin figured out how to turn the Dark Side inside out. We end up on the Dark Side when we grope around the bottom of the ocean lapping at the boundaries of the visible world. Beyond the boundaries of the Dark Side, there is something else even deeper, even more enigmatic. No one but Mynin has ever been there, with the possible exception of a few ancient sorcerers. But they didn't bother to take any travel notes. No need to bore a hole in me with your eyes, Max. I've never been there, either. Honest."

"How does anyone even know about this 'inside out' place, then?"

"From ancient legends that are virtually unfathomable. And from Mynin himself, naturally. And Mynin, unlike the ancient legends, you can trust. He was reputed to be the most honest person in the World. From childhood on, he was aware of the power of his own words and managed to shun the habit of lying. When every fancy that strikes you comes true and takes on a life of its own, life can become unbearable. Bear that in mind for the future, by the way."

"Done," I said, sighing. "The Dark Side inside out, you say? Wow."

"Ah, your eyes are glittering, I see," Juffin said, laughing. "I don't recognize you, Sir Max. When you have to learn a trifling little trick, you announce to the World that I terrorize you by forcing you to learn some two-bit wonder. But as soon as the talk turns to things that strike terror even into me, you start drooling in anticipation. Maybe you're just bored?"

"Maybe," I said. "But more likely I just don't want to live in the *Middle of the Woods*."

"What's that?"

"Don't you remember? Melifaro once talked your ear off about the strange characters who put us up for the night when we traveled to Landaland. They're people who think that their house and their forest are the whole World because that's what their late parents told them."

"Ah, yes, now I remember." Juffin looked at me searchingly, then smiled a pensive, sad smile. "Don't fret, Sir Max. The fate of the inhabitants of the *Middle of the Woods* wouldn't befall you even if you begged for it."

"I believe you," I said. "And it's for the best, though you'll no doubt have to hear my wails of terror."

"That I can deal with. I've heard plenty in my time."

After dinner we parted ways. The boss left for the House by the Bridge, and I decided to take a stroll through town. There was nothing else to do anyway. I had agreed to meet up with the nomads at sunset, which was still two hours away. That didn't leave me enough time to go home, but it was too long for me to continue warming the stool with my buns at the *Bunba*.

I rambled through the Old City. A light breeze from the Xuron tumbled about like a puppy, nipping me now from the left, now from the right, and even tugging amiably at my clothes. The occasional passerby preferred to keep a good distance away from me—the Mantle of Death neutralized all my charm.

At the intersection of the Street of Gloomy Clouds and the Street of Lanterns, I paused, trying to decide which one to take. And just then, one of my hearts knocked at my ribcage—a single but insistent thud. I shuddered, turned around, and discovered that a shady-looking character was following just a few steps behind me. I couldn't quite make out the face, and I had no time to gauge his intentions. My left hand started jerking, and my fingers snapped, releasing a Lethal Sphere.

A moment later I was staring in perplexity at a body lying immobile on the ground. This time my Lethal Sphere had not turned the poor fellow into my trusty slave. In the blink of an eye, the tiny ball of green light had fulfilled its function: killing a stranger instantaneously and, judging by the peaceful expression on his face, completely painlessly.

I sat down on my haunches next to the body of my victim. Only then did I notice that the stranger was wearing round eyeglasses with dark-violet, nearly opaque lenses. Until then I had never seen glasses like this on any of the Echo inhabitants.

Gosh, was he blind or something? I thought, horrified. Congratulations on the greatest victory in your life, Sir Max. It seems you've finally snuffed out a completely innocent person. And a blind one, to boot.

Then I sent an incoherent call to Juffin and reported my crime.

Did you say your hand trembled of its own accord? he responded. *Interesting. Please refrain from any pangs of conscience at this stage in the game. You'll have plenty of time to water all the pavements of Echo with your tears of remorse. Better pick up the corpse and bring it to the House by the Bridge. I'm dying to have a look at it.*

My silent conversation with the boss had the effect of a tranquilizer strong enough to knock out a horse. My surging emotions seemed to pack themselves away in mounds of fluffy cotton, then subside altogether. Life suddenly got a whole lot better.

I ran my left hand along the dead body. It hid itself obediently in my fist. Now I just had to get it to the House by the Bridge without incident. I rushed through the city as though there were a warrant out for my arrest and my only refuge was the office of Sir Juffin Hully in the Ministry of Perfect Public Order.

I had just shot like a bullet into that very office, heaving a sigh of relief as though the hounds really were after me, when I noticed that Juffin had a visitor. He was an emaciated, bent figure. His face was splotchy with age, and he had the streaming red eyes of a veteran tippler. His long, greasy, tangled locks of hair hung all over our long-suffering desk. He was dressed in rags so old, they looked like they were pushing eternity. The occasional beggars that you came across now and then in the port were dapper men-about-town compared to this guy.

"You run almost as fast as you drive," Juffin said, smiling. "Well, you'll just have to wait a bit. It's your own fault."

I nodded and went out to the Hall of Common Labor. I was in an abysmal funk. I had plenty of grounds for it. Those grounds were located right between the thumb and the index finger of my left hand.

"Whence the expression of bitterness on thy noble countenance?" Melifaro said, suddenly appearing out of nowhere. "Is being a cuckold really so bad? You should have thought about that sooner. Now it's too late."

"What? Oh, that. To each his own, but the naked sure need a bath."

Melifaro blinked, unable to follow the sudden twist in the narrative.

"What, you mean it really is 'too late' already?" I said, alarmed. "You managed to seduce the poor innocent?"

"That's none of your business," Melifaro said defensively. Then he added in a softer tone, "And the question is, who seduced whom?"

He seemed eager to continue the conversation, but the door to Juffin's office was flung open just then and the aforementioned bedraggled gentleman emerged. He walked on bent legs, but his step was so light, he seemed to weigh nothing at all.

Melifaro watched the spectacle in perplexity. He seemed even more surprised by it than I was. Paying no attention to us, the pathetic creature tripped his way over to the exit and disappeared.

"An elf," Melifaro said finally. "I wonder what he's doing in Echo."

"An *elf*?" I thought I had misheard.

"Of course, wasn't it obvious? Ordinary people can't descend to such a benighted state and still remain alive."

"Surprised, boys?" Juffin said merrily. "I must admit, my jaw dropped, too, when he appeared on my doorstep. And if you knew what sort of present he brought me . . ."

"But was he a real elf?" I said, my voice dropping a register.

"Of course. Ah, you don't know about elves."

"I thought I knew until a moment ago. What happened to him? He looks like he's been on a drinking binge for the past hundred years."

"Oh, come now. When have you ever seen such a youthful elf? They've usually been drinking since childhood, anyway. This specimen has been at the bottle without stopping for the past millennium, at the very least."

"What was he doing in the Capital?" Melifaro said.

"All in due time. First, I want to make a short trip to the morgue for the benefit of our Nocturnal Representative here. In a few minutes we'll return, and I'll explain everything," Juffin said. "Come on, Max. Let's see what you've done."

"Oh, I see you've been killing poor defenseless people again," Melifaro said with a snort.

I smiled a crooked smile and went out into the hallway. For the first time since we had met, his idiotic joke had really hit home. And with what devastating effect.

❦

"Okay, Max. Let's see your trophy," Juffin said, leading the way into the tiny, dark morgue.

His good mood was indestructible. It even seemed to grow more jubilant by the second, if that were at all possible.

I shook my hand, and the body of the unfortunate blind man tumbled to the floor. Juffin crouched down beside the dead man and removed his dark glasses. Then he examined him carefully, hemmed with satisfaction, and looked up at me as if I were the newest addition to the city zoo.

"What was that you said about your hand, Max? That it trembled of its own accord?"

"Yes," I said with a sinking feeling.

"And now you're wracked with guilt," Juffin said with feigned sympathy. "Fine. Now I'll relieve you of it. Watch."

He carefully opened the convulsively cramped fingers of the corpse and removed a long, lethal-looking needle from its fist. Juffin turned around to face me triumphantly and waved the object under my nose. The needle emitted a faint scent of fine perfume.

"I understand that as a weapon it looks rather flimsy, but believe me, it is fatal in a practiced hand. This little knickknack was dipped in the poison known as Choice. Can you smell it? It's unmistakable. At one time the court doctors of the kings of the Old Dynasty distilled this masterpiece from thousands of ingredients, specifically tailored to the needs of their clients. Remnants of this historical luxury keep turning up in the most unexpected places, to my deep regret. A needle dipped in Choice must be thrust into the victim precisely at the base of the neck. This is mandatory—otherwise the poison rarely leads to a fatal outcome unless the victim is of particularly weak constitution. But if it hits the mark, the victim doesn't just expire; the body disappears completely, along with the clothes and boots, which is truly uncanny."

"Holy smokes," I muttered. "So you mean I was about to disappear, too? Delightful."

"That's about the long and short of it," said Juffin. "Your wise heart sensed misfortune in the offing, and your hand took it upon itself to deal with it while you were dithering and trying to grasp what was going on. Amazing. If I were still the Kettarian Hunter, I'd try to recruit you as my apprentice."

"You've already managed to waste Magicians know how much time teaching me," I said.

"Naturally. But I'm no longer the Kettarian Hunter. I'm just Sir Venerable Head these days. I'm far less demanding now."

"I wonder who it was that felt the urge to rid this wonderful World of my no less wonderful body?" I said.

"To answer that we have to do some work. I, for one, have no idea who he is. Never laid eyes on him before."

"But why would such an important task have been entrusted to a blind man?" I said.

"What makes you think he was blind?" said Juffin. "His eyes look like they're in the right place to me."

"And the eyeglasses? Blind people wear glasses like that in my homeland."

"Well, I wouldn't know who wears them there. But tell me this. How can someone with both his eyes intact be blind? That's why we have wisemen, after all. As for the eyeglasses, they are needed so as not to miss the mark. Try them on, you'll see what I mean."

I put the glasses on and understood at once what they were for. I could hardly make out the figure of my boss in front of me, but I could see several bright dots on his body that formed an asymmetrical geometric shape.

"The topmost dot is the one you need to hit if you're using Choice poison," said Juffin. "Come on now, take off that piece of antique junk. Simple, isn't it? They must have belonged to some court assassin at one time. The ancient kings held such experts in very high regard."

"So what do we do now?" I said anxiously.

"While you're amusing yourself with your subjects, I'll try to revive this lovely specimen. And when you come back, we'll have a little confidential talk with him. That should be easy. Since we found out that you're able to get resurrected dead men to talk, investigation has become a simple and nauseatingly boring routine. You won't be disappointed if I deprive you of the opportunity to contemplate this dead body?"

"Not really. Of course, I'll run off to sob in the bathroom, but not for more than half an hour. I promise."

"That's reassuring. Let's go. Melifaro's waiting for us. That is, if he hasn't died of curiosity."

"I'm dying of curiosity, too, by the way," I said, closing the door of the morgue behind me. "That hideous elf of yours, a hole in the heavens above his hoary head! Tell me, Juffin, are all elves really that unsightly?"

"Most of them are even uglier. Why does that surprise you?"

"I've read heaps of books about elves. Not here, of course, but at home. For the most part they were just fairy tales, but they were based on ancient legends. The stories they tell about them vary a great deal, but they all seem to agree on one thing: elves are wonderful, immortal, magical beings. And now along comes this bedraggled old wino."

"Wonderful, immortal, magical beings—precisely," Juffin said, nodding. "This is what they were at one time. But they were destroyed by their love of pleasure. Everything was fine until they transgressed an ancient prohibition and tasted wine. They liked it so much that since that time their lives are completely given over to satisfying this craving. Remember that elves are still immortal, so they can't drink themselves into the grave. The poor things are doomed to live on the edge of it, and this, as you yourself noticed, is a joyless spectacle."

"Why have I never seen them before now?"

"Because they live in the enchanted Shimured Forest, to the west of Uguland. Echoers don't exactly welcome them with open arms, and other towns aren't very accommodating, either. The fellow you saw in my office came to me on an important matter. He worked quite a few wonders to avoid falling into the welcoming hands of the vigilant police force. It's a miracle the poor guy still knows how."

We caught up with Melifaro. "Well, Sir Melifaro, are you still dying of curiosity?" Juffin said.

"Consider me dead. All is lost, you might say. My dear mama always predicted that no good would come of my serving in the Secret Investigative Force. Tell her she was right."

"I will," Juffin said. "Let's go to the office, boys. You won't believe what I'm about to show you."

Melifaro and I guffawed since we had a ready-made retort to that question: "What, your butt?" The effects were all the more exhilarating when the retort remained unexpressed.

Juffin paid no attention to us, however. He had no time for such nonsense. He had to put all his effort into undoing his own spell and opening the bookcase. This flimsy excuse for office furniture from a bygone era preserved the secrets of the Secret Investigative Force much more reliably than a fireproof safe. I wouldn't envy the fate of the madman who tried to break into it without permission. I suspected that even Juffin was taking a big risk every time he tried to open it. And he was the one who had cast the spell in the first place.

This time it didn't take him very long to open the bookcase. He only resorted to a couple of strong expletives. Normally, he was much less restrained at such moments.

"Behold," Juffin said triumphantly, taking from the bookcase a large, messy bundle and carefully unwrapping the tattered cloth.

We stared in perplexity at a large piece of greenish metal that prompted one to wonder whether, thousands of years ago, some naive human being could seriously have considered this lump of scrap iron to be a weapon.

"What is it?" Melifaro said, breaking the silence.

"I'll bet it's the Sword of King Arthur," I said grinning.

"Who's King Arthur? We've never had a king by that name," Melifaro said. "Or did we?"

"Ahem. Your friend got carried away again, that's all," Juffin said.

"Nevertheless, he was almost right—in that it actually is a sword. Only it belonged not to some mystery king named Arthur but to our own King Mynin."

"That's the actual Sword of King Mynin?" Melifaro stared reverently, standing on tiptoe to see it better. Then he sighed. "It certainly looks like it's seen better days."

"Yes, it's a sorry sight now," Juffin said. "But fret not. I'll perform some hocus-pocus on it, and tomorrow King Mynin's Sword will be a sight for sore eyes. I'll restore it to its former gleaming splendor. It's a wonder that it still exists. That besotted elf buried this legendary weapon at the roots of a tree fifteen hundred years ago when he realized that he wouldn't be able to cut his hair with it. Early this spring he finally dug it up again. He was in the throes of a terrible hangover and was looking for a stash he thought he had somewhere—hair of the dog, you know. Fortunately, he hit upon the idea of selling this relic to a dealer in the Capital. Like all the others, this elf had long ago forgotten his own name, but I suspect it might have been Toklian the Bright. Even in poor health he was still of sound mind. Can you imagine, he even tried to haggle with me?"

"The Bright Master of Shimured, legendary Elf King, childhood friend and teacher of King Mynin? Sinning Magicians, better he had died in battle by the Bay of Gokki," Melifaro mused.

"That would have been preferable, of course, but no one asked us," Juffin said drily.

"Wait a minute. There's one thing I still don't get. How did he get the Sword of Mynin in the first place? And did he really show up here just to sell it?"

"Yes," Juffin said. "That's exactly why he came. He had no thought of *giving* it away. Luckily, the poor fellow recalls very well those times when one crown was considered to be a fortune. Those are the only times he does recall since he played no active part in what happened subsequently. So Mynin's Sword only cost me eleven crowns. And boy, did we haggle! The fellow demanded a dozen, and

I was so intent on beating down the price that I began to believe myself that it was a substantial amount. I insisted on ten. We finally agreed on eleven. Buying King Mynin's Sword for eleven crowns, cheaper than any thrift store junk from the late Code Epoch—unbelievable! I don't feel a bit of remorse, either. The Shimured Elves only want money to buy 'real Capital city hooch'—to use the expression of our guest. He's grown tired of just drinking elfin moonshine, especially over the past thousand years. Imagine how many bottles of Jubatic Juice you could buy with eleven crowns. Sir Dondi Melixis can sleep peacefully, though. I won't demand that the Treasury compensate me for expenses. It will be enough for me to have Mynin's Sword in my possession."

"Can I play with it?" I said.

"Maybe," said Juffin. Unlike me, he was completely serious. "As for your previous question, when it comes to our legendary king, you can never be sure what his motives were. I'm almost certain, however, that he gave his sword to the elves himself. Why not? In those days the Shimured Elves were the 'magical beings' you read about in all your books. It would never have occurred to anyone that they would one day violate the only ban they were under."

"It's good I'm not an elf," Melifaro said somberly. "Still, I think I'll pass up that drink tonight. Tomorrow I may reconsider."

"My, my, what impressionable employees I have!"

"Oh, shucks! I've got to be off," I said. "It's almost sunset. If I don't take my subjects out to dinner, they'll lose faith in the goodness of humanity and take to drink, too."

"That's all we need, a bunch of nomadic tipplers," Juffin said, laughing. "Go on, then. But don't forget to come back. If you return before midnight, I'll be happy."

"I'll try," I promised. "I'm going to explain to my military commander that exemplary subjects must obey their monarch, eat well, and hit the sack early. I lack the brainpower to come up with anything more original."

"Do your wives also have to take part in this dubious outing?" said Melifaro. "Remember, Lady Kenlex has made other plans for the evening."

"It makes no difference to me what kinds of plans she has," I growled. I made a threatening face, but then I took pity on the lovesick fellow. "All right, all right. I'll try to get along without the girls."

Actually, the sisters made the decision all on their own. I ran into them just as they were leaving the Furry House. Three chic young ladies, dressed to the nines—who would have thought that not even a year had gone by since the frightened girls had exchanged their quilted jackets and short trousers for elegant looxis.

"Sinning magicians, you look absolutely gorgeous!" I said without a trace of sarcasm. "I've never seen anything like it."

"Thank you," the triplets said in unison.

"That wasn't a compliment. I was just calling a spade a spade." I beamed at them. "Are you going out on the town? Good for you. Tired of being queens?"

"Not at all," Xeilax said. "We were happy to see our people and to hear all the news from home. So much has happened since we left! But they're expecting you now, and we decided that we could step out for a bit. We may, may we not?" she said timidly.

"Of course you may. You may do whatever you wish. I've told you that a thousand times."

They smiled and said goodbye, then hurried off into the orange mist cast by the streetlamps. I gazed after them in approval. The girls were quickly getting used to their newfound freedom. Now they were already finding their way around the Capital of the Unified Kingdom, making friends, and even losing their hearts. This was just as it should be.

Droopy interrupted my musings. He ran up wagging his shaggy ears, stood on his hind legs, and placed his front paws squarely on my shoulders, but I managed to stay on my feet. The huge mobile mound of snow-white fur was already half a head taller than me, and it didn't look like he was planning on abandoning his growth spurt just yet. I groaned and begged the dog to stop his shenanigans. Droopy licked my nose in ecstasy and obediently resumed his four-legged perspective on the world.

I grabbed my pet by his ruff, and we entered the house.

The delegation of nomads had already gathered there. It was so quiet in the hall that not only did it seem they weren't talking, they weren't even breathing.

"Good evening!" I almost shouted. "Let's go eat."

The tavern that was fated to suffer our intrusion was the *Sated Skeleton*, for the simple reason that it was close by. From my interactions with the sister trio, I had come to understand that my people had a sweet tooth of inconceivable proportions, so I knew just what to order: a triple dessert course, with ten dozen pastries, for starters.

I had exaggerated when I described for Tekki the horrors of the impending social event. It was actually very pleasant, quite homey and cozy: the nomads sat around the large table, listening attentively to my confused words about the battles they would be waging and waxing enthusiastic about the sweets they were being treated to. Their stern faces, spotted with whipped cream, expressed utter bliss.

The other customers looked on in curiosity and wonder. Of course, my Mantle of Death put something of a damper on the prospects for a spontaneous international exchange, but that was probably all for the best.

After this gastronomical orgy, I led my subjects in disorderly formation back to the Furry House. I was brimming with paternal pride. For that reason, in addition to the envelope with the king's directives, I gave Barxa Bachoy a hundred crowns and ordered him to spend the money solely on acquiring sweets for my heroic people. That was approximately enough to get a dozen cartloads of the best pastries. The only remaining problem was how to deliver the valuable cargo to the steppes of their homeland.

"You still didn't tell us what to do with Esra, sire," Barxa Bachoy reminded me.

"Ah, yes, your prisoner, the Lord of the Manooks," I said. "You must bring him to Echo so that he can swear allegiance to me on behalf of his people. Can they be trusted to keep their word?"

"Some of them can," Barxa Bachoy said. "I will make sure that Fairiba accompanies him here. His wisdom is great enough to distinguish a genuine oath from empty promises."

"Great. Then we can let him go. I don't really feel like becoming Lord of the Manooks, as well.

"Of course you couldn't wish such a thing!" My commander seemed horror-struck. "Lord Fanghaxra cannot allow himself to sink so low as to rule over some paltry mouse-eaters."

"It's a good thing that our views on this matter coincide. But why do you call the Manooks 'mouse-eaters'? Do they really eat rodents?"

"Yes, it happens that nowadays they do eat mice. In fact, they shun no food of any sort. But our elders still remember the time when mice ate the Manooks," Barxa Bachoy said with contempt. "Those cowardly lumps of dung fed their own newborn babies to the Mouse Lord, a dozen per year, to appease that filthy spawn of darkness. They say he worked some loathsome wonders in exchange. But do you really wish me to talk of such matters, sire?"

"Nah, not really," I said. "I must leave you now. It's time for me to report to duty."

I couldn't keep back a smile, in view of the incongruity of the situation—the king admitting to his subjects that he's beholden to his own boss.

"When should we go back home, sire?" Barxa Bachoy said, with dry but admirable pragmatism.

"As soon as you've stocked up on souvenirs."

"Everything will be done as you request, sire. Tomorrow morning we will do our shopping, and we will leave just after midday. There is one more thing I should tell you. We have brought you offerings. It is that portion of the plunder of war that we consider worthy of you. Will you accept it from us?"

"I hope it isn't a new lot of girls wishing to be my wives," I said warily.

"No. They are not living creatures at all, sire. Only things. We will show them to you, if you wish."

"I want very much to see my gifts, but I don't have the time. Let's do this: I'll go to work, and you give the presents to Lady Xeilax. That way I'll be accepting them, only indirectly. And tomorrow I'll take a look at them. You won't feel hurt or insulted by that, will you?"

"How could we feel hurt or insulted by you, O Fanghaxra?" Barxa Bachoy exclaimed. "We're happy that you've agreed to accept our offerings. We couldn't hope for more."

After bestowing my paternal blessings on my trusty vassals, I left for the House by the Bridge.

"You'll have to wait a bit, Max." Juffin said, poking his head out of the morgue. "You did such a thorough job killing this poor soul that there was nothing I could do to revive him at first. Sit down in the office. I'll call for you shortly."

To be honest, I was grateful. If there was anything I was dreaming of at that moment, it was a cigarette. I wanted to smoke in peace. I went into the office and dropped into the armchair, propped up my feet on the desk, and stared out the window. I sat like that for a long time, not moving. My thoughts abandoned me one by one, like rats leaving a sinking ship.

Juffin jolted me back to reality.

You may proceed with the interrogation.

I stared in surprise at the crumpled cigarette I hadn't gotten around to lighting up, then made a dash for the morgue.

The body of the failed assassin lay prostrate in the far corner. Juffin was sitting in the doorway.

"Come on, Max. This creep, Magicians be praised, will never walk again. Even I can't help him there. But he's quite capable of whispering a few words to us."

"Okay," I said, sitting down beside him. "Let me have a cigarette and collect my thoughts."

"Go ahead, collect away," the boss said.

By the time I had smoked half my cigarette, I knew I was ready. I really did have a few questions for this lately revived dead man. I could only hope that my Lethal Spheres would obey my conscious desires as they had heretofore obeyed my unconscious impulses. I raised my left hand and snapped my fingers. I had grown increasingly sensitive to the aesthetic impression made by this laconic magical gesture. Juffin looked on, bemused by my vanity, but said nothing.

"I am with you, Master," the dead man mumbled faintly after the tiny sphere of green light that leaped from my fingers had melted and swathed his body in an almost invisible mist.

I instinctively took a step back when I noticed the corpse begin to stir. The dead man clearly wanted to crawl closer to me, but praise be the Magicians, he couldn't even manage to budge an inch.

"Why are you so jittery?" Juffin said, laughing. "I told you he couldn't move. And what if he could? You're being absurd."

"So I am."

"Come on, don't dawdle. I don't want to stay here till the Last Day of the Year," the boss said, urging me on.

"Tell me who commanded you to kill me," I said, turning to the dead man.

"No one commanded me. It was my own decision," he said.

His reply irked me no end. I had thought the killer would tell us the name of his employer, and that would be the end of it. Juffin was surprised, too—if I interpreted the angle of his slightly raised eyebrow correctly.

"Fine. You it was, then. But why?" I said, perplexed.

"Because I thought you were a bad man," the dead man said.

"Thank you for the elucidation," Juffin said with a laugh. "Max, I think your interrogation has reached an impasse. Here's a piece of advice: ask him who he is and where he got hold of the Choice. Maybe then we'll get somewhere."

"Thank you," I said, smiling. "By the way, right up until this happened I was absolutely certain of the power of my charms."

"Please stay focused. We have a whole life ahead of us that we can devote to the subject of 'Sir Max: Is He Good, or Is He Evil?' Now it's time to deal with this gentleman. Unlike us, he's in a big hurry. They're eagerly awaiting him in the next world."

"Certainly," I said with a sigh. I faced our interlocutor again. "Tell us your name."

"Donboni Goulvax."

I gave Juffin an inquiring look.

"Never heard of him. Go on."

I turned to the dead man again.

"Where did you get the poison and the spectacles?"

"I have always had them. My grandfather was the Secret Executioner at the court of His Majesty Gurig I. They belonged to him."

I looked helplessly at Juffin. "I'm not getting anywhere. Maybe I should just command him to answer your questions."

"My thoughts exactly. Why didn't you do that in the first place?" The boss chuckled and put his finger on the tip of my nose, pressing it like a doorbell. "Some investigator you are, your majesty."

"I'm just not having any luck with this one," I said, rubbing my nose. "Any ordinary criminal would have spilled the beans long ago. This one is just a rare bird."

"I couldn't agree more," Juffin said in a conciliatory manner.

"You must answer all the Venerable Head's questions," I said, turning to my "rare bird."

"Yes, Master," the corpse said.

"Why did you think Sir Max was a bad man?" Juffin said.

"Because that is what my mistress told me."

"Now we're getting somewhere. Who is your mistress?"

"Lady Atissa Blimm."

"Ah, it all makes sense to me now, more or less," Juffin said. "What about you, Max?"

"Is this one of Lady Melamori's relatives?"

"You might say that. Actually, it's her mother."

"Oh, brother," I said, sighing. "You said I would have to hide from Sir Korva Blimm."

"I was slightly off the mark. It happens," said Juffin and turned to the dead man again. "Let's take it from the top. What exactly did your mistress tell you about Sir Max?"

"She told me nothing at all."

"Fine. What did she say about him in your presence, then?"

"Many times she told Sir Korva that it was Sir Max's fault that Lady Melamori fled to Arvarox. I heard all their conversations. It has been my duty to stay by Lady Atissa's side at all times, since—"

"Since she began to lose her mind," Juffin said, nodding impatiently. "So you were in effect her bodyguard. Did Lady Atissa ask you to kill Sir Max?"

"No. She never asked me. Sometimes she commanded me to do things, but her commands concerned only household affairs."

"What made you try, then?"

"From her words I understood that she would be happy if Sir Max were to die. My lady said many times that her daughter had run off to Arvarox to avoid having to see this terrible person. She was sure that Lady Melamori would return if—"

"I see," Juffin said, interrupting him. "But what made you decide to do her that kind of favor? You should know how little credence the words of a madwoman deserve since you make a living protecting these unfortunate people."

"I was very happy to do something to please Lady Atissa," the dead man said. "Even now I have no regrets about it, though I realize death is not something we should strive for. At this moment, at least, I can say that I do not like being dead."

"Fine," Juffin said with a short nod. "Tell me something else. Did Lady Atissa know your family history? Did you ever tell her about your ancestor, the court executioner?"

"Lady Atissa never talked to me about matters like my family. She never talked to me at all. She just gave orders."

"Indeed," Juffin said, "she had other ways of finding out about a person they had hired to watch over her. And to realize that she is in the presence of someone who is madly in love with her is well within the power of any woman. Insane or not, Lady Atissa has always been very astute. And a brilliant schemer. You can release our prisoner, Max. I've found out everything I needed to know."

"Release him?" I said, surprised. Then I understood and turned to the dead man. "I release you from the necessity of staying alive."

I was shocked at my own words. I'm usually not so eloquent. Juffin wasted no time in approaching the dead man to make sure he had ended his unnatural posthumous existence.

"Good. Let's get out of here, Max," he said with a yawn.

We went up to the office without talking. The boss stared at the empty desk in annoyance.

"I sent a call to the *Glutton* fifteen minutes ago," he grumbled. "Where's the food?"

Just then the door creaked. A young assistant to Madam Zizinda hoisted a huge tray onto the desk. Juffin's gaze grew warmer. He looked at me with sympathy.

"Are you upset, Max?"

"Fair to middling. It's just unfortunate that Melamori is connected with this is any way. It's as if some bloody joker had befouled the hem of her looxi, and she hasn't noticed it yet."

"Don't exaggerate. Lady Melamori, Magicians be praised, is slumbering peacefully right now in a stateroom of *The Surf Thorn*, floating somewhere between the water and the sky, halfway to that sinning Arvarox. So the hem of her looxi is fine. Some people get along with their parents, some don't. That's just how it is. The one I really feel sorry for is Sir Korva Blimm. In his time he fought tooth and nail to keep his wife out of the Refuge for the Mad. Even for someone as well connected as he is, it was almost impossible, since her madness was not only incurable, but she was also a danger to those around her. It can be contagious, as the fate of her bodyguard proves. He flipped his lid, too. But Korva is as stubborn as our Melamori. That's why Lady Atissa was able to stay at home. Now we're going to have to intervene. Better late than never."

"Looks like you didn't forget my lecture on 'flipping one's lid,'" I said, smiling.

"How could I forget? I consider the expression to be your personal contribution to the wiseman's arts," Juffin said. "And why, might I ask, is your mouth still empty, while your plate is full of food? Perhaps you need a drink? If so, be my guest. Praise be the Magicians, you're not an elf."

"I'm so far from being an elf that I never feel like getting sloshed. Not even now."

"That's terrible," Juffin said, drawing the cork from a small ceramic bottle. "I've never in all my days seen such a positive young man. It's no surprise that the humble inhabitants of Echo are trying to take your life. Another's person perfection always rankles. I definitely need a drink, though, considering the kind of conversation I'll have to have with Korva."

He sniffed the contents of the bottle, nodded in approval, poured it into a glass, and took a big gulp.

"Maybe we should just leave everything as it is?" I said.

"Nothing really happened. A lovelorn orderly tried to make a rather nonstandard present to his patient, who was not in her right mind. So what? I'm still alive, and the would-be killer is in the morgue. I don't see it as a problem."

"You have rather strange ideas about what qualifies as a problem," Juffin said. "You don't have to extend your affection for Melamori to her parents, Max. Unlike me, you don't even know these people. Lady Atissa and her daughter are not one and the same person, believe me."

"I understand that very well. It's just that I feel guilty toward the Blimms. Not guilty enough to deserve being stalked by a killer, but still. I put a lot of effort into supporting Melamori's brave undertaking, the bravest in her life so far. But even that's not the point. Sometimes I feel that the reason she left *was* because of me. Not because she couldn't stand seeing me, of course. No, I think that she believed it was a way to finally catch up with me, and even outdo me."

"Outdo you?"

"Yes. You know, she desperately wanted to learn to drive the amobiler faster than I do. Once we even joked that she would catch up with me one day. But it wasn't really about the amobiler, you understand. Melamori wants to surpass me on a grand scale. Or at least catch up. It's not even really about me—but I did become a pretty important event in her life. I'm like a novelty that she once feared. But Melamori isn't the type to forgive herself for such lapses. Now she thinks there's only one way out—she thinks she has to be like me. A mysterious creature up to my ears in miracles. It's possible she went to Arvarox only because she knows I decided to leave my World one day and set out for Magicians-know-where. For ordinary Capital-city dwellers, Arvarox is almost the same as another World. Am I right?"

"Most likely."

I shuddered under the weight of his gaze. Even a statistically average heavy gaze from Juffin weighs a ton, but this one set a new record.

"All right," he said abruptly. "We'll visit them together, and then we'll see. Let's go, Max. Korva usually goes to bed late, but he doesn't stay up till the crack of dawn."

The enormous Blimm mansion in the heart of the Left Bank looked more like an ancient castle. Which, in fact, it was. It had been rebuilt and renovated, and boasted a patchwork of annexes and extensions, but it was steeped in the same ineffable, disturbing smell of ancient mysteries and secrets that had tickled my nostrils that morning in Rulx Castle.

"Like it?" Juffin said. "Lady Atissa's ancestors were distant relatives of the Ancient Royal dynasty. This little house is actually a few centuries older than Rulx. At one time it lay outside the city bounds. In those days every distinguished person had to have his own castle, especially if he wanted to enjoy nature at his leisure."

Sir Korva Blimm, Lady Melamori's father, about whose difficult nature she had complained more than once, met us at the door. He greeted us with calm reserve. He had the same bright-blue eyes as his amicable brother Kima, keeper of the wine cellars of the Order of the Seven-Leaf Clover, but their similarity ended there. Sir Korva Blimm wasn't like any of my acquaintances, including his daughter. His grave and haughty countenance might be a welcome addition to any grandiose, formal undertaking—from a modest crusade to the conquest of the Universe.

This handsome fellow must have made quite a contribution to the Battle for the Code, I thought to myself.

"Did something happened to Melamori?" he said first thing.

"Why should something have happened to her?" Juffin said. "As far as I know, she's just fine. Max, you've spoken to her recently, haven't you?"

"The last time I heard from her was the day before yesterday," I said, nodding. "She said she was taking part in a hunt for some enormous fish. If her words are anything to go by, the fish was several times larger than the House by the Bridge."

"I'm glad to hear that," Sir Korva Blimm said drily. "I doubt that the size of the fish corresponds to the description, though. In all likelihood my daughter won a wrestling match with some overfed herring."

Suddenly I started thinking that Melamori and I were comrades in sorrow. My own father also liked to downplay my achievements in public. I think if I were to go on safari and drag home a lion I had killed, he would no doubt refer to my trophy as a dead alley cat.

Of course, unlike Melamori, I had learned not to let it bother me. There were plenty of other places in the world where I could show off the lions I killed. Deep down inside, I also consider them to be just dead alley cats, but this doesn't stop me. What's clear is that the actual dimensions of a lion can be measured objectively. Public opinion, and even that of the hunter, doesn't affect them in the least.

"It would be nice if you would invite us into the living room, Korva," Juffin said. "That is not to say I have any objection to smelling the scents of a summer night, of course."

"Please come in," said the host.

His face showed no embarrassment whatsoever, making a seamless transition to a grimace of gracious hospitality. He looked rather annoyed, like any normal person who receives uninvited guests at home in the middle of the night.

"I need to talk to you, Korva, and Sir Max desperately needs to see your wife," said Juffin, making himself comfortable in a sumptuous ancient armchair that might easily have served as a throne for some forgotten king.

"What kind of nonsense is this?" Korva Blimm said coldly. "Atissa is already asleep. Besides, you know very well that—"

"I know a lot of things," Juffin said. "For instance, I know that your wife's caretaker disappeared today. Do you want to know what happened to him? The poor fellow tried to kill Sir Max here. He was so fatigued by his failed attempt that he ended up in the morgue of the Ministry of Perfect Public Order. At first I was just going to drop in for a minute on my way home and tell you the bad news. And worse news, as well—that your wife would have to be taken away. Then I was going to sleep the sleep of the just."

Juffin made a dramatic pause, as if to say, "Now is the moment when you start to tear out your hair and beat your chest in despair." If I were Korva, that's probably what I would have done. But he turned out to be a worthy match. Not a single muscle on his face so much as trembled. He eyes reflected only polite interest.

Juffin seemed impressed by his restraint and continued magnanimously:

"But this eccentric young fellow here doesn't share my views on life. He believes that Lady Atissa should stay at home. I was too lazy to argue with him, and I brought him along so he could personally make the acquaintance of the woman whose cause he was pleading. It's just possible that he still won't change his mind, and I'll again be too lazy to argue with him. And then there will be one less piece of bad news."

"I understand," Sir Korva said, nodding. "As you might guess, the aforementioned grievous events are as much a surprise for me as they were for you. There is no need to look upon me with reproach. I know that one should express gratitude in a situation like this, but saying thank you sounds senseless and incongruous." Sir Korva looked intently at me. "What made you decide to intervene, Sir Max? It would have been logical for you to retaliate."

"To be honest, I don't know myself," I said. "It just seemed like the right thing to do. That was the logic."

"Very well," he said. "I like that answer. Kima was right when he said that it was easy to get along with you. I'll take you to see Lady Atissa. You do know that she is not necessarily the most pleasant interlocutor? But you seem to know everything already. Actually, my wife is not really that mad. Sometimes it seems to me that there are plenty of people walking the streets of Echo who are far more dangerous. They just don't have caretakers at home who are ready to sound the alarm at a moment's notice. Sometimes Atissa sees things that aren't there; other times she fails to notice what's right in front of her eyes. And she reacts too emotionally to what she sees, that's all. The wisemen say that she's a danger to others. I don't believe this. She hates you because once, a year or two ago, she imagined that our daughter ran into her bedroom to hide from you. Melamori and I could never persuade her that this never happened, although the girl tried very hard. In my view, she tried too hard . . . But never mind. Please, come with me."

I stood up and followed my host in silence. It took a long time to reach his wife's quarters. To be honest, my own little palace wasn't much to boast about in comparison with the Blimms'. From a million miles away you could smell the vulgar scent of luxury available to any nouveau riche in the brand-new carpets that covered the floors of my residence. Here I was stepping on creaky floorboards covered with ancient tapestries. It was not unlikely that they had been woven by the fingers of real elves, in those days of yore before the poor devils succumbed to the temptations of drink.

"In here," Korva said, stopping by a door encrusted with studs of some glistening substance. "Atissa's still awake. Try not to distress her with your presence for too long, if you can."

He turned around and left. His tread had seemed very heavy to me from the very first, and now I noticed that Sir Korva's soft house slippers left such deep traces in the carpets that he would seem to be made of lead.

I opened the door carefully and entered a huge chamber plunged in semidarkness. In the farthest reaches of the room shone a small sphere of blue gas, casting a light that was too weak to penetrate the other corners.

"Is that you, Korva?" a woman's voice said nervously. The voice sounded so much like Melamori's that it made me question my own sanity.

"No," I said, for some reason in a whisper. "It's me. Excuse me for visiting you at such a late hour, my lady."

"Come here," she commanded. "I can't see you."

I went closer and stared in astonishment at a face that was almost an exact replica of Melamori's. It was somewhat older, a bit fuller. A hardly noticeable crease between the brows and the blurred outline of the lips made Lady Atissa's face look helpless and vulnerable—feelings our Melamori would never show to the world—but I couldn't get over the resemblance.

"Ah, you look like a kind guest," she said hospitably.

This surprised me. After Sir Korva's dramatic preface, I was prepared for a pillow fight, at the very least. On the way to the chamber I had decided that it wasn't strictly necessary to tell Lady Atissa who I was. But I was so flustered that I told her anyway.

"I'm Max," I said. Then I added, "They say you don't like me very much."

"Nonsense," she said. "Sir Max doesn't look like you at all. I know."

"And yet—" I began, but Lady Atissa shook her head stubbornly.

"Never mind. If you don't want to tell me your real name, don't. It doesn't matter to me a bit. Do what you came to do. I know you have come to heal me. This morning my caretaker disappeared. That's a good sign. If he disappeared, it means I don't need a caretaker anymore, doesn't it?"

"I have come only to make your acquaintance," I said in confusion. "I don't think I am able to—"

Lady Atissa shook her head stubbornly again, as if to say, "Don't try to wriggle out of it now, friend."

"Do you see what's over there?" she asked all of a sudden, pointing into the darkness.

I turned around quickly but saw nothing.

"You're as blind as all the others," she said, sighing. "But I see everything. There's a man standing there. He doesn't have a face. It's quite unpleasant. But wait!"

With surprising agility Lady Atissa got down on all fours and crawled to the very edge of her huge bed. She stared fixedly into the darkness, as if she were trying to make out a message written on the far wall, a very important but unintelligible message upon which her whole life depended.

I hesitated. I had never had any dealings with madwomen before —I felt very much out of my element. And the element I found myself *in* was a complete mystery to me.

Finally Lady Atissa began staring at me relentlessly. "The person without a face says you can do anything you wish to someone. Don't you wish to help me? Tell me. Why are you trying to fool me?"

"I do want to help you," I said, sighing.

I knew what Lady Atissa was trying to achieve. She wanted me to strike her down with my Lethal Sphere and then command her to be cured of her madness. It was a good bargain, but I would have preferred to practice on guinea pigs for a couple of years first.

"If you want to, then help," Lady Atissa urged.

Her likeness to Melamori made my head spin, and it was already hard for me to keep track of who it was that was begging me.

"It's dangerous," I mumbled.

"Well, what of it?" she said coldly. "Why did you come here if you weren't going to do anything?"

Why not? I thought.

I had recently had to undertake so many tasks that were beyond what I considered to be my abilities that I was getting used to the idea that I could. After all, the powers of my Lethal Spheres had sufficed to release the dead Jiffa Savanxa from this World, and very recently I had sent the dying Magician Glenke Taval into the unknown. It seemed that he had decided to make an appearance to Lady Atissa and tell her everything.

I snapped the fingers of my left hand—for the third time in this seemingly endless day. I did it without even thinking that there would be no going back. Goodness gracious, I thought, if only it doesn't turn out that I've killed her! Anything but that.

But thinking about it wouldn't change anything. The green sphere had already gently stuck Lady Atissa in the chest and then melted.

She didn't die. She simply shuddered and stared at me with her beautiful gray eyes. Gosh, how much she looked like Melamori!

"What do you want from me?" she said in a quiet voice.

Up until now, the victims of my Lethal Spheres had announced, "I am with you, Master"—every last one of them. But it seemed that Lady Atissa's aristocratic upbringing would not allow her to resort to such idiotic platitudes.

"You must get well," I commanded. "You must become completely healthy again, as happy and lighthearted as you were in your youth. And no more delusions. Ever again."

"Very well," she said. "I will do as you wish. Anything else?"

"Now you must free yourself from my power."

"What, may I ask, are you doing in my bedchamber, young man?" Lady Atissa said haughtily, scrambling to wrap herself up in the blanket. "Who are you?"

"I am Sir Max. I have already introduced myself, but you wouldn't believe me when I told you the first time."

"Ah, the secret police," she said with a wry smile. "Still, I don't understand what you're doing in my bedchamber. Are you searching for felons and malefactors, or are you simply interested in the color of my nightgown? You could have acquired that information by questioning one of the maids. They have a strong sense of civic responsibility. Too strong, even. Hold on a minute. Has there been a palace coup while I was sleeping? And is the Secret Investigative Force now hunting down everyone connected to the Order of the Seven-Leaf Clover? In that case you could simply give orders to my own daughter to arrest me. I am certain that Melamori would derive great satisfaction from it.

Her presence in my bedchamber would have been slightly more appropriate than yours." Lady Atissa rubbed her forehead. "By the way, do you realize that you woke me up? And that it is the middle of the night? Or are such trifling facts unworthy of your attention?"

I laughed out loud from a sense of indescribable relief. It seemed I wasn't half bad as a psychiatrist. Lady Atissa was behaving not only like an ordinary healthy woman but like an ordinary healthy woman with nerves of steel. How and why I had entered her bedroom had been completely erased from her memory. Nevertheless, she showed not a trace of panic. I doubt that I could have addressed a stranger who had suddenly appeared in my bedroom with such calm sarcasm.

"I do beg your pardon, Lady Atissa," I said, with a feeling of sudden levity. "I'll be going now."

"You're leaving?" she said. "Frankly, I would have thought that you were here with some purpose, having already forced your way into my bedchamber."

"You are absolutely right. My purpose was to make sure that you weren't sleeping with your head to the South. That's very important. I see now that you don't. Good night to you."

"Is it truly dangerous, to sleep with your head to the South?" Lady Atissa said.

"It certainly is. The most dangerous delusions, the ones that waylay sleepers, come from the South."

It was shameless to lie so brazenly, of course, but it was the first thing that came into my head.

When I had found my way back into the passageway, I glanced around in confusion. Which way did I turn to get back to the living room?

"This way, Sir Max." Korva Blimm's voice came to me from somewhere down below. I made my way to him down a narrow spiral staircase.

"Your timing was impeccable. I would definitely have lost my way," I said.

"My wife just sent me a call and said that the Echo secret police had stormed her bedchamber," said Korva gloomily. "Is she imagining things again?"

"No," I said smiling. "I think this time she was joking."

"Joking? Where did that come from? Atissa hasn't been able to joke for ages. At least since—"

"I think she's cured," I said softly. "And I also think that she doesn't even remember she was ill. In any case, she has no recollection at all of the first part of my visit. We even had to make each other's acquaintance twice."

"Atissa? Cured?" Korva said in disbelief. "Her illness is incurable. Otherwise she would have been well again long ago. Do you think I've just been waiting passively for her to get better on her own?"

"No, I don't think that you have. But I'm quite sure that she is cured now. Go up to her and see for yourself. But first tell me how to get back to the reception hall, or I'll spend the rest of my life wandering the passageways. A grim prospect."

"Around that corner you'll find one more stairway. It leads directly to the living room. Please don't leave before I return. I don't understand a thing at this point."

Following my host's instructions, I reached the living room without incident. Juffin was sitting there by himself, and he didn't look at all like he was the most carefree fellow in the Universe. In fact, he even overdid it a little when he knitted his brow.

"Well, how was your romantic encounter?"

"Marvelous. I liked it so much I advised Sir Korva to do the same."

"What happened up there, anyway?" His impatience was bordering on real annoyance.

"I think I cured her," I said. "Don't tell anyone, though. Otherwise there will be a long line of mad people waiting in front of Tekki's tavern tomorrow. I think she might show me the door after this anyway. And it's probably the right thing to do."

"Wait a minute, quit your jabbering. Are you sure you cured her, Max? You aren't exaggerating?"

"Lady Atissa herself asked me to launch a Lethal Sphere at her," I said. "I couldn't refuse. Beautiful women can wrap me around their little fingers. She got wind of this extravagant form of amusement in a conversation with one of her hallucinations. She told me about a 'man without a face' that visited her. Ring a bell? Gosh, I don't understand a thing myself anymore!"

"Your Lethal Sphere?" Juffin said. Then he grinned in approval. "Why not? It would be funny if you really cured her that way. And did the smell of madness go away, too?"

"You know I could never discern it. But Sir Korva has gone up to see her. Send him a call and ask him about the smell."

"You can be so resourceful sometimes," Juffin said.

The boss followed my advice and began staring intently into space. Several moments later he raised his eyes to me. Now they showed only merriment.

"Let's go home, Max. There's nothing for us to do in the middle of the night in someone else's home. Especially when the hosts are very busy themselves."

"But Sir Korva requested that I stay until he returned," I said.

"Of course he requested that. At that moment he didn't realize he wouldn't be able to return to the living room for the next day and night. Use your imagination, Max, and you should be able to figure out why he has better things to do now," Juffin said. "Let's go, Mr. Brainiac."

"So did I really cure her?" I said, getting up reluctantly from the comfortable armchair.

"As if you didn't know. I'm sure your Lethal Spheres can do far more than that."

"Well, that's good," I said. "I like them both very much. But I can understand Melamori. People like that make better friends than parents. They probably aren't all that easy to get along with."

"Right you are," said Juffin, making himself comfortable in the front seat of the amobiler. "I don't know about 'friends,' but today you've made two acquaintances who will be eternally grateful to you. If you want a third, just drive me home. It's not far from here."

"Give me directions, though. I've never been able to find my way around the Left Bank, especially at night. That would take a miracle."

"Now turn left," Juffin said after we drove out through the gates of the Blimm estate. "And don't go too fast. There are lots of unexpected twists and turns ahead."

"I'd like to believe that this is not a grim prophecy, just information about the upcoming journey," I said with a grin. "Speaking of unexpected twists and turns, today is supposed to be my Day of Freedom from Care, remember?"

"Didn't you get enough rest today?" Juffin said with perfect calm. "We've had a great time. All right, don't pout. Tomorrow you can take the day off."

"Do you think I'll be able to pull it off?" I said.

"Why not? Wonders happen even to bores like yourself. By the way, we're here already, didn't you notice? Will you survive if I don't invite you in for a mug of kamra? I've had enough of you for one day. I hope the feeling is mutual."

"I can survive even worse things. I'm very resilient. Besides, my girlfriend makes better kamra than your butler."

"Well, that's a matter of taste. Good night, Max."

I watched as Juffin's shimmering silver looxi receded into the darkness of the garden. Then I turned toward home. I desperately needed a good dose of ordinary human life: whispering to Tekki in the semidarkness of the already closed tavern, laughing with her about the day's crazy events, scratching the kitties' soft furry necks, things like that.

Wonder of wonders, all of this—and nearly a dozen hours of the soundest sleep, to boot—I got. When I woke up just after midday, I allowed myself to loll around as long as I wished, even making some plans for passing a pleasant evening. Tekki was the protagonist of these plans, of course, though the proposed setting for the act changed with frightening speed.

Melifaro's call reached me not long before sundown. I was just planning to diversify my R&R. Having something to eat, for example.

Where have the girls gone, Max? Do you know what's going on?

If it had been an ordinary conversation, he would have roared out the question. Silent Speech is not the best means for expressing emotion, but I understood all the same that something was very wrong.

No idea. Why?

No one is at the Furry House. Everyone has disappeared: the girls, your servants, even your dog. To be honest, I am at my wit's end. The boss went to Xolomi to interrogate some conspirator they're afraid even to let out of his cell. What lousy timing! So it's impossible to contact him. Come to the Furry House, all right?

Have you tried to send a call to the girls? Maybe they've just run back to their native steppe. After all, I'm a pretty bad husband.

I've sent calls to all of them. To Kenlex, her sisters, even the servants. They're not there. It's uncanny. It doesn't feel like they died. It feels like they were never even born. I did find something here, though . . . Hurry over, you should see this for yourself.

I'm on my way.

I ran downstairs at a gallop.

Tekki stared at my contorted features. "Has relaxing tired you out that much?"

"Relaxing is tired of me, not the other way around. Melifaro says that everyone in the Furry House has disappeared. No one answers his calls. I hope it's just some kind of misunderstanding."

"What could have happened to them? Why would they just up and leave?" said Tekki.

"I hope I'll be back today. Or someday, anyway," I said. "Sinning

Magicians, why oh why does this have to happen now? I had such well-laid plans for our evening, and even better ones for the night! It was to be a classic scene—nothing original, mind you, but who needs originality when—"

"I believe you," Tekki said. "Just try not to forget what you thought up. Sooner or later we'll put your plan into action."

"Down to the last detail?"

"Every last one. And then some."

She waved goodbye, and I disappeared from her life—for a while, anyway.

※

The pitiful remains of what was once Melifaro were waiting for me in the main hall of the Furry House. The downcast creature was so unlike the force of nature I was familiar with that their similarity seemed shocking rather than reassuring.

"That bad?" I said.

"I'm not sure." Melifaro did a weak impression of a sad smile. "Maybe you'll be able to take the situation in hand. You'll kill a couple dozen villains and a few hundred innocent civilians in one fell swoop. Then it will turn out that everything really is bad, but not that bad. Here, take a look at this, Max."

Only then did I notice that Melifaro was turning some object over and over in his hands. Peering closer at it, I realized that it was a stuffed toy, a small figure that looked like a little boy in a looxi. On the floor was a neat pile of similar toys. What are they doing here and where did they come from? I wondered.

"What are these things? The promised trophies of war, former property of the hapless Manooks? My subjects brought me a bunch of gifts that I had no time to look at. Anyway, I've never seen these before in my life. Or anything like them."

"Neither have I," Melifaro said. "But I've had some time to think about it. Doesn't the boy's looxi remind you of anything?"

"No."

Just in case, I examined the clothes on the toy, then shook my head with even more certainty.

"Well, naturally, since you hardly ever put in an appearance here. And if you do, you wander around through the bookcases like a sleep-walker or chase after the dog, squealing hysterically."

Melifaro's cutting tone testified to his emotional resilience. I could only dream of making such a quick recovery.

"The designs on his looxi exactly replicate the designs on the uniforms of the servants who flooded your palace on the command of our solicitous Majesty Gurig. How many do you have, by the way? Any idea?"

"As a matter of fact, yes, I do know. Last spring I wrote the king about them. I thanked him for his concern for the welfare of the occupants of the Furry House, and at the end of the letter I delicately suggested that three dozen servants was too many. I assured him that in such a small dwelling there was no purpose in keeping more than a dozen of these useless fellows. In my opinion, two of them would be enough to keep the house clean and to feed my dog. But I lacked the courage to tell His Majesty the honest truth. Since that time, there have been only a dozen servants trying to keep themselves occupied around my house."

"Well, that's exactly right. One dozen," Melifaro said, nodding. "I already searched the house and found exactly twelve of these dolls. By the way, the one I found in the kitchen is wearing a chef's cap. See for yourself."

He thrust another rag doll under my nose. Its hands were holding something that resembled a spoon. It was made of the same soft material as the figure itself.

"Do you mean to tell me that my servants have turned into dolls?" I said.

"You got it. Want some more proof? Just don't faint."

He pulled a shaggy little dog from the pile of toys.

"Is that all that's left of Droopy?" I said, horrified, as I took the toy into my hands. "A hole in the heavens above you, I'm afraid you're right. Look, that's his collar—just very tiny."

"Are you sure it's his collar?"

"Absolutely," I said. "You see how there's a stone missing on the clasp? I scraped it off by mistake myself when I was putting it on him for the first time. He kept fidgeting . . . Well, don't look at me like I'm the Capital's number-one cannibal. I was just confirming your hypothesis."

"I just realized how much I hoped I was wrong! I'm afraid the same fate has befallen the girls. That's why I can't reach any of them— neither Kenlex, nor her sisters."

"Have you found anything that . . . that looks like them?"

"No. But I didn't look very thoroughly. I ran all over the whole house, looking into the bedrooms, the kitchen—everywhere."

"Shall we go together to look for them?"

"Let's go," Melifaro said like a doomed man.

The search plunged me into despondency. I just wasn't used to dealing with this grief-stricken hypostasis of Melifaro. To be honest, his emotional state distressed me far more than the horrible mystery of the dolls. My own heart winced from his pain, and my thoughts grew confused from his despair. Now I would even have preferred that Melifaro be the same delightfully insensitive brute he seems to be the first time you meet him. Actually, the second, third, fourth, and even the three thousand eight hundred twenty-fifth time, too.

"Where could they have gone?" Melifaro moaned when we had returned to the first floor after three-quarters of an hour of fruitless searching. "Maybe you have some sort of Secret Door around here?"

"Even if there were one, I wouldn't know. Anyway, why should there be one at all? This is just a former university library, not Rulx Castle. There's probably not another person in this World who is less familiar with his own house than I am. Still, I'm sure that we haven't searched the whole place yet. For instance, we haven't been to the room where my subjects dumped their gifts. I would have noticed the bales, or whatever they are."

"Of course! What's wrong with me? There have to be storerooms here," Melifaro said. "They're probably near the bathroom and the bathing pools, and we haven't gone downstairs yet."

"I know nothing about any storerooms or whatever else is down there," I said.

"Give me a break! You mean to say you've never used the bathroom in your own house?"

"Kings like me don't engage in such petty activities," I said, bristling.

"Well, never mind, I do. I've been there a number of times, in fact. So I can show you the way. Please don't be squeamish, your majesty."

When we had descended to the cellar, we checked the bathroom and the bathing pools, just to make sure. I discovered to my horror that I had exactly two dozen bathing pools. Such an abundance of facilities was even beyond the expectation of Lonli-Lokli himself. That aficionado of all things watery only had eighteen.

"And it is widely believed that I live here. Imagine," I said with a sigh.

"Max, I've found the storeroom," Melifaro said in a wooden voice. "The girls are here. See for yourself."

I followed him into the spacious room, illuminated by three gas spheres. Melifaro stood among the fat bales and neat piles of brightly colored woven material. My naive subjects probably thought they had made me the happy owner of the most beautiful carpets in the Unified Kingdom.

"Here they are," Melifaro said, his voice trembling, as he handed me three small rag dolls. "Your entire harem, Monster."

I took one of the dolls and examined it carefully.

"I think this one is Xeilax, judging by the bright-red looxi. The poor thing has the same terrible taste as you."

"You've told me that eight hundred thousand times," Melifaro said. He stroked the head of one of the dolls. "Here's Kenlex. She was wearing a funny little metal earring. There it is, see? It's so tiny, but you can still make it out. I kept asking her why she didn't take it off, and I tried to give her some prettier ones. But she insisted that she couldn't remove it. She was born with it, and it was a sign of an unusual fate and luck. What nonsense! And this is our Xelvi. See? She keeps smiling, no matter what. Max, do you think we'll be able to get to the bottom of this madness? I've never seen the likes of it."

"I guess it won't surprise you if I say I haven't either," I said morosely. "I could try to find some alien trace here, of course, but . . . my heart isn't in the right place for it, buddy. To be honest, ever since we entered this room, I keep thinking that you and I are going to turn into something, too. Let's get hold of Juffin first. Maybe he has something insightful to say about the matter."

"Send him a call, will you?" Melifaro said. "If I start recounting the story from the beginning, I'm afraid I might just break down. And what if the boss says they're doomed to stay that way forever? If you said it, I might survive. You're always talking nonsense anyway."

"Okay, whatever you say," I said, putting my hand on his shoulder. "We'll figure this out, friend. There's nothing we can't do together."

"I want to believe you so much that maybe I even do," Melifaro said with a crooked grin.

He clutched at the soft rag dolls so desperately that I feared for his sanity. This really was crazy. Perhaps Lady Atissa's madness actually was catching. Korva should have listened to the doctors.

Luckily, Juffin had already finished his business at Xolomi—the only place in the entire United Kingdom where it was impossible to receive a call in Silent Speech. I caught him on his way home. I told him somewhat incoherently what had happened. I never knew it was possible for me to tell a story that was so laconic and so garbled at the same time. Luckily, Juffin has a very high IQ, and he has honed his skills in dealing with idiots over many long centuries. He knew just where we had to start.

Gather the dolls together and try to arrange them more comfortably, just as if they were alive, he commanded. *Then come over to the House by the Bridge. I think I'll get there before you do. I'm telling Kimpa to turn around, so consider me there already. That's it, over and out.*

"Over and out," I said out loud in my own absurd turn of phrase. Melifaro stared at me.

"The boss advises us to play with dolls," I said, smiling. "He says it will calm our nerves. And he believes, of course, that they are still alive. In some sense of the word, anyway. So we have to make them as comfortable as possible."

"Of course," Melifaro said, nodding. "Hey, you really seem to bring luck. If the boss believes they're still alive . . . Anyway, that news is better than if he told us to burn all the traces."

"Let's take them into the bedroom. And move it, mister. Juffin will be at Headquarters in five minutes. I don't want him to turn into an old man before we get there."

To be honest, I was really hoping that nature would answer in kind, and Melifaro would dump a load of garbage on my head, in turn. Nothing doing. He just shuffled along behind me in silence. I couldn't even get a rise out of him, poor guy.

I went into the hall where we had left the rest of the dolls, gathered them up, and started upstairs to the huge sumptuous room that was considered to be my bedchamber. I had never once slept in these impersonal and forbidding quarters, designed especially for the relaxation of my royal person, and I hoped I'd never have to. Nevertheless, I laid out my poor servants so they could experience the utmost comfort. Some I placed carefully on the pillows, others on the soft carpets; the chef I seated in the armchair. He was an important personage, after all.

Gazing at the fruits of my labors, I realized that I would probably never make a good interior designer. The arrangement of the furnishings and accoutrements attested to a complete lack of taste and common sense. I shrugged and headed for the door. Suddenly, I turned around and went back to pick up the little white dog.

"Do you want to come with me, boy? That's right. There's no reason for you to stay here in the company of strangers. And you're so compact these days."

I hid the toy carefully in the inner pocket of my Mantle of Death. If anyone had tried to frisk me, the poor fellow would have been in for a shock: the terrible Sir Max is walking around town clutching a toy dog to his chest. There was, however, little chance that anyone was going to try frisking me for the next millennium.

I found Melifaro in the next room. He was tenderly wrapping the remains of my wonderful wives in a warm blanket.

"I hope they'll be comfortable," he said.

That was the last straw. I burst out in a wild guffaw. "I'm sorry," I mumbled, trying to stifle my laughter. "It's just that seeing you this way . . . I just did the same thing, but I couldn't see myself, of course."

"Actually, it's not hard for me to imagine," Melifaro said, smiling suddenly. "Come on, let's get out of here."

Then I noticed that only two dolls' heads were peeking out from under the blanket. "But where's Kenlex? Did you bring her along with you?"

"It will make me feel better," Melifaro murmured. "At least I won't be overcome with panic when I recall that fires can sometimes break out in empty homes. Also, I've still never been able to persuade her to spend the night with me. Now the poor girl doesn't have a choice." This time it was Melifaro's turn to break into hysterical laughter.

"It's pure pleasure getting to work with you," I said. "No matter what happens, we just laugh like madmen."

"We *are* madmen," Melifaro said. "That's the only reason we're still alive. Let's go, Max. You'd better hide your dog a little better. His shaggy ear is sticking out from under your armpit like a wilted chrysanthemum. Which don't even grow in our World."

"How do you know about them, then?"

"From the movies. Where else?" he said with a deep sigh.

Juffin was already sitting in the office. And he wasn't alone. Sir Lookfi Pence was perching on the edge of another chair. He looked confused and even somewhat affronted. The fellow had long ago come to take it for granted that his working day ended at sundown, when the buriwoks from the Main Archive preferred to be left alone to pursue their own lives.

"Sinning Magicians, talk about hangdog looks, boys!" Juffin said by way of greeting. "I hope you've brought some of these poor dolls with you to show me."

I drew the small, shaggy Droopy out of the folds of my Mantle of Death and handed him to Juffin.

"Is this what happened to your dog? I've never seen anything like it in my life. To be honest, I like him more in this state than the former one. He's so tiny and quiet—a perfect charm." Juffin handed me my dog back and smiled in sympathy. "Don't be angry, Max. It really is a terrible thing, of course. I just had to insult your dignity a bit, to humor Melifaro. He likes that kind of thing, as far as I know."

"I can't live without it," Melifaro said, gloomier than ever.

"Well, I'm glad to have pleased you. Now we'll proceed upstairs, where we'll try to talk the clever beaks from the Main Archive into breaking with custom. I hope they'll see the gravity of the situation. Our Kurush, of course, is a genius, but he doesn't have any information about the magic rites of the Barren Lands stored in his memory. Whoever would have thought I'd need it one day—and so urgently."

"Do we really need the information about the magic rites of the Barren Lands?" I said.

"A hole in the heavens above your head, Nightmare! You haven't understood a thing!" Melifaro was jubilant. "What do you think happened? You said yourself that your trusty vassals brought you some war trophies that you had never laid eyes on. And where did we find the girls?"

"In the storeroom." It started to dawn on me what he was driving at.

"Exactly. Earlier today, after the girls said goodbye to their countrymen, they went downstairs to examine the gifts. Unlike you, they were very curious about them. They unpacked a few of the bales, and at that moment, as far as I can gather, some horrible mysterious nasty thing happened."

"You guessed it," Juffin said. "The rest is piffle. We just have to find out what the nasty thing was. It looks to me like the defeated Manooks decided to wreak their vengeance on the sovereign of their enemies. Poor, poor Sir Max. To think that I inveigled you into this sorry venture, certain that His Majesty Gurig and I were only playing a harmless practical joke on you. Let's go up the Main Archive, boys."

"You don't think the buriwoks will tell us to take a hike till morning?"

"I think they'll agree to help us. Sir Lookfi thinks they won't. Now we'll find out who's right."

"If Melamori were here, the matter would definitely end in a bet," I said with a smile.

"You can bet with me if you have such a burning desire," Juffin suggested.

"No, that won't work. I wanted to bet *on* you, but you would no doubt bet on yourself, too."

"Perhaps you could submit your request to the buriwoks yourself, sir?" Lookfi said to Juffin. "I feel a little awkward about it, to tell the truth."

At these words, the poor fellow got inextricably tangled in his looxi. I had to take precautionary measures to prevent him from tumbling down the stairs headfirst.

"Of course I will," Juffin said to reassure him. "I will even tell him that you were categorically against this break with tradition."

"That's very kind of you," Lookfi said, brightening. "My relations with the buriwoks are founded on mutual respect for one another's habits, and I would like—"

"As I said, don't worry about it," Juffin said, reaching for the door that led to the Main Archive. "Wait here."

A few minutes later he poked his head out from behind the door. He wore an expression of triumph.

"Come in. I told you our buriwoks are very understanding."

We greeted the buriwoks far more ceremoniously than we would have greeted even His Majesty Gurig VIII. Lookfi mumbled his excuses. Melifaro and I kept bowing humbly and held our tongues. Juffin waited until it was possible to get down to business.

"Which of the buriwoks keeps information about the customs of the Manooks, Lookfi?" he said finally.

"Tunlipuxi keeps all the information about dwellers in the Barren Lands."

Lookfi approached one of the buriwoks. How he was able to distinguish between a hundred or so rotund, bright-eyed birds that all looked exactly alike, I'll never understand.

"Tell us all you know about the Manooks, Tunlipuxi," said our Master Keeper of Knowledge.

"No, no, not everything," Juffin said. "Please, not everything. A lecture like that could last until dawn, and that's something that neither I, nor you, nor our feathered colleagues need. The secret magic of the Manooks—this is what we're after."

"Very well," the buriwok said. "But if you wish to receive information about the secret magic of the Manooks, I'll have to give you a short historical overview."

"Tell us whatever you consider to be necessary, my dear friend," said Juffin tenderly.

When the boss converses with buriwoks, he is unrecognizable. Honeyed words drip from his mouth. The birds seem very pleased with his attentions.

"Unlike the other peoples who make their homes in the Barren Lands, the Manook people are not indigenous dwellers of Xonxona," the buriwok began. "It is beyond dispute that they are descendants of people from the Uandook continent who once made up the Secret Retinue of King Mynin. Allegedly, they inhabited the Great Red Xmiro Desert. Some sources claim that Mynin selected his Secret Retinue exclusively from dwellers of the enchanted city Cherxavla. Unfortunately, I have no information about Cherxavla. You must consult with Kuvan if you wish to have it."

"Thank you, Tunlipuxi. I think we can manage without the legend of Cherxavla for now, dear. How did these remarkable people end up in the Barren Lands, though?"

"After King Mynin disappeared, his Secret Retinue fell into disgrace—primarily because they refused to submit to the laws that bound all citizens of the Unified Kingdom. Moreover, they weren't able to see eye to eye with the retinue of the new king. It would hardly be possible to enumerate all the reasons for their banishment. The fact was, however, that the Manooks and their families were forced to leave Echo, and then even Uguland. They liked the Barren Lands because they could live there according to their own laws. Several thousand years of an isolated existence in the vast steppe turned the Manooks into a fairly ragtag nomadic tribe. My own view is that their impoverished existence was a result of the Manooks living by rules that were far from perfect. I don't think it would really interest you, however, to hear my personal opinion of these somewhat abject people."

"Of course we are interested in your opinion," Juffin said. "We are grateful that you told us. But if I have understood correctly, you explained the origins of the Manooks to us so that we would understand that the roots of their magic go back to the ancient traditions of the continent of Uandook. To be honest, this is not something about which I can boast of having any precise knowledge. In fact, even the current inhabitants of Uandook have only a superficial knowledge of the magic arts of their remote ancestors. And how lucky it is that those few who guard these dangerous secrets don't turn up on my doorstep every day to wreak havoc. Go on, Tunlipuxi."

"Keep in mind that from this moment, I will be imparting only unverified information to you," the bird warned. "It is not my fault that not one of your men of letters has managed to separate true fact from whimsical fabrication. The fact is that the secret magical rites of the Manooks right up to the beginning of our present epoch were connected with certain mythical beasts known as the Mice of the Red Desert, which no one has ever laid eyes on—apart from the Manooks, of course. The legends of the Manooks claim that the mysterious mice arrived from Uandook with their forebears. Furthermore, the Manooks believe that it was the mice who made up the real Secret Retinue of Mynin and their ancestors were only intermediaries between the king and these creatures. The name Doroth figures in all the known legends. According to the Manooks, this was the name of the ruler of the Uandook mice.

"The traditions surrounding the cult of Doroth are rather unseemly. It is rumored that the Manooks fed him with the bodies of children raised for this purpose. In return, Doroth shared his might with their leaders. It is supposed, for example, that Manooks were able to change the climate and even the terrain at will. Some say that the Barren Lands were transformed into an almost infertile desert through the machinations of the Manooks. They wanted their surroundings to resemble, at least in part, the homeland of their ancestors from the Red Xmiro Desert. The Manooks had never been good warriors. Nevertheless, in spite of that, no one had ever succeeded in causing them harm. If the Manooks' neighbors tried to cause trouble for them, they simply disappeared. There are reports of the sudden disappearance of the Nougva people, about two thousand years ago, and the also fairly large warrior tribes of the Nexrexo and the Shaluvex. This happened only six hundred years before the end of the Code Epoch."

"But how did my guys manage to beat them if they're so invincible?"

"I anticipated that you would ask this question before I had time to elucidate the reasons for the Manooks' defeat in the recent battle," the buriwok said. "The Manooks lost their superior might much earlier, about three hundred years ago. Legend has it that Doroth, the leader of the Mice of the Red Desert, fell into hibernation. Some of the other mice were eaten by the Manooks, who hoped in this way to acquire their former power; others simply ran away. Without their leader they reverted to ordinary rodents. Until now, the Manooks have made no attempts to awaken Doroth since their fear of his wrath is boundless."

"I see," Juffin said, nodding. "One last question, Tunlipuxi. Do you have any information about the events that accompanied the disappearance of the Nougva people? And the others—I forget their names."

"The Nexrexo and the Shaluvex," the bird said. "I have no information on this subject. You know it is not customary to burden the Main Archive with unverified information. I think I managed to recall everything I've already told you only because there is no verifiable information about the Manooks at all. In such unfortunate cases one is forced to choose between the information that is to a greater or lesser degree reliable."

"Well, thank you, at least, for that," Juffin said with a sigh. "In any case, now we won't be barking up *all* the wrong trees. Good night, my clever ones. Thank you all. And I would like to apologize once more for disturbing you after sundown."

"We hold our traditions dear, but not so much as to refuse to share your grief," the buriwok said with an air of solemnity.

We left the Main Archive feeling despondent. Mice, some Doroth or other, and not a single clue about what to do to revive the rag dolls and restore them to their former existence.

"Go home, Lookfi," Juffin said. "You've already stayed here past the call of duty."

"I'm terribly sorry that your daughters have experienced such a calamity, Max" Lookfi said. "But don't despair. Maybe everything will come right in the end."

He turned around and left, and I stared after him.

"My what?" I said. But it was already too late. Lookfi was gone.

"Yeah, well, that's Lookfi for you," said Juffin.

"What are we going to do?" Melifaro said. "Did you understand anything that plumed genius told us, gentlemen?"

"I, for one, understood absolutely everything," Juffin said. "The fact that the information isn't useful at this stage in the game is another matter."

"Maybe there are other more useful informants," I said. "My subjects have been living among the Manooks for some time. By the way, my general—Barxa Bachoy, that is—called them 'mouse-eaters.'"

"Perfect," Juffin said, brightening. "They left not long ago to go back home, didn't they?"

"Today after lunch. Moreover, they have several cartloads of sweets in tow, so it won't be hard to catch up with them. I can set out in pursuit this very second."

"No, I'll go," Melifaro said. "And don't argue. I want to do something. Wanting is one thing, but aside from personal motives, there are practical considerations. When it's a matter of going off to claim the head of some half-dead Magician, I will gladly hide behind your back. But when it comes to interrogating a few potential witnesses . . . Excuse me, Nightmare, but 'the dinner's over,' as your absurd little rotund friend used to say. You'll ask them a million questions, get a million answers, half of which you'll promptly forget and the other half of which you'll garble so much that they will become useless. Then it will turn out that you didn't ask about the most important thing, and you'll have to turn back again."

"I agree with you one hundred percent," I said, smiling. "But how do we make those sweet folks listen to you in the first place? Maybe we should go together."

"That's an idea. I feel so miserable that even a long trip in your company seems bearable."

"Out of the question," Juffin piped up suddenly. "I'm sorry, boys, but there won't be any joint outing followed by a picnic. You go,

Melifaro. Max has a few things to do here in Echo. Besides, his rank won't permit him to go chasing after his subjects down country roads. The nomads will be shocked by such extravagant behavior on the part of a crowned personage. We don't need to invent extra problems for ourselves; we've got plenty of already existing ones as it is. You just write them a note, Max. Your general knows how to read, I take it?"

"He does. I'll jot something down for him right now. But let's order something from the *Glutton*, all right? It has been my habit to indulge in literary pursuits while digesting ever since my days as a budding poet, writing dreary hogwash—preferably about death; if worse came to worst, about unrequited love. But invariably in the kitchen, stuffing my face with a piece of mom's homemade pie."

"A marvelous tradition," Juffin said. "What would be a good substitute for your mother's pie? Have you already decided?"

Then I spent half an hour writing a missive to Barxa Bachoy. It turned out to be rather hard. Much harder than writing poems about death and love. I realized that my field commander was not the sort to read for pleasure, so I tried to be concise and clear. Finally I finished a letter that met with even Juffin's approval. Of course, the boss is too magnanimous to be a successful literary critic. A former hired killer without a solid educational background in the humanities—Juffin would never fit the bill.

"I hope I'll be able to chase them down before sunrise," said Melifaro, taking the letter from me. "I'll send you a call as soon as I find out something. Max, how should I introduce myself to your subjects so that they tremble in holy terror?"

"Tell them you're my favorite slave." I still hoped to distract him from his dark brooding thoughts. If I couldn't make him laugh, at least I might infuriate him. But it was a no-go.

"I'd tell them I was your favorite chamber pot if I thought it would convince that ragtag bunch to help us," he said with a sigh. "Okay, I'll think of something myself. Good night, gentlemen."

He got up from the chair and made a beeline out of the office. I watched him go, then turned to Juffin.

"Things are looking pretty grim," the boss said, summing up all that had happened. "Magicians be praised that you didn't start digging through those sinning war trophies yourself. Right now I just can't imagine what we can do to help those poor girls. Not to mention all the others."

"I'm sure we can do something." I was surprised at my own confidence. "I'm not sure what, but . . . In any case, I sense an alien presence in the Furry House. I'm absolutely certain that someone else was there. Especially in the cellar. I didn't like the feeling a bit. I didn't even try to follow the trace of this stranger. I'm ashamed to say it, but I was really afraid that Melifaro and I could also be turned into dolls at any moment. But you and I should go there together and look for the trace now."

"No, we shouldn't," Juffin said firmly. "For the time being, anyway. If you sensed that you could also turn into toys, then there was a real danger of that. You're not given to vain imaginings, but you sense real danger with your backside, and it tells you to move it. So we won't hurry things. It's better to lose time than to lose our lives. I'll go there on the way home, but I'll go alone. Maybe I'll pick up some clues, maybe I won't, but I don't plan to step on anyone's trace, either. At least not before we get some concrete news from Melifaro. Then we'll see. Kofa will be coming in soon. You go on home. And don't try to play the hero on your own, okay?"

"Of course, I'm happy to go home," I said, surprised. "But you told Melifaro that you'd find something for me to do here?"

"Maybe I will," Juffin said. "Any second now some unhappy soul could run in here wailing that his whole household had been turned into these sinning toys. But for now I want you to just spend a pleasant evening at home. It might be a long time before you get another chance. If there is the slightest possibility that we can unravel this dirty mess, you'll be the one who has to take action."

"Is that because they were my subjects who brought the gifts that started it all?"

"Of course not," the boss said, laughing. "According to that logic, Gurig and I would have to take the responsibility. We were the ones who dragged you into this mess."

"But why, then?"

Juffin shrugged. He mused for a few seconds, then waved his hand dismissively.

"I don't know myself. Let's just say I shared my premonition with you."

"Okay. In any case, I really like your suggestion."

"You see how things fall into place? Now scram. I can't stand looking at you. Nor can anyone else, you bad, evil man. With the exception of one marvelous lady—so go to her."

"Gladly. And you send me a call after you stop by the Furry House, all right? I won't be sleeping for a long time yet."

"I can imagine," he said, grinning. "Fine, I'll tell you everything as it unfolds, if there's anything to tell at all."

Everything seemed to be decided, but for some reason I still couldn't force myself to turn around and leave.

"Listen, if even you have no clue about what's going on, shouldn't we ask Maba Kalox?" I said.

"All in good time. If I go to Maba right now, he'll say he's glad to see me, treat me to some revolting otherworldly drink, and send me home, blessing me with friendly advice so as not to vex his valuable person with trifles. You know him. But to be honest, I doubt that this time even Maba could help. If we're dealing with people whose ancestors made up the Secret Retinue of King Mynin . . ."

"How about Lady Sotofa?"

"I don't think so. But we can try if it comes to that. We'll stop at nothing, believe me. Go home already. I need to be alone for a bit. It's my only chance to think in peace. And not only to think."

"I'm sorry. Here I am, dawdling and giving you idiotic advice.

Naturally, it would have occurred to you to consult Maba without my prompting."

"I suppose it would have occurred to me. I've got a bit of ingenuity up my sleeve," Juffin said, laughing. "How do you think I managed to survive the last seven hundred years before such an ingenious adviser as yourself came along?"

§

The boss's good mood (insofar as it could be considered good under the circumstances) helped to boost my own. At least I didn't have to hide my misery from Tekki when I dove into the cozy semi-darkness of the *Armstrong & Ella*. She saw through me right away, though.

"That bad, huh?"

"I was hoping you wouldn't notice. Yeah, it's all pretty darn lousy. I even wanted to hang myself in the bathroom, but I changed my plans for the evening. Where is your mythical assistant?"

"Why mythical? She's as real as can be. She just stepped out for a while—to the bathroom, if you really must know. Praise be the Magicians you didn't hang yourself in there. That would have been awkward."

"I still don't really believe this woman exists," I said. "You keep saying you hired her especially so she could work evenings instead of you. But every evening I discover you behind the bar all alone. Are you sure she's not a figment of your imagination?"

"The poor thing is just afraid of you, like all normal people. I even have to give her extra hardship pay," Tekki said, laughing. "But she still hides whenever you're around."

"Well, let her come out of hiding, then. Juffin gave me strict instructions to enjoy my evening. I couldn't possibly disobey him. You know how scared I am of him."

"I know. You just take one look at him and fall into a faint," Tekki said. "But what does my assistant have to do with anything?

Does she have to undress and dance on the table for you? Is that what you have in mind when you say you want to enjoy your evening?"

"Almost. Of course, it's you I want to undress. Not just yet, but after we have something to eat and I dump all my problems on you. That's how I envision a good evening. Really banal, isn't it? Dancing on the table isn't a prerequisite. And all your assistant has to do is take your place behind the bar. I thought of everything, didn't I?"

"You did. Believe it or not, that's just what I want to do. Have something to eat, and then get undressed. I'm really sick of these duds"

The rest of the evening was great. First, we went out to eat at the *Three-Horned Moon*. I knew that in this wonderful club you could rub elbows with some living literary legend *and* get excellent food to boot.

It was still a long time before the new moon, so there were no poetry readings that night. Nevertheless, we found ourselves in the midst of a large number of people with pensive expressions and shining eyes. The regulars here were already used to seeing me and greeted me amiably, but they didn't force their conversation on me. And what was even more agreeable, they didn't stare at Tekki and me like we were aliens from outer space. They were concerned with their own affairs.

In a word, the *Three-Horned Moon* was the perfect place for talking about the events that had befallen us. In this setting my story recalled a desperate attempt by a young fabulist to impress his girlfriend with the subject of his forthcoming fantasy novel in verse. In fact, if I had gone on a bit longer, I might have stopped believing my own true story.

"Things are looking pretty grim," she said, echoing Juffin, and summing up my long saga.

"Well, I guess it's not really dinner-table conversation," I said. "You know, on top of everything else, I feel guilty. I could have taken precautions—looked into the sinning bales, sensed something evil, and told the girls not to unpack them. But I just let everything take its own course. And, of course, I'll have to be the one to get us out of this mess now. So it's a good thing that you and I have this evening together."

"Well, it's not all that bad," Tekki said softly. "You're going to be all right, Max. You can deal with it. Others, maybe not. But you? Sure you can. Trust me."

"That's good to hear," I said smiling. "How do you know it for sure?"

"This tells me," she said, tapping her breastbone with her delicate fingers. "The most reliable source of information."

Juffin's call reached me when we were on our way home.

I walked around your residence for two whole hours. You were right not to try to step on anyone's trace. If you had found the trace of the beast that had the run of the place, I would also have acquired a favorite toy to clutch to my chest.

You mean Melifaro and I might have turned into those dratted dolls, too? I said. The idea horrified me. So it wasn't a fit of paranoia but an ordinary human presentiment?

Well, I wouldn't go so far as to say "normal" and "human," but your presentiment was right on the mark. In fact, the happy prospect of continuing your existence as a cute stuffed toy would have been your privilege alone. Melifaro is not a Master of Pursuit, and he never will be. To become cute and fluffy, he'd need to have his own personal meeting with the unknown beast.

And how will we search for this creature if we can't step on its trace?

Don't worry about that. Its trace is so potent that I can smell it. It resembles somewhat the everyday smell of madness, with the smell of a wild animal thrown in. I'm about to follow the path of our unknown friend right now. So try not to sleep too soundly. I might need your help at any moment.

Maybe I should just come and join you right now?

No. There's no need. I'm not sure you're indispensable to me just yet. I'm not sure of anything right now. Besides, I don't want your girlfriend to scratch my eyes out. This is not a good time to run afoul of such a formidable lady. When we try to get to the bottom of those souvenirs from your Manook friends, it will be a different story.

I'll pass it on to her. Happy hunting.

Thanks. Very apt wish indeed.

✵

About two hours later, when I didn't really feel much like sleeping yet but already foresaw the possibility in the immediate future, the boss sent me another call.

Come to Rulx Castle. Hurry like there's no tomorrow. I need your Lethal Spheres. Mine don't cut it. The Palace Guard has been warned. They'll meet you and lead you to me.

I'm on my way.

I threw off the blanket like the bed was on fire.

"Max, even if the World is collapsing, it doesn't mean you have to wear my skaba, and definitely not inside out," Tekki said matter-of-factly.

"You're right. You could help me, though. I'm all tangled up in these sinning rags."

✵

It took me just a few minutes to get from the New City to the gates of Rulx Castle. A remarkable tempo—yet it also felt like I had wasted an eternity getting there.

A healthy, pink-cheeked giant in a patterned looxi bowed to me in silence and gestured to me to follow him. The Palace Guards are discouraged from entering into conversation with guests except out of dire necessity. For this reason I didn't ask him what the matter was,

239

whether the king was safe, how loud Juffin Hully was cursing, and which choice expletives he was throwing about. Knowing the boss as I did, I could get a pretty good idea about what was going on if I knew the approximate number of vampires under the blanket he was urging on his opponent.

The fact that they did not send a palanquin after me further attested to the seriousness of the situation. I had to desecrate the shiny surfaces of the floors of the meandering hallways of Rulx with my boots. Needless to say, it saved me a great deal of time.

I found Juffin in an enormous, brightly illuminated hall. All manner of odd and ornate objects hung on the walls. My imagination prompted me to think that they were ancient sorcerer's weapons, formal portraits of the kings of the Old Dynasty executed in the abstract mode, or some sort of elfin spinning wheels from the Early Binge period.

"You were fast," the boss said sadly, "but still not fast enough. The beast got away."

"Got away? From you?" I said, astonished. "Is that even possible?"

"It happens," Juffin said. "I have to admit that I got off easy. You and Melifaro almost had the chance to add me your collection of stuffed toys. I still can't get over it. A rotten, good-for-nothing little mouse, but what power! I'm not surprised that Rulx Castle let him in, though it's usually very difficult for creatures with evil designs to enter here."

"So it was a mouse?" I said in disbelief.

"A mouse it was. Can you imagine? Hefty and rather ugly, with a huge head. Quite a creature. It only had a few tricks at its disposal—but what tricks they were! I couldn't counter them in any way. It would be easier to destroy the World and then create a new one without mice of any kind—whether ordinary or mighty."

"But where could this mouse have run off to? It's probably wreaking havoc here somewhere!"

"No, no, that's very unlikely. Not now, anyway. The mouse hid on the Dark Side. And that's the most remarkable thing. Rulx Castle is a special place, you see. It's almost impossible to pass over to the

Dark Side from here. I wasn't able to follow the creature there, in any case. You probably could, though. King Mynin, our one and only Origin, built Rulx Castle exclusively with his personal comfort in mind. He could leave here at any time he wanted, and even go over to the Dark Side. If one Origin could manage it, another one certainly could, too."

"Time to get down to work, huh?" I said. "To go into the unknown, perform a few inexplicable novelties, and try not to soil my britches?"

"You hit the nail on the head, my boy. I'm glad you have such a good grasp of your duties. But this doesn't mean you should rush off in hot pursuit of that mouse. Haste is not the wisest course of action. I sped over here like lightning, and now we've got a very big problem on our hands, which could have been avoided. We should first wait for news from Melifaro and listen carefully to everything he has to tell us. Then you and I should think long and hard about it. And have a few requisite dreams. That's the main thing now."

"Dreams, you say? Sounds tempting. But why do you think this mouse broke into Rulx? To cast a spell on the king?"

"No, I don't think so. Most likely he was looking for you. You see, his outstanding might doesn't prevent this creature from thinking in a very primitive way. I suppose it decided to look for the king in the biggest palace. Our little animal doesn't seem to have known about the existence of His Majesty Gurig. This powerful little wretch behaves and thinks like the most unenlightened nomad."

"Has anyone turned into a doll in Rulx?"

"Unfortunately, yes. Since I ordered the castle to be searched, they've found forty-six dolls, most of them servants, plus several sentries and five dignitaries. It's pure luck that Gurig himself set out in the morning to inspect his summer residence and was so pleased with what he found that he decided to stay there until the end of the summer. Most of his retinue left to go there immediately after lunch. If the king's caprice had not been so timely, there certainly would have been far more victims. Let's get out of here, Max."

"But what if the mouse returns from the Dark Side and wants to continue his hunt?"

"That would be even better. There are no windows or chinks to the outside here, and I already cast a spell on all the doors except the one you entered from. I'll take care of that now. Not a single living creature has ever been known to use a door I whispered a few tender words to at the right time. Besides, I don't think the mouse will be returning any time soon. I gave it a pretty good scare."

"I can imagine," I said, turning toward the only remaining exit.

It didn't take long for Juffin to cast a spell on the door. He caught up with me in the courtyard and clapped a hot, heavy hand on my shoulder. It occurred to me that his hand would make a good space heater in wintertime.

"We'll have to spend the night in the House by the Bridge, Sir Max, so say goodbye to your favorite blanket for tonight. I'm truly sorry, but for the kinds of dreams that are in store for you and me, even my bedroom won't work."

"Sounds like we're in it up to our waists, if not higher."

"Not unlikely. I don't know myself just yet," Juffin said. "I think this darn mouse really was the leader of Mynin's Secret Retinue at one time, though. I think we have been graced by the presence of that creature of legend—what was his name again?"

"Doroth."

"That's right. He came with the sole purpose of telling our buriwoks that the information about the secret rituals of the Manooks they keep in the Main Archive can be filed under 'Verified.' This would explain everything: the unearthly might of the mouse, whose roots go back to the ancient mysteries of the continent of Uandook, and even his flight to the Dark Side of Rulx Castle. No doubt Doroth had made that journey many times before when he accompanied Mynin as leader of his retinue. Our legendary king loved to surround himself with dangerous toys. All of you Origins have the craziest quirks."

"Not true. I don't know about your King Mynin, but I certainly don't have any crazy quirks. A bit of crazy foolhardiness here and there—I won't deny that, of course."

"Is that really what you think? Well, thank you very much. You're quite amusing!" Juffin laughed so loud that a few leaves fell off the trees.

"Did I say something funny? Well, at least I can do something useful."

Once we crossed the threshold of the Ministry of Perfect Public Order, my mood improved, simply out of habit.

"It will be pleasant in my office now. Too pleasant for our purposes," Juffin said. "Kofa will be there, and the table will be groaning under the weight of good things to eat. We need to speak in a more subdued setting. I don't want you stuffing your face with junk and agreeing placidly to everything I say. Right now I need your undivided attention."

"We should go to Sir Shurf's office, then," I said. "Its walls are so used to the gloomy face of its occupant that I'll feel obliged to satisfy their expectations with my own glum countenance. Furthermore, there's only one chair there, which you will sit in. It's unlikely that I'll be able to nod complacently when I'm sitting on a hard floor."

"Well, you can always sit on the windowsill. But I must say I like the idea."

It was dark in Lonli-Lokli's office. Juffin and I agreed that it was just what we needed. Just as I had predicted, Juffin sat down in the only chair: hard and uncomfortable, as Shurf liked it. After a moment's hesitation, I plumped down on the desk. Sacrilege!

"Just don't tell Shurf I sat here," I said. "He tried to kill me once. I don't want it to become a habit."

"Don't be silly," Juffin said absentmindedly. "Sir Shurf himself sits on it from time to time. He says that in certain cases it stimulates his thinking. I can't imagine how, but I'm sure he knows best."

"So what kinds of mysteries are you planning to unleash on me?" I said.

Juffin was silent, drumming his fingers on the tabletop—annoying at first, yet soon it started to have a calming effect on me. Then I realized that the boss was tapping out this jagged rhythm to help me concentrate.

"That's more like it," he said after a few minutes. "Now I think I *will* lay a few mysteries on you—some terrible, some not so. Here's the first one. Look."

Juffin went over to the open window and raised his right hand. His palm began to glow with a warm light. Then he made a smooth circular motion with his hand. I didn't dare blink, and yet I missed the moment when the warm orange glow began to fade. A few seconds later I saw that Juffin's hand was now wearing a *fedora*. It was a completely ordinary gray fedora—the kind that no one here wore except for His Majesty King Gurig VIII. It was, in fact, considered to be his crown.

"Do you recognize it? King Mynin's Hat. You gave it to me yourself, remember?"

"I do. But this hat was given to me by someone named Ron. I don't understand how it could be the hat of your King Mynin, who lived Magicians know how many thousands of years ago."

"Don't exaggerate. It's only three thousand years since Mynin disappeared. There's no two ways about it, though—it's his hat. But let me get down to business already."

"Translation: Shut up."

"Precisely. Take the hat. Just take it—don't try to put it on your head yet. Now listen carefully."

I nodded. I began feeling extremely uncomfortable, as though at any minute the boss might turn to me, smiling graciously, and say, "You know, actually, we eat people like you here. That's why I invited you to come live with us a while. How about I go ahead and eat you right now, before Lady Tekki beats me to it? I'm sure her mouth has been watering for ages."

I shook my head to rid it of these uncanny thoughts and looked at Juffin in confusion. I had known for a long time that he was privy to all the follies that went on in my poor head. This time it was very awkward.

"You don't have to look so guilty, Max," Juffin said. He was very serious. "It's a good thing that these fears visit you. At any given time, the most outlandish fancy could become the only reality at your disposal, and you must take such a possibility into account, along with many others that are far worse. You must always be aware of them and still love this wonderful World and us—the mysterious strangers who surround you. Love, no matter what."

I nodded again. I seemed to have temporarily lost the gift of speech, but I knew very well what Juffin meant. I also realized that I truly was able to "love, no matter what." I was still a surprise to myself sometimes.

"Good," Juffin said, smiling. "The lyrical digression is over. I see you're ready for more."

I could only nod. Magicians be praised, this time that exercise of the neck muscles did not give rise to anomalous cognitive phenomena in my head. Apparently, I was now really ready to listen.

"As you have already understood, we're in big trouble. Not so much you and I as your girls—and all the others who had the misfortune to be in the path of that dratted mouse, too, of course. Since we are dealing with a creature that in its time was drafted into the service of King Mynin, we stand some chance of getting help from Mynin himself. Unlike ordinary people, the Origins bear responsibility for their actions regardless of whether they are alive or not."

I raised my brows. Juffin shook his head, as if to say, "Slow down, you'll understand it all soon enough."

"There's a trick known—or, rather, unknown by almost everyone these days—as Mynin's Dream. It's the ability to consciously and intentionally summon up in your dreams a certain dimension in which it is possible to meet up with the Shadow of any human being—whether living, dead, or lost in another Universe. That's where I found your Shadow, by the way, when you urgently needed to acquire a new heart. It is thought that one must enter Mynin's Dream from underground. The deeper you go before you go to sleep, the better. But on that evening, I managed to set out to meet your Shadow directly from Tekki's room on the second floor, proving again that anything is possible when you're up against the wall. We're not going to do any tests today, though. There's no need to. We have at our disposal any number of excellent dungeons. It's funny. Long ago King Mynin discovered in some old manuscripts some allusions to a forgotten path used by the ancient sorcerers of Xonxona. He was the first to try it out and to leave a record of the results. Now you and I are going to disturb his own Shadow. I'll bet it will turn out that we are going to be the first to try *this*, in turn."

"How can that be?" I was so surprised I found my tongue again. "Do you mean to say that this idea never occurred to a single one of your crazy Magicians?"

"Well, I can't be absolutely sure, but I doubt it. King Mynin's Shadow is a mystery that protects itself. Few people nowadays even suspect the existence of Shadows. Among the initiated, it is customary to consider a possible encounter with Mynin's Shadow to be a less than pleasant prospect in the life of a wonder hunter. I personally think it's pure superstition, but I must warn you that this time I'm not even sure myself what will come out of our undertaking. I would gladly set out to meet him alone, but I'm certain that Mynin's Shadow would sooner agree to meet with you than with me. You and he will find a common language much more easily."

"Because I'm an Origin, too?" I said, my voice dropping.

"Precisely," Juffin said. "Also, because one of your hearts belongs to your Shadow—another reason for mutual understanding. Usually I skip the explanations before dragging people into these kinds of undertakings and rely on fortune instead. But I need your consent. Even more than your consent. You must *want* to see Mynin's Dream; otherwise it won't work. If you end up there not on your own volition but simply to keep me company, you won't be able to act independently. And chances are you'll need to."

"Well, you're my main supplier of first-class adventure, and you know it doesn't take long to convince me," I said. "I mean, right this second I want to turn around and go home before it's too late, but I'm too intrigued. I won't be able to rest until I see this Mynin's Dream with my own eyes. Besides, until today I didn't dare hope that I'd ever have the chance to meet this legendary king. How can I pass it up?"

"Not Mynin himself, only his Shadow," Juffin said.

"Doesn't it come down to the same thing?"

The boss shook his head. "I don't know what you mean by 'coming down to the same thing,' but the Shadow is strikingly different from its source. The odd thing is that they also consider us to be *their* Shadows. To be honest, it's not clear which of us is right."

"Okay, so his Shadow, then," I said. "Anyway, who am I to turn down a mystery?"

"Never a truer word spoken," Juffin said. "All the better. Wait a moment, I'll be right back."

He left the office, and I stared at the orange mist surrounding the streetlights outside the window. I didn't want to contemplate the boss's words, nor did I want to think about the symptoms of my own madness, which for some time had been whispering to me that for the sake of some promised mysteries it was worth even putting your own head in a noose. Why wrack your brains over some nonsense when you could look out the window at the myriad paving stones on the Street of Copper Pots? You could also raise your eyes and see the greenish saucer of a waning moon in an inky sky, the glow above the city, and two pale stars through a rent in the clouds. One needed to remember what this marvelous and still unknown World looked like. There was no guarantee it would be possible to return to it, and no guarantee that what returned would be *me*.

"We're off, Max. Don't forget the hat."

Juffin came in so quietly that I first took his words to be my own thoughts—sudden and so very clear they seemed almost palpable. I turned around and saw a bright silhouette in the doorway. The boss looked so much like a phantom that I thought, *What if it turns out that Sir Juffin Hully, the Venerable Head of the Secret Investigative Force, is my personal delusion? That would be a showstopper.*

We made our way downward for a long time. The underground levels of the Headquarters of the Ministry of Perfect Public Order seemed to go on forever. It's completely beyond me how for three years I could have thought there was nothing down there but dreary bathrooms.

Finally our long descent segued into a brief sprint through a dark passageway, at the end of which Juffin fumbled around with a tiny door.

"Crawl in, Max," he said after the door had opened with a long protesting creak. "Technically, this room belongs to the Order of the Seven-Leaf Clover, as do all the dungeons under the Xuron. A half-hour walk through the corridor would take us directly into the reception hall of Magician Nuflin himself. Long ago, however, I bargained for the right to use a large part of these underground spaces, which are extremely useful for practicing magic in your spare time, as we are going to do now. I'm almost certain that Nuflin made this door small on purpose before handing the room over to us, just so I'd have to kowtow to him. A little jest."

"Do you really think he'd be such a scoundrel?" I said, laughing.

"Oh, I don't just think so. I know it."

Juffin locked the door behind us, and I looked around. The room was extremely tiny. No more than sixty square feet. Here in Echo, where the smallest rooms are about the size of a school gym, this room would be too small even for a closet.

"You're not claustrophobic, are you?" said Juffin. "Some strong people start feeling unwell in here, and it isn't surprising. Yet this little room is the perfect place for entering Mynin's Dream."

"Not to worry," I said. "If I start feeling sick, it won't be from the dimensions of the room."

"Good, then. You see the pile of blankets in the corner? Take as many as you need, and try to get comfortable."

"Gladly," I said, starting to dig through a mound of thick fur pelts. "I have no idea what kind of sleep you're preparing me for, but it's getting harder and harder for me to stay awake."

"Now take off your turban," Juffin commanded, "and put on the hat. A person who wants to enter Mynin's Dream must have on him an object belonging to the one whose Shadow he intends to seek."

"And you've brought the Sword, right? Oh, I'll bet you have. That tipsy elf's timing couldn't have been better."

"Elves always have an impeccable timing. That's just the way they are. Even thousands of years on a drinking binge are powerless to change that."

I managed to fashion a perfect little nest from the blankets. Then I lay down, curled up in a little ball, and realized that I liked burrowing like this very much. A little room with a low ceiling, fresh air—I had no idea how the scent reached this underground space, but it smelled like a park after rain here. All of this filled me with a sense of peace and well-being.

Juffin sat down on the ground, his back resting against the wall. I could see the pallid gleam of the Sword resting on his knees. I didn't know when the boss had found time to clean it off and polish it, but the formerly rusty lump of iron had turned into a splendid specimen of ancient weaponry, forged from a light-greenish metal.

"Am I supposed to do something now?" I said, donning the hat that had once belonged to Ron, the guy I had run into in a New York café.

"No. Just close your eyes and let the slumber wash over you. Don't worry, it will all happen of its own accord."

I closed my eyes. The dream pounced on me like a strangler who had been lurking in the shadows of a dark bedroom, waiting for his victim.

At a certain moment it seemed to me that I woke up. I was no longer lying on the heap of soft fur blankets. I was sitting with my legs crossed on the threshold of an enormous dark room, as though expecting the next meeting with the official delegation of my subjects. I stared around the room for a few seconds, trying to make out where exactly I was and what was going on. Little by little I remembered the circumstances that had preceded my awakening.

"Juffin, are you here?" I called out in fright.

Not completely, the boss said in Silent Speech. *I'm already in, but you're still on the threshold. So we're in different places.*

But why— I began, but Juffin didn't let me finish.

It will be easier for us to talk if you come into the room. Stand up and take a step forward. According to the laws of this place, you must come in yourself, voluntarily. And you're still not able to make up your mind what you want—to see Mynin's Dream or just to have a good long sleep. That's why you're on the threshold. Come on, then, step inside.

I stood up and took a step forward. I have to admit I was completely unprepared for such strong resistance. Actually, I wasn't prepared for any problems at all. I thought that in this dream everything would be as easy and simple as it had been in the past—boom, and you're there. But this was not the case. Far from it.

An invisible wall grew between the dark room and me. I was stuck in a thick substance, like warm jelly. I couldn't move forward or back. I desperately wanted to call out to Juffin, but I had no access to speech at all—either ordinary or Silent. I thought of the dead insects that show up sometimes in amber. I seemed to be in the same kind of mess.

I wasn't afraid. What I felt was more like anger—my own helplessness always infuriates me. A part of me lurched forward with such an effort that it seemed my body was a plane on fire and I was trying to escape. Whether with a parachute, or without, was the last thing that mattered.

"Got stuck, huh?" Juffin said. He caught me just before my nose hit the floor. "Don't worry," he said. "That happens here. Especially to those who waver. Indecisiveness isn't a luxury you can afford here. But you entered, that's the important thing."

I took a deep breath and looked around. The huge room wasn't dark, as it had seemed to me on the threshold. It was fairly bright. I couldn't focus my eyes enough, though, to make out the details of the interior. They looked like melting pools of color, as though I were nearsighted and had forgotten my eyeglasses.

"I can't see very well," I said. "Is that normal?"

"Yes, it's normal," Juffin said, nodding. "You see me, don't you?"

"You I can see," I said, surprised.

"That's because I don't belong to this place, just like you. It's a good sign that you can make out something, at least. When I was here for the first time, I could only see a colored mist in front of my eyes. In time you learn to see here. Now I can see almost as well as I usually do."

"What kind of room is this?" I said. "Is it just the apartment of one of the Shadows? Or a meeting room for tiresome visitors so they don't wander through your whole house?"

"I don't know myself what kind of room this is," Juffin said. "I've seen Mynin's Dream many times, but each time I ended up in a different place. I think this space is as large as any inhabited World."

"What do we do now? Will Mynin's Shadow come here to us? Or do we have to go somewhere to find it?"

"We wait. We have the hat and the sword with us—that should be enough. His Shadow knows that we came to see it. I don't think it has any reason to avoid us. Also, we don't have to wait standing up: there's a couch here."

With these words, the boss lowered himself onto a bright-blue spot. I bravely took his lead and discovered that I had sat down on something soft and comfortable.

"We have company. We didn't even have to wait," Juffin said in a whisper.

Then he put his arm around my shoulders, as if to shield me from invisible misfortune. I almost got scared—and praise be the Magicians it was "almost." It would have been ridiculous to wake up on a heap of blankets, wailing in terror. I guess we would have had to start all over again.

I strained my eyes to make out the presence that Juffin sensed. An invisible danger is, of course, always more frightening. I stared into the kaleidoscope of colored spots and suddenly perceived at the other end of the room a small human figure wrapped in a long overcoat that resembled our looxis. It approached us at a leisurely pace, moving in a way that seemed coquettish rather than threatening. That was not surprising since I was almost certain that the figure coming toward us was a woman, and I was used to thinking that women were not a source of danger. That was foolish of me, of course. There have been some dangerous creatures even among my girlfriends.

"Mynin's Shadow is a woman?" I said in a whisper. "How can that be?"

"A woman? Why a woman?" Juffin said. "Well, yes, in some sense you're right. Mynin's Shadow is not a man, in any case. Wait a minute, did you really think that a Shadow had a sex and correspon-ding attachments on the body so there's no mistaking it? My, my, Sir Max—you're a piece of work. Even here you make me laugh."

"Well, I have to earn my royal salary somehow," I said sighing. "I thought that Shadows of men were also men, and vice versa."

"I thought you thought that. Congratulations."

In the meantime, the dim silhouette had come right up to us. I peered into the face of the Shadow. It seemed very ordinary to me. I expected to see something that made more of an impression. Deep inside, I was sure that the legendary King Mynin and, accordingly, his Shadow were bound to have glittering eyes, a noble forehead, a chiseled Roman nose—and so forth and so on.

I discovered nothing of the sort on the face of the Shadow that approached us, which I continued to perceive as a woman. Her countenance showed no clear signs of age, sex, or even character. It was the dispassionate face of a Greek statue, with regular but inexpressive features.

"The hat is on the wrong head, the sword in the wrong hands. Switch," the Shadow said. She spoke in a high voice that grated on the ear, but I immediately sensed the tremendous power lurking behind that falsetto.

Juffin took the Hat from me and placed the Sword on my knees. I gripped the carved hilt mechanically, and suddenly I felt something I had never before experienced: I knew with absolute certainty, beyond the shadow of a doubt, that everything in my life now was *right*. At last.

"It is now yours," the Shadow said. "Return to your friend the money he paid poor Toklian for it."

I groped around in the pocket of my Mantle of Death, where I actually did find a whole fistful of coins. I counted out eleven crowns and handed them to Juffin. He took the money with perfect calm and put it in his pocket. I laughed in spite of myself.

"Money has always slipped through my fingers, but I never thought I'd be a spendthrift even in a dream."

Juffin smiled, too. The Shadow waited until we returned to sobriety, then trained her attention on me.

"You are a good boy," she said, "but you are too alive for an Origin. It is not fitting. Will you come with me?"

I looked at Juffin uncertainly. He shrugged. "It's up to you. I would accept the invitation if I were you," he said. Then he added, with a hint of anger in his tone, "To be honest, I'm mortally envious of you."

"I cannot take you with me, Hunter." Now the Shadow trained her gaze on Juffin. "But I can let you take another stroll. You love mystery, do you not? That is the only thing you do love, and it will always be thus. I know how it is."

"I'm sure you do."

"Walk along the left wall of this room," said the Shadow. "Try to find the door. I think you'll manage. This will be a nice stroll. You'll find several secrets, exactly to your liking. You will not find the secret you came here for, however. That one is for your companion only. There are matters that are only for Origins—you know that yourself."

"I do know," Juffin said. "I will follow your advice without fail. Thank you."

"You are welcome. I like giving such gifts. But there are not many who are so willing to accept them."

The Shadow turned and slowly moved away. I understood that I was to follow her. Parting with Juffin was the last thing on earth I wanted at this moment, but I didn't seem to have a choice.

I got up from the blue couch and shuddered in horror: I couldn't take a single step. I was again stuck in the viscous air like an insect in amber. The Shadow didn't even turn to look at me. Apparently, I was supposed to deal with this problem on my own.

"I told you that indecisiveness is a luxury you can't indulge in here," Juffin reminded me. "Vacillating between curiosity and the desire to leave everything as it is may be lethal. Choose one or the other."

Hell, I *already* chose, I thought angrily. Sure, I don't feel like following into the unknown this strange creature who considers me "too alive." Who doesn't have a moment of weakness now and then? But I made the choice ages ago when I stuffed my backpack full of sandwiches and set off to find the streetcar stop on Green Street. Although, no, it was much earlier, when I read the story about the green door in a white wall, shed angry tears for the protagonist, and vowed to myself that I'd never pass up my chance. I didn't pass it up. Here I am. I'm not going to regret it. It was the right choice. The best one I ever made in my long and pointless life.

This incoherent inner monologue worked on me like a powerful incantation. I was suddenly free again, and took one step and then another, without even noticing it. I set out in pursuit of the slowly receding Shadow of King Mynin, who had disappeared three thousand years before. I followed without hesitation and without looking around, clutching in my untrained hand his own Sword.

I caught up with my guide, and we continued side by side.

Several endless minutes later, I finally realized that a great deal of time had passed since we had left the room where Juffin still remained. We were wandering through a deserted space that felt to me more like being *outside* than inside a room. My perceptions about these things were hardly valid, however, like any attempt to attach familiar notions to incomprehensible experiences.

"Do you know that meeting me is the greatest fortune in your life?" the Shadow asked out of the blue.

I nodded.

"My own experience attests to the fact that Origins are obscenely powerful yet too vulnerable," the Shadow said in the tone of a university professor. "The one who was called Mynin paid a high price to learn of his own vulnerability. The joy of becoming invulnerable will cost you very little. Only eleven crowns, and a bit more in fear and pain. In truth, very little, believe me."

"May I know what happened to you . . . to him?" Of course, I needed urgently to distract myself from my panicky thoughts about the promised fear and pain. This seemed to be the only way. Besides, I really was burning with curiosity, so I went on. "More than once I heard that King Mynin disappeared, but the word 'disappeared' only means something for those who stay behind. But the one who is said to have 'disappeared' in fact undergoes something more concrete. Death, or another life, or even—"

"Consider that with Mynin it was 'or even.' In any case, it was neither death nor another life. Perhaps someday you will find the precise answer, perhaps not. Stop here. There is no need to go farther. This place is no worse than the others."

I stopped and looked around. I was still as helpless as a four-eyes who had sat on his glasses. There were colored spots dancing and swaying all around me.

"It is beautiful here, is it not?" the Shadow said. "You will have ample opportunity to understand this in time. Show me your left hand, Origin."

I obeyed. Her hands were unexpectedly soft and warm. The Shadow opened my fingers carefully and examined the marks that had appeared on my left palm after the old nomad Fairiba pronounced my unwieldy True Name. I regret to say I didn't remember it myself.

"This is the most remarkable inscription I have ever witnessed," the Shadow said. "I know the ancient alphabet of the Xonxona, but I cannot read your True Name. It slips away. All the better for you. Now give me the Sword."

I was very reluctant to give the Shadow my new toy. It wasn't that I seriously intended to fight for my life with this ungainly object, but merely touching the Sword gave me a sense of calm and protection.

Still, I held out the Sword to her. Something told me I had to, because . . . Actually, this "something" didn't go into detail. It was more like, "Do as you're told and zip it."

As soon as I let go of the Sword, I felt defenseless and terribly alone. I was terrified because it became clear to me why King Mynin's Shadow had taken the Sword away.

"Do not be afraid," the Shadow said softly. "I will not bring you harm. On the contrary. You are too alive. That is why you always want something, and why you are always afraid. Your feelings gush over; their scent attracts death to you like a magnet. Sooner or later death will take you, however many protective amulets and powerful friends you have to guard you from it. Death craves Origins. We are its tastiest delicacies. It always gobbles us whole. People want to believe that nothing ends past the Threshold. This turns out to be true for some of them, but not for Origins. Our death is always the end. This is the price for the power that almost none of us succeeds in using well. You sensed this yourself, did you not?"

I nodded, trembling from unprecedented horror. It was so strong, it felt like physical pain. I had always thought that the myths of life after death were just reassuring lullabies that kept us from falling into despair and madness. I strongly suspected that these promises of life beyond the grave didn't pertain to me. This knowledge felt like a gnawing pain in my chest, and I could only be thankful that it wasn't as bad as a toothache, so excruciating you feel like you're losing your mind.

"Now be calm. Do nothing. Just look at your left hand," the Shadow commanded. "And fear not. All will be well. It is not possible to die here for real."

"Only for pretend?" I said, my face twisting into a grin.

Then I stared at the intricate interwoven patterns on my palm. I stared at them while the sword's greenish steel pierced my breast as though I were a lump of soft butter. I noticed this with curious indifference, like an outside observer and not the protagonist of this scene from a medieval romance. A moment later I had no doubts that the ache in my chest was a normal, human, nearly unbearable pain. I wanted to scream out, but I couldn't utter a sound. My mouth twitched convulsively, and my face was wet with sweat or tears—or both at once.

"The pain will subside soon," said the Shadow. "It is a wonder that you are still standing. That is a good sign."

The pain did lessen to the degree that it became bearable.

"Look what happened to the Sword," said the Shadow.

I lowered my gaze and saw that the ancient blade had penetrated my breast so deeply that it had nearly disappeared. The sword was melting like ice in the hot sun. As the pain receded, it carried away something else with it as well. Maybe it was that absurd boy I had once been—and not so very long ago.

"Now the Sword will always be with you. This is better for both of you. You need a good protector, and the Sword has long needed a trustworthy refuge. Your chest is just the place. It is far better than a wretched hole in the Shimured Forest. Is the pain gone now?"

"Almost," I said, nodding. "For a person who was just killed, I feel superb. Just a bit achy, like I sat too long in a draft."

"A draft? Is that a kind of wind?"

"A close relative, anyway."

"Yes, they certainly are close. Death is like the wind: an invisible but palpable power that is always ready to knock us off our feet. Perhaps this pain will return to you from time to time, but not for long. It is not too high a price to pay for invulnerability."

"Do you mean to say I'm immortal now?"

"Not immortal but invulnerable. This means that death will truly get out of your way—for the time being. At some point it will find a way to reach even you. Never mind, you will have the chance to find out how Origins outsmart death. You are still too young yet. I find it hard to believe you are so young."

"I am," I said. "Though sometimes I feel I was born a very long time ago. Only my 'very long time ago' can't be measured in hours or days."

"All Origins belong to eternity, and you will gradually come to understand that," the Shadow said. "Now let us talk of practical matters. You wish to hunt down my mouse, do you not?"

"It's not really that I *wish* to hunt it down, but it looks like I'm going to have to. People I am responsible for have suffered. Can you help me?"

"You do not need my help. I can give you with a piece of advice, however. You can now easily pass over to the Dark Side from Rulx Castle. My Sword is part of you now, and it is the best key for one who intends to set out for the Dark Side and farther, to its Inside-Out. If you wish, you may take with you someone who belongs to the Dark Side. Origins should bear gifts such as this. You will without doubt find Doroth in some secluded nook. He is frightened and hiding. In spite of all his power and his more than ripe old age, Doroth is just a foolish little beast. You must also take with you all those whom he enchanted. Perhaps on the Inside-Out of the Dark Side, you will find a way to bring them back to life. This is their only chance. Only beyond the boundaries of the World can you hope to overmaster the ancient spells of the red heart of the continent of Uandook."

The Shadow fell silent and stared at me with her cold, gray eyes.

"You look like Pallas Athena," I said all of a sudden. Then I grew confused and decided to make up for my blundering remark by explaining myself. "In the World where I was born, there was a gray-eyed goddess named Athena. There were people who believed in her, anyway. I saw depictions of her, and you resemble her."

"No need to explain. While you are here with me, I know every-thing you know, including all the fairy tales that fascinate you. You speak of the goddess who sometimes helped people, but only those she liked. You have a beautiful legend about an Origin by the name of Ulysses, who for a very long time could not return home. Keep in mind that the reason he couldn't return was because he did not wish to—the curses of the gods had nothing to do with it. His story is noth-ing like yours, but it's still one and the same story. All Origins are wanderers among people because they do not wish to come home. Perhaps we all still remember that home is a terrifying place."

"You don't mean the home where I was born, do you?" I said quietly.

"Of course not. The home where you were born, and the home where you count on waking up tonight, and the home where you, pre-sumably, will return on an evening a thousand years hence—these are all just pieces of land, surrounded by walls and covered over to pro-tect them from the sky. Places where you can lie down in your bed and close your eyes briefly at dawn. Nothing more. Do you understand my meaning? Now go. They are waiting for you."

The Shadow came right up and embraced me, pressing her heavy, cold body against mine. Her touch felt almost unendurable. It was as if we were made of different, incompatible matter. I steeled myself, and then suddenly I was alone.

The ground shifted beneath my feet, and a warm wind blew against my face. It grew stronger and stronger, and I knew I shouldn't try to resist it. Let it have its way. After all, I had never promised to stand my ground, come what may.

Then I learned what the wind feels when it blows above empty expanses, bending stalks of dry grass down to the earth. I can't describe these sensations. Human languages do not have words for them; human experience does not encompass such experiences. It was not possible to say, "It was like . . ."—for it was unlike anything else.

"Well, well, well, if it isn't Sir Max, alive and kicking," Juffin said in his most jocular manner.

His voice jerked me out of the somnolent darkness, at the bottom of which my inarticulate but sweet adventures had safely landed me and drawn to a close. I opened my eyes, saw the smiling face of the boss, and closed them again. When Sir Juffin Hully smiles like that, it means all is well. And if all is well, I can safely hit the snooze button.

"I get it," Juffin said. "You think I'm going to pick you up, put you into your crib, and stick your thumb in your mouth. Well, tough. You've got two legs, so move them."

"Is it necessary?" I said.

"It's necessary. I'm not planning on carrying you piggyback up all those stairs. If you decide to close your peepers right here, keep in mind that you don't have much chance of getting a good night's sleep in this cellar. Unless you want to go back to Mynin's Dream, of course."

"Oh, no. I've had enough for now."

I managed to struggle to my feet and take a few uncertain steps. Surprised at this recently reacquired ability, I walked out into the corridor.

By the time we had finished dragging our long-suffering feet up the endless steps of the staircase, I was more or less awake. My condition, however, still prevented me from feeling I was a full-fledged representative of organic life.

"Maybe I can tell you about everything tomorrow?" I said. "If I have to give you a report here and now, it won't turn out too well."

"You don't have to report anything to me," Juffin said, smiling. "Not today. Not tomorrow."

"You probably know everything already."

"I don't know, but I can guess. Rather, I draw conclusions based on observations. Mynin's Sword—the bargain of a lifetime, by the way—is missing. Your clothes are stained in blood, and there's an impressive hole in your looxi. At the same time you don't look like you're wounded. From all that I infer that I'd better not stick my long nose into any mysteries of Origins. I'd like to, naturally, but that's just out of habit. You'd call it a 'conditional reflex.'"

"I might," I said. "I'm going home, okay? I'll get some shut-eye, and then I'll mop the floor with this Doroth."

"Of course," the boss said. "I intend to remind myself what it's like to sleep in my own bed, too. By the way, it's already nearly noon."

"And Melifaro hasn't shown up yet?" I said, suddenly alarmed.

"I sent him a call while we were climbing the stairs. I had to do something to amuse myself. His conversation with your subjects was in full swing, but I told him to take himself in hand and give up this unearthly pleasure immediately. He's coming back this evening. I think you should be awake by then."

"I wouldn't count on it," I said, yawning. "I'm almost sure I could sleep for several days running."

"Doesn't matter how sure you are," the boss said. "If I say you'll wake up, you will. Any more questions?"

"Nope," I said with a sigh. "No questions. And no me, either. I'm gone."

✺

I barely managed to get behind the lever of the amobiler. After that, everything was much easier. I was hardly aware of braking next to my house on the Street of Yellow Stones. I didn't want to barge in on Tekki in a bloodstained Mantle of Death with an eloquent hole in my chest. And I had no idea what my face looked like. I forgot to look into the mirror in the hallway at the Ministry of Perfect Public Order. But it wasn't just that. I felt the need to be alone, like a dying cat.

This time the spacious empty apartment where I almost never spent any time these days finally seemed like the perfect place to come home to after . . . I wasn't yet ready to put into words what had happened to me.

I went up to the second floor and took off my clothes, still sticky with blood. Then I studied my chest, somehow noncommittally. There was not a mark to be seen where it had been pierced with the Sword. Odd. The blood was very real, and the rent in the Mantle of Death, too. Well, whaddaya know.

Then I rolled up into a ball on the edge of the bed, pulled several blankets over myself, and finally dozed off.

Of course, Juffin's call jolted me awake. It was the most reliable alarm clock—and the most merciless—in the Universe. When I looked out the window, I saw that it was already dark. This alone suggested that I had been able to sleep my fill, though my own body told me otherwise.

You'll get a headache, the boss said. *Too much sleep is worse than a hangover.*

No, it's not, I protested.

Let's continue this enlightening discussion in my office. In thirty minutes.

An hour, I countered.

Then I went all the way downstairs, because Echo had turned me into an awful sybarite. From time to time I catch myself thinking that a person who has just woken up must splash around in at least eight bathing pools in succession.

An hour later, as promised, I crossed the threshold of the House by the Bridge. In addition to Juffin himself, Lonli-Lokli was sitting in the office. They were both munching away. This cheered me up. I had already worked up an appetite during my watery orgy, but there had been no time for breakfast.

"Has Melifaro crawled back to Echo yet?" I said, looking up from the mug of kamra I was already guzzling. "No? Why did you wake me up then?"

"Sir Max decided to economize on breakfast again," Juffin said, like he was plumbing the depths of the human soul.

I sighed histrionically. The boss could elaborate on this subject endlessly. But he did deign to answer my question.

"Melifaro should be here shortly. He sent me a call saying that he was just driving through the Gates of Kexervar the Conqueror."

"Oh, no, that means the speed demon should be here by tomorrow morning," I said.

"Max, don't get so uppity," Juffin said. "If I had known that that sinning Shadow would mess with your mood and turn you into a grouch, I would never have invited you to spend time in her company."

"I think she really did mess with my mood," I said. "I don't feel myself tonight."

"I, too, think you have changed, but it is for the better," said Lonli-Lokli. "You have certainly become calmer. Before, even the furniture would get nervous once you walked into a room."

"Calmer? Perhaps. I guess I just stopped being 'too alive.' I'm glad you like me this way," I said with a crooked grin. "Then again, I put up with your exacting nature for so long that you should welcome me into the ranks of grumblers and mumblers."

"Well, never mind your temper, present or past," Juffin put in. "Before you went to sleep, you threatened to wipe the floor with our little rascal of a mouse when you woke up. Perhaps you would care to preface this exploit with a little introductory lecture?"

"Only if you would be so kind as to preface my lecture with another order from the *Glutton Bunba*. I never thought it possible that a person who was still hardly awake could be so famished. Now I know it is."

"Congratulations. Learning something firsthand is always more convincing," Juffin said. "By the way, I sent a call to the *Glutton* as soon as I saw the vampirish gaze on your face. It should arrive any minute now."

"Excellent. Then I probably won't have time to eat alive any of those present. As for the mouse, I'm planning to follow its trace to the Dark Side of Rulx Castle. Mynin's Shadow promised me that I'd succeed. In everything. I hope it wasn't just a sick joke. Do you happen to know whether King Mynin had a sense of humor? What do the ancient legends say about it?"

"Don't digress," Juffin said. "You know, Max, I think you're as alive as ever."

"My hunger is making me cranky. If you don't feed me, watch out, I may set out in search of human flesh."

As if to ward off that possibility, the door to the office flew open and a young messenger from the *Bunba* came in with a tray laden with contents I lost no time in trying to devour.

"I'll have to take all his poor victims with me," I said with my mouth full. "The dolls, I mean. Here in the World there is no way to help them, but there is still a chance there, they say. I won't be able to carry the goods all by myself, and I don't want to hide them in my fist. My hands need to be free, at least. So I'll need an assistant." I winked at Lonli-Lokli. "Well, Sir Shurf, do you feel like taking a walk with me to the Dark Side of Rulx Castle and back?"

"I'd consider it an honor," he said solemnly. He made it sound like I'd offered him the post of prime minister in a newly formed government. After pausing for a moment to think, Shurf said, "Do I have an hour and a half to take care of a few matters?"

"You have an hour and a half," I said like a rich man passing out alms.

"Very well. In that case, I will not say goodbye to you, gentlemen," he said and hastened out the door.

"Can you really take him with you?" There was a note of surprise in Juffin's voice. At another time I might have swelled with pride, but now I just shrugged.

"Sure. That is, if your legendary King Mynin didn't have a passion for practical jokes." I smiled at Juffin. "I would be very glad to invite you, but to expect you to carry the luggage—that would be going too far."

"How long have you been studying the art of diplomacy, your majesty?" Juffin said caustically. Then he softened and smiled an almost sad smile. "Of course you made the right decision. You can't bestow a gift like that on me. Although you are perfectly capable of saddling others with your horrible souvenirs. Sir Shurf is the prime candidate for them: you have made a mockery of his life and reason many times already."

"Are you saying that by way of praise?"

"A hole in the heavens above you! You can already read my mind," the boss said with feigned horror. "If things keep going like this, you'll soon be sitting in my chair or in Xolomi. One of the two."

"Let's leave everything as it is," I suggested. "Xolomi isn't bad, but Tekki won't like it. She'll tattle on me to her dad. And I already sit in your chair nearly every night. It's just an ordinary chair."

In the doorway appeared all that was left of Melifaro. It wasn't much, to be honest. The poor guy looked so exhausted that it seemed he had walked the whole way. He struggled to restore his habitual smile to his weary, beleaguered face.

"Good evening. Do you have anything here to eat that isn't sweet? The nomads decided that any close friend of their sovereign leader deserved to be nourished only with cheap candy and cookies. I was afraid that if I refused, the only alternative would be the traditional dish of menkal dung. So I ate my sweet things like a good boy."

"It looks like my subjects really wore you out."

"'Wore me out' is putting it mildly. During the sugar orgy I had to listen to forty-nine original versions of the legend of Doroth, Master of the Manooks. Praise be the Magicians, another two dozen volunteers wanting to shed the light of their wisdom on me turned out to be third-rate storytellers, so Sir Barxa Bachoy ordered them—and I quote—to 'stuff their mouths full of moldy dung and shove off.' But I shouldn't gripe. I found out a great deal about that sinning Doroth. By the way, the nomads are sure that the Manooks hid their sleeping leader in one of the bales with the booty of the conquerors, in the hopes that he would wake up in Echo and avenge their defeat. They unanimously agree that he is to blame for what happened to the girls."

"And they are absolutely right. I'm sorry, Sir Melifaro," Juffin said. "It seems we sent you there for nothing. While you were enjoying your banquet with the worthy sons of the Barren Lands, I had a personal encounter with the legendary Doroth. Then Max and I undertook an exploratory expedition to find out about him, and—"

"Just tell me one thing. Can we save them?" Melifaro implored.

"I'm going to try, anyway," I said. "If you want to, we can go to the Furry House together. I have to gather all the victims into one big sack."

"Why in a sack?" Melifaro said. He sounded indignant.

"To take them to the fair in Numban. At least we'll be able to make some money off this misfortune," I said.

When I saw his crumpled face, I was sorry I had said it. I hurried to make amends.

"I'm taking them to the Dark Side. That's where our friend Doroth is scampering about now."

"So we're going to the Dark Side?" Melifaro sounded happy.

"To the Dark Side of Rulx Castle," I said softly. "So your mission will be the hardest of all: you'll have to stay behind and wait to see how it all ends."

"The Dark Side of Rulx Castle?" He was alarmed. "But that's impossible. Juffin, what is he going on about? Ah, I understand. Some tipsy elf must have shown up again, bringing along a dozen lumps of rust for sale, and you all drank yourselves into oblivion to seal the deal."

"Magicians be praised, Max means every word. And he's being surprisingly straightforward," the boss said, laughing. "So go with him to the Furry House, and after that go home. I can see you're dying to get some sleep."

"I am," Melifaro said, "but I'd feel much better if I could take part in the hunt for that omnipotent piece of mouse turd. If only as a Sentry. After all, the lousy scoundrel cast a spell on my girlfriend."

"I understand you completely," Juffin said, "but someone who passes over to the Dark Side of Rulx Castle doesn't need a Sentry. Max is right. You must stay home and wait. As we both know, this isn't easy, but you are a brave man and a great hero, and people like you are few and far between. You'll manage. Remember when you had just arrived here to take up your post and your life felt like one long bout of insomnia, with or without cause?"

"I remember," Melifaro said glumly. "You taught me the Moffaruna lullaby. Are you hinting that it will come in handy again? Don't worry, Juffin, I won't get underfoot or trouble you in any way. I'm not a kid anymore. I'll help Max gather up the dolls, and then I'll go home to sleep. After this trip I don't think I'll be needed a lullaby, either. I'm beat. Let's go, Monster."

"I'll be right back," I said to Juffin.

"Of course you will," he said.

"Are you sure this outing of yours will work out?" Melifaro said, settling in beside me on the front seat of the amobiler.

"How can I be sure?"

"But do you know how to get back?"

"There's only one way to find out," I said, smiling. "Besides, I stand a good chance of surviving. I'll be in the company of Sir Shurf. He'll whack their butts, if push comes to shove."

Melifaro let out a guffaw. "Whack their butts!" he groaned in delight. "I can see it now."

"Yep, me too," I said, pulling up in front of the Furry House.

"Oh, I almost forgot," he said, crossing the threshold of my residence. "Your subjects asked me to tell you that they won't go any farther until they learn about how everything turns out. Can you imagine, they set up camp right in the garden of some poor farmer. I had to negotiate with him. I had to explain that it's not the beginning of a war, and to swear that His Majesty Gurig VIII will find a way to compensate him for the inconvenience. Anyway, keep in mind that when all this mouse business is over, you'll have to send a messenger to them. Otherwise your subjects will never return to their Barren Lands and will be the first nomadic tribe in Uguland. Then all their pining relatives and neighbors will join them. Imagine what that will be like."

"I can imagine," I said. "So nice of my subjects to be concerned about my domestic affairs, although I'd rather they just went home."

We went up to the bedroom, where I collected the rag doll servants I had so solicitously arranged on the pillows the day before. While I looked around for something to pack them in, Melifaro gave the edge of the curtain a sharp tug. The material ripped, and a large piece of lilac checked fabric lay at my feet.

"How thoughtless of you. This is royal property," I said. "His Majesty Gurig took such care to choose the right pattern and color. I'm sure he even lost sleep over it."

"Right, I'm sure he wanted the curtains to match all the colors of your crazy eyes. Well, are they all packed away?"

"All except for the girls. They're in the next room. Perhaps I should put them in my pockets. Young ladies shouldn't travel in such close proximity to strange men."

Melifaro nodded and dashed out of the room. He returned with two daintily dressed dolls.

"Tuck them away in your pockets, Mister Lucky Break," Melifaro said. He paused and then put his hand under his armpit. He took out one more doll and smoothed the mussed-up threads that had once been the short dark hair of Lady Kenlex. I saw how hard it was for him to part with her.

"I will comport myself like a true gentleman," I promised. "Not a single attempt to fulfill my conjugal duties, honest."

Melifaro grinned, almost like he used to in the good old days. "Come off it, I know you better than that!"

I drove Melifaro home. He dawdled a bit in front of his house.

"Maybe you want to come in?" he said uncertainly. "The last thing I want to do right now is sit in my own living room all by myself. 'The dinner will be over once and for all,' as your rotund friend would say. And after a visit from such a terrible, rude, and disgusting guest as you, solitude will feel like a gift of fortune. Do you still have half an hour to spare?"

"No, but I'll come in anyway. After all those insults, I'm duty bound to ruin your evening."

"Awesome," Melifaro said, beaming. "Now we'll have a little tussle, and when I'm all tired out, I'll fall asleep right on the floor. Do you want a drink? When I was home the last time, I think I saw a bottle of some kind of firewater or other. True, after seeing that miserable elf, I was so distressed I might have thrown it away. You'll have to rummage around in the trash for it."

"That doesn't sound too inviting. You'd never make a career in advertising," I said. "Besides, I don't want anything, except maybe some coffee. You can't help me there, so I'll have to forage on my own."

I stuck my hand under the table and tried to remember the heavenly cappuccino I had tasted a whole eternity ago in a tiny Italian restaurant in . . . I didn't even remember which city it was. My memories were shrouded in a thick mist. They stayed with me, but now, instead of clear, unchanging pictures, I found scattered fragments, mutable and shifting, like the patterns in a kaleidoscope. The reliable glue that had linked them together in a chain of cause and effect had expired. I never noticed how it had happened.

This did not prevent me from drawing a cappuccino out of the

Chink between Worlds, however. My hand grew numb, but my disobedient fingers didn't drop their valuable plunder: a pink porcelain
cup with a white foamy cloud resting on top of its contents. There was
even a little cookie on the edge of the saucer.

"What's that?" said Melifaro.

"Coffee. It used to be my favorite drink. A million years ago, it
seems. Want to try it?"

"Sure."

I handed him the cup. Melifaro carefully dipped his tongue in the
milky froth and melted into a blissful smile.

"I see. I need to fetch another another cup for myself," I said,
thrusting my hand under the table again.

It took me less than a minute to produce a second pink cup. I took
the first—and always the tastiest—sip and looked at Melifaro. He
looked like a kid who was longing for ice cream and suddenly found
one in his hand. Until then I hadn't come across a single kindred spirit. My new countrymen were not enamored of the taste, or even the
aroma, of coffee. Some asked in alarm whether I didn't feel sick from
drinking yet another portion of that bilgewater; others said there were
more pleasant ways of parting with life.

I ransacked my pockets for cigarettes. Melifaro's eyes began to
glitter.

"Me too!" he demanded, in the desperate tone of a person who
had decided to drink away his inheritance in one night.

"But you don't smoke. You can't even stand being around cigarette smoke."

"I don't smoke Uguland tobacco. I've never tried yours."

"Help yourself." I passed him a cigarette and watched how awk-
wardly he drew in the smoke. "It looks like you need to emigrate to my
native land. You like both coffee and cigarettes, and that's a good start."

"Gladly. At least for a vacation," Melifaro said. "After all those
movies you brought back with you . . ."

"Exactly: the movies. Real day-to-day life is far less exciting.

Maybe that's why we have so many good films. It's a safe, artificial dream—the same one for everybody. My compatriots bend over backward to escape their reality for a while, each in his own way. They don't all admit it, of course. I've managed to find the most radical way of all. What's true is true."

"You can say that again," Melifaro said, then yawned. "You know, strange as it may sound, you've made me feel a lot better, Monster. It's nice to think that somewhere far, far away there are a bunch of miserable nutcases like you. So get lost, Sir Nightmare. Go do what you've gotta do. Go to the Dark Side and catch that blasted mouse. Rescue my girl and the rest of humanity in the bargain. I'm going to hit the sack. Now I won't have any trouble falling asleep, that's for sure."

"Welcome back, Sir Melifaro," I said softly. "Finally. Who would have thought that I would be so glad to see your brazen face again?"

"Your whole life is about getting pleasure from looking at other people's brazen faces. That's the only kind of pleasure you understand," Melifaro said with admiration, leaning over the railing of the stairs leading to the bedroom.

His eyes were already fluttering shut as he ascended. I dare anyone to tell me yet again that coffee causes insomnia. There's more common sense and truth in tales about the bogeyman.

"Are you the wiseman now?" Sir Juffin said. "Did you tuck Melifaro in and send him off to dreamland?"

"So they say."

"Good for you." Juffin looked at me and shook his head in surprise. "In time you're going to make a very passable Sir Venerable Head, Max. You've begun to decide for others how they should proceed in life and to force them to dance to your tune. The surprising bit is that everyone seems to like it."

"I'm not deciding for others. I only . . ." My voice trailed off, because it seemed to me that Juffin knew best. If he says it, that's how it is. How could I understand what was happening to me when for some time it had seemed to happen even without my participation?

"Exactly," Juffin said. "Besides, you've almost stopped saying silly things altogether. When you do, you break off your sentence in the middle. I never dared hope that you'd learn this old man's art so fast."

"I'm a fast learner. If, of course, it's really happening to me. Sometimes I think that there's not much of me left. Do you remember the kid who wandered around your house, his eyes wide with astonishment? He doesn't seem to exist anymore."

"Good riddance. I knew he wasn't the one I wanted from the get-go. I wanted someone more like the fellow who's sitting here in front of me now."

"Really? Well, everything's great, then. That means you're not going to fire me this year, anyway." I smiled.

"Not only am I not going to fire you, I'm not even going to give you a vacation."

"Never?"

"Never," Juffin said, looking very serious. "You had one long vacation from work the first thirty years of your life. You didn't like it, as I recall."

"No, I didn't like it," I said.

"If you were waiting for me, we can go now."

We turned around. Shurf Lonli-Lokli stood in the doorway, serious and composed as usual.

"Let's go."

I was surprised at the buoyant force that ejected me from the armchair. It seemed I no longer needed to borrow Shurf's holey cup to walk without touching the ground. If anything, I needed to carry a weight around so as not to float up to the ceiling.

Metaphorically speaking, of course.

This time when I strode down the mirrored corridors of Rulx Castle, I felt, to my surprise, that I was coming home. A pleasant feeling, granted—but somewhat strange under the circumstances.

"It's the Sword," Juffin explained. "Unlike you, it really is at home here. It was forged in one of the underground armories of the castle. If I understand correctly, you and the Sword are now one whole, so you share all of its feelings and sensations, as well."

"Of course you understand correctly. Have I already told you that you are always right? I don't think you're capable of making mistakes. Nature has cruelly deprived you of that particular knack."

"Oh, if you only knew how well I made mistakes in my time, though," Juffin mused. "I admit, I'm a bit out of practice now."

We stopped in front of the door to the hall where Juffin had met Doroth, Master of the Manooks. The boss had to engage in a fierce struggle with the spell that he himself had cast on it. His angry fuming and fumbling reminded me of trying to use a duplicate key to get into an apartment—in theory, it should open the door, but it only works after a great deal of fiddling and sweating. This undoubtedly builds character.

"Where are the other victims of the Uandook mouse?" said Lonli-Lokli. "As I understand it, my primary task in our undertaking is to transport this valuable cargo."

"They will arrive shortly. I've already sent a call to the Palace Guard chief," Juffin said. "Don't distract me, or I'll never get this sinning door open."

A few minutes later, the feisty door creaked and opened just a crack.

"I think I should enter the room first. It's my duty," Lonli-Lokli said.

"Not here you won't." I was surprised at the commanding tone of my own voice. Shurf looked at me sharply and moved aside.

"As you wish."

A silent guard in a patterned uniform looxi placed a neat parcel at our feet and waited respectfully some distance away.

"Is that all?" said Juffin.

"Yes, sir. Forty-eight dolls. Forty-six were found in your presence, and two more were discovered after you left."

"Good, you may leave." The boss dismissed him with a nod and stared at me quizzically. It was my turn to make a move. I had no idea what I should do next.

"Take the parcel, Shurf. And take mine, as well, if you don't mind."

To be honest, I felt awkward issuing commands to Sir Lonli-Lokli. The Master Who Snuffs Out Unnecessary Lives nodded and took the package with calm equanimity. From his point of view, I guess, everything was just as it should be.

I pushed open the door all the way and saw a narrow silvery path glinting in the semidarkness of the room.

Up until then I had tried not to think about how I was going to find the path to the Dark Side. Before, I had been taken by the hand and led there, but now I could only rely on the soothing effect of the "we'll get there somehow" mantra.

As it turned out, my feet knew very well how to get there. They stepped onto the shimmering pathway all by themselves. I even laughed in relief. King Mynin's Shadow had known what she was talking about—this was as easy as Chakatta Pie.

"Just follow me down the path, Shurf," I said.

"I have no doubt that you are about to walk down some pathway or another, which you also find very funny, judging by your heightened spirits. To my utmost regret, however, I do not see it," said Lonli-Lokli.

"Okay, then just follow in my footsteps. Literally."

"Do as he says," said Juffin. "Our Sir Max is at the peak of his wisdom now. I hope it will pass in time, like the common cold. Happy hunting, boys."

"Thanks," I said as I took another step down the narrow strip of shimmering light. "Thanks for the good-luck wishes, and for everything. I'm not sure who's going to come back from that Dark Side, me or someone else, so I just have to tell you that it's been great. I mean the green moon over Echo, our endless lunches in the *Glutton Bunba*, your adorable acerbity, my second heart, the H. G. Wells story that your friend Glenke ghostwrote, and of course the streetcar on Green Street. I wouldn't have been able to imagine it all in a million years."

Then I began walking down the silver pathway that existed for me and me alone. I walked without looking back or worrying about anything. I knew Shurf was walking behind me, following scrupulously in my footsteps with the pedantry that only he was capable of. I caught myself staring down—first, because I was afraid of straying off the pathway; then because I couldn't take my eyes off the play of light. Its rhythmic quivering mesmerized me. I felt like I was sleepwalking.

The narrow path was getting wider fast. It engulfed me in silvery light and obscured the rest of the World, as happens only in a dream. Then there came a moment when I realized there was no more path. I was wandering somewhere through a bright, empty space.

I felt sand crunching under my feet and heard water splashing somewhere nearby. A damp purple leaf with an intricate asymmetrical shape fell down and landed on my boot. A pale wisp of wind came close to my face and veered off at the last moment without touching it. I looked up. The sky above my head was as bright as the sky over Echo in the morning. The ground under my feet seemed firm and reliable, as it was supposed to be.

"We're here, Shurf," I said, dropping to the ground heavily. "I don't know where 'here' is, but here we are."

"By golly, we are," he said, amazed. "We are here, where one cannot be. Or, at least, that is what I have heard since childhood: 'Impossible.' The Dark Side of Rulx Castle—unbelievable! You, Max, have led me into an ancient myth. It can't get any better."

"You know what's funny? I have this immense craving for a huge mug of Madam Zizinda's kamra," I said, smiling. "Wouldn't it be great if it was in my power to conjure up something like that?"

"The odd part is that there is a mug just to the right of you," said Shurf.

I turned around and saw a steaming mug sitting not two feet from my right boot. I picked it up, took a few sips, and handed it to Shurf.

"Well, I'll be! It *is* kamra, and I'll be darned if it isn't Madam Zizinda's kamra. Here, try it."

"Thank you," said Lonli-Lokli. He shuffled around behind me for a few moments, hesitating, then came up and sat beside me, taking the mug from my hands.

"I was afraid I would disappear as soon as I stepped off of your trace," he said. "But perhaps that danger exists only while one is on the way to the Dark Side."

"Perhaps," I said. "But you know that I'm a lousy theoretician."

I allowed myself a few moments to enjoy life: I lit up, took the mug with the remains of kamra away from Lonli-Lokli, and thought with a smirk that anything could change except for my habits. Well, think about it: my chest was still sore from the invisible Sword of King Mynin stuck inside it, I was no longer "too alive," and I had made it safely to the Dark Side of Rulx Castle—something that the most powerful Magicians of this World didn't dare dream about. Yet I needed to smoke a cigarette and take a few sips of some lukewarm beverage or other to feel tranquil and happy.

"Let's go find Doroth, Shurf," I said, getting up. "I wish I knew where we were supposed to look for him. Then again—"

"Look," said Lonli-Lokli, tugging gently at the fold of my looxi. "There are some words written here. They were not here a moment ago."

I looked down and saw a phrase written in the sand in large, neat letters. The missive read:

> move away from the river and you'll see
> the tracks of the mouse from the red desert

"Sinning Magicians," I said. "What are they, words from an anonymous well-wisher?"

Then I realized what had happened. On the Dark Side, my words turned into powerful spells, so the writing was the comprehensive answer to the question I had addressed to the emptiness.

"Now that's what I call good service," I said, laughing. "Shurf, do you know what just happened?"

"I think I do," he said. "Has it ever occurred to you that you can simply command the mouse to come here? Why go somewhere yourself when your words have this power?"

"This *obscene* power," I said. "Last night, one gray-eyed Shadow told me that the Origins were obscenely powerful. Now I'm beginning to understand why she chose that word."

"Then summon the mouse here and let's be done with it," Lonli-Lokli said impatiently.

"Gosh, I love you even more on the Dark Side, Shurf," I said. "But if we were sitting in your office in the Headquarters of the Ministry of Perfect Public Order, you'd frown and say in a stern voice that we should do just what the message tells us to do. Think about it: if I could just summon Doroth, the message would have said something like, 'Call him and he will come.'"

"That is true," said Shurf. "All right, let us move away from the river."

❀

For some time we wandered through pearl-colored dunes. My feet touched the ground but left no footprints, so Lonli-Lokli's were the only boots that marked our path. Nothing surprised me anymore; it just registered with me.

"Look at these trees," Shurf said rapturously. "I've been to the

Dark Side many times, but I've never seen anything like this."

"I haven't either," I said, raptly touching the semitransparent trunk with my finger.

I had always known that trees were beings as sentient as I was, but until then this knowledge had been purely academic. I knew the tree whose bark I had just stroked was undeniably, unequivocally alive, though. It trembled under my palm and purred quietly, like a kitten.

We walked around in circles a bit longer in this wondrous grove. I tried to concentrate on looking underfoot—somewhere here we were supposed to discover the footprints of Doroth. So far the expedition had been extraordinarily pleasant. I had expected something far more dismal and heroic from this outing. In comparison with the scenes churned up by my imagination, and after my recent encounter with King Mynin's Shadow, who was enamored of cold steel, this was like a Sunday picnic in the park.

Soon I saw Doroth's tracks. The small dark paw prints on the silvery ground looked clear and deep.

"Here are the tracks, Shurf," I said. "See them?"

"No, but it is not strictly necessary. It is enough that you see them," he said. "My task is to carry your bales and thank the heavens that this mouse turns people into rag dolls and not stone effigies. So follow the trail, Sir Origin, and I will humbly bear the luggage."

"I have the strange sensation that we've traded places," I said. "Next thing you know, I'll be asking you to be a bit more serious."

"Do not, I beg you," Lonli-Lokli said with a laugh. "If I ever hear such advice from you, I will lose my wits all over again."

"Thank you," I said, bowing ceremoniously. "Now that's what I call a compliment."

Bathed in the milky-white breezes that dodged in and out between the transparent tree trunks that nestled in the dark grass, we followed the tiny tracks of Doroth. My sense of time had always been far from perfect, but here time seemed to be suspended altogether. I have no idea how long we wandered through the strange transparent forest. Somewhat longer than half an hour, a bit less than an eternity.

❦

"Wait a minute, please," Lonli-Lokli said suddenly. "There is something preventing me from going any farther. And I can hardly see anything at all anymore."

I turned to him. Shurf was standing with his back against one of the trees, and the bales with toys were lying on the ground. At first I couldn't figure out what was wrong with him, but then it dawned on me.

The tree trunk was absolutely real, dark and wrinkled. It was covered with thick dark-green moss. It had none of the ghostly diaphanous shimmer of the other trees. Instead, the body of my companion had become almost transparent. Sir Shurf Lonli-Lokli was slowly melting before my very eyes, like a lump of ice cream in a hot room.

For an entire second I stood there blinking, not knowing what to do. Then I realized that I had no choice but to believe my words really were powerful incantations—which would definitely come in handy just about now.

"I want Shurf to be all right so he can accompany me farther."

I'm afraid I spoke in the frightened voice of a child who was suddenly told to pick out a present for himself, and who took the risk of asking for the impossible—a motorcycle or a live hippopotamus—knowing beforehand that he was going too far, and that they would rap him over the knuckles or stand him in a corner for his impudence.

"You do not understand. This is no longer the Dark Side, Max," Lonli-Lokli said in a hoarse, weak voice. "This is most likely that infamous Inside-Out. I once read in an old manuscript that people disappear when they stray into this place. They melt, like shadows in the dark. Now it is happening to me. I am not complaining. At least I made it here. I have had many opportunities in my lifetime to die in far more ignoble ways."

"I don't give a damn about your blasted legends!" I was shocked at the sharpness of my tone. "So don't you even think about dying on me like an imbecile. And don't you dare disappear! Sir Shurf, I'm talking to you! Now unstick yourself from that sinning tree. This instant! Then pick up your bales and follow me. You will not melt into the dark but come with me like a good boy. Because that's the way I want it!" By the end of my rant I was screaming.

This flash of rage completely undid me. I saw little spots of color dancing in front of my eyes, followed by thick, murky brown darkness, as bold and out of place as a psychotic policeman. I had to seat myself carefully on the ground, lest I collapse on it altogether a moment later.

"Some fit of fury that was. Thank you for not launching into fisticuffs with me." Lonli-Lokli's voice no longer rustled like the wings of a dead butterfly. It was a regular human voice. Fairly ironic, I might add.

"Yeah, all it took was for me to get really mad," I said, smiling weakly. "I couldn't bear seeing you disappear on me like that. Help me up, will you?"

"Of course."

Lonli-Lokli picked me up from the ground like I was a newborn kitten. If he made any effort at all, it was so as not to crush me by accident.

I stared at him. He was no longer transparent. He was Sir Shurf in the flesh, as real as day, now and then driving me nuts with his almost total likeness to the young Charlie Watts.

"It's good you didn't disappear," I said. "Who would I have gotten to drag around these stupid bales if you had?"

"It truly is a good thing I did not disappear," Lonli-Lokli said seriously. "I am standing here with you on the Inside-Out of the Dark Side and not going anywhere. Who would have thought it possible?"

"But why are you so sure that we are on the Inside-Out?"

"Praise be the Magicians that your practical skills far exceed your theoretical background," he said. "Or else I would have known exactly what happens to madmen who wander into these nonexistent realms. Just look around you. Do you see how everything has changed?"

"That's true," I said, staring at my feet.

I was standing on the most mundane wet asphalt. That was the last thing I was expecting to see. Some sort of predatory grass latching onto my boots, talking pebbles that spew out four-letter words when a careless hiker stepped on them, or any other kind of everyday hallucination—these all would have made perfect sense to me. Anything but cracked asphalt, dark and wet, like it had recently been drenched in a downpour.

"You have the expression of someone who has just been to his own funeral," Shurf said, surprised.

"Yep. Something like that. You know, this road looks suspiciously like a road in the World I was born in. And everything else does, too . . ."

I looked around. A dark-gray sky, wet trees, their leaves dripping, a few streetlamps surrounded by aureoles glowing salad-green, almost imperceptible in the slightly thickening twilight, the velvety surface of a hedge in the distance. All of this was very reminiscent of a landscape cut out of a picture of my World. Not a concrete, familiar place, but a general suggestion of one.

"What difference does it make what it looks like?" Shurf said, unfazed. "Maybe it looks this way to please you. Or maybe it has always looked like this. Are you sure that it is so important? What I would rather know is whether you still see the mouse tracks."

I looked down. On the dark surface of the street, there really were the footprints of tiny paws, as distinct as if the creature had scampered across when it was freshly laid and soft and left a timeless trace in it. Timeless, that is, until the road was scheduled to be paved again.

"I see them," I said. "Let's go."

We hurried into the bluish twilight gloom, where Doroth, the Elusive Avenger, was hiding from us. The road started to rise rather steeply, and soon I had to stop to catch my breath.

"You are panting and breathing as heavily on this incline as a fat farmer's son on his wedding night, Sir Origin," said Lonli-Lokli. "I seem to have wasted my effort when I tried to teach you my breathing exercises. Perhaps there really are things you will never learn?"

"You said yourself that it would take me at least forty years to learn them," I mumbled.

When I had caught my breath, we continued walking along the aromatic hedge. Finally the slope ended, and we stopped in front of an ordinary wooden gate. It was open, and it squeaked quietly, swinging back and forth in the cold wind. The little tracks led into a garden, in the depths of which nestled an old three-story house topped with a small tower.

"I wouldn't mind knowing where it is we've ended up," I said.

"In a myth," Shurf said. "Forward, Max."

"Your eyes are glittering like the eyes of my cats when I fill their food bowl."

"That is a mild comparison," he said, laughing out loud. "Do you not realize what you have done for me? I could never have dreamed about an adventure like this."

"You call this an adventure? While we were wandering about on the Dark Side, everything was absolutely strange and unprecedented, like a proper adventure. This, though, is pretty humdrum. A stroll through the Old City is way more interesting than this."

"Sometimes it seems to me that you have an overactive imagination, and sometimes it seems to me that you do not have any imagination at all," Lonli-Lokli said. "We are probably just very different in the way we see things."

"That's no surprise," I said. "All right, let's go. Speaking of adventures, keep behind my back. Like I'm the omnipotent Sir Lonli-Lokli, and you're some clueless weakling like me."

"Anything you say."

We went into the garden and headed for the house. I had only put my foot onto the first step leading up to a massive stone veranda when a remorseless gush of memories poured over me, tearing to shreds my last bastion of common sense.

"What is it, Max?" Lonli-Lokli said, alarmed.

I guess the expression on my face reflected what I was feeling. What I wanted to know was, who was this tall stranger, and what was he doing on the veranda of *my house*?

A sharp pain pierced my chest, as though the Sword of King Mynin that was concealed there was shifting from side to side, trying to find a more comfortable position. It couldn't have happened at a better time. The pain returned my memory to me and allowed me to grab onto the tatters of my former self—if only to restore the illusion that I was again the all-powerful Sir Max of Echo who could grapple with even greater problems than this. Anything to keep me from turning into a terrified lump of flesh and nerves, pathetic and helpless.

Then everything suddenly fell into place. The invisible traffic controller of my life decided to throw the right switch and avert disaster. About time.

"Okay, we're good to go," I said. "You are Shurf Lonli-Lokli, as I recall. I'm Max. I now live in Echo, I scare passersby with my Mantle of Death, and I work doing Magicians know what in the House by the Bridge. Before that . . . Well, never mind what happened before. But I remember that, too. Perfect. You know, just now I was absolutely sure that I had returned home. Actually, there's a part of me that still considers this to be my own home. I've dreamed about this house many times, but I always forgot about it when I woke up. I . . . work here, or something. I guard the house at night. I come here at twilight and sit down in a chair covered in tattered old red velvet, in the large hall on the first floor. The people who live in the house always seemed to me to be ghosts. I think I was the ghost, and they were just ordinary people. They could never see me, but they sensed my presence. They never tried to sit in my chair, anyway. But wait, now I realize that this was all just a dream. Probably a dream."

"Sometimes our memories surprise us," Lonli-Lokli said with a nod. "Dreams and illusions can bear a very strong likeness to memories, and vice versa."

"True."

I opened the heavy door with some difficulty, leaning against it with the weight of my whole body. Even the weight of the door felt familiar. I remembered that my right shoulder always ached from having to struggle with the door every evening. I overpowered the door, and the first thing we saw was the marble floor of the entrance hall and an umbrella stand to the right of the stairs with two umbrellas: one white and one gray, with old-fashioned wooden handles. They had been sticking out of this umbrella stand for as long as I could remember . . . Wait, what?

"Shurf, you're right. Illusions do resemble memories, so much so that it makes me dizzy," I said. "Now we'll go into the great hall. On the left is a door leading to a glassed-in terrace. At the end of the hall are a black leather divan, a chair similarly upholstered, and a table for newspapers. To the right is a wooden staircase, and behind it, my red chair and a mirror on the wall. I have never seen myself in the mirror, by the way. There's also a small marble table and a table lamp with a green lampshade. Sometimes someone switches it on, but I've never done it myself . . . Well, let's go. And take my hand, will you? My knees are trembling, if you want to know the truth."

"Mine, too," Lonli-Lokli said. "There is something in this place that makes me tremble from cold and loneliness. I was such a fool as to think that cold and loneliness had long ago lost their power over me."

He held out his hand, encased in its huge leather protective glove. I latched on to it like a drowning man clutches at the neck of his hapless rescuer, and we entered the great hall. It looked exactly how I had described it. In fact, I hadn't doubted for a second that it would.

"Sit down on the divan, Shurf," I said, letting go of his hand reluctantly. "A front-row seat for the only spectator. You probably shouldn't intervene in what's going to happen. I never know myself what that will be, but—"

"I understand, Max," he said softly. "You are in some sense at home here. I am not. Therefore, I will simply sit and watch."

"Good," I said.

I went up to my chair covered with tattered red velvet, sat down, and sighed with inexpressible relief. I had wandered the devil knows where, for the devil knows how long, but now I had come home. I could rest. I so needed to rest.

I closed my eyes and almost let the gentle waves of slumber carry me off. I still can't bring myself even to think where it might have taken me, if a familiar pain in the chest hadn't forced me to open my eyes and shake my head vigorously. This is no time to relax, I told myself in fury. Later you'll go home and make yourself comfortable in your armchair, and then you can turn into warm jelly. You can do whatever you want—only not here, and not now.

The pain didn't subside. I looked down at my chest and discovered that King Mynin's Sword was visible and palpable. Its carved hilt was protruding from my chest. The sight was so horrendous that I wouldn't have been ashamed to fall down in a dead faint. I didn't, though. I simply coughed and cleared my throat, making sure at the same time that I was still alive.

Then I raised my eyes to the staircase ascending into the gloom, and called out, in a voice not loud but still commanding:

"Doroth. Come here. No more hiding."

I had no doubt that my command would be fulfilled instantly. The Sword of King Mynin, which had become part of me, was its previous owner's plenipotentiary, so the frightened little beast had no choice but to obey. His master had summoned him.

Doroth made haste to scramble down the staircase. Never in my life had I seen a more absurd sight: a diminutive, gray, short-legged creature with a head twice as big as its body. It looked more like a teddy bear put together in a slapdash fashion than a mouse. Only its tail looked like it belonged to a proper mouse, or even a rat—it was a long, thin shoelace of lively pink flesh.

285

The creature dashed head over heels up to my boots and peeped a few times. Doroth wanted to make amends, by the looks of it. He was asking for mercy.

"Sorry, no," I said. "Peeping just doesn't cut it. I want you to turn the people you enchanted back into human form. Peeping I can do myself."

Doroth rushed around in circles and peeped still more beseechingly. I held out my hand and, obeying a sudden urge, picked him up off the floor. For a moment I stared at him, not knowing what to do next. Then I did something that I would never have expected of myself: I carefully placed the base of his tail on the transparent edge of the sword protruding from my chest. The severed tail fell into my lap. Doroth gave a desperate shriek, thrashed about in my hand, then went limp. Several drops of viscous bluish liquid formed an intricate new pattern on my left palm, crossing out the signs depicting my True Name with fanciful swirls and lines.

I licked my soiled hand mechanically, obeying the same atavistic instinct that makes kids put any unfamiliar trash into their mouths to try it. Only then did I realize that it was Doroth's blood—as bitter and aromatic as an apricot pit. For a few seconds my poor head tried to work through this information. Then I shook off my muddled ponderings and concentrated on what I was feeling. A heavy hot wave seemed to rise up out from the depths of my body. It softly but peremptorily announced its dominion over me, and there was only one thing I could do: let this ruthless power bear me off wherever it wished.

At last, the force that was spinning me around grew tired of its game, and it mercifully threw its new toy upon the shore of what passed nominally as reality.

I opened my eyes and looked around. I discovered that the hilt of Mynin's Sword had again become invisible and intangible. Wonderful. Otherwise what had happened would look too much like a low-budget movie about the adventures of the living dead starring me, my favorite actor.

Everything had settled into place. I was sitting in the red chair and holding Doroth's tail in my left fist—a smooth pink cord of flesh, still alive and almost all-powerful. The magic tail of the last mouse king of this World. Now I knew everything about Doroth and the Manooks who served him, about the Great Red Xmiro Desert and the ancient magic of Uandook, available to animals and plants but not to people. I felt as if I had known these facts forever—since childhood, at least, like the alphabet or multiplication tables. I had simply forgotten them for a while, but now that I had remembered, all was well.

In particular, I knew that Doroth was born in the very heart of the Red Xmiro Desert many thousands of years ago and had fled from it, leaving behind no descendants. He left not of his own volition but on the command of an extravagant young Origin by the name of Mynin, who had decided to bustle about collecting all the wonders of the Universe.

The Manooks, of course, were descendants of the Maxxa, a small ancient tribe of rodent charmers, cursed by all the mice kings of Uandook in succession. The curse ensured that the lands surrounding the Maxxa settlements would never bear fruit, children would inherit only the bad qualities of their parents, and good actions would never be rewarded in kind. Even King Mynin, who accepted help from these unfortunates, never showered blessings upon them. The Maxxa followed him eagerly, hoping that the good fortune of the Origin would be stronger than their curse. And so it was for a while.

Beside these curious but useless historical facts, I knew everything I needed to know about saving the people who had turned into rag dolls. That was the only thing that mattered now.

I turned to Lonli-Lokli.

"Come on, Sir Shurf, unpack our treasures."

He really is the most perfect creature in the Universe. The whole time he had been sitting on the black leather divan at the end of the room, not betraying his presence with so much as a sigh. Now he calmly got down to work.

"You know what to do, if I understand correctly?" he said finally.

I nodded, taking the white dog from the pocket of my Mantle of Death. "You'll be first, boy. I was born in a terrible place where it was the custom to try out experiments on dogs, and only then on people. Now you'll be the first to come back to life—that's a serious advantage."

I placed the toy on the marble table under the mirror, rummaged around in my pockets, and found that the dagger I had been given on the first day of service was still with me. That would come in handy. I cut off a piece of the rat's tail that was wriggling about in my hand like an eel, and made a neat little incision in the tummy of the dog. Into the cut I placed the small scrap of still living, warm, protesting flesh.

"There we go," I said, carefully depositing Droopy's soft cloth body on the floor. "Now we just have to wait. Let's turn away. If you look too closely into the eyes of a miracle, it can get shy and not work—if only because people's eyes aren't used to seeing wonders. Even our eyes, my friend. Even ours."

I hid Doroth's tail in my pocket and went over to Shurf. He was laying out the dolls on the reading table.

"Would you like a bite to eat?" I said. "I still have the feeling that I'm the master of the house."

"Of course I would. Can we even do that here?"

I didn't bother to speak my wishes out loud or even to rummage around in the Chink between Worlds. I simply opened the door to the glassed-in veranda. I knew there was a table there already laid for tea. It was always set to welcome guests. The tea in the cups was always hot, and the strawberry pie was always fresh.

"After you," I said. "I'm becoming like Kofa. No matter what happens, I always have a table laden with food and drink at my disposal."

"How appropriate," Shurf said, sipping the tea. "Mmm, delicious!"

"Indeed. Now try the pie. I am as staunch a patriot of the Unified Kingdom as any other loyal immigrant, but boy have I missed strawberries."

I took such a huge bite of the pie, I almost choked. I had to swallow it without chewing. I was more cautious with the next bite, but alas I had no time to savor it. I heard the door bang, and a moment later, Droopy rushed in, yelping in ecstasy. His shaggy paws were launched straight in the direction of my shoulders. Five hundred odd pounds of happy, completely unbridled fur descended on me, sending the pie and me sprawling out on the floor. Droopy demonstrated his undying affection by slobbering all over my nose, boots, and ears, and everything else he could reach. He chose to ignore the pie.

"I'm starting to regret my good deed already," I groaned, trying to shield myself from the wet black tongue. "You used to be so small and quiet and good . . . Sit! And calm down!"

I am, of course, an Origin, and on the Dark Side my words acquire the instantaneous power of a magic spell. For my dog, however, these words remained just a chaotic string of meaningless sounds. I had to put up with his friendly outpourings for a while.

Finally Droopy removed his heavy paws from my chest—not because I'm such a great dog trainer but because he finally noticed the pie. He finished it off in one go, licked off all the extra crumbs from my Mantle of Death, and started sniffing around for more.

"Your dog resembles you," Lonli-Lokli said.

"Huh? When did you ever see me greet you like that?" I said, picking up an overturned chair.

"Magicians forbid," he said, grinning. "Still, the resemblance is obvious. When you come into a room or into someone's life, one finds it very difficult to continue with what one was doing before the intrusion. It is utterly impossible to pay attention to anything but you."

"Really?" I was nonplussed. I was trying to keep the piece of pie I had just cut for myself away from Droopy. "Wait, is that a compliment or a reproach?"

"Neither one nor the other. A statement of fact, no more. But tell me, what are you planning to do now?"

"Well, I'll do what we came here for: bring all these poor rag dolls back to life. Naturally, I'll have to sweat a bit. There are more than five dozen of them, but I'll manage. I hope those guys will express their gratitude with more restraint than Droopy."

"That's not what I meant. What happens next? How will you get all of us out of here?"

"I'll think of something," I said flippantly, but then I felt a tremor of concern.

I had to get sixty odd people out of the Inside-Out of the Dark Side—the nature of which I had only the dimmest notions at that point—and deliver them to safety, preferably to their homes. Shurf had almost melted on the way here, and I had managed to save his life only by some miracle. What if the others started to melt and disappear as soon as I had turned them back in to people? Even if that didn't happen, who knew what else could happen on the way back?

"That's what I thought," Shurf said, picking up on my gloomy train of thought.

"But Droopy didn't disappear," I said finally. "That means the others will be fine, too. When I start to think too much, it doesn't end well. It's better that we act now and think later. Finish your tea, Shurf. I hope I can polish off the rest of this divine pie. Then we'll go back into the house and do what we can. That's the best idea I can come up with at this point."

"All right," Lonli-Lokli said. "I am sorry, Max. I should not have importuned you with my questions. I have not yet gotten used to the idea that you are the one who decides everything here, and that I do not have to supervise you."

"Believe me, it's even harder for me to get used to it," I said. "I would gladly shift the responsibility onto your powerful shoulders— or someone else's—but I'm afraid that's not on the menu."

I finished my piece of strawberry pie, paying almost no attention to the taste. I didn't really want it anymore. I had been wanting it for so long, though, that finishing it was a matter of principle.

We went back into the great hall, where Doroth's lifeless little body was still lying on the floor. I didn't try to pick him up. I didn't want to touch him.

Then I got down to work. I made incisions in the cloth bodies and carefully inserted small pieces of Doroth's still wiggling tail in them. Never in my life had I imagined I would have to save so many people in such an absurd manner.

Lonli-Lokli would have made an excellent surgeon's assistant. He orchestrated the procedure beautifully, passing me new dolls, then adroitly arranging off to the side the ones that had already been treated. When Droopy tried to get his wet nose in on the act, Shurf bellowed at him so loudly that the dog went to lie down in the far corner of the hall. He looked like he wanted to plead that he was physically incapable of disturbing me at my work, and the very thought of licking my face made him shudder.

"Aha, we've found the way to keep you in check," I said gloatingly. I looked over at Lonli-Lokli with admiration, hardly able to contain my untimely desire to ask for his autograph.

After the first dozen dolls, I decided that I was already a fairly qualified specialist and felt around under my Mantle of Death, where I had placed the rag doll bodies of Xeilax, Kenlex, and Xelvi close to my chest for safekeeping. My hands were shaking. The girls were good acquaintances of mine—not girlfriends, certainly, but not unlike nieces, as I had called them in the dorky lecture about our familial relations that I'd subjected them to in the *Sated Skeleton*.

"Do not fret, Max," Lonli-Lokli said. "It all worked out with Droopy; it will work with the others, too. Do you feel you are more responsible for the girls?"

"I guess so."

"Yet you are just as responsible for all the others, including me, while we are here. There is no difference."

"You're right, of course," I said as I made a small, careful cut in

Lady Xeilax's stomach. She had always seemed older to me than her sisters, so I decided to begin with her.

Half an hour later, everything was over. The postoperative toys were lying on the leather divan, in the armchair, and right on the floor—there were too many of them to fit in any one place comfortably. Droopy's feelings were so hurt that he had fallen asleep in the same far corner to which he had been exiled under the stern gaze of Sir Lonli-Lokli. Still, his strawberry-smeared snout looked perfectly contented.

"Now we must leave them in peace for a while," I said to Shurf, surveying the surreal panorama in the great hall. "Would you like some more tea? Or perhaps we can go up to the library."

This idea suggested itself to me spontaneously, taking me quite by surprise. Then I discovered that I had not been led astray. High under the eaves of the third floor of this house there really was a library; I had always known about it. Well, not all of me, but the part of my consciousness that felt right at home here.

"To the library?" Shurf said. "A hole in the heavens above you, Max. What library? Do you really think . . ."

"You are right again," I said. "If we are indeed in the Inside-Out of the Dark Side, it could very well be that legendary library. Let's check it out."

I strode up the creaking stairs, almost mechanically pressing the light switches along the way as I ascended. Unlike me, my hands knew just where they were. Opaque white spheres lighted our way upward with a dull glow. Under the lampshades burned ordinary electric light-bulbs.

We made it up to the third floor, and from there continued up into the attic. The final staircase turned out to be ancient and rickety, and the wooden steps felt springy under my feet. The condition of the attic floor was just as precarious as that of the stairs. But I liked this. If the floor-boards had not been so pliant and our progress so touch-and-go, our journey through the house might have seemed like a confused dream.

"I can't believe my eyes," Lonli-Lokli said in a whisper, placing his hand on my shoulder. "This *is* a library."

"No, these are just bookshelves stacked with old books," I said, also lowering my voice. "The real library is farther down. See the little white door over there in the corner?"

"No," he said with a sigh. "I do not see any door. The entrance to the library probably exists only for you. Will you go in?"

"Sure. Since we've come this far . . . Will you wait for me? I'll be quick."

"Yes, go ahead. I'll look through the books out here in the meantime."

"I don't doubt it will be time well spent."

I smiled at him and opened the shabby white door, as small as the door of an antique icebox. I had to crawl inside on all fours, so it was hard for me to come to grips with the significance of the act. Besides, that's sometimes for the best.

A cozy half-light reigned in the place where I found myself. It was the sort of weak, dispersed light you find in the darkest corner of an enormous room on an overcast day before rain. I stood up and looked around. Everything looked just as I had always imagined the mysterious "upstairs library" would look when I was warming the red velvet chair with my backside on the first floor of this house. There were neither windows nor walls. There was not even a ceiling. If they existed, they were lost somewhere in the shimmering mist that was like the very fabric of this place—or its movable, constantly shifting frame. Besides the mist, there were only green carpet runners on the floor and books lined up in neat rows on the shelves—eternity in its most reassuring form.

I took several steps forward. The distorted spatial perspectives of the library made my head spin. To be honest, I was afraid to move away from the door. I couldn't allow myself the dubious luxury of getting stuck here forever. Someone still had to transport the five dozen people who were coming back to life on the first floor of this enigmatic building back to Echo.

My disobedient legs carried me off to the left, and I crashed into the corner of a desk. The desk was very real, just as real as the future bruise that would soon bloom on my left thigh in all its multihued glory. Beating back my childish urge to curse, I stared at the polished surface of my tormenter. There was a sheet of thick blue paper, scribbled on all over with fairly small writing. Only the first line was spelled out in large letters: *Dear Max.*

I grabbed the page and stared at it in almost superstitious horror. Can you imagine the state of a devout Catholic who discovers on the altar a letter with his name on it, signed by St. Peter? Such was my shock.

For a few minutes I read and reread the greeting, which had struck me as so absurd that I couldn't force myself to read further. But curiosity is a powerful force. Especially mine. So I gave myself a good hard kick and fell out of my trance with a thud.

I am very glad that you found your way to the library.

My eyes started wandering easily down the page.

Now a few words of friendly advice of a practical nature. First, you should not stroll around through the library. I am not sure that you are ready for such an endeavor. Do not hurry. Everything in its own time. Second, do not try to find your unwritten book here. As far as I can tell, this idea had occurred to you. It will not work, in any case, but if it did . . . In short, you must abstain from this. You may keep taking my books by means of the Chink between Worlds. But don't try walking out of here with one of them under your arm.

"What does he think I am, a kleptomaniac?" I said aloud, somewhat miffed.

A soft, eerie chuckle was the only response. It welled up quietly

from nowhere, from everywhere, and it struck me as the most horrific sound effect imaginable. That brought me up short, and I continued reading.

That, however, doesn't hold for the books under the eaves,
beyond the confines of the library. Those are bona fide books,
written by all kinds of ordinary people. I really don't know why
they did it, to be honest. You can take those away by the armful.
Personally, though, I doubt whether you'll find anything interest-
ing in them.

Now, one last piece of advice—the piece most relevant to you.
It is not at all necessary for you to leave here on the same path by
which you came, following the tracks of Doroth. "Not at all nec-
essary" usually means, coming from my mouth, "you ought not
to," and in the current situation it would not be an exaggeration
to add "under any circumstances"—an expression I have no spe-
cial liking for, to tell the truth, and try not to use at all.

I hope you remember that in certain circumstances any door
opened in darkness can become the Door between Worlds. You
have already experienced this yourself. I do not think that just any
door will work this time, as you will be traveling in a large group.
The garden behind the house is surrounded by a wall, and there is
an opening in it. Precisely what you need.

Keep in mind that you'll have to do without my advice in the
future. Giving advice is not my policy, but today I had a duty to
help you. After all, it was my whim—summoning to Echo a crazy
mouse from the Red Xmiro Desert, with his witless servants in
tow. This letter is a form of apology.

After this followed some illegible scrawl. Lower still was a postscript, clearly dashed off in haste.

P.S. Do not try to understand why this place feels familiar to
you. Try to persuade yourself that you only dreamed it, like many

other very convincing places. Do not hurry, Sir Max. It is not that crucial to understand absolutely everything. In fact, you should never hurry with anything—if you can help it, of course.

I folded the piece of paper carefully, thought a bit, then decided that it would be better to burn it. I didn't want to take it with me, and I was reluctant to leave it here. Deep in my heart, I was afraid that if the letter addressed to me stayed here on the desk, some "dear Max" or other who looked frighteningly like me would start coming here on a daily basis. He would put the letter back on the table and leave, making way for the next in a series of doppelgängers . . . The thought of it made me feel queasy.

I burned the letter and carefully rubbed away the charred remains. I didn't feel I could relax until I caught myself staring at my own palms, smeared with ashes.

Let's scram, buddy, I said to myself. I can't stand looking at your face anymore, all stunned with wonder. Just try to get back home in one piece, okay?

I was able to salvage the pathetic remains of myself and make it out of the library, thanks to the little white door that was still at my service.

＊

"That was fast," Lonli-Lokli said, tearing himself away from the piles of books. "Everything is still quiet downstairs. By the way, there are real ghosts haunting this place. Two of them were here just now. I was ready for anything, but they did not pay any attention to me. They just went past me, then oozed through the wall and disappeared."

"I don't think they disappeared," I said with a smile. "I know for a fact that somewhere here there is another invisible door leading upstairs to the tower. The beings that inhabit the house are able to use the door, but you and I are not. I don't know why. But I don't think they are ghosts. I am almost sure that they are absolutely ordinary denizens of this place. Unlike you and me."

"I do not understand," Shurf said, frowning.

"I'm not sure I understand it myself, but I'm beginning to have some idea of what the Inside-Out of the Dark Side really is. It's not a parallel World, not a neighboring Universe, but the potential to change once and for all your own nature, to become someone different, and then to go wherever your heart takes you. Or wherever you are whisked off to. That's why the people who live here don't even notice us. And that is probably why you almost disappeared when we crossed the boundary . . . I'm sorry, my friend, I can't explain it more clearly. I guess I just don't have the proper terminology yet."

"On the contrary, that was very clear indeed. Your version is not the worst distortion of the truth, which we will in any case never reach. Let us not distract ourselves with too much thinking. Look here at what I found. All the other books are in some language I don't understand. Even the alphabets are unfamiliar. But this one looks like the books you fetched for me from the Chink between Worlds. It says here that it is 'very scary.'"

"Where does it say that?"

He handed me a thick book in a smooth, dark-brown binding. It had no name or author on it—like books with their dust jackets removed. On the spine of the book was a broad strip of tape with thick letters in black magic marker: *VERY SCARY BOOK.* I opened it up and a burst out laughing: Stephen King. *The Tommyknockers.* That's Shurf's "luck" for you. There's nothing more I can say.

"Max, is it really so funny, or do you have a case of nerves?" my friend said, looking worried.

"Both, most likely. At least it's a real book, written by a real person. And it's yours, if you want it."

"Of course I do. Do you think I can take it?"

"I'm absolutely sure. I found out in the library precisely what is permitted and what isn't."

"Who told you, if I might ask?"

"King Mynin," I said. "He wrote me a letter and politely gave me to understand that it was not advisable for young whippersnappers like me to hang around in his library. At the same time he offered his apologies for the bad behavior of his former favorite Doroth and things like that. So grab your book. In the words of Mynin, you can take them by the armful. But you don't need that many, do you?"

"To be honest, I would not refuse them. Even though the alphabets are unfamiliar to me, and I cannot read them, just holding them in my hands is a pleasure. But I will content myself with just one."

Then he looked at my face searchingly, as though he had observed some visible change in me, or as though he was about to question me further. At that moment I heard a commotion downstairs. I grabbed my head and cursed myself. Where did I get off thinking that my enchanted patients would just lie there meekly on the floor until I decided to do something about them? I flew downstairs, three steps at a time. Lonli-Lokli followed behind at a measured pace; nevertheless, we both made it to the first floor at the same time.

The spacious hall now looked like a hastily equipped field hospital in the epicenter of an earthquake, with Red Cross workers rushing about. Terrified adults, looking as helpless and confused as lost children, were scattered about on the floor, in armchairs, on the table and windowsills. My girls had managed to crowd onto the red chair all together. They were clinging to one another and to Droopy, who was howling in sympathy with them.

"Everything is under control, people," I said, trying to up the volume of my voice. "The worst is over. Now we will be going home, so there is no need to fear."

"Max, is that you?" one member of the trio screeched.

A second later all three of them were hanging on my neck. It was pleasant, but pretty darn heavy.

"Well, you've finally dropped the 'Sir.' It's about time," I said, trying to pat all their heads at once with my two hands. "Just stop strangling me to death. You need me alive, trust me."

While I was struggling for my inalienable right to breathe, Lonli-Lokli sauntered into the hall, greeting people here and there and offering a laconic but digestible version of what had happened. He had a number of old acquaintances among the courtiers who were victims of this sorry affair. His presence was as effective as the strongest calmative, and I could sense the tension in the room subsiding.

"Girls, if you don't let go of me, I'll have to put a spell on you," I moaned, trying to speak sternly at the same time.

No go. The sisters just sighed in delight and gripped my neck still more tightly, which by that point I would not have thought possible.

"I absolutely and wholeheartedly share your delight, young ladies, but now you must release Sir Max for a time," Lonli-Lokli said sternly. "He still has to make sure that we return home safely. Then you may do anything with him that you see fit. Agreed?"

"That's a somewhat daring claim. If everyone who wishes does anything with me they see fit . . ." I muttered, hurrying to put the girls, who were quite taken with this splendid speech, back into the red chair. I kissed three little noses, one after the other. "Sir Shurf is right, girls. Now we will go home, and all will be well. I promise."

They gasped in delight and nodded. Three pairs of eyes looked up at me trustingly. There were sixty more pairs of eyes staring at me with the same expression. There is nothing worse than being the one everyone else depends on, but it seemed I had to get used to this awkward position.

"Now we'll go outside into the garden," I said in the jaunty manner of a Boy Scout leader. "I ask all of you to follow me, and not to lag behind or to go off on your own. It would be really swell if you would try to step in my tracks. It could turn out that your very lives depend on it. We'll soon be home, and then you can rejoice, get angry, be afraid, ask questions, and do anything that you wish—even dance on the table naked. Sir Shurf, you will have to bring up the rear and make sure that everything goes smoothly. Let's roll, folks!"

I winked at the triplets, who had finally quieted down after my address, and flung open the door leading into the garden.

It was night. I had already forgotten that night could be so dark— no moon, no streetlights, just the murky, dark-purple stain of a cloud-covered sky. But I knew exactly where to go. Turn right, into the thickest undergrowth of the neglected old garden. There were ancient stone steps by which you could descend the incline of a steep hill, feeling your way along, to a place where a wrought-iron fence glistened after a recent rain. I guessed which opening Mynin had been referring to. I even remembered where the fence was missing one bar, and the one next to it was bent out in such a way that there was enough room for a strapping young lad to slip through and raid someone else's orchard. Even a sizable grown-up who was not averse to the idea could squeeze through. This was very convenient in the present situation, seeing as how I was shepherding an entire group of adults who were not particularly scrawny.

I must give credit where credit is due, though: my traveling companions did not cause me any trouble whatsoever. After all, they were not a bunch of frightened farmers but educated members of the court of His Majesty King Gurig VIII. They followed behind me in silence, not making any kind of fuss and not looking around. The sisters also followed in my footsteps, holding each other by the hand. It seemed that losing one another was their greatest fear. Even Droopy sensed the seriousness of the situation and pressed close to my leg instead of leaping and frolicking through the ancient garden, which was what I had feared he might do.

I found the opening immediately and stopped next to it. "Now I will crawl through the fence, and you must follow after me. Do not hurry, and don't be anxious. All will be well. I will be there on the other side to help you, if necessary. Sir Shurf, you must bring up the rear again and make sure no one gets left behind. That is your bitter fate."

"Why bitter?" he said, surprised. "You do love to exaggerate."

"I won't deny it," I said.

I allowed myself a moment—no more than a second—of weakness. I stared fearfully at the gap in the fence, behind which lay only the impenetrable fog of the unknown, and whispered softly, "Please let everything be all right."

I inhaled, taking in a last gulp of fresh night air that smelled of dampness, dead grass, and last year's pine needles, and slithered through the bars of the fence. I still consider it to be another gift from the magnanimous King Mynin that I managed not to snag my Mantle of Death on a fragment of the broken wrought-iron bar. My own powers are usually not sufficient to prevent such things.

As soon as my feet touched the ground on the other side of the fence I had to jump aside: Droopy the Brave was right at my heels.

"Good boy. Now sit!" I said sternly. The dog clearly wanted to play, though. It was written in huge letters across his happy snout.

"I'll call Uncle Shurf!" I threatened.

Droopy whimpered and sat down obediently a few feet from me. I shook my head in delight. Sir Lonli-Lokli was surely the most amazing creature in the Universe. Just the sound of his name was enough to calm the indomitable shaggy force of nature known as Droopy.

"Sir Max, where are you?"

I thrust my hand into the fog in the direction of the voice and felt a little warm hand grasp it. "Come over here," I said, trying to speak quietly and gently. "That's good. Is that you, Kenlex?"

"Yes," she peeped.

"You see, I don't mix you up anymore. By the way, no more 'Sirring,' remember?"

"Yes," she said, poking her nose into my shoulder. "I just forgot. Max, I was so frightened! I followed you through the gap, and there was suddenly nothing there and no earth beneath my feet. Then you gave me your hand, and everything reappeared."

"That was my fault," I said. "I should have realized right away that I needed to give you my hand. Now you must move aside, or you may get shoved."

She let go reluctantly and took a step back.

I thrust my hand into the darkness where Lady Kenlex had just materialized and shouted, just in case, "Over here!" A few seconds later I was wiping away the tears of the terrified Xeilax with one hand, while with the other I pulled the giggling Xelvi out of the dark fog. A kindred spirit: I probably would have been giggling too, if I had been her.

Things got easier after that. I quickly got the hang of thrusting my hand into the darkness in just the right place at the right moment. The courtiers, Gurig's and my own, had stronger nerves than the girls did. A few moments later I winced involuntarily, feeling Lonli-Lokli's iron grip. The rough leather of his protective gloves ruled out the possibility of a soft touch.

"Thank you, Sir Max," he said courteously. "What is this place?"

"I'm not sure, but it smells like Echo. Though it doesn't really smell like anything here."

"I understand just what you mean," he said. "I feel almost certain that we are in Echo, too. But where?"

"I think we might be in Xolomi," one of the courtiers piped up. "This is one of the cells. It looks like one, in any case."

"In Xolomi?" I said, surprised. "Well, that's just what I deserve."

Then I roared with laughter. I laughed so hard I couldn't stop. Lonli-Lokli had to call the guards and explain what had happened. His explanation was remarkably tactful and convincing, naturally.

When I was finally laughed out, I discovered that the room was almost empty. Droopy was sitting on the floor next to me. A few feet away from us the inseparable trio was huddled on the floor. Sir Shurf stood in the doorway, his arms crossed over his chest. He shook his head in disapproval.

"All the same, you must try to control yourself," he said softly. "Are you all right, Sir Origin?"

"I've been all right all along," I lied. "Where did everyone go?"

"I suppose the warden is treating them to kamra in his office."

"So we really have landed in Xolomi? Amazing. It's good the cell was empty." I shook my head in amusement, then asked anxiously, "Have you found out how long we were gone?"

"One day and one night," Shurf said. "Did you think we were away for longer?"

"Yes. Juffin says that time can play practical jokes on those who loaf around on the Dark Side. Since then I've been afraid that I'd leave for half an hour and return a hundred years later or more. Actually, I've always been afraid of that—disappearing for many years and then returning to find that everyone had gotten along fine without me the whole time. That would be terrible."

"Most likely you will have to go through that at some point," Shurf said in a melancholy voice. "All of us, sooner or later, have to undergo our biggest fears. Tell me, do you really have to sit here on the floor, or are you just unable to stand up?"

"I can get up, of course. You know, I really want to go home. No chitchat in Sir Kamshi's office, no tears of gratitude, no pestering with incoherent questions. Everything can wait until tomorrow. Even seeing Sir Juffin. I don't think I'll make much sense now, anyway. I want to steal home and hide under my blanket. What do you think, is that possible?"

"Very well. That means it is my turn to make miracles," he said. "I'll accompany you to the amobiler. I'll manage all the rest, as well. Do you have the strength to take these young ladies home? And your dog, of course."

"I think I'll be able to manage that." I smiled and winked at the sisters. "Ready to go home, girls?"

They nodded vigorously. Even Droopy wagged his ears in ecstasy, his own version of wagging his tail.

Magicians be praised, Lonli-Lokli was an unsurpassed expert in navigating the labyrinthine passages of the Royal Prison of Xolomi. A few minutes later he led us into the fresh air, called the head of the guards, ordered him to furnish me with an official amobiler, and accompanied us to the ferry.

"Thank you, Shurf," I said. "You've saved my skin, of course. Not to mention my sanity. I am not exaggerating in the least!"

"And I thank you," he said. "I could never in my life have imagined anything like the walk we took together."

"Same here, believe me. You haven't forgotten your book, have you?"

"Sometimes you say the most surprising things," Lonli-Lokli said, shaking his head. "How, may I ask, could I have ever left it behind?"

I stopped the amobiler in front of the Furry House.

"We're here, girls." They didn't budge. Three pairs of pleading eyes stared at me.

"Shall I come in with you?" I said, smiling. "Oh, that's right. It's dark, empty, and cold in there, and your servants are being plied with free kamra by the warden of the Royal Prison. You want me to turn on the lights, sit for a spell in the living room, and wish you all a good night. Of course I'll come in. Only not for too long, so please don't get angry with me."

They beamed and made a dash for the door. Droopy, just about to doze off, raised one ear, sized up the situation, and leaped from the amobiler. I yawned, desperate for sleep, then followed after them.

Despite my expectations, it was light in the hallway and smelled of good food. The enormous living room was plunged in a cozy semidarkness, so I didn't notice right away that we had guests.

"Didn't I tell you that this nasty brute was gallivanting around who knows where with a pack of pretty women?" Melifaro said to Tekki.

"What are you doing here?" I was so glad to see them, and so confused, that I asked them the dorkiest question of all.

"What do you mean? Tekki made a date with me here," Melifaro said, grinning. "Everything was great until you showed up."

I looked over at Tekki.

"Did you know we were getting back today? And that I would be stopping by here? But I had planned to go immediately to your place, only the girls didn't want to go home to an empty house . . . What if I had gone straight to the New City?"

"Well, if the girls had come home without you, I would have just sent you a call," said Tekki. "Isn't that what Silent Speech is for?"

"Still, how did you know that we were coming back today?" I said, hugging her.

"What difference does it make, Max?" Tekki said, laughing. "The last thing on earth you want to do now is uncover this secret since you're so weary of your own mysteries. What you really want to do is sleep. And maybe just one mug of my kamra—there is it, on the table."

"You know everything about me," I said. "Am I really such a predictable bore?"

"Yes," she said, nodding.

I sat down next to her, then shifted my attention to Melifaro. The fellow looked like he hadn't had the easiest day, but now he was glowing with happiness. He didn't even try to outdo Tekki by flinging some outrageous insult at me. Kenlex, shy but pleased, sat down next to him, and her sisters gazed at the couple indulgently.

Meanwhile, Xelvi, the flibbertigibbet, took a small gray object from the pocket of her looxi and showed it to her sister. Xeilax smiled approvingly.

"What do you have there, Xelvi?" I said in alarm. "Come on, let me see."

"It's just a toy," she said, embarrassed. "I found it in that house where we woke up today. It was lying there on the red chair. You're not angry?"

"Of course not."

I reached out and took the souvenir. Then I regretted that I had expended my quota of laughter at Xolomi. Now was just the time for another such outburst of hysterical merriment, but I had no strength left. Xelvi had brought home Doroth himself, the Master of the Manooks, the main culprit in our recent misfortunes. Now that he was missing his tail, he himself had become a stuffed toy. Doroth looked almost sweet in this state and didn't seem to pose the least bit of danger. I handed him back to Xelvi.

"Let me introduce you. This cute little mouse is Doroth. He once lived in Uandook, in the very heart of the Red Xmiro Desert, by the walls of the enchanted city of Cherxavla. Then he served King Mynin and spent his later years in the Barren Lands, where he ruled over your neighbors, the ill-starred Manooks. Now he will be your toy. I think this little rodent should make quite a powerful talisman."

"That same Doroth from the ancient legends, once sung by the Manooks?" Xeilax said.

"The very same. Don't be afraid. Without his tail he can't cast a spell on anyone."

"Will you tell us everything?" Xelvi said hopefully.

"Everything? Well, probably not. But I will certainly tell you about what happened to you. Tomorrow. Or the next day."

"Max's trademark promise," said Tekki. "Tomorrow, or the day after, or the Last Day of the Year."

"Can't say it's not," I agreed.

Then I dropped off to sleep right there in the armchair, with a full mug of kamra in my hand. That was a first.

When I woke up, I discovered that I was no longer sitting in the armchair but lying under a blanket. I had no clue how I'd gotten there, but it was great. I floated off into the sweet darkness of sleep again.

It didn't stay sweet for long. I was beset by alarming dreams, confusing but distinct, like frames in a newsreel. I dreamed that I was lost in the forest, and I was approached by some crazy, pathetic creatures who had at one time been elves of this World. Unsteady on their legs, they shuffled around, staring at me with their turbid, teary eyes. They said nothing, but they didn't leave, as if they were waiting for something. Suddenly I knew what they wanted from me.

I drew the invisible Sword of King Mynin from my aching chest and plunged it into the throat of the nearest elf. He fell to the ground quietly and slowly, like a dry leaf in autumn, and I shouted, "Next!" Then I lost my wits altogether. Remarkably, I seemed to wield the sword like I had been practicing fencing all my life. Rather, it seemed the sword was wielding me, and not the other way around.

My dream was full of senseless rage, emerald-green blood, and indescribable relief. But whether it was me or my victims who were experiencing it, I didn't know.

When it was all over, King Mynin's Sword wanted to return to its sheath—to my chest, that is.

I woke up from my own screaming. I shouted from an excruciating pain in my chest and between my shoulder blades—as though a skewer was turning inside of me. A few seconds later the pain subsided, leaving behind just a slight numbness in my chest muscles and a bad memory. I buried my head in the pillow and laughed out loud from relief. Actually, I didn't so much laugh as cry. I sobbed, gasping for breath like an orphaned child.

"What's wrong, Max?" Tekki, pale with fright, was standing in the doorway. She looked at me, took a deep breath, and smiled. It seemed my wet cheeks were not in the least incompatible with her knowledge of the world. And I, idiot that I am, had so often feared revealing to her my wretchedness of spirit, hiding out on the Street of Yellow Stones with my head buried under the blankets. Why? I now wondered.

"Well, praise be the Magicians, you're alive. Did you have a nightmare?"

"Something like that. I'm sorry, I didn't mean to scare you," I said, wiping my nose. I smiled weakly, then looked around. "Where are we?"

"In your little palace. You nodded off right in the living room, remember?"

"Well, let's just say I do. So this is my royal bedchamber, huh? Jeepers." I twisted the checkered pillow, wet with my tears, in my hands, then threw it into the far corner of the bed, as big as a football field. "Now I see why I had such a hideous dream."

"I liked sleeping here," Tekki objected. "Today I felt like a true royal concubine, in spite of the fact that you were here with me in name only."

"But I was here?" I said cautiously.

"I hope so," Tekki said with a shrug. "When I lay down to sleep, you were here. When I woke up, you were still here somewhere under a pile of blankets. At least I think you were. I didn't want to wake you up, so I just got up and went down to the bathing pools. The rest of the time I was watching one remarkable dream. And you were definitely not there . . . Do you think you might have been somewhere else?"

"I don't know. To be honest, you are so beautiful that I don't even care."

"You have terrible taste."

I could hear unfeigned sadness in Tekki's voice. This was our oldest and most stubborn controversy. She held great attraction for me— but for herself, not a drop.

※

I made it to Juffin's office just after lunch. He greeted me with the heaviest of his trademark gazes. I settled myself in the armchair opposite him and gazed back. A few moments later I realized that this stare-down contest was not really what he had in mind, and I started to talk.

"This is the first time it's happened to me. So much to tell, but I don't seem to have a single word to describe it. Sinning Magicians, where is my good old motormouth now?"

"It's all right," Juffin said, interrupting me. "It's over now. The rag dolls are people again. Sir Shurf Lonli-Lokli is whole and unharmed, snoozing at home, and you're here. You did everything that was required. I don't need a report. It's better without it. You're a big boy now. You have every right to your own secrets."

"I guess so," I said. "As for Shurf, I doubt he's snoozing. I think he's reading. Stephen King, believe it or not," I said and laughed uncontrollably.

"Is it really so amusing?" Juffin said.

"Yep. Only for me, though. I'm afraid Shurf will be shaken to the depths of his noble soul, and in the evening it will turn out that I owe him a good dinner, what with certain writers from my World making up horrific stories. That's always how I have to pay for their rash literary experiments."

"Wait a minute," the boss said. "The name sounds familiar: Stephen King. Does he by any chance make movies?"

"Not directly, no, but there must be a few film adaptations of his books. You've probably seen them."

"*The Langoliers*," Juffin said confidently. "I watched it last night while you and Shurf were gadding about on the Inside-Out of the Dark Side. What a word! Sounds like the worst of the old incantations. He wrote that story up, didn't he?"

"Yes. What did you think of it?

"It's the most terrifying tale I've ever heard. And such verisimilitude," Juffin said. "At first it was very hard for me to believe in a huge flying machine that contained so many people, but I've seen them so often now in the movies that I've gotten used to the idea. They really do exist in your world, don't they?"

"Airplanes? Yes, of course they do. When I become a very old and powerful sorcerer, I'll get hold of one and give it to you as a gift on the Last Day of some far-off year or other. Would you accept it?"

"Thank you, but no thanks," the boss said. "If one is to believe what one sees in the movies, nothing good can come of them. By the way, Max, have you already sent a messenger to your subjects? Sir

Melifaro, as you will recall, said that they had occupied someone's garden a few hours' ride outside Echo."

"I'd rather go there myself. It will be much faster, and it will be a pleasurable outing for me into the bargain. Will you give me some time off?"

"Who am I to stop a foreign monarch from visiting his subjects?" Juffin said, laughing. "Plus, you'll come right back, won't you?"

"Sure. In the evening. Well, during the night, at the latest."

"Hey, hold your horses! During the night? Who's going to work while I'm watching movies?"

"Okay, the evening, then. It's still very easy to come to an understanding with me."

Melifaro caught up with me on the way out of Headquarters. Reason suggested he should be very tired and very happy just about now. My guess was only partly correct, however. He wasn't able to get a good night's sleep, of course, but the lover boy's brow showed telltale creases of brooding contemplation. Still, when he saw me, he smiled from ear to ear.

"It's definitely time for me to kill you, Nightmare. As though it wasn't enough that my girlfriend happens to be your wife, now she's crazy about you after all your mutual adventures."

"Yeah, some adventures. But what I'd like to know is, why are you so bent out of shape, man? Is anything wrong?"

"Yes. Everything's wrong. Are you in a hurry?"

"Theoretically, I'm already late. I am due to meet with my subjects in someone else's garden. At the same time I'm about to faint from hunger. So while I'm devouring delicacies, you may humbly report to me on your suddenly discombobulated life."

"Where did you get the idea that it's discombobulated? You are truly a great man, O Fanghaxra!" said Melifaro. "Where are you going to stuff yourself?"

"One should stuff oneself in the *Glutton*, naturally," I said.

And we set off for the establishment of the incomparable Madam Zizinda.

"You've chosen just the right moment to visit your subjects," Melifaro said, after we had made ourselves comfortable at a table. "You couldn't have chosen a better time."

"What's with this sudden interest in the foreign policy of the Unified Kingdom?" I grinned at him, trying to come to grips with the endless list of dishes the menu had to offer.

"Quit mocking me," he grumbled.

"Well, this is rich. Sir Melifaro is telling *me* to stop mocking *him*? Are you feeling all right, buddy?"

"Fine, fine," he said, sighing. "You see, Max, it breaks down like this. I'm feeling so fine, I'm planning to get married. And not just to anyone but to your wife."

"Well, I already guessed that part. But why? I mean, why get married? Everything's fine just the way it is, isn't it?"

"Oh, everything's wonderful," he said. "But you see, I want Kenlex to move in with me. Did you really think I'd allow my girlfriend to stay on in your enchanted palace that's infested with horrible little magical mice? Moreover, you show up there from time to time—and you're no picnic yourself, when you think about it. Besides, I've never been married. Why not try it? Manga will be delighted, not to mention Mama."

"Well, it's your funeral. But why bring me into it? Do you need my parental blessing?"

"Kenlex does," he said morosely. "And it's not just yours she needs, unfortunately. This morning she told me that besides you, the Xenxa people have some 'wise elders,' headed by your ingenious military commander Barxa Bachoy. Without their consent, Kenlex will never risk becoming my wife. The poor girl doesn't want to quarrel with all her people at once, and that's understandable."

"And what am I supposed to do? Explain to Barxa Bachoy and his

friends that my wife felt a sudden urge to get married again to someone else? Okay. I suppose I can do that. Send a call to Kenlex. You're
coming with me."

"Do you think that would be better?" Melifaro said.

"Of course. I'll tell my subjects that I can't live without you, so I
decided to give you my wife as a keepsake. I'll come up with some elevated nonsense. If something goes wrong, we'll all be in it together. I
don't want to take the rap for you alone."

"You're a true Monster, Max," Melifaro said gently. "And the
most genuine barbarian from the borderlands, whatever mystical nonsense you may have made up about your former life in some faraway
world. Giving away your wife to any stranger like an old, worn-out
skaba . . . Well, to be honest—I adore you!"

"How can you adore an uncouth barbarian from the borderlands
who gives away his wives to any strangers . . . and his old skabas at
the same time?"

When I was a child, I didn't dream that Santa Claus would come
to me bearing gifts. I had bigger ambitions. My dream was to become
that generous Christmas magician with a sack of presents myself. It
looked like the dream had come true.

Surprisingly, it only took Kenlex thirty minutes to get to the
Glutton. I seated the lovebirds in the back seat of the amobiler, and
we were off.

"Prepare yourself for the worst, Ken," Melifaro said as we
approached the Gates of Kexervar the Conqueror. "Do you know
how fast our worthy Master Fanghaxra drives along country roads?
You're about to find out."

"Don't be a fearmonger," I snarled as the amobiler gathered
speed. "Maybe she'll like it."

"I do like it, though it is a bit scary," Kenlex said politely. "We
won't crash, will we?"

"Well, that depends," I said. Then I checked myself and said, "No, no. Of course we won't. Word of honor."

"Really? Then I won't worry," she said with relief.

I realized with horror that this young girl believed implicitly every word I said. And I had thought I'd have to bite my tongue only when I was roaming around on the Dark Side.

After about half an hour, I saw we had arrived. Next to the road antlered menkals were roaming about among carts piled high with goods. The Supreme Military Commander Barxa Bachoy spied my black turban from afar and dashed over to greet us.

"What an honor, sire!" my top brass said, trying to prostrate himself before me. He looked at Kenlex and nodded knowingly. "I see you were able to lift the Manook mouse's curse from her, Fanghaxra."

"From her and from all the others, too," I said. "I need to speak with you, Barxa. Please sit down next to me."

"In your chariot?"

"Yes. It's more comfortable to sit in here than on the ground, even when it's covered with a rug."

Barxa Bachoy nodded submissively and got into the amobiler. He had the look of a person determined to undertake an exploit.

"What did you want to speak to me about, sire?" he said. "About the Manooks?"

"Yes, about them, too. This silly idea about bringing their captive king to me to swear his allegiance and all that other nonsense—I don't like it. Forget about it, Barxa."

"What will we do with the Manooks?" he said pragmatically.

"Kill them," I said curtly. I was surprised at the indifference in my own voice. It was like I had been issuing orders for mass execution every day for years on end, and I considered it the most routine aspect of my job.

"All of them?" Barxa said, as though he couldn't believe his ears.

"To a man. Children and grown-ups, men and women. Not because they set their monstrous mouse leader on me. I am not vengeful, and if it were up to me, I would leave everything just as it is. But I know things about the Manooks now that I didn't know before. These unfortunates are laboring under three hundred eighteen curses—and what curses! Their ancestors were cursed by all the mouse kings of the Uandook continent in succession. All except the last one, Doroth, who decided to cooperate with them. After that moment, luck deserted him, too. First, he lost his freedom when King Mynin pressed the lot of them into service. In fact, when they were with Mynin, their affairs didn't go too badly. Sometimes the luck and good-will of the Origin is enough to counteract a curse. But Mynin's successor, who banished the Manooks from Echo—he knew what he was doing. A curse is catching, like disease. Remember this, Barxa. This is why you must kill the Manooks—so you may survive and not be destroyed yourselves. Do you understand?"

"I understand, sire," my commander said reluctantly.

"Can you explain to my people why this is necessary?"

"I cannot, but old Fairiba, can. He has been telling me the same thing since the very first war with the Manooks. He knows that the Manooks are cursed. But I did not want to kill them. When you kill an innocent, his spirit will visit you every night to ask you, 'Why?'"

"That is appalling, I agree," I said. "But I have a proposition. You may tell those you kill that you are doing it on my orders. Let them come to me if they have the urge, straight to the House by the Bridge. I'm usually there at night. After all, battling restless corpses is part of our job. Right, Sir Melifaro?" I turned to the couple, who were sitting quietly in the back seat.

"Man, give me a break," Melifaro said, heaving a sigh. "Until today I was sure I was only joking when I called you Monster. I sure hoped I was, at least."

"Maybe you yourself foretold it," I cut him off sharply. "You can't keep hammering away with one joke, year after year, and expect it to go unpunished."

"So you are giving me permission to tell the children of the

Manooks that I am killing them on your orders?" Barxa Bachoy said.

"Of course," I said with a shrug. "Who am I to prevent a good man from telling the truth?"

"Then I will do as you say, sire." My brave commander said this with unconcealed relief.

"Okay, that's that," I said, pounding my knee with my fist. "Now I must ask your advice."

"You need *my* advice, sire?" Barxa said.

"That's right. Listen carefully. I have something of a family problem, Barxa. I have three whole wives, and I have one very good friend. My friend is very distressed that I have so many wives while he has none. He cries into his pillow at night and refuses to eat. I am unable to endure his suffering any longer."

"Why doesn't he just get married?" Barxa said.

"Just look at him, Barxa. He's so ugly that women run away when they see him."

"Wha—?" Melifaro bellowed.

Take it easy, my friend. I had to resort to Silent Speech to soothe the ruffled feathers of the insulted and injured in the back seat. *Do you want to marry Kenlex? Then just shut up and sit tight.*

You're really pushing it, he said, but he held his tongue after that.

"In fact, not one woman would freely consent to be his wife," I went on, turning back to Barxa. "But since this unfortunate person is my best friend, I have decided to help him. I want to give him one of my wives as a gift. This is the only solution. I have been trying to persuade Kenlex for some time, and now she has agreed to submit to my decision. She insists, however, on getting your permission. The opinion of the elder of her people is very important to her."

"You are the best of the women of Xenxa, Kenlex," Barxa said in a heartfelt manner. "You are prepared to refuse the title of queen and give your life to an ugly man whom all other women shun." At this point I clearly heard the gnashing of poor Melifaro's teeth. "And you are prepared to do this in order to fulfill the wishes of your king. This is an act worthy of the daughters of Isnouri!"

"So you are giving me your permission to become his wife, Uncle Barxa?" Kenlex said timidly. "And you will tell the others that there is no need to be angry with me?"

"Angry? We will fall at your feet, daughter," Barxa said solemnly. "We will sing hundreds of ballads in your honor. You are the first of the daughters of Xenxa to sacrifice herself in this way to her king."

"Well, okey-doke, then," I said. "I am glad that you appreciate her courage, Barxa. I myself will never forget this immortal deed. Now I must go greet the others, I suppose, and say goodbye at the same time. We must return to Echo, and you have a long journey home ahead of you."

After a short consultation with the nomads on the occasion of my surprise visit, we were free as birds. We could get back into the amobiler and drive to our hearts' content in whatever direction we wished. The direction my heart was seeking at that moment led straight back to the marvelous Capital of the Unified Kingdom.

"You know, Nightmare, that was too much," Melifaro said angrily. "It was awfully kind of you to organize everything so quickly and easily, but it's been a long time since I felt such an overwhelming urge to punch someone in the nose."

"Well, go ahead and do it. What does that have to do with me? And what are you so miffed about, anyway? You wanted to get married to Kenlex. Be my guest. If she hasn't reconsidered in the meantime, of course. You haven't reconsidered, have you, Kenlex?"

"No," she said, smiling. Then she added shyly, "Max, you were fooling Uncle Barxa, I think, weren't you? I mean, Sir Melifaro is certainly not that ugly."

"I like how precisely you put it," I said, feeling quite happy. "'Not that ugly'—how true!"

"Maybe I will punch you in the nose," Melifaro said pensively. "Otherwise I might just explode."

"Don't even dream of it," I said sternly. "Now you are my subject, buddy. Your duty is a small one: to bow down before me and await my command."

"No, I won't punch you," Melifaro said, sighing. "I will just strangle you. And I will be saving our wondrous World from its worst scourge at the same time. What's Loiso Pondoxo compared to you!"

"You are just joking, aren't you?" Kenlex said unhappily. "Or are you really fighting?"

"See what you've done?" I said. "Don't scare the child, Sir Secret Investigator."

"Of course we're joking," Melifaro whispered to her. "We sometimes joke even worse than this, so you should try to get used to it . . . The sire's cruisin' for a bruisin' one of these days, though."

The last remark was loud enough for me to hear it. I shook it off, then picked up speed. They have their simple pleasures—and I have mine.

I dropped them off on the Street of Gloomy Clouds, next to Melifaro's house. He didn't invite me in this time. He was right not to. If they needed me for anything else, it wouldn't be this evening, in any case.

Then I set out for the House by the Bridge. Where else?

"I'm glad you made it back so soon," Juffin said, pleased.

He was still sitting in his office, but he didn't look like he was doing any work. He was probably just waiting for me. He examined me closely and said, "How are things, Sir Max?"

"Okay, I guess. Only I just gave orders for the genocide of a people. While I was at it, I helped some lovers get hitched. Great, huh?"

"Well, that's just how it goes," Juffin said. "Just a regular working day. You're not going to make a big tragedy out of it now, are you?"

"No. A few days ago it wouldn't have seemed like 'nothing much.'

Back when I was still 'too alive.' I'm not anymore, and now I think I'm starting to feel the difference."

"Don't fret, Max," the boss said, smiling sympathetically. "Everything that is happening to you—they are good changes. The *right* changes. You like that word more, don't you?"

"Yes," I said. "I know it's right. But it's all happening so fast. So fast I feel I was left behind long ago, and now I'm lost. Although that's probably 'right,' too."

"That is, too," Juffin said. "Can you deal with one more bit of news, Max?"

"Good or bad?"

"Neither one nor the other. Probably just interesting."

"Let me hear it."

"While you were chasing down your nomads, I got a call from the Shimured forester. He says all the Shimured Elves—"

"Were killed?" I said, my heart stopping in my throat.

"Exactly," Juffin said. "You see, Max, killing elves is nearly impossible. That's why they stayed alive so long, in spite of everything that had happened to them. King Mynin's Sword, on the other hand, is just the right tool for the job."

"I don't need to hear more. I know I killed them all. I remember my dream down to the last detail. But why did I kill them? What business was it of mine? The history of the elves that had taken to drink was simply sad and somewhat absurd to me. I forgot all about it. I had other things on my mind. If I had been in a conscious state, it would never have entered my mind to hurt the poor things."

"Of course you didn't want to kill the Elves of the Shimured Forest," Juffin said. "You had no reason to want to. But, you see, in his time King Mynin took an Oath of Supreme Allegiance to the King of Shimured, Toklian the Bright. An oath like that is worth a great deal."

The boss fell into a brooding silence.

"And?" I said.

"The Oath of Supreme Allegiance is a very powerful thing. There are many legends that tell of people who returned from great distances, even from the Threshold of Death, to fulfill their oath. I think Mynin considered it his duty to sever the life of Toklian and his people, since their senseless existence was far worse than death. Perhaps Toklian himself had requested that he do this, if it ever became necessary; perhaps not. Who knows? You had to help Mynin against your will since you are the protector of his sword. That's just the way it turned out. It fell to you to do it."

"But how come? Praise be the Magicians, I never gave an oath to anyone. Not one of supreme allegiance, not even one of half-baked allegiance. It would be one thing if I had decided myself that it was necessary, but—"

"It fell to you to do it," Juffin repeated softly. "Some people have the luxury of naively assuming their whole lives that they can act just as they please and do just what they consider necessary. Others are deprived of this pleasant illusion early on. You are one of the latter. That's just the way it turned out, Max. Those words would be a fitting postscript for any human life, don't you think?"

"Maybe," I said. "I still don't like it."

"I'm not too fond of it myself," Juffin said. "But the power that governs our lives and fates isn't concerned in the least about whether we like its designs or not. Let's go for a walk."

"Into some Dream of King Mynin again? Or just back to the Dark Side?"

"No, no, silly. We're just going to take a stroll through the city. We'll stop into some wretched dive and have something to drink there. A breath of fresh air and some simple human pleasures won't do you any harm."

"That makes me think 'the power that governs our lives and fates' wants to make a good impression on me," I said, laughing.

The summer night was bathed in the orange glow of the street-lamps. When we stepped out into the soft air, my head started spinning from happiness. The World around me seemed like such a wondrous place that I could hardly believe it was real. All the same, I knew that the small colored paving stones under my feet, sheathed in their absurd boots with the dragons' heads on the toes, were real. Those were things you couldn't dream up . . .

"You know, Juffin," I said. "I think the gray-eyed Shadow was wrong when she said that I was no longer 'too alive.' I'm still alive, probably more alive than ever. And it's so amazing that I can't even begin to describe it."

"Well, that's just the way it turned out, Max," the boss said, grinning. "Just the way it turned out."